Wild Horses of Currituck

Lily

Michael Justus Murray

Text copyright © 2020 by Michael Justus Murray

ISBN: 978-0-578-70234-6

Front cover portrait: Michael Justus Murray

Website: http://www.wildhorsesofcurrituck.com

CHAPTER ONE

Beth and I are kissing by the sundial in front of Swasey Chapel in the moonlight with the fall leaves swirling around us. My fingers are sensually entwined in her lustrous chocolatey hair. Her doe eyes are gazing into my eyes ardently.

I'm so happy—

I'm jarred awake by the finale of Tchaikovsky's 1812 Overture—including cathedral bells and cannon fire—blaring from the bedroom wall speaker.

She's...she's just a dream...

Her loving eyes vanish. My heart sinks like a stone...

Over the intercom my old man's voice barks, "Leo! Get your butt out of bed! Answer me, Leo!"

I tumble out of bed, stagger across my room to the intercom on the wall, and press the talk switch. "What?" I mutter.

In a chipper voice, he says, "Rise and shine. Time to get up."

What day is it? My brain is groggy from staying up last night till 3:00 a.m. partying with my brother, Jack.

He instructs, "Mow the lawn today. The grass is long so use the bag. Dump the grass clippings back in the woods. Do not cut off any of the heads of the automatic sprinklers. And trim around the trees with the grass clippers. You hear me?"

I recall that today is Monday, May 31, 1976—Memorial Day. Pressing the talk switch, I point out, "Dad, today's a holiday."

"Not for me. I'm going to the office today. Every day has been a holiday for you. Do something today to earn your keep."

I sigh. His gibe makes me feel guilty about being unemployed and living in his basement—sponging off him.

"And get a haircut," he orders.

This irks me. I curtly reply, "Roger, over and out."

The alarm clock beside my bed says seven twenty. Falling back into bed, I try to go back to sleep but can't. I'm haunted by my dream. I realize I dreamed about our first kiss. A feeling of melancholy grips me…

Dad subscribes to the Sunday Cleveland Plain Dealer and showed me Beth's wedding announcement which said she got married on May 1 in Shaker Heights. What especially hurts is how beautiful she looked in her wedding dress.

I made a big mistake. I should've married her.

But she wasn't Lara.

Shit…I thought I was over her. I haven't dreamed about her in months.

I have to find my Lara.

I can't think about it—it's too painful. Get up.

After breakfast I mow the lawn. I live at 566 Greenbrier Lane in Mansfield, which is a small city approximately seventy miles south of Cleveland in north-central Ohio. Our house is set on a large, wooded lot on the corner of Greenbrier Lane and Possum Run Parkway in the heart of Woodland. I roll our self-propelled lawn mower out of the garage into the driveway, attach the side discharge bag, fill the gas tank, and yank the starter cord. The buzz-roar of the engine drowns out the world. As I mow the grass, I keep an eye out for any sprinklers that failed to drop back into the ground after the sprinkler system was turned off.

Eventually, I begin to daydream and remember the night Beth and I clandestinely climbed to the bell tower high atop Swasey Chapel at Denison University when the door was left unlocked by the cleaning crew—then daringly had sex. Coincidentally, she orgasmed when the bell rang at midnight—I kidded her I was such a stud that I made her hear bells when she came. Sighing, I squelch the fond memory.

Every few minutes I have to shut off the mower, detach the heavy, bulging bag, and dump the grass clippings in the woods behind our house. While emptying the bag, I see sunlight glint off a tree trunk in the woods. Curious, I check it out. Someone has hidden a half empty bottle of vodka in a hollow in the bark. My old man must have stashed it there to nip on when he sits on the patio. Knowing that stashing booze is a sign of alcoholism, I pour the vodka on the ground and put the empty bottle back in the knothole.

It takes me all morning to mow the expansive front and side lawns and trim the numerous tree trunks. By the time I finish, my melancholy is long gone, and I'm in a good mood again.

Back in the house, I ponder what to do today—my last day of freedom. Tomorrow I start work at Boals-Corrigan Vitreous China Plant. I've never worked in a factory before with blue-collar workers, so I feel a little nervous. Every summer until now I've had a cushy job as either a lifeguard or the pool manager at the Stonehaven Country Club. My old man says it's time I get a "real job"—one that pays more than minimum wage. Hot and sweaty, I decide to go swimming. Cool off. Work on my tan. Just take it easy. I'm hoping that some sexy college women in bikinis may be there.

Before I can slip out the door, Mom nags, "Leo, your father said you need a haircut."

"No, I don't."

"Yes, you do. You're not in college anymore. You're going to work at a factory."

"Mom, it's my hair. I don't tell you and Dad how to wear your hair. Besides, I don't have any money. I'm broke."

"He left money for it." She hands it to me.

My beloved sports car is parked in our four-car garage. I own a red '57 Triumph TR3A. I think of my car as a sexy woman and nicknamed her Red. She's parked next to my Dad's Jaguar XKE, which I nicknamed Sean after the suave Scottish actor, Sean Connery. I greet "Good afternoon, Red, Sean. How are you two lovebirds today? It's a beautiful day, Red, so let's put the top down." Even though it's a royal pain in the ass to remove the snap on convertible top and clear vinyl side windows and put them in the boot, I do it because I love riding with the top down. I hop in the driver's seat, put on my aviator sunglasses, and start the engine. She purrs like a kitten.

With the hot sun shining on my face and the cool wind blowing through my hair, I cruise through my hilly, wooded neighborhood. Located on the southwest side of town, Woodland is a white, upper class residential development where many doctors, lawyers, bankers, industrialists, and merchants reside. Singing along with the radio, I admire the stately homes on Woodhill Road.

Exiting Woodland, I drive past Windsor Woods. The Windsors are said to be the richest family in Mansfield. According to my dad, Archibald Windsor founded the Richland Iron Company in the late 1800s. In the early 1920s, he built an elegant brick mansion on approximately eight hundred acres of pristine, wooded land on the southwest side of Mansfield. His home was modelled after an eighteenth century English country manor house. A long, brick horse stable and a spacious, brick equestrian arena are situated on the grounds. After Archibald died, his son, Andrew, inherited the estate and presently lives there with his wife, Lois. When I was a kid, my friends and I used to play army in Windsor Woods. Ever since then, I've wondered what the horse arena looks like inside.

Traveling north on Trimble Road, I skirt Brinkerhoff, which is a white, middle class neighborhood named after Roeliff Brinkerhoff, who was a Colonel in the Union Army during the Civil War and an eyewitness to the tragic assassination of President Abraham Lincoln at Ford's Theater. At the northern perimeter of Brinkerhoff, I drive past the historic Richardson Park, which was built in 1926 by Harry Richardson, President of Richland Iron. As a member of the Richardson Garden Club, my mother proudly says the magnificent mansion and gardens are visited by people from all over the world.

If you live in Woodland or Brinkerhoff, Mansfielders say you live on "the rich side of town" or "the right side of the tracks." After opening his law office, my dad bought a starter home in

Brinkerhoff, and I lived happily there throughout grade school. By building a successful law practice, he then purchased one of the most expensive homes in Woodland and achieved his lifelong dream.

Soon, I pass the high school football stadium, Arlin Field, cross a railroad tracks, and enter Roseland. Roseland is a white, lower class neighborhood on the north side of Mansfield. The north side of town is called the Flats and is where the train station, factories, and slums are. Roseland was developed to provide homes for blue-collar steelworkers employed at the nearby Empire Detroit and Cyclops Steel Mill. Snobbish people in town derisively call the neighborhood "Little Kentucky" because many "hillbillies" who resided in Olive Hill, Kentucky, moved there to work at the mill in the 1950s. If you live in Roseland, Mansfielders say you live on "the poor side of town" or "the wrong side of the tracks."

Turning onto Springmill Street, I drive east to the Stonehaven Country Club. Constructed in 1921, the clubhouse and golf course are situated high atop the prominent Country Club Hill. Entering the gate, I shift into low gear and ascend the steep lane to the clubhouse, which looks like Tara in the movie, *Gone with the Wind*. Designed by an eminent golf course designer to resemble a park on the coast of Scotland, the beautiful golf course is surrounded by Roseland and the steel mill. Enclosed by a chain-link fence, the country club is the last bastion of wealth on the poor side of town.

Starving, I have a cheeseburger, onion rings, and a chocolate milkshake for lunch in the clubhouse grill, which I pay for with my haircut money.

While I lounge beside the pool in my Hang Loose pro surfer swim trunks and aviator shades, I discreetly check out the scenery. All I see are teenyboppers in two-piece bathing suits, no hot college women in bikinis. My roving eyes spot a nubile lifeguard in a black bikini sitting under an umbrella in her lifeguard chair. Bored, she's twirling her whistle on a lanyard. She blows it and tells a kid to stop running. A pretty brunette, she reminds me of Beth. I actually feel slightly attracted to her, but she looks to be high school age, which is too young for me.

I read my book, *The Hobbit,* until the lifeguards blow their whistles for rest period and climb down out of their lifeguard chairs. The kids exit the pool at a snail's pace. The adults exclusively have the pool for ten minutes. Standing at the shallow end where No Diving is painted in bright orange letters on the concrete pool deck, I do a racing dive and swim breaststroke four hundred yards; then swim fifty yards underwater without taking a breath. I almost pass out—I actually see a few black, dancing dots before I surface gasping for air. I'm pleased I could still hold my breath that long.

Late in the afternoon I discover that I'm sunburned and go home, where I read my book on the screened porch. My parents are having a cookout to celebrate the holiday. Mom is laying out food and plates and silverware on the picnic table on the screen porch. Dad is grilling T-bone steaks on the patio. Sitting in a lawn chair beside the grill, he's holding a martini in his right hand and a cigarette in his left. He's wearing his olive Marine Corp fatigue cap, black plastic sunglasses, a T-shirt that says Sue the bastards!, Hawaiian print Bermuda shorts, and burgundy penny loafers with no socks. He thinks he looks cool.

"Hey, Faye. Put on Don Ho," he yells. Dad has loved Do Ho ever since he and Mom vacationed in Hawaii and saw the pop singer perform at a nightclub. Mom dutifully goes into the family room to the stereo console and inserts a cassette in the tape deck. Music begins to play out of the in-wall speakers on the screen porch. Don Ho is singing "Tiny Bubbles." I hear my old man singing along with him—slurring the words. He's bombed as usual.

Suddenly, I smell something burning. On the patio smoke is billowing from the grill. Flames are engulfing the steaks from the fat dripping onto the coals. My old man is oblivious.

"Hey, Dad, the steaks are on fire."

For a moment he observes the steaks nonchalantly. Not wanting to spill a drop of his precious booze, he carefully sets his martini down on the bench beside him; then calmly puts his cigarette in the ashtray on the bench. Standing up, he picks up a jug of water, dips his fingers into it, and flicks water on the flames. When that has no effect on the fire, he pours the whole jug on it—fsssst! A cloud of ash erupts like a volcano. The coals smolder and hiss…

With a blasé expression on his face, Dad checks the steaks. Placing his thumb and index finger against his lips, he whistles loudly; then hollers "Time to eat." Putting his cigarette back in his mouth, he removes the steaks from the grill with tongs and sets them on a platter. Balancing the platter in one hand and his martini in his other, he tells me to hold the screen door open. I check out the steaks as he goes by—they're charred. Adding insult to injury, cigarette ashes fall onto them.

The three of us sit down at the picnic table. Dad gives me the biggest steak. Mom has fixed bacon-wrapped potatoes. I mash one with my fork and smother it in butter and sour cream; then dish up baked beans. Scraping the charcoal and cigarette ashes off my steak with my knife as best I can, I eat a bite—it's like chewing burnt leather coated with gritty, nicotine-flavored ash. I have to wash it down with a gulp of lemonade.

"So how's your steak, Leo?" Dad asks.

"Well, I asked for medium-rare, and I got well-charred."

"If you don't like it, you can stick it where the sun don't shine."

"Hey, I love ash," I reply drolly.

"John, you burned the steaks again. Why do you keep doing that?" Mom asks.

Because he's bombed. Are you blind?

"Faye, don't sweat the small stuff," Dad replies.

I make a meal out of Mom's side dishes. I notice my old man barely touches his steak. He just polishes off his martini.

"So where's Jack and Lynn?" I ask.

"They couldn't make it. Jack's studying for the bar exam," Mom answers.

"He's always studying for the bar exam," I grumble even though I spent last night partying with him.

"Leo, the law is a jealous mistress. Which you'll soon find out," Dad says.

"So you think he'll pass?"

"Yeah. He has my genes."

"So when's Olivia coming home?" I ask.

"Two weeks," Mom answers.

"What's she doing this summer?"

"She's gonna work at Rainbow School."

"What's that?"

"It's a school for kids with Down syndrome. It'll be a good experience for her."

"Your sister has a big heart, Leo. She wants to save the world. She was always bringing home a stray kitten to save," Dad remarks.

I don't reply.

"Do you know if she's seeing anyone?" he asks, squinting as cigarette smoke wafts away. He worries about the guys Olivia dates because he believes she's attracted to losers who need saving.

"No," I answer.

"No—you don't know? Or no—she's not dating anyone?"

"I don't know."

Even if I did know, I wouldn't tell you.

For dessert Mom serves her delicious strawberry shortcake with vanilla ice cream and whipped cream. After we finish she clears the dishes from the table.

"Faye, put on Don Ho again," Dad slurs.

"No. I'm putting on something I like."

A few minutes later I hear a song being played on a piano.

"Mom, that song is really beautiful. What is it?"

"'This Nearly Was Mine.' It's by Rodgers and Hammerstein from the musical, *South Pacific.*"

"Who's playing it?"

"Don Shirley."

"He's really good."

"Yeah. We saw him perform at the Ohio Theater. I just love him."

"So what album is that?"

"*Water Boy.*"

Dad and I sit at the table bullshitting. He lights up another cigarette. I feed my leftover steak to our German shepherd, Shepa. Despite his jaws of steel, he has trouble chewing it.

"Leo, you shouldn't feed him from the table. It teaches him to beg," Mom says.

"Aw, you're no fun. Watch this," I tell Dad.

I feed Shepa a green olive from the relish plate. His huge canine jaws chew the small green olive for at least a minute—his big, hairy muzzle twists in complex contortions. Then he spits out the tiny red pimento perfectly intact on the floor. Chuckling, I remark, "I think that's hilarious. He doesn't like pimentos."

Dad cracks a smile. "So where'd they hire you to work—the foundry downtown?"

"No. The Vitreous China Plant on West Fourth Street."

"What department?"

"Packing."

"What's your job title?"

"Toilet packer."

"What shift?"

"First shift. Seven to three thirty."

"You better hit the hay early tonight. Get a good night's sleep."

I nod.

Suddenly, he frowns and says, "You didn't get a haircut today."

"Dad, I tried. But the barbershop was closed because of the holiday," I lie. I stand up to go back to my book.

He takes a quick drag on his cigarette. "Leo, wait a second. Before you go we need to have a man-to-man talk."

Shit—here comes a lecture.

"Dad, I can't right now. I gotta go do my laundry," I lie.

"This will just take a minute."

"No, it won't."

"Sit down," he orders.

Resigning myself to the inevitable, I sit back down.

Do not argue with him. I can't win. He's a lawyer.

Taking a long, last drag on his cigarette, he stamps out the butt on my dessert plate. Then he tells me in a beneficent manner, "I paid for Denison. I was glad to pay for your college—I want each of my kids to have a college education. And I supported you when you were lost—"

Throwing up my hands, I protest, "Dad, I wasn't lost."

"Yes, you were. You've been trying to find yourself ever since you graduated."

I shake my head uncomprehendingly. "I don't know what you're talking about."

"You know what I'm talking about. First you gave up on med school. And then—"

"Dad, I did not give up on med school."

"After four years of pre-med, you failed to apply to med school."

"I just decided I didn't wanna be a doctor. I didn't feel like looking up people's orifices the rest of my life."

Not finding me funny, he replies, "You quit. You're a quitter."

"Dad, I'm allowed to change careers. Lots of people do it."

"Bullshit. You blew med school. And then you blew it with Beth. Which was a big mistake. I really like that girl. She's not just another pretty face. That girl's got a head on her shoulders. She's the best thing that ever happened to you, and you've lost her forever."

I flinch at his rubbing salt in the wound.

"What'sa matter—the truth hurt?" he asks nastily.

You don't know the truth.

"You were a fool," he says.

I sigh.

Don't even try to explain it to him. He'd never understand—she's not Lara.

"Then you took that screwy job drawing portraits at Cedar Point. Had to move back home when you couldn't cut it on your own."

Last summer I worked at Cedar Point Amusement Park at Lake Erie drawing people's portraits. Unfortunately, I couldn't make a living as an artist and had to move back home when I ran out of money.

"Then you wasted a year chasing some pie in the sky dream of being a paperback writer."

"Dad, I didn't waste it. I wrote a novel. And it didn't take a year. It only took seven months."

"I've tried to be patient. I let you live in the guest suite while you found yourself."

"Dad, someday my novel will get published. It'll be a bestseller, and they'll make it into a movie. I'm gonna make it big. Just you wait and see—"

"Shut up, Leo. I've heard all this before."

I shut up and let him ridicule me.

"You graduated from college over a year ago, and you're still living at home. Face it—so far you're a flop."

This makes me feel like shit…

"I'm telling you this for your own good. I don't wanna see you end up a starving artist. I wanna see you living in Woodland someday."

"Dad, living in Woodland is your American dream. I have a different American dream. One not so materialistic."

"That's easy for you to say when you're living under my roof, eating my food."

I bite my tongue.

In his sternest voice, he says, "Listen to me. I'm not supporting you any longer while you achieve your American dream. No more free room and board to write the great American novel. I'm not subsidizing Leo's Folly anymore." He calls my novel Leo's Folly, mocking my title *Incognito's Folly*.

"You need to quit living in never-never land and start being an adult. Stop sponging off me."

"Dad, I plan on paying you back with interest."

"Leo, you know what you are?"

I wait for him to tell me.

"You're a freeloader."

Just agree with him.

"Okay. I'm a freeloader. Now that I got a job I'll move out."

"I'm not saying you hafta move out. Paying rent would be counterproductive. You need to save your summer earnings to pay for law school.

"What I'm telling you is this is where I draw the line. I'm not paying for law school. You're gonna hafta pay for it. You'll value it more if you pay for it. You understand?"

In a bad mood now, I say what he wants to hear. "I understand."

"I had to pull some strings with Floyd Verekee to get you hired there. Called in a personal favor," he divulges.

"What personal favor?"

"A few years ago, when his son was in law school, I hired him to intern over the summer. In return, he hired you even though it was against his better judgment because most college kids quit. They couldn't cut the mustard. I assured him that you can cut it. The only reason he hired you is he owes me. Understand?"

I nod.

He gazes at me steely-eyed—sizing me up. "So…you gotta cut the mustard, Leo. I don't care how hard this job is, you gotta tough it out. Be a man. Understand?"

I nod again.

"No matter what, you cannot quit. You hear me?"

"I hear you."

I hear Shepa barking.

"Working in a factory will be good for you. It'll teach you the value of getting an education. I remember working at Westinghouse before I went to law school. I learned real fast that I didn't wanna work on an assembly line the rest of my life. It'll motivate you to put your nose to the grindstone."

I tune him out by eyeing the interesting geometric mosaic of wooden blocks in the floor…

"I can't try cases forever, Leo. Someday I'd like to handoff my practice to your brother and you."

"Leo, Reese Soliday's here to see you," Mom calls.

"Gotta go, Dad. I got company."

Reese and Mom are standing in the foyer. "Come on in, Reese," she tells him and leads him down the steps into the sunken family room.

"Hey, Reese."

"Hi, Leo."

"Long time no see."

"Not since high school."

"How ya doing?"

"Good. And you?"

"Fine."

Gazing appreciatively around the family room, Reese makes the mistake of saying, "This house is so cool, Mrs. Locke."

Mom can't resist informing him, "It's a Prairie-style home designed by an apprentice of Frank Lloyd Wright."

"I actually majored in architecture my first two years of college so I appreciate modern architecture. I really like this picture window," he replies. The family room has a ten-foot-high, twenty-foot-wide wall of tempered glass, affording a panoramic view of the wooded back yard.

"And this fireplace is really cool." In the center of the house is a massive, cream-colored limestone fireplace, featuring a two-sided, see-through design that opens into both the family room and the living room.

"And I like this parquet floor. It's really beautiful. What wood is this?"

"Cypress. All of the woodwork and cabinets in the house are cypress. The architect used building materials that Wright used," Mom answers.

"It has a warm, golden color," I chime in.

What really catches Reese's eye are the three sectional wall panels made of acrylic with inlaid silk flowers and iridescent air bubbles. Mom demonstrates how the cypress-framed panels roll smoothly on wheels in tracks, so you can close off the den for privacy or roll the panels together for open space.

"That's an ingenious design—the way it creates a screen but still allows light to pass through," he observes.

"The home has a Japanese motif. Wright lived in Japan and was influenced by their architecture. The cabinets have inlaid jade doors. And there's a Japanese garden out front," she expounds.

When my old man is drinking, Mom tends to talk compulsively, trying to maintain an appearance that our home life is normal. I'm afraid she's going to give him a tour of the Japanese garden outside.

"Mom, he came here to see me about something."

She stops talking.

"So…what's up, Reese?"

"I hear you're going to law school at Toledo."

I nod.

"I just got accepted there," he informs me.

"That's great."

"Congratulations, Reese," Mom says.

"Thanks. You wanna get an apartment together in Toledo?" he asks.

"Yeah. Sure."

"We could split the rent and utilities."

"Good idea. We could save money. Definitely."

"Great."

"Man, this is really good news—having a friend to room with at law school," I remark.

"Yeah. We could help each other."

"It'll be just like old times on swim team. We'll sink or swim together."

In a good mood again, I take him downstairs to the guest suite where we can shoot the breeze in private.

"Welcome to my humble abode," I say. The guest suite is comprised of a rec room with a TV, my stereo, and a bar; kitchenette; bedroom; and full bath. "Want a beer? Pop?"

"I'll have a beer."

Sitting at the bar, Reese watches me play bartender, dispensing beer from a tap into a mug. "You got your own tap. Decent, man."

"Yep. The guy who built the house was a beer and soda distributor," I explain, while I dispense root beer into an ice-filled mug for myself.

We go sit down in the rec area. Casting his eyes around the room, he observes, "This is a nice bachelor pad."

"Yeah. Especially since I got my own private entrance, so I can come and go as I please," I reply, pointing at the sliding glass door out of the walkout basement.

"So, uh…what're you doing this summer?" he asks.

"I just got hired at Boals-Corrigan. I start tomorrow."

"Boals-Corrigan?"

"Yeah. They make toilets."

Reese grins. "You're shitting me. No pun intended."

"I shit you not."

"You're gonna make toilets?"

"No. Pack them."

"So how'd you get hired there?"

"My dad and the president of the company have a symbiotic relationship."

"Symbiotic relationship?"

"My dad is his lawyer and hired his son to work in his law office one summer. So the president hired me to work in his factory this summer."

"It sure helps to have a connection, doesn't it?"

"It does. I gotta admit I'm not looking forward to it. I hear it's a hard place to work. I just gotta make it three months. Earn enough money to pay for law school."

Nodding like he can relate to my situation, he replies, "I just got hired at the steel mill."

"Doing what?"

"I'm gonna fill in for guys on vacation. Dig slag out of the pit during shutdown."

"Slag?"

"The waste material from smelting ore."

"Shit, that sounds worse than packing toilets. How'd you get a job there?"

"My uncle is the personnel manager. I start after I get my physical tomorrow."

"My old man just lectured me on the Protestant work ethic. Working in a factory will motivate me to put my nose to the grindstone at law school," I say, rolling my eyes.

"Hey, I got the same lecture from my old man."

"I shouldn't complain. He's alluded to a job in his firm if I make it."

"My dad said the same thing."

We catch up on our lives since we graduated from high school. I tell him about going to college at Denison; that I loved living in

Granville, Ohio, and wish I could live in the quaint college town the rest of my life.

He tells me about Colorado State University in Fort Collins, where he attended on a swimming scholarship. He says he loved it there because he could go skiing all winter in the Rocky Mountains. Unfortunately, he blew out his knee in a skiing accident necessitating surgery and lost his swimming scholarship.

"I thought you were pre-med," he says.

"I decided I wasn't cut out to be a doctor."

"I started out in architecture. Switched to psychology. And ended up in law."

"Like father, like son."

"Afraid so...do you have a girlfriend?" he asks.

"No. I'm free."

"I heard that you had a serious girlfriend."

Trying to act like I'm over her, I tell him, "I dated this girl named Beth Brooks all through college. We lived together our junior and senior years but broke up when we graduated."

"Why'd you break up?"

Not wanting to resurrect painful feelings, I answer glibly, "It's a long story. Suffice to say, we had irreconcilable differences. You got a girlfriend?"

"Nope. I dated this girl from Colorado—Nancy Ludwig—off and on in college. After we graduated she moved to LA to become an actress. So what'd you do after you graduated?"

"I lived here at home and wrote a novel."

Impressed, he asks, "What's the title?"

"Incognito's Folly."

"Hmm...that's cryptic."

"It's science fiction."

"I like science fiction. Can I read it?"

"Sure—as soon as I finish it. It's a work in progress. So what'd you do last year?"

"I went to Europe."

"Really? Where?"

"Italy, Switzerland, France, Belgium, and the Netherlands. I backpacked and traveled on a Eurail pass, staying at hostels till my money ran out. I wanna go back and see the countries I missed."

"Wow…that sounds like fun. I'll go with you."

"I had a blast, Leo. Europe blew my mind."

I wonder if he gets high. "Hey, uh…you like to get stoned?"

Grinning waggishly, he answers, "I love to get stoned. I smoked some great hashish in Amsterdam."

"Let's get high and listen to music."

Standing on the couch, I lift up a drop ceiling tile and fish out my stash—this small verdigris mosaic box containing a baggie of marijuana, cigarette rolling papers, a roach clip, and a derringer. I take the derringer out of the box and aim it at Reese.

His eyes get big.

I pull the trigger—a flame emits from the barrel. "It's a cigarette lighter."

He laughs. "Man, it looks real. Where the hell did you get that?"

"A curio shop in New Orleans. I collect novelties."

We step outside on the deck so my parents won't smell the weed and smoke a joint. We get really stoned.

Back inside, I stack the following records on my turntable: *Revolver* by the Beatles, the first *Led Zeppelin* album, *Who's Next* by the Who, *Retrospective* by Buffalo Springfield, and *Dreams and All That Stuff* by Leo Kottke.

Lounging in a comfortable bean bag chair, I say, "I wanna hear all about Europe."

For the next three hours, he regales me with stories of his adventures in Europe.

At midnight, we get the munchies and raid the kitchenette, devouring ice cream sandwiches and a whole package of devil's food cookies.

Reese doesn't leave until 2:00 a.m.

I have trouble sleeping. The pain from my sunburn keeps waking me up. I have to sleep on top of the sheets.

CHAPTER TWO

I'm luxuriating in a deep sleep when my alarm clock goes off at ten till six. I hit the snooze button and roll over onto my stomach— "Ow!" My sunburn hurts.

No sooner do I fall back to sleep than the alarm goes off again and Mom's voice squawks over the intercom, "Leo, time to get up."

Shutting off the alarm, I struggle to wake up…my brain is groggy…my limbs feel paralyzed…

Eight and a half hours of sleep over the last two nights are not enough.

Mom sticks her head in my room. "Leo, get up. You're gonna be late for work," she says in a shrill voice.

"No, I'm not. I've got plenty of time…"

"You stayed up too late last night. They say you need eight hours of sleep. Chronic sleep deprivation is unhealthy," she lectures.

"I'll go to bed early tonight. Catch up on my sleep."

I drag my ass out of bed. Trying not to touch my sunburn, I put on a T-shirt, jeans, white socks, and my new steel-toed work shoes.

Running late, I rush into the bathroom, take a leak, comb my hair, and brush my teeth; then dash upstairs.

Mom is in the kitchen, packing my lunch in a brown paper bag. She has fixed me bacon and eggs for breakfast.

The bacon aroma makes my mouth water. Glancing at my watch,

I tell her, "I don't have time."

"You don't wanna skip breakfast. They say it's the most important meal of the day."

Instead, I scarf down a stale glazed donut.

As she hands me my lunch, she says again, "You're gonna be late."

"Mom, don't worry. I have everything under control."

"You need to go to bed earlier and get up in time to eat a healthy —"

"Gotta go. Bye."

"Don't speed."

I run out the door to my car.

"Damn it…"

I forgot to put the top and side windows back on my car. Since it looks like it might rain today, I put them back on as fast as I can.

Keeping an eye out for cops, I sail through Woodland, rolling through stop signs, flying through the yellow light at the intersection of Marion Avenue and Millsboro Road.

I speed north on Home Road. As I approach a railroad track, the red warning lights start to flash and the gates begin to come down. A train is coming in the distance. "Of all the rotten luck…"

Drive around the gates. I can beat it.

What if my car stalls?

I visualize color film footage from a driver's education movie I saw in high school. The gory road safety film showed a man's corpse in the tangled wreckage of a car that had been struck by a train. From the waist down, his body was sitting upright behind the steering wheel in the blood-soaked driver's seat. From the waist up, his body was laying on the tracks with his entrails hanging out. The sheer force of the collision had torn his body in half and decorticated the skin on his face from his skull like a hideous Halloween mask. The gruesome images are forever etched in my eidetic memory.

Nope. Bad idea.

As the train rolls by slowly, precious minutes tick away.

"Hurry up…"

Finally, the caboose goes by, and the flashing red lights turn off and the gates go up. I check the time—it's going to be close.

Bouncing over the bumpy tracks, I speed to Fourth Street. Up ahead is a large factory with a sign in the front lawn that reads Boals-Corrigan Vitreous China Plant. Tires squealing, I turn into the driveway. Several factory workers are entering the plant through a side entrance. As I zoom by, they gawk at Red.

I zip around four semi tractor-trailers backed up against loading docks and turn into the employee parking lot. Driving up and down the rows of parked cars, I find a spot in the last row beside a gigantic pile of what looks like scrap vitreous china. My watch says seven o'clock.

I mutter, "Oh, shit…I'm gonna be late…"

I sprint across the parking lot and dash through the door. In the vestibule an elderly, uniformed watchman and a gray-haired man with a crew cut and black safety glasses, who looks authoritative, are talking about the Cleveland Indians game last night.

Panting hard, I say, "Hello."

"Are you Leo Locke?" the authoritative man asks.

"Yes, sir."

Extending his hand to shake mine, he says, "I'm Mr. Castor, the foreman of the packing department." His hand almost crushes mine.

"Nice to meet you."

He takes me to the time clock where he demonstrates how to clock in. My time card reads 7:05.

"Son, you're five minutes late. You'll be docked an hour's pay on your first paycheck," he says matter-of-factly.

Shit…

"That's not starting off on the right foot," he says with raised eyebrows.

"No, sir. I'm sorry. I got held up by a train."

"You need to leave home earlier."

"Yes, sir."

Mr. Castor escorts me down a short concrete corridor, where he points out a drinking fountain with a salt tablet dispenser. Showing me the restroom, he warns me not to enter when there's a red sign on the doorknob—that means it's being used by a woman. I didn't realize any women worked in the shop.

Entering the shop, he shows me the cooling area. Sinks, toilet tanks, and toilets, which he calls ware, are exiting long tunnel kilns. I see fire in the bowels of the kilns and feel heat blasting out of the exit openings. Heat waves are radiating off the ware. Two guys wearing fireproof gloves and aprons are stacking the ware on long, flat-bedded wagons to cool.

He shows me the packing department. It consists of six parallel gravity roller conveyors each approximately a hundred feet long, which he calls the lines. There are two sink lines, two toilet tank lines, and two toilet lines. A sink inspector, a toilet tank inspector, and a toilet inspector are standing at their workbenches at one end of the lines. If an inspector finds defective ware, he scraps it. If it passes inspection, he places it on a wooden pallet on one of his two lines. Gravity conveys the ware down the metal rollers. Two sink packers, two toilet tank packers, and two toilet packers are standing at their packing presses at the other end of the lines. They lift the ware off the lines and pack it in cardboard boxes. The boxes roll out of the packing presses down six parallel gravity roller conveyors each approximately thirty feet long to an electric belt conveyor.

Mr. Castor flags down a guy driving a tow motor. A mean-looking, bald-headed man in a white A-shirt and greasy work pants turns off the engine and climbs off.

"Leo, this is Merle Fields. He's your group leader. Merle, this is Leo Locke. He's the summer help I told you about."

I extend my hand to Merle.

Frowning with disdain at me, he shakes it brusquely.

Mr. Castor instructs me, "You do what Merle tells you to do. You have any questions, you ask him."

"Yes, sir."

He disappears.

Merle leads me down an aisle between the packing presses and the assembly lines of metal rollers. As we walk by the packers, they each glance at me curiously. The second toilet tank packer is a tall, lean black man, who's singing "I'm a Soul Man" by Sam and Dave. "Hey, man," he says to me with a friendly grin on his face.

Smiling back, I reply, "Hey."

Further along, we go past a short, stocky guy, who's briskly packing toilets like an automaton. He doesn't pay any attention to me.

Lastly, we come to the packing press next to the wall, where a young guy with a beer belly is packing a toilet at a leisurely pace. His auburn hair is slicked back in a ducktail, and he has long, scraggly sideburns and stubble on his chin. He literally has a red neck. A pack of Camels is rolled up inside the left sleeve of his holey, short-sleeved T-shirt.

Merle says perfunctorily, "Locke, this is Bill Barnes. Barnes, this is the new guy, Leo Locke."

Barnes stops packing. In his left hand, he's holding an open cardboard box containing a toilet on the press's table; in his right hand, he's holding a glue brush. A cigarette is dangling from his mouth.

Smiling, I extend my hand and say, "Hi."

Sneering at me, Barnes says, "Shit, Merle—he looks like a fucking, long-haired hippie. He ain't gonna make it two days." As he speaks, his cigarette flaps up and down, and the ashes break off and flutter down into the toilet bowl.

I revoke my smile and withdraw my hand.

Merle replies, "Look, Barnes, don't give me no shit. If it was up to me, I wouldn't hire a college kid. But it ain't up to me. This come down from the plant manager. The sooner you train him, the sooner we transfer you to the mold shop."

Turning to me, Merle says, "Barnes is your trainer. That means you do what he tells you to do. You got any questions, you ask him."

I nod.

He disappears.

Curling his lip, Barnes asks, "So you're a college kid, huh?"

"Yeah."

"Well, that don't mean shit around here."

Okay…

He finishes packing the toilet and shoves the cardboard box into his packing press. He lays his glue brush in a metal dish mounted on the right upper corner of his press. After taking a last drag on his cigarette, he drops it in an empty coffee can on top of the press—it sizzles. Then he picks up a clipboard and pencil from beside the coffee can and explains the time sheet to me. I'm required to specify the toilet model number and color and to tally the number of toilets that I pack in a day; if I pack over six hundred, I get paid an additional piece-rate. "You gotta know how to add to do this job," he declares like one has to have brains to do this job. "Get it?"

"Got it."

"Alright, hippie, let me show you how you pack toilets. I'm a pro. First, you get your cardboard boxes."

He leads me around the side of the packing press. Immediately, I spot a photograph torn out of a cheap, pornographic newspaper of a nude woman lying on a bed, spreading her beaver with her fingers. The raunchy photo is taped to the side of the press.

With a shit-eating grin on his face, Barnes says, "Admit you wanna fuck that."

No thanks. I'll pass.

"Damn—you read my mind. Did you put that up there?"

"Huh-uh. That's Herb's pussy. He tacked it up."

"Who's Herb?"

"That asshole," he answers, pointing at the wiry toilet inspector at the other end of the line. Herb picks up the toilet and sets it on a small wooden pallet on the line that leads straight toward my packing press. "He used to be a toilet packer. He brings in literature every Friday for the guys to look at."

Literature—I love it.

Barnes shows me where the cardboard boxes are stored. Packs of twenty flat, unopened cardboard boxes are stacked higher than my head on wooden skids in the storage bay between the two lines of metal rollers running from the two toilet packing presses to the conveyor belt. Using metal shears, he cuts the metal bands that bind two packs of boxes; then grabs the stack of forty boxes, carries them to the packing press, and props them vertically against the side of the press. Pointing at the toilets on the line, he identifies them as model 4720s. Then he tallies forty white 4720s on the time sheet.

"Okay. Now you gotta stamp the model number and color on the box." After squirting black ink on an ink pad, he rapidly stamps "4720" and "WHITE" with rubber stamps on each of the forty flat cardboard boxes propped against the press's frame.

"Now you get your glue." With a screwdriver he pries the lid off a metal drum of glue on the floor beside the packing press. Stirring the glue with a wooden paint stirrer coated with dried glue, he instructs, "You gotta stir it with the stir stick till the glue drips off."

"Now you pour your glue in the glue bucket." He lifts the heavy glue drum by its handle and pours clear, syrupy glue into the plastic bucket sitting on a shelf on the right side of the packing press. Pounding the lid back on the drum with his fist, he warns, "And don't forget to put the lid back on tight or the glue hardens like rock."

Barnes pauses. He picks his nose, looks cross-eyed at his booger, rolls it between his thumb and index finder, and flicks it onto the floor.

"Now you're ready to pack toilets," he declares, looking up the line. Approximately twenty toilets are sitting on the line of metal rollers ready for us to pack. Barnes whistles and motions for Herb to send them down. Pushing the train of toilets, Herb starts them rolling. Gravity propels them faster and faster until they are rolling toward us like a runaway freight train. Running up the line a few yards, Barnes grabs hold of the first two toilets and slowly brings the train to a halt at the rubber bumper at our end of the line. "When he sends them down the line, you gotta catch them. If they fall and break, them bookkeeping fuckers will take it out of your pay," he warns me.

Next, he demonstrates the fastest technique to break open a flat cardboard box, apply glue to the bottom and top flaps of the box, lift a toilet off the line and drop it in the box without breaking it—or "them bookkeeping fuckers" will take it out of my pay—and shove the box into the packing press. He explains that the press holds eight boxes. When you shove the ninth box into the front end of the press, it forces the first box out of the back end of the press. By this time the glue has dried on the first box, and it rolls down the line of metal rollers to the conveyor belt, which transports it to the warehouse, where a warehouse worker lifts it off the line and stacks it on a wooden skid to be loaded on a truck.

Handing me the glue brush, he says, "Okay, hippie. That's all there is to it. She's all yours. Don't fuck up."

I start packing toilets. Barnes sits on the glue drum, leaning against the wall—overseeing me. After packing several, I get the hang of it—the truth is any moron could do it.

Fifteen minutes later I'm sweating like a pig. After a half an hour, I'm bored shitless. My sunburn hurts. As the morning creeps by, it gets hotter and hotter in here…

Finally, at nine o'clock the black tank packer yells, "Break time." Barnes has me put my glue brush in the water-filled coffee can so the brush doesn't get gummy over break. My T-shirt is drenched in sweat. My hair is sopping wet. The thermometer mounted on the wall beside my press reads ninety-six degrees already. I'm so thirsty—all I want is something to drink.

I follow Barnes to the breakroom. As I plod down the main corridor through the heart of the plant, heat is emanating from the adjacent wall of the tunnel kiln. When I enter the air-conditioned breakroom, it feels like I'm walking into a refrigerator—it's paradise.

Barnes sits down at a table with Herb and the other ware inspectors. I go over to the pop machine, drop my quarter in the slot, and hit the selection button. A paper cup drops down and fills with ice; then slowly fills with fizzing soda. I sit down at a table by myself and guzzle it. It tastes so refreshing on my parched throat. I devour the ice.

After guzzling another soda, I walk over to the drinking fountain and fill my cup with ice-cold water—

"Goose!" somebody yells and simultaneously pokes me in the ass.

Startled, I jump and spill my cup of water.

Spinning around, I see Herb standing there—his hand is shaped like a fist with his thumb pointing upward. With an inane grin on his face, he exclaims, "Got'cha!"

Everyone laughs at his prank. As the new guy, I realize I'm going to be the butt of jokes. Trying to be someone who can take a joke, I smile. Keeping an eye on Herb, I refill my cup and guzzle it, refill and guzzle it again, and refill it.

I sit back down and sip the water. I am so tired. I realize I'm out of shape. How the hell am I going to make it to three thirty?

When I walk out of the air-conditioned breakroom, it feels like a sauna. Wilting, I plod back to my press and start packing again. Barnes sits on the glue drum, chain-smoking. He doesn't help me. He just bosses me around and tells me, "You fucked up, hippie," every time I do something wrong.

The black tank packer keeps singing soul songs. Barnes informs me his name is Percy, remarking, "Fucking management won't let us have a radio. So Percy's our radio."

As I listen to Percy sing, I set my sights on making it to lunch at eleven thirty.

I hear someone making weird "wa-wa" sounds. Looking where the sounds are coming from, I see a guy standing at a workstation in between the two toilet tank lines midway betwixt the tank inspector and the tank packers. He's installing parts inside each tank. After each installation, he sends the tank down the line to one of the tank packers.

"Hey, hippie. Don't pay no attention to that dumbfuck. That's Beanie. He's a deaf mute. He makes them goofy sounds. He's just talking to himself."

Beanie sees me looking at him and waves. I wave back.

"Don't stop packing," Barnes orders.

At a quarter till eleven, Barnes checks the tally on the clipboard. "You pussy—you've only packed one hundred fifty-eight." Pointing at the guy furiously packing toilets next to me, he says, "Mr. Machine can pack over a thousand a day."

Mr. Machine imitates the sound of a racecar shifting gears while he packs and the sound of tires squealing when he runs around the corner of his packing press to get another batch of cardboard boxes.

I crack a smile. Yep—Mr. Machine…

Prodding me with the glue stirrer, Barnes goads me, "Pick up the pace, hippie."

"I'm packing as fast as I can."

"It ain't fast enough."

"Haste makes waste," I retort.

"You're a fucking pussy," he retorts.

I try to pack faster. Sweat is streaming down my face, dripping off my brow onto the toilets…

I just got to make it half an hour.

I'm so bored my brain keeps fading out…

All of a sudden, a burly, bowlegged guy appears out of nowhere. He's carrying a toilet with a broken base in one hand and a used cardboard box in his other hand. He looks pissed.

Barnes sees him and quickly says, "It ain't my fault, Jessie. It's the fucking new guy's fault."

"What'd I do?" I ask meekly.

Jessie sticks his face about two inches from my face—he's really intimidating—and growls, "You dumbshit—you forgot to glue the bottom of the box."

"I did?"

He shows me the box. Sure enough, there's no glue on the bottom flaps—only the top flaps. He sets the broken toilet and the box down on the floor right at my feet. Scowling, he asks, "You know what happened when my man in the warehouse tried to lift this off the line?"

"Uh…I can imagine."

He shouts in my face, "The fucking toilet fell out right on his foot!"

"Sorry…"

"You're the new college kid, right?"

I nod.

"Well, you may be smart enough to go to college, but you're too dumb to glue the bottom of the box."

"It won't happen again."

"It better not," he threatens; then storms off in a huff.

Chortling, Barnes says, "Man, he just ripped you a new asshole."

I stammer, "I…I don't know why he's so mad at me. It was an accident. It's not like I did it on purpose."

"Shit, man, you got Jessie pissed off at you. Buddy, you don't want him pissed off at you. He boxes Golden Gloves. You better not do it again, or he'll come back here and kick your fucking ass."

Discouraged, I stare at the broken toilet…

Barnes makes me go dump it in the scrap vitreous china bin. Marking the scrapped toilet on my time sheet, he informs me that I'll have to pay for it. He instructs me to re-use the cardboard box and pack the toilet upside down. "You gotta quit fucking up, hippie. I bid on a job in the mold shop, which pays fifty-nine cents more an hour. And it's third shift, so it's a hell of a lot cooler. But they ain't gonna transfer me till you quit fucking up."

Fearful of Jessie kicking my ass, I double-check each box to make sure that I glued the bottom. This really slows me down.

The minutes crawl by…

Finally, Percy yells, "Lunchtime."

I've made it half way through the day.

My shirt and jeans down to my crotch are soaked with sweat. It's now a hundred and four degrees in here. Barnes makes me put my glue brush in the water can and pour a cup of water in my glue bucket so the glue doesn't skim over. Then he tells me he's going to a bar to drink his lunch and hightails it out of here.

I trudge to the breakroom and plop down at a table by myself, basking in the wonderful air-conditioning. After cooling off, I go to the pop machine. While keeping an eye on Herb, I fish a sweaty dollar bill out of my wet wallet and buy three sodas, which I line up in a row at my table to drink one by one. Opening my lunch bag, I discover Mom has packed two baloney sandwiches, potato chips, and an apple.

I decide to heat my sandwich in the microwave oven. A chart on the machine indicates the cooking time for sandwiches to be three minutes. I place the baloney sandwich, which wrapped in cellophane, on a paper plate inside the microwave, set the timer, and press the start button. The machine starts humming…

"You set the timer too long," a female voice behind me says.

Turning around, I see a young woman looking at the timer. Her face is ravishing. She has sparkling eyes with long, curly eyelashes, high cheekbones, a pretty nose, sensual lips, and an ivory complexion. Her cinnamon hair is beautifully braided in a long ponytail.

She's wearing a tight, red T-shirt that sculpts her shapely breasts. I gaze at them, trying to undress her in my mind's eye…

I realize I'm leering rudely at her. Prying my eyes away, I ask, "Uh…what'd you say?"

"You set the timer too long," she repeats more emphatically.

I don't know what she's talking about. Having followed the chart, I reply, "I think it's okay."

"You're the new guy, huh?"

I'm so hot and bothered by her my brain is unable to think clearly. I stammer, "Uh…yeah…today's my first day. They're training me to be a toilet packer."

"That's a really hard job." She has a calm, clear voice with the slightest country twang—it sounds so sensuous.

She's holding a Tupperware container in her hand. I gaze at her slender arms and pretty hands with red fingernail polish. I'm mesmerized by her shimmering, milky white skin sprinkled with a few pink freckles.

She's wearing close-fitting, faded blue jeans. I take a step backwards and discreetly eye her from behind.

Wow.

My fingertips are tingling with desire…

Inside the humming microwave, my baloney sandwich is spitting and popping.

But I can't take my eyes off her…

My sandwich explodes.

"I think you better get it out of there," she tells me.

I fumble around with the buttons on the microwave but can't stop it. She hits a button and stops it for me. My sandwich is a mushy mess inside the cellophane. Hot grease drips off the paper plate and runs down my hands, burning my fingers.

"Ow!" I mutter and blow on them. "Whoops, heh. My baloney sandwich is a little overheated."

"That's what I was trying to tell you."

"The chart says three minutes for sandwiches. I set it on three minutes."

"That's for frozen sandwiches out of the vending machine. For a sandwich that ain't frozen, I wouldn't set it over half a minute."

Grinning, I say, "Oh well...at least I don't hafta worry about botulism. Any Clostridium botulinum bacteria have undoubtedly been eradicated."

"I don't think you hafta worry about getting botulism from a baloney sandwich. Botulism is caused by food that ain't canned right. I know cuz my mama taught me how to can fruit and vegetables."

"Right...I was just joking."

She looks at me like she didn't get it.

"Thanks for the tip," I tell her and go sit down at my table.

Man alive! I just felt the strongest sexual attraction that I've ever felt for any woman in my life—lust at first sight.

While I unwrap my soggy, shriveled baloney sandwich, it occurs to me that it metaphorically overheated like me, and I chuckle.

Guzzling a soda, I watch her warm her lunch in the microwave…

She's the sexiest woman I've ever seen.

I wonder if she's married.

I look at her ring finger—don't see a wedding ring.

She sits all by herself at a table back in the corner. While she eats her lunch, she reads a *Western Horseman* magazine.

I realize I should've introduced myself to her.

I heat my second sandwich in the microwave for thirty seconds. It comes out perfect.

Lunchtime ends at noon. I follow the redhead out of the breakroom—it feels like a blast furnace hits me. As she strolls up the main corridor toward the packing department, I watch her hips swivel back and forth. She turns left and disappears down a side corridor.

When I return to my packing press, Barnes is sitting on the glue drum, smoking a cigarette. He looks smashed.

"Hey, Bill. Who's the red-haired girl who works here?"

"Lily."

"Is she married?"

"Nope. Divorced."

"She's really sexy."

He staggers to his feet. Draping his arm around my shoulder, he leans close to me and belches right in my face. I smell alcohol on his breath. Slurring his words, he mutters in my ear, "She's a stuck-up bitch. She thinks she's better than everybody. But she ain't. She's trailer trash."

He takes a long drag on his cigarette. "And she's a fuckin' whore. She got knocked up in high school. Had to drop out. My sister went to school with her. She clued me in." He blows a smoke ring. "And she's got a shitload of baggage."

"How so?"

"She's got three fuckin' kids."

Shaking my head disbelievingly, I reply, "No way. She looks way too young to have three kids."

"I seen her at the fair with 'em."

Despite being a drunken lout, Bill has a valid point. If she really has three kids, there's no way I would consider getting involved with her romantically.

Handing me my glue brush, he tells me, "Buddy, I wouldn't fuck her if you paid me. Now quit jawin' and get back to work. The line's backin' up."

Toilets are backed up the line half way to Herb's work table.

"Herb's gonna be pissed if he has to stop and wait on you. He's paid piece-rate. You'll be costin' him money," he scolds me.

Not wanting to cost Herb money, I hurriedly resume packing. Immediately, sweat starts pouring down my face. "God, it's hot in here."

Barnes checks the thermometer. "Aw, you fuckin' pussy—it's only a hundred six. This ain't nothin'. I seen it hit a hundred fifteen."

As the afternoon creeps by, it gets hotter and hotter. Barnes enjoys the temperature rising. He loves watching me suffer. The temperature rises to a hundred and nine. My jeans are now soaked down to my knees. I wish he would spell me, but he won't lift a finger to help.

After a while, I'm so exhausted my arms start to tremble...

I got to somehow make it to break time.

I check my watch.

Just fifteen minutes.

I go to lift a toilet off the line—I can't believe my eyes. A huge, dark brown turd is floating in a pool of bright yellow piss in the toilet bowl.

"Jesus Christ!" I exclaim, jumping back

"What'sa matter?" Barnes asks.

Wrinkling my nose in revulsion, I point to it.

Feigning disgust, he remarks, "Shit—this one's used." He's laughing his ass off.

"Who did it?"

"Beats me."

Not only do I suspect he knows who did it, I get the distinct feeling he's in on it. "What do I do with it?"

"You gotta clean it out. You can't pack it that way."

"I'm not doing it. That's gross."

"Do it."

I shake my head.

"Look, hippie, you heard Merle. You're my fuckin' trainee. You gotta do what I say."

"Screw you." I drop my glue brush in the water can and lean against my packing press with my arms folded across my chest.

"We'll see about that," he replies and walks off.

The other packers, except Mr. Machine, come take a look at the foul toilet. They think it's funny. I ask them who did it, but they play dumb.

Five minutes later, Barnes returns with Merle.

"What's the problem, Locke?" Merle asks.

I show him the problem. He doesn't look shocked.

Pointing at Barnes, I say, "He says I hafta clean it out."

"He's right. Chain of command. I'm the group leader. I sure as hell ain't gonna do it. Barnes has seniority over you. You're his trainee. You're low man on the totem pole."

With his hands on his hips, Barnes looks at me with a big smirk on his face.

"Can't we just scrap it?" I ask.

Merle sighs like I'm trying his patience. "No. I ain't scrapping it. It passed inspection. It ain't defective."

"But...but I didn't do it. I'm innocent. This isn't fair," I protest.

With a callous expression on his face, he replies, "Fair don't mean shit. Now, if you was in the union, you could file a grievance. But you ain't in the union. You ain't got no rights. You're just summer help. You're expendable, boy."

"You're discriminating against me because I'm a college kid."

"Tough shit. Go clean it out. Now."

"I'm not doing it. I'm going on strike."

"Goddamn it! You do it or I'll fire your ass!" he yells. His face is crimson and a blue vein is bulging in his neck.

Shit! He's going to fire me.

"Okay, okay... how do I clean it?"

"You take it up to the restroom. Dump it out in the shitter. Then take it in the janitor's closet next door and wash it out. There's a sink in there," he instructs.

I lift the toilet off the line and carry it past the other packers, who scoot out of my way in case I spill it. While lugging it to the restroom, piss sloshes over the rim of the bowl and down the front of my shirt and pants. I go in the toilet stall and dump the contents in the toilet. The smell stinks so bad it makes me gag.

I lug the bowl to the janitor's closet and rinse it out in the utility sink. On the way back to my press, I get a cramp in my right bicep and have to set it down for a minute.

When I return to my press, it's break time. Everyone has gone to the breakroom. Hot and thirsty, I desperately want to walk down to the air-conditioned breakroom and get something to drink, but I don't think I can make it—my legs feel like rubber. I'm so weak and lightheaded I have to sit down on Barnes' glue drum…

Everybody's harassing me because I'm a college kid. I'm on Jessie's shit list, and he'll kick my ass if I forget to glue the bottom of the box again. I have to clean shit and piss out of toilets or they'll fire me. Disheartened, I want to quit…

"'No matter what, you can't quit. You gotta tough it out. Be a man,' " I hear Dad's voice say in my mind.

"Dad, I…I can't make it…"

Suddenly, I feel disoriented…my vision and hearing start to fade…I can't hold my head up…I'm going to faint—

Quickly, I put my head between my knees; then breathe in deeply though my nose and exhale through my mouth…

"Are you okay?" I hear the red-haired girl's sensuous voice ask.

I look up. There she is, looking down at me with a concerned expression on her face. I mumble, "I'm…I'm really hot…"

"You look flushed. You're probably dehydrated." She vanishes.

I'm not sure she was real. Closing my eyes, I imagine her bringing me a big glass of cold water…

"Here—drink this."

Opening my eyes, I see her ravishing face again. She hands me a thermos of cold water, which I gulp. "Oh man…that's the most thirst-quenching water I've ever had. Thank you."

"Don't drink too fast. Take these. They're salt tablets. They prevent heat exhaustion." She hands me several white tablets.

I swallow them with some water.

She fastens a sponge headband that has been soaked in cold water to my forehead—it feels wonderful. Gradually, it cools my head…

I drink all the water and hand the thermos to her. Smiling feebly at her, I ask, "Are you Florence Nightingale?"

"Who's she?"

"A famous nurse."

She smiles compassionately.

"The guy training me won't help me," I tell her.

"Bill Barnes?"

"Yeah."

"I can't stand him. He's a real asshole."

"No shit."

"He don't like me either. When I first started working here, he kept hitting on me. I complained to Mr. Castor, and he wrote him up. Then one night I had a run-in with him at a bar. He was drunk and tried to pick me up. I told him to get lost. Then he tried to proposition me. I told him to fuck off—I ain't no whore. My brothers told him to leave me alone—or they'll kick his ass. He don't bother me no more."

I tell her about the prank they pulled on me and that Merle made me clean out the toilet. She tells me they pull that prank on all the new guys. Shaking her head in disgust, she says, "I don't understand men. They can be so gross."

"Scatological."

She looks at me blankly.

"Never mind."

Glancing at her watch, she asks, "You feeling better?"

"Yeah…I think so. I was so weak and dizzy I was afraid I was gonna pass out. This heat is killing me."

"You get used to it."

If I don't quit first…

Searching my eyes, she asks, "You gonna quit?"

"Why do you ask that?"

"Cuz Barnes is talking shit about you down in the breakroom."

"What's he saying?"

"He's saying you can't take it. You're a pussy college kid. You're gonna quit."

"That dumbass…"

"So are you gonna quit?"

"I'm thinking about it…"

"Don't quit. Prove him wrong."

"I don't know…"

"You can do it. They all said I was gonna quit. You know—cuz I'm a woman. But I proved them wrong."

I nod half-heartedly. "So…what's your name?"

"Lily…Lily Wyatt. What's yours?"

"Leo Locke."

At this moment, Barnes returns from break. "Hey, sexy lady," he slurs.

"Bill, it's his first day. Why don't you help him?"

"Mind yer own business, Lily."

"Give him a break."

"He's my trainee. I'm trainin' him my way."

"You asshole."

"You bitch."

"Barnes…"

"What?"

"Kiss my ass!" she fires back. Then turns around and walks away.

Damn…she's a real spitfire.

Barnes just stands there with his mouth hanging open, trying to think of an insult to hurl back at her. "Bare it, bitch!" he yells. But he's too late—she's long gone. "I guess I told her a thing or two," he says to me.

"I don't think she heard you, Bill. You weren't quick enough."

"Hey, hippie, you're sittin' on my chair."

I get up off his glue drum.

"You gonna make it, hippie?"

I'm revived. "Yep…actually, Bill, this job ain't that hard."

"Is that so?"

"Yeah. As a matter of fact, I don't think it's as hard as swim team in college."

I resume packing. I don't even look at my watch. I just keep thinking about Lily Wyatt bringing me that cold water…picturing her ravishing face…hearing her sensuous voice…

In my mind, I sing "Cinnamon Girl" by Neil Young again and again…

The next thing I know, Barnes says, "Hey, hippie, it's quittin' time."

I check my watch—it's ten after three. I barely noticed the last hour.

I made it through my first day. Now all I got to do is somehow make it through the rest of the summer.

He has me pour the leftover glue in my bucket back into the glue drum and put the lid on tightly. Then we tally the toilets that I packed today on the time sheet.

"Shit, man, you only packed three hundred fifty-seven. You college kids are all fuckin' pussies."

Maybe I am a pussy. But come September, when you're slaving away in the mold shop, I'm out of here, asshole.

Smiling, I pat him on the back and reply, "Bill, you're all heart."

He's oblivious to what I said. Evidently, sarcasm goes over his head.

While we clean up our workstation, Merle shuts down the conveyor belt and breaks it open. With a forklift he restocks the skids of cardboard boxes in the storage bays between the packing presses. Afterwards, he picks up my time sheet. Perusing it, he grunts likes he's satisfied. "This ain't too bad for your first day, Locke. I think you're trained. Starting tomorrow, you're on your own. Boy—we just might make a toilet packer out of you."

CHAPTER THREE

During breaks and lunch at work, I sit alone and discreetly observe Lily Wyatt. She routinely sits by herself at her table back in the corner reading her horse magazines.

I also see her when she rolls big, plastic bins filled to the brim with tank parts to Beanie's workstation. She communicates with him through sign language. I can't believe it—she actually looks sexy speaking animatedly to him with her fingers and facial expressions.

When I go to bed on Thursday night, I lie awake visualizing her ravishing face and sexy body. I realize I desire her. I need to find out if it's true that she has three kids and is a high school dropout and lives in a trailer park. If it's true, I could rule her out romantically. She couldn't be Lara. But if it's not true, who knows? Perhaps she could be Lara.

At lunch the next day, I sit down facing her at a table beside her table. She's sitting with her back against the wall, reading a book. When she glances up from it, our eyes meet. She smiles and says, "You haven't quit."

"Nope. I'm drinking lots of water and taking salt tablets and wearing my sponge headband soaked in cold water—like you showed me."

"Looks like the college kid is gonna prove everybody wrong."

"Yep. I figure if you could do it, I can do it. Thanks again. You know—for helping me get through my first day. I...I don't think I could've made it without you."

"The first day is the hardest. Then it gets easier."

"Every muscle in my body is sore. I figure this'll get me in shape."

Munching on a carrot stick, she nods.

This is my chance to find out about her. "You mind if I join you?"

"Sure."

I gather up my lunch and sit down across from her. "So what are you reading?"

"A book on horse breeding."

"Horse breeding?"

"Yeah." She shows me the cover. The title of the book is *Veterinary Guide to Horse Breeding.* "I have a stallion, and a farmer at my church has a broodmare. We're gonna breed them. I work for a vet part-time. He loaned me the book."

"So what's his name?"

"Dr. Hall."

"No, I mean your horse's name."

"Oh. Appaloosa."

"Appaloosa—that's a kind of horse, isn't it?"

"A breed. They're spotted. Appaloosa is his name, too."

"It's a nice name."

She's eating a peanut butter and jelly sandwich. Unscrewing the lid on her thermos, she pours what looks like tomato juice into her thermos cup. Smiling conspiratorially, she whispers, "I'm having a cocktail. I treat myself on Fridays. Want one?"

"No thanks."

"You sure? I make a mean Bloody Mary. I used to be a bartender."

"I'm sure."

"I didn't drink out of it."

"That's not the reason." I don't tell her the reason is that I suspect my dad has a drinking problem. I characterize it as a drinking problem because that only means he overindulges in alcohol regularly. I don't call him an alcoholic because that means he's addicted to alcohol, and it's too frightening to think of him as a drug addict. Actually, I fear he may be an alcoholic, and, being his son, I'm afraid I may have the same genes, so I avoid alcohol. But I don't want to get into all this with her, so I simply tell her, "I…I just don't feel like it."

There's an awkward silence…

"So, uh…are you the only woman who works here?"

"Uh-huh. I'm the only woman in the shop. Some women work in the office."

"What do you do?"

"I assemble ballcocks."

"Ballcocks?"

Grinning, she says, "I know—it sounds dirty, don't it?"

"Yeah."

"It's the valve in the tank that turns on and off the water. You know—after you flush."

"The rubber ball?"

"Uh-huh. That's part of it, the float. There ain't too many jobs around here for women. Most of them require too much heavy lifting."

"Right."

"I just bid on a job driving a forklift in the warehouse. I figure I got a good chance of getting it. Me and Jessie are friends. He's the warehouse group leader."

"Yeah…I'm acquainted with him. I'm afraid I'm on his shit list because I accidently forgot to glue the bottom of a box, and a toilet fell out on some guy's foot."

"Yeah. I heard about that."

"He implied he'd kick my ass if it happened again. Barnes told me he boxes Golden Gloves."

"That's true. I seen him box. He's a real tiger in the ring. But don't worry about Jessie. He's all bark and no bite here at work."

"I sure hope so. Because I couldn't punch my way out of a paper bag. My motto is, Make love, not war," I joke.

LILY

She smiles. Eyeing me curiously, she says, "I hear you're a rich kid."

"If I was rich, would I be working here?"

She sips her Bloody Mary. "Jessie said you're going to college."

"I went to college. I graduated a year ago."

She looks impressed. "I don't really know any college guys. All I know is horny guys that work in factories."

"College guys are just horny guys with a bachelor's degree," I joke.

She laughs. "So what the hell are you doing packing toilets? Ain't you supposed to be sitting at a desk in a suit in the air-conditioned offices?"

With a straight face, I answer, "Ever since I was a little kid it's been my dream in life to be a toilet packer."

For a second, she falls for it; but then she realizes I'm kidding her and says, "Get out of here. You're putting me on."

I can't resist trying to impress her more. I tell her matter-of-factly, "Actually, this is just a summer job. I'm working here to save money to go to law school in September."

She looks even more impressed. "You're gonna be a lawyer?"

"That's the plan."

"What kind of lawyer?"

"A trial lawyer."

"Like Perry Mason?"

"No. He tries criminal cases. I wanna be an insurance defense lawyer. I plan on going to work for my dad. That's what he does. He defends civil tort actions."

"Torte? Ain't that a dessert?"

Smiling, I say, "You're talking about t-o-r-t-e. I'm talking about t-o-r-t. They're homonyms."

"Oh…"

"He litigates personal injury cases. Uh…hypothetically, let's say you run over a little, old lady crossing the street and break her leg."

She interjects, "I know somebody that actually did that."

"Really?"

"Yeah. My ex. He ran over a little, old lady and broke her ankle."

Cringing, I reply, "That's too bad. Anyhow, so the little, old lady sues you for negligence. You got car insurance, right?"

"Yeah."

"Your insurance company hires my dad to defend you. That's what an insurance defense lawyer does."

She nods like she understands.

I further hypothesize, "Now let's say you go in the hospital to have your gall bladder removed and the doctor negligently leaves his scalpel inside you. So you sue the doctor for malpractice. My dad defends him."

"Your dad defends doctors?"

"Yeah. He specializes in medical malpractice."

She looks at me apprehensively.

"What's the matter?"

Shaking her head, she answers, "Nothing. So...where'd you go to college?"

"Denison University."

"Never heard of it."

"It's a small, liberal arts college in Granville, Ohio."

"I ain't ever been there."

"It's a quaint village."

There's another awkward silence...

"So...where do you live?" I ask.

"Roseland. You probably don't know where that is. I live on the poor side of town. You know—Little Kentucky. Ain't that what rich people call it?"

"Snobbish rich people," I answer.

"I don't care if you call it Little Kentucky. I'm a hillbilly and proud of it."

I laugh. "I know where it is. It's near the steel mill. My dad used to take me there when I was a kid to watch them pour steel at night. I loved to watch the light show in the sky."

"I live in Roseland Trailer Park. I can sit on my front stoop and watch them pour steel at night."

"That's convenient. My aunt and uncle live in a doublewide mobile home in Florida. It's really nice."

"Yeah? Well, mine ain't no doublewide mobile home."

There's another long, awkward silence…

"Where'd you go to high school?" I ask.

"Mansfield Senior." Mansfield Senior High School is the old, deteriorating high school on the north side of town.

"Where'd you go?"

"Malabar." Malabar is the new, state-of-the-art high school on the south side of town. The Dean of Admissions at Denison once told me he considered it to be one of the top ten public high schools in Ohio.

"So…where do you live?" she asks.

"Woodland."

"You live on the rich side of town. Do you live in one of them old mansions?"

"No. Our house is modern."

Trying not to sound like I'm bragging, I describe our house. "It was designed by an architect who was an apprentice of Frank Lloyd Wright. So it's a Prairie-style home. It has a steel frame instead of wood. It's made of limestone and cypress and has huge walls of glass and a flat roof with skylights."

"Is it big?"

"I guess so. Counting the guest suite, it has five bedrooms, five full baths, and two half baths."

"That's big. Is it fancy?"

"My parents' bedroom is pretty luxurious. It has a stone fireplace and adjoining his and her dressing rooms. And their bathroom has his and her toilets and sinks and a walk-in shower for my dad and a soaking tub for my mom."

"That's fancy."

"Each of the bathrooms on the main floor has a skylight, so you feel kind of exposed when you're sitting on the toilet and an airplane flies overhead," I joke.

She laughs. "I like the way you talk. I can picture it."

This makes me smile. "I try to be descriptive. Paint a picture with words. The most unique feature is the half-completed bomb shelter. The guy who built the house was so afraid of nuclear war after the

Cuban missile crisis that he started construction of a fallout shelter in the basement. But he didn't finish it because he keeled over from a heart attack at forty-nine. Life is absurd, Lily," I remark with a sigh.

She sips her drink. "So is your dad gonna finish it?"

"Nope. He says, 'When your time's up, it's up.' "

"He must make a lot of money. He's a lawyer."

"He makes a lot of money, but he spends it as fast as he makes it. He lives like there's no tomorrow because of the war. Actually, he started out poor. He grew up on the north side of town in the flats near Westinghouse. Living the American dream, he made it to Woodland."

I feel like I'm talking about myself too much. "So, uh…how long have you worked here?"

"Two years."

"You like working here?"

"It ain't that bad. I'm used to the heat in the summer. And the dust. And the boredom. And the guys hitting on me…"

I nod sympathetically.

She polishes off her cocktail. Looking me straight in the eye, she asks, "You wanna know the truth?"

"Yeah."

"I hate this sweatshop."

"Right…so, uh…why don't you find another job?"

"I can't."

"Why not?"

"Cuz nobody else will hire me. Cuz I don't have a high school diploma. I had to drop out when I was sixteen. Cuz I got knocked up.

"And I need this job. I'm divorced, and my ex don't pay no child support. I got three kids I'm raising by myself. They need a roof over their heads. Food. Clothes. Health insurance…"

How the hell can someone who looks so young be the mother of three kids?

"Yeah. I see what you mean. So, uh…how old are you?"

"Twenty-five."

Unbelievable…

How the hell can someone who's only twenty-five years old have three kids?

"You must bathe in the Fountain of Youth. You look so young," I remark.

She smiles. "How old are you?"

"Twenty-two. I'll be twenty-three on October thirty-first."

"October thirty-first—you was born on Halloween."

"Yeah. I'm a Halloween baby, which probably explains why I am the way I am."

"What do you mean?"

"Well, all my friends tell me I'm kind of weird. But not in a bad way. In a good way."

She looks at me quizzically…

So Barnes told the truth. She's a divorced high school dropout with three kids who lives in a trailer park.

Shit…

She's not Lara.

No way…

Our conversation is at a standstill. It doesn't seem to bother her one iota. She just sits there peeling her orange. I become so uncomfortable with the awkward silence that I think maybe I should take her up on her offer of a drink—to lubricate the conversation. After all, it is Friday afternoon. All I have to do is make it three and a half more hours, and I'm free for the weekend.

I won't get addicted on one drink.

"Uh…hey, Lily. I changed my mind. I think I will take you up on your offer."

"What?" She pops an orange slice in her mouth.

"I think I will have a cocktail."

"Okay." She fills her thermos cup full of Bloody Mary and pushes it across the table to me.

"Thanks."

I take a swig—it tastes cold and tangy. I drink the whole cup.

"You can finish it off." She hands me her thermos.

I drink straight from the thermos. "So, uh…tell me about your kids."

Eyeing me skeptically, she asks, "You really wanna hear about my kids?"

"Sure. Why not?"

"Most guys ain't interested in them."

"Yeah, well, I'm not most guys. I like kids."

As long as they're not mine.

"Okay. You asked for it." She collects her thoughts for a moment. Smiling reflectively, she says, "Sean's my oldest. He just turned eight. He's all boy. Loves sports. Sarah's six and loves animals. Rachel's my baby. She's four.

"They can't wait for school to be out. They get to stay at my mama's this summer. She lives right around the corner from me. They love it there. She's got a farm with a barn and a lake and horses."

"It sounds like summer camp," I remark.

"I only trust family to watch them cuz there's just too many sickos in this world. There's a path that runs from my trailer to the farm, so they can walk over there without going out on the road or even leaving our property."

I empty her thermos and sit here chewing ice, feeling a nice buzz. She's happy, I'm happy. There are no more awkward silences. While I listen to her talk about her kids, I think about how someday I'd like to have my own kids when I'm ready financially and emotionally—but I don't tell her this. Before we know it, it's eleven fifty-nine—we're the only people still sitting in here.

"Shit! Time to get back to the salt mines," I exclaim.

We jump up and dash back to the packing department. She turns at the corridor that leads to her workstation.

"See ya at afternoon break," I holler.

As I pack, I think about Lily. I'm struck by how easy she is to talk to. Then I realize her hillbilly characteristics actually turn me on in an earthy way.

I can't stop picturing her ravishing face. Then I imagine kissing her rose lips and caressing her cinnamon hair and ivory skin…

My mind goes around in circles—I want her. I wanted her from the moment I first saw her. Ask her out.

Are you crazy? She has three kids. She's a high school dropout. She lives in a trailer. She's poor. Don't be a fool.

I feel myself swaying.

Whoa…I'm tipsy.

I picture her phenomenal body…

What the fuck? Lily, I don't care if you do have three kids…and are a high school dropout…and live in a trailer…and are poor. I don't give a damn if you aren't Lara…she ain't real…she's a fictional character…I ain't ever gonna find her. All I know is I want you…

Ask her out tonight. I could borrow Dad's Cadillac and take her to a drive-in movie.

I imagine making out in the back seat…taking her clothes off…seeing and feeling her fabulous body…then screwing—

Lifting a toilet off the line, it slips out of my hands and drops on the concrete floor—making a horrendous crash and shattering into shards of vitreous china.

I stand here mortified…

The other packers all whistle and hoot.

Merle appears out of nowhere. I'm scared he's going to notice that I'm tipsy and fire me; but all he does is tell me that it'll be deducted from my pay and make me sweep up the mess and dump it in the scrap bin.

At break, Lily is waiting for me where the corridor to her workstation intersects with the main corridor to the breakroom. Smirking, she says, "I hear you dropped a toilet."

Grinning sheepishly, I answer, "Yeah. I guess I'm not used to drinking. How'd you find out?"

"Beanie. Did Merle bust you for drinking on the job?"

"Luckily, he didn't notice."

"That's good." She pulls a lever on a machine, and a stream of water gushes downward out of a big nozzle into a tank with a drain. She washes her hands in the water.

"What the hell is that?"

"A toilet tester. Hey, you wanna see my workstation?"

"Sure."

She takes me to a storeroom off the corridor to the warehouse. Seated at a workbench is an old geezer who's working through his break. Lily introduces me to him. His name is Rufus. He grins toothlessly at me—his chin almost touches his nose. He spits a huge cud of chewing tobacco into an empty coffee can. A long, string of brown saliva dangles from his lips, which he breaks off with his fingers. He extends his leathery hand to shake my hand.

I shake it.

"Howdy," he drawls.

"Nice to meet you, Rufus," I say, covertly wiping the tobacco spit on my hand onto my pant leg.

"Rufus assembles part bags. He's been doing it forever."

Rufus packs another cud of chewing tobacco inside his cheek. He drawls, "Twenty-one years."

"He's my boyfriend. Ain't cha, Rufus?" she teases him.

He just grins at her bashfully.

As we walk away, she whispers, "He's a sweet old man that wouldn't hurt a flea. He just sits there farting all day. He don't ever take a break. He lives for his paycheck."

Lily shows me her workbench. On one side of it are several big cardboard boxes filled with ballcock parts: float balls, fill valves, flush valves, refill tubes, and overflow pipes. On the other side of it is a large plastic bin on rollers, which is half-filled with assembled ballcocks. She demonstrates how to assemble one.

I look at the photographs tacked up at her workbench.

"Those are my kids. Sean, Sarah, and Rachel," she says, pointing at each one.

I notice they all have sandy hair. "They look really cute."

Smiling proudly, she says, "They can be ornery, but I love them."

I look closely at a photograph of a man and a woman posing on a Harley Hog in front of a red barn. The man is wearing goggles and holding onto the handlebars with a big grin on his face. He looks tall and lean and has sandy hair. The woman is sitting high up behind him with her arms wrapped around his waist and is smiling serenely. She has long, wavy red hair and looks strikingly beautiful.

"That's my dad and mama. Sean and Ruby…"

"I see where you all get your red hair."

"My mama was a real beauty when she was young."

"I see that."

"And that's my dog, Cajin."

"C-a-j-u-n?"

"No. C-a-j-i-n."

"Is he a Golden Retriever?"

"Yeah. They have gentle temperaments. He's good with the kids. And that's Appaloosa. He's a Snowflake Appaloosa." She's pointing at a photograph of her sitting on a black horse with white spots. In the background is the same red barn. "He's my pride and joy."

"He's beautiful."

"That's why I'm breeding him. He'll make me a big stud fee."

Sitting on a golden horse next to her is another young woman with red hair and a body similar to Lily's. "That's me and my sister going horseback riding."

"What's her name?"

"Karen. That's her horse, Palomino."

"Palomino—that's a breed, right?"

"Not really. It's a coat color."

"Oh. So…where do you ride?"

"At my mama's farm. We got horse trails all through the woods."

Glancing at my watch, I exclaim, "Whoa. I'm late."

I dash back to my press. As I pack, I sober up…

So…should I ask her out?

I logically analyze it, evaluating what we have in common. I went to college and am going to law school. She's a high school dropout. I can't imagine smoking a joint and philosophizing about Dostoevsky with her.

I live in Woodland—the right side of the tracks. She lives in Little Kentucky—the wrong side of the tracks. I doubt our families will be socializing together at the country club.

I'm going to be a lawyer. I'm going to be white-collar. She assembles ballcocks. She's blue-collar. It's classic management versus labor. We'd be on opposite sides in a labor strike.

The truth is we have nothing in common.

I imagine what it would be like dating a woman who is the mother of three young children from a prior marriage. I realize I could not pretend they don't exist. The reality is she comes with three kids; they are a family. If I would date her, sooner or later I would have to get involved in their lives, which would mean taking on difficult parental duties and responsibilities. This would take considerable time and money, not to mention having to deal with her deadbeat ex-husband, which could be difficult. In three months I'm moving to Toledo to start law school. All my time will be spent studying; all my money will be spent paying for tuition, room, and board.

I want to be a father when I can financially support a family and am emotionally mature. I'm not ready to have my own kids right now—let alone take on the task of raising some other guy's kids. I'm still living at home with my parents. I can't even support myself—much less three stepchildren. The challenge is too daunting.

So…it's this simple: I don't want to be responsible for taking care of her children, and I'm too young to be a stepfather.

There is only one reason to get romantically involved with her— I'm sexually attracted to her more than any woman I've ever met. If I ask her out and we have fun, it'll lead to a first kiss, which will lead to making out, which will lead to sex. If I have sex with her, I run the risk of falling in love with her.

I recall falling in love with Beth and then breaking up with her. I know what happens when I fall in love with the wrong woman— pain and sorrow. When I go to law school, I would have to break up with Lily. The pain and sorrow would outweigh the pleasure and happiness.

Face it, man—the rational thing to do is not get involved with her romantically in the first place. I need to just be friends.

So do not ask her out.

I let out a long sigh…

Well, Lily…no more flirting with you.

Reluctantly, I squelch my sexual desire for her. Forcing her out of my mind, I count down the minutes to the weekend.

Finally, it's quitting time. I made it through my first week. While I'm filling out my time sheet, Mr. Castor and Merle stop by my packing press. I'm afraid they are going to bust me for drinking on the job. Instead, they tell me I have to work on Saturday because I'm not packing fast enough and the toilets are backing up in the cooling area. I'm concerned Mr. Machine and Herb are going to be mad at me for making them have to come in on Saturday; but, to my surprise, they thank me—they're glad to work overtime because they'll get paid time and a half. Me—I'm bummed out. I couldn't care less about getting paid time and a half. I just wanted two days off.

As I walk out of the plant with Lily, I complain to her that I have to work tomorrow. Since the tank packers aren't behind on ware, she doesn't have to. She tells me she's taking her kids fishing. I'm envious of her for having Saturday off. She's envious of me for earning time and a half on Saturday.

CHAPTER FOUR

On Monday morning, I look for Lily in the breakroom to sit with, but I don't see her. I wonder if she's sick today. At lunchtime she's waiting for me at the toilet tester. While walking to the breakroom, she tells me she had to call her union rep over break this morning. We eat lunch at her table back in the corner where we can talk in private.

"So how was your weekend?" she asks.

"Lousy. Saturday was beautiful, and I was stuck in this windowless, sweltering factory packing toilets all day. And then Sunday it rained, and I was stuck in the house all day. So how was yours?"

"Fun. Saturday I took my kids to Emerald Lake."

She tells me Emerald Lake is a private lake out in the country where she has a family membership; it has a beach, picnic and playground areas, tennis courts, a pavilion, and summer cottages.

"It sounds nice. What'd you do?"

"We went swimming and fishing."

"You catch anything?"

"Yeah. The fish was really biting."

"What'd you catch?"

"Mostly blue gill. A few bass. And three catfish. We threw back the blue gill and bass. The catfish we ate for supper. My kids love fried catfish with cornmeal breading."

"You know how to fish, huh?"

"Yeah. I'm a country girl. My dad took me fishing. What about you? You like to fish?"

"I don't know. I've never done it."

"You've never gone fishing?"

"Nope. I'm a city boy. My dad never took me. He doesn't like to fish. He thinks it's boring."

"I love to fish. It's free fun. You wanna go fishing with us sometime?"

While I think it'd be fun to go fishing, I don't want to get involved in her personal life. I just want to be friends with her at work. "Yeah. Sure," I fib. I figure I can always make up an excuse to get out of going if she actually invites me.

Changing the subject, I ask, "So…uh…how's the horse breeding going?"

"Fine. Yesterday I gave Dakota a physical. She's the broodmare. I wanted to make sure she's sound for breeding."

"So how'd you do that?"

"By examining her reproductive organs."

"How'd you examine her reproductive organs?"

"First, I palpated her mammary system for mastitis. Then I cleaned and disinfected her perineal area and wrapped and tied her tail. And then checked her vulva and palpated her ovaries, uterus, and cervix."

"How'd you do that?"

"By inserting my hand up her rectum and feeling them through the recto-vaginal wall."

"Where'd you learn to do that?"

"Dr. Hall trained me. He takes me along on house visits and has me do it for him. And I studied the *Veterinary Guide to Horse Breeding*. It has illustrations."

As an ex-biologist, I find this interesting. "When will you breed them?"

"The farmer that owns her is bringing her to Mama's farm after work. Now is the natural breeding season for horses in North

America. More sunlight causes mares to come into heat. That's cuz the gestation period for a foal is eleven to twelve months. So the weather will be warm, and there'll be plenty of grass for the foal to graze on when it's born next summer."

"Huh."

"Like Dr. Hall says, you can't beat Mother Nature. I'm breeding her the natural way. Live cover."

"Meaning?"

"The stallion covers the mare live. He mounts her, sticks his penis into her vagina, and screws her till he ejaculates. Then he dismounts. You ever seen horses screw?"

"Can't say that I have."

"It's amazing. I'll house her in the barn with Appaloosa during her heat cycles so they can get acquainted. When she's in heat, I'll turn them out in the pasture together without people being around to distract them. I'm trying to imitate nature—like free-roaming horses mate in the wild. This'll give them time to court." She gives me a sly smile.

"How do horses court?"

"She might sniff and lick and nuzzle him. He might nudge her and neigh. Smell her urine. Or do the Flehmen response where he lifts his nose up in the air and curls his upper lip. He's trying to see if she's in heat. If she ain't really in heat, she'll let him know by squealing or laying back her ears. Maybe even bite or kick him."

"Interesting."

"With her at my mama's place, I can check her daily. I'll see the signs when she's really in heat. She'll raise her tail and get in the mating stance and squat and urinate or squirt mucus out her vulva."

This girl is not dumb. Just because she uses bad English doesn't mean she's not smart. She's just not formally educated.

"Damn, Lily—you know a lot about horse breeding."

Smiling proudly, she tells me, "I could've impregnated her by artificial insemination. I perform AI for Dr. Hall's clients."

Now I'm really fascinated. "So how do you perform artificial insemination?"

"I insert my arm up a mare's vagina and inject semen into her uterus with a syringe during ovulation."

I'm blown away that she knows how to do this. "How much does a horse weigh?"

"The average mare weighs about a thousand pounds."

"And how much do you weigh?"

"A hundred pounds."

"Sounds dangerous."

"It can be if you don't know what you're doing. Mares in heat are unpredictable. Some don't take kindly to an inseminator sticking their arm up their vagina. Dr. Hall told me about a guy that got kicked in the stomach. It ruptured his spleen, and he almost bled to death."

"You're a hundred pound woman sticking your arm up the vagina of an unpredictable, thousand pound horse. One kick can kill you. You're fearless."

She shrugs like it's no big deal. "Dr. Hall calls me a natural-born inseminator. He says mares like me cuz I got gentle hands. Says I can relate to them cuz I'm female."

"Inseminator—that's a unique profession. You're the first inseminator I've met."

With a devilish twinkle in her eye, she says, "I could've inseminated her, but I want Appaloosa to get laid."

"I agree wholeheartedly. I'm sure he'll appreciate it. Artificial insemination would be a drag for him."

She laughs.

When she laughs, her eyes sparkle. Peering into them, I remark, "Hey, I just noticed something. You're eyes are different colors, aren't they?"

"Yeah. My left eye is blue. My right eye is green."

"Wow…I've never seen that before. That must be rare."

"I don't know. You like them?"

Scrutinizing them, I answer, "Yeah. They're brilliant shades of blue and green."

"My blue eye is good Lily." She smiles with an expression of pure innocence—she looks like a seventeen-year-old girl.

"My green eye is bad Lily." She looks at me with a sexually provocative expression on her face that makes my pulse quicken.

"Bad? C'mon, Lily—you have a good heart. You rescued me on my first day."

"You think you know me, but you don't really know me, Leo."

"I don't?"

"Nope. I can be dirty." She sticks the sucker that she's eating for dessert in her mouth and sucks on it…

She's flirting with me.

"How do you think I got three kids?"

"Uh…immaculate conception?" I joke. I marvel how she can change from innocent girl to seductress like that. It's unreal.

After lunch I think about her flirting with me. I wonder if she just likes to flirt or if she's interested in me romantically.

Opening her thermos, Lily tells me, "Cajin charged a skunk by the bird feeder last night and got sprayed. He stinks. This ain't the first time. That damn dog never learns his lesson."

"Dogs will be dogs," I reply philosophically. I recount how our German shepherd attacked a porcupine when we went on vacation to Lake George. My parents had to take him to a vet to have quills removed from his muzzle. Then he did it again two days later.

She winces. "I couldn't get the skunk smell out of him. I tried dog shampoo. Tomato juice. Nothing worked. Then he wondered why I wouldn't let him sleep with me on the bed."

"You let him sleep with you?"

"Yeah. He keeps me company. He lays his head on the pillow right beside me."

"I wanna come back reincarnated as your dog," I joke.

She laughs.

I tell her about Shepa spitting out pimentos. She thinks it's funny. To my surprise, I realize I enjoy listening to her tell me about her life. It's my entertainment when I'm bored shitless from packing toilets in the sweltering heat.

LILY

∞◊∞◊∞◊∞◊∞◊∞

"Mama's taking my kids to Vacation Bible School. She's afraid I ain't raising them to be religious cuz I don't take them to church. Sarah loves it—she likes to color and sing. But Sean hates it. He says it's boring. He wants to stay at the farm. What do you think I should do?"

Munching on a chip, I reply, "I remember my mom made me go to Vacation Bible School one summer when I was a kid. I hated it. After being cooped up in school all year, the last thing I wanted was to be stuck inside a church reading Bible verses on a beautiful summer day. I wanted to be outside playing with my friends. My two cents worth is that you should let him stay at the farm. It's summer vacation. Let him be free."

She nods like she's going to follow my advice. I wonder why she's asking me for parenting advice and not her ex-husband. I figure he must not be in the picture. I notice that she doesn't talk about him, and I don't ask. He's none of my business.

∞◊∞◊∞◊∞◊∞◊∞

On Saturday, Reese and I go to the country club. While lounging beside the pool, we debate which factory is the worst place to work—the steel mill or the toilet factory. He argues it's harder to shovel slag out of the pit. I argue it's harder to lift a fifty pound toilet five hundred times a day—that's twelve and a half tons a day. He argues the steel mill is hotter because of the blast furnaces. I argue the toilet factory is hotter because of the kilns. Ultimately, we agree that they are both sweatshops. Then it occurs to me that Boals-Corrigan is a much better place to work because of Lily.

During rest period, Reese and I go for a dip. Several young kids are sitting on the side of the pool alongside the high board, waiting for rest period to end. Regressing, we show off for them by performing trick dives off the high diving board. I do a forward one-and-a-half somersault, ending in a watermelon dive. Then

Reese does a full gainer, ending in a can-opener, which splashes them. I do a front flip with a half twist, ending in a can-opener, which splashes them again.

Standing on the high dive with a panoramic view of the surrounding golf course, I tell Reese, who's standing on the top rung of the ladder, "Reese, I hafta tell you about this girl I met at work—"

"Splash us," the kids beg.

I'm six foot one inch, a hundred and seventy-five pounds, so when I do a can-opener off the high board, I make a big splash. Springing as high as I can off the board, I lean backwards with my one leg extended downward and my other leg drawn up to my chest. As I enter the water, I feel the vacuum under my butt—whoom!

I drench the kids. They scream, "Do it again. Do it again."

Reese does a huge can-opener that soaks them.

Climbing back up the ladder, I ask him, "How high was my splash?"

"High."

"As high as the high board?"

"Higher."

"I knew I nailed it."

In between doing can-openers off the high board, I tell him about Lily rescuing me on my first day of work and her altercation with Bill Barnes. "She's a real spitfire," I say admiringly.

"It sounds like she likes you."

"Yeah. She's incredibly sexy, Reese. I think she just might be the sexiest woman I've ever seen. Ordinarily, I think sexy is as sexy does. But I've never seen a woman with such innate sex appeal. It's not just her ravishing face and phenomenal body—it's her nature. It's the way she walks and talks, the way she eats her peanut butter and jelly sandwich or reads her magazine. I'm more sexually attracted to her than I've ever been toward any woman. She's a redhead, and I have this thing about redheads. She...she just really turns me on..."

"So why don't you ask her out?"

"I don't wanna get involved with her romantically. She's not what I'm looking for."

"So? You don't hafta marry her. Just have a one-night stand. Love 'em and leave 'em. You know—like James Bond."

"No. I don't wanna do that. I really like this girl. We eat lunch together every day and just talk. She likes the way I talk, and I enjoy listening to her tell me about her life. We're becoming good friends. I'm afraid that would screw up our friendship."

"Hey, man, it's the '70s. The sexual revolution. Women's liberation. Free love. Get with it," he razzes me.

He does another can-opener. Then Coach Swigart, who's the new pool manager, tells us to knock it off because we're emptying the pool.

∞()∞()∞()∞()∞()∞

"So what'd you do this weekend?" Lily asks me.

"I went swimming with my friend, Reese Soliday."

"What's he do?"

"He's working at the steel mill this summer. He's going to Toledo State Law School in the fall. We're gonna be roommates."

"Where'd you go swimming?"

"The country club."

"I don't like that place. I was a waitress at the fancy restaurant there in high school. They was snooty."

"Who?"

"My boss. The members."

"Some members are snobs. They belong because it's a status symbol," I acknowledge. "That's not why my dad belongs. He hates golf. He joined for business reasons. His junior partner is the country club's lawyer, and his firm represents a lot of corporate clients who belong."

"And rich people are lousy tippers."

"Not my dad. He's a big tipper," I reply. When my old man drinks, he leaves huge tips. It drives my mom crazy.

"So what else do you do for fun?" she asks.

"Not much. I read." I tell her that I'm reading *The Lord of the Rings* trilogy by J.R.R. Tolkien; currently, I'm reading *The Fellowship of the Ring*. She's never heard of it, so I try to describe it to her.

"That sounds like something Sean would like. He loves monsters and sword-fighting. So what else?"

"Uh...nothing. I'm just treading water till I go to law school." I don't tell her about *Incognito's Folly*. I'm saving it for my true love— Lara. "So what'd you do on the weekend?"

"Saturday I took Sean to the motorcycle races. He loves motorcycles cuz his uncle Tommy races them. He wants to be a motocross racer like him. Mama bought him a dirt bike. He loves to race around the farm on the horse trails."

"I like motorcycles. I had a Honda 90 in high school and a Honda 350 Scrambler in college."

"Have you heard of Evel Knievel?" she asks.

"Sure. He performs stunts on his motorcycle."

"He's Sean's hero."

"He's my hero too. He's incredible. I gave a speech on him in speech class in college. He jumped his motorcycle over a twenty-foot-long box of rattlesnakes and two mountain lions. And the fountains at Caesars Palace. And tried to jump the Snake River Canyon on his rocket-powered Skycycle."

"Sean built this ramp in our back yard and jumps his motorcycle off it. He keeps jumping higher and higher."

"He sounds like a daredevil."

"He takes after me. I was a daredevil when I was young. I performed trick horse riding."

"What tricks?"

"I stood on a galloping horse holding the American flag."

I imagine her doing that. "Damn, Lily. You never cease to amaze me. Man, I would've loved to have seen that."

She smiles. Changing the subject back to Sean, she says, "I don't know if I should let him jump his cycle. I don't want him to be a sissy. But I don't want him to hurt himself either."

"Does he wear a helmet?"

"Tommy gave him one. But he don't wear it. He don't like how it feels."

"If he was my kid, I'd make him wear it. An ounce of prevention is worth a pound of cure."

She nods thoughtfully. "We're going to the races on Saturday. You wanna come with us? It's really fun."

While I'd like to go to the motorcycle races with her, I don't want to socialize with her children. Not wanting to hurt her feelings, I tell a white lie. "I can't, Lily. I've already made plans to play tennis with Reese this Saturday."

She tries to hide it, but I can tell she's disappointed.

"So where'd you learn to trick ride?"

"I grew up on a horse farm in Kentucky. My dad trained and bred horses. Rich people boarded their horses there. I rode them to exercise them. That's how I learned to ride.

"I got my first horse when I turned thirteen. My dad gave me a quarter horse for my birthday. I named her Roan cuz she had a roan coat. He taught me how to trick ride. Roan had the perfect temperament for trick riding. Smart, steady, and forgiving. I started performing for money."

"Where?"

"Horse shows. Rodeos. Fairs. I wore a red, white, and blue spandex costume. Country folk are patriotic. I loved performing stunts in front of a crowd. The cheers. But I quit."

"Why'd you quit?"

Frowning, she tells me, "Roan got killed in a wreck going home from a fair. A semi rear-ended us. We was riding in a pickup truck towing the horse trailer. The trailer probably saved our lives—it absorbed the brunt of the collision. But Roan's back was broken. The vet had to put her down. It broke my heart, Leo. I loved that horse. I cried for a week."

Listening to her story, I get a lump in my throat. "That's really sad."

"After she died my heart just wasn't in it no more."

I just look at her sympathetically.

"Mama's taking Sean and Sarah to swim lessons every morning at Emerald Lake. They don't wanna go. They say the water is freezing—it makes their lips turn blue and their teeth chatter. You think I should make them go?"

I'm starting to feel like I'm Abigail Van Buren dispensing parenting advice in her newspaper column, *Dear Abby.* "Absolutely. They need to learn how to swim. It could save their lives. They'll thank you someday."

"You think so?"

"I know so. I said the same thing when my mom made me take swim lessons as a kid. She told me she never learned how to swim and always regretted it because it curtailed her recreational activities. She said I'd thank her someday, and she was right."

She nods like she's going to follow my advice.

"I taught swim lessons at the country club and was the swim team coach. I think the fastest way to teach kids how to swim is put them on swim team where they hafta swim lengths at practice—it's sink or swim. By the end of the summer, they swim like fish."

"There ain't no swim team at Emerald Lake."

"Join the country club. They have a heated pool," I say facetiously.

"Right," she says sarcastically. "I ain't rich like you."

∞◊∞◊∞◊∞◊∞

One day the janitor comes in the breakroom during lunch. He's a little, squirrelly-looking guy. When he empties the trash barrel at the end of our table, he smiles at Lily in a creepy way. She ignores him. He moves on to the trash barrel at the next table.

She whispers, "I don't like him."

"Why?" I whisper back.

She waits until he's out of hearing range. "He's a creep. He spied on me going to toilet."

"Are you kidding?"

"I was sitting on the toilet when I heard a noise and looked up and seen him peeping over the top of the stall at me."

"What'd you do?"

"I complained to Mr. Castor."

She tells me Mr. Castor investigated her complaint. The janitor claimed he was innocently changing a ceiling light bulb and didn't know she was in there; but Mr. Castor didn't believe him because he set the ladder beside the toilet stall, which was too far away from the light socket. Management suspended him two weeks without pay and instituted a written policy prohibiting men from entering the restroom when she's using it. She has to hang a red sign on the outside door knob warning men not to enter.

"So you're the first woman they've ever hired to work in the shop, huh?" I ask.

"No. I'm the second. They told me the first woman didn't make it through the first day."

"It must be hard."

"My biggest problem is men coming on to me. But I just tell them I have three kids—that usually scares them away."

It scares me away.

"Actually, I've discovered that I like working with men more than women. They ain't catty like women. If they don't like you, they tell you to your face. Now they treat me like one of the guys. You know—they swear and tell dirty jokes in front of me. Some are even trying to help me get ahead. Like Jessie, he's trying to help me become a forklift operator. But it does get lonely cuz I don't really have any friends here I can talk to—except you and Jessie. Most guys ain't interested in what I'm interested in..."

"I think you're interesting to talk to."

"Really?"

"Really. I'm learning all about horse breeding."

She smiles. "I remember it was hard at first. Some guys resented me just cuz I'm a woman. They gave me shit about being a women's libber. Asked me if I burned my bras. I told them, 'Nope. They're too expensive.' "

I laugh.

"And some guys resented me cuz they thought I got special

treatment. You know—cuz I get the whole restroom to myself, and they hafta share it with other guys.

"And some guys thought I was stealing a job from a man. I remember my first day Merle told me I don't belong here. I should get a job as a waitress or a cleaning lady. I took a good job away from a man with a family to feed. I should've told him, 'I'm a woman with a family to feed,' but I ain't that quick. He said he warned them not to hire me. That it would cause problems. But they didn't listen to him. He hoped I'd quit. That made me feel really welcome."

"That Merle—he's a jerk."

"He's a bully. That's why everybody calls him Mean Merle. But I ain't scared of him. My dad taught me if you stand up to a bully, they back down."

"Sounds like sex discrimination to me. Did you complain to anyone?"

"No. He said if I told anybody, he'd just deny it. It'd be his word against mine. Like my dad said, I gotta choose my battles wisely. Only fight the ones I know I can win."

"Your dad sounds like a wise man."

"And I figured if I complained, everybody would think I'm a bitch and hate me. I gotta work with these guys. I couldn't stand it here if everybody hated me."

I nod.

"I'll stand up for myself if somebody's really trying to screw me. I ain't afraid to fight for my legal rights. I'm fighting right now. I filed a grievance over equal pay. It went to arbitration and I won. But they still haven't paid me my money."

"I'm impressed, Lily. You have intestinal fortitude to be the first and only woman to work here."

"I'm just doing what I gotta do to support my family."

"You're a trailblazer."

She smiles. "Management made a big deal out of it when they hired me. They tried to get free publicity. They got the newspaper to run a story on me—saying I was breaking gender barriers in the workplace. My picture was on the front page standing at my workbench. They printed my job title—Ballcock Handler. Brother! That was a big mistake. I got obscene phone calls for a month—guys asking me to come over and handle their ballcocks. So much for breaking gender barriers."

I laugh.

"The reporter was some girl right out of college. She interviewed me in the breakroom where there was air-conditioning. It was too hot for her at my workbench. She wanted to know why I took the job. You know—if I was a women's libber. I told her no—I took the job cuz I needed the money. Why else would you take a shitty job like this? Then she asked me if I was trying to break the glass ceiling in the workplace. I didn't know what she was talking about. I told her I thought the ceiling here was made of corrugated steel. She thought I was joking, but I wasn't."

I laugh.

"She kept talking about fighting for women's rights and some women's libber named Gloria Steiner that I hadn't ever heard of."

"Uh...I think you mean Gloria Steinem. She's a famous feminist. She's a founder of *Ms.* Magazine."

"Do you know everything?"

"Almost," I answer with a smirk on my face.

"Well, she kept talking about her and women's liberation. She made me feel dumb. I think I disappointed her."

"How so?"

"I think she wanted me to say I'm fighting for women's rights. You know—she wanted me to be like Gloria Steinem. But that ain't me. I ain't into protesting. I don't have time. I'm working two jobs. And trying to raise three kids."

I nod like I understand.

"I'm just an ordinary girl trying to make a living and be a good mama."

I think about what she just said for a moment. "Believe me, Lily, you're no ordinary girl. As a matter of fact, I think you're extraordinary."

As she comprehends what I said, her eyes begin to twinkle and she smiles at me affectionately...

My heart skips a beat.

Don't even think of it. She's not Lara. You've ruled her out.

Friday is my first payday. While everyone is waiting at the time clock to punch out, Merle hands out our paychecks. Initially, I'm somewhat disappointed with my take-home pay. Withholding taxes take a big chunk out of my wages. But then I realize I'll get a sizeable tax refund next spring just about the time I'll be running out of money for law school.

He hands Lily her paycheck.

Examining it, Lily frowns. "Damn it, Merle. They screwed up my paycheck again. Look!" She thrusts it back in his face.

He looks at her paycheck with a knitted brow…

She points out, "They're still paying me the lower rate."

"You're right. Sorry, Lily," he replies perfunctorily.

Exasperated, she says, "This is the third time."

"I know. It won't happen again."

"That's what you said last time."

He sighs impatiently. "I promise, Lily."

"You promised last time. You guys are trying to screw me."

"Look, Lily, don't bitch to me about it. It ain't my fault. Go bitch to bookkeeping. It's their fault. If you don't like how I'm handling it, you can deal with them. It ain't my problem."

Moving on, he hands Beanie his paycheck.

"Come back here, Merle!"

Stopping dead in his tracks, he looks at her surprised.

"I can't. I'd be violating our contract. It says I'm supposed to take any workplace grievance to the group leader. That's what my union rep told me. You're the group leader, ain't you?"

He nods grudgingly.

"So it is your problem," she corrects him.

Annoyed, he asks, "So what do you want me to do about it?"

"I want you to go to bookkeeping and get me a new paycheck at the right rate. And I want my back pay plus interest."

LILY

"Right now?"

"Yeah. Right now."

Rolling his eyes like she's being totally unreasonable, he says, "Lily, it's quitting time Friday afternoon. I'm tired. All I wanna do is go home and have a beer. I'll take care of it first thing Monday morning."

Shaking her head vehemently, she replies, "No, Merle. I ain't waiting any longer."

"Why are you being such a bitch?"

"I ain't being a bitch. I just want my money."

He mutters under his breath to Herb, "She's probably on the rag."

"I ain't on the rag. Get me my money."

Bristling, he replies, "Lily, you're starting to piss me off."

"I mean it, Merle. I ain't backing down. Go do it."

"No woman's gonna tell me what to do."

"Now, Merle."

Merle goes ballistic. Sticking his finger in her face, he shouts, "Don't be a raging bitch!"

Glaring at him fiercely, Lily stands her ground. "Don't you dare try to bully me, Merle. I ain't scared of you. I know my rights."

Fuming, he replies, "This...this is why they shouldn't let women work here. You're all raging bitches."

Trying to control her temper, she takes a deep breath. "I'm onto you guys. I know what you're doing. Chuck Skiles told me," she says coolly.

"And just what the hell do you think we're doing?"

"You're retaliating against me—that's what."

"Retaliating?" he scoffs.

"You're retaliating against me cuz I won my grievance, and there ain't a damn thing you can do about it cuz our contract says binding arbitration. That means the arbitrator's decision is final. So quit jerking me around and pay me my money."

He backs up a step and protests, "I ain't jerking you around, Lily."

She has fire in her eyes. Sparks are flying off her. Stepping toward him, she says, "This…this makes me really mad, Merle. Chuck Skiles told me retaliation is an unfair labor practice. You know what I'm gonna do? I'm gonna file a charge with the NLRB."

That strikes fear in Merle's heart. He stammers, "Just—just wait a minute, Lily."

"And you know what else this is? This is sex discrimination. You're discriminating against me cuz I'm a woman. You ain't paying me equal pay. And you just called me a raging bitch. You know what else I'm gonna do? I'm gonnna file an EEO complaint against you personally, Merle."

Merle panics. Trying to placate her, he tells her, "Okay, okay. I hear you. I'll take care of it. Just calm down. You don't hafta do that."

"I am calm, Merle. I'm perfectly calm. I'm gonna call Chuck Skiles right now. He told me he'd get me a free labor lawyer if you guys kept jerking me around. I'm gonna sue all of you. Every last one of you who's trying to screw me out of my hard-earned money."

Then she just turns around and walks away.

Scurrying after her, he begs, "Hold your horses, Lily. Please…please don't do that."

She spins back around and faces him. Shooting daggers with her eyes at him, she demands, "Fix it. Right now."

"Yes, ma'am."

"And don't you ever call me a raging bitch again."

He's cowed by her threats. "Lily, I'm sorry. I shouldn't've called you that. Please don't call him. I'll be right back with your money."

He trots off toward bookkeeping.

Everyone is staring at Lily in awe…

"Whoa, Lily—I don't believe you. You just stood up to Mean Merle. I love it," I tell her.

"I ain't gonna let him bully me. Not when I'm in the right."

"Man, you ripped him a new asshole. I don't think he's gonna call you a raging bitch again."

Grinning, she winks at me. "Like my brother, Ray, says, the squeaky wheel gets the grease. I guess that lit a fire under his lazy ass. I've got them by the balls cuz they screwed up legally. I can't believe he had the nerve to say he was tired when all he does is drive a tow motor all day. He don't lift nothing."

"Man, I wouldn't want you pissed off at me. You're a real tigress."

"You don't wanna mess with my money. I got three mouths to feed. I'm a pussycat most of the time. But I can be a raging bi—tigress when I get mad."

"I'll try to remember that."

Snickering, she replies, "Just don't do me wrong."

"Man, you should be a lawyer. You know the law."

"That's cuz my union rep told me."

"You're the one who should be going to law school."

At quitting time, everybody clocks out except Lily and me. I hang around and keep her company while she waits on Merle. About forty-five minutes later, he hands her two paychecks—a new paycheck at the correct pay rate and a paycheck for her back pay plus interest for all the time they had her pay rate wrong. Looking at her contritely, he says, "Sorry it took so long, Lily."

She thanks him and walks out the door triumphantly.

"Leo, I feel like celebrating—I'm rich. C'mon, I'll buy you a drink."

Happy for her, I'm tempted to have a drink with her.

"Take me for a ride in your sports car. I'd love to go for a ride with the top down," she says eagerly.

But then I remind myself that I'm not interested in socializing with her after work. I lie, "I can't, Lily. I'm meeting Reese at the pool." I figure if I keep turning her down, sooner or later she'll get the message.

On the way home, I think about Lily standing up to mean Merle for her rights. I truly admire her courage and marvel at how articulate she was in her own way.

I sigh.

Too bad it's impossible for me to fall in love with her.

CHAPTER FIVE

Monday, Tuesday, and Wednesday Lily is absent. She must be sick. During lunch, I sit at a table with Percy and Mel, who's the other tank packer and Percy's white sidekick. I enjoy shooting the breeze with them, but, I have to admit, I miss Lily. Much to my surprise, I realize she's more fun to talk to.

Even though they know I'm a college kid, I can tell they're beginning to accept me as one of them, so now is my chance to find out who pulled that prank on me. "So tell me—who was the joker who shit in the toilet on my first day?" I ask.

They just grin at each other knowingly.

"C'mon, tell me. I'm not gonna rat on him."

"You didn't hear it from me—Herb. He plays that prank on all the new guys," Percy divulges.

"Someday he's gonna play it on the wrong person, and it's gonna backfire on him," I reply.

When I arrive at work on Thursday, I'm glad to see Lily's car in the parking lot. At break time I look forward to seeing her, but, to my disappointment, she's not waiting for me at the toilet tester. I look for her in the breakroom, but she's not here either. Sitting with Percy and Mel, I wonder where she is.

After morning break, we have a line jam. The conveyor belt running from the packers' presses to the warehouse becomes jammed with boxes of ware; boxes are backing up and falling off the conveyor belt onto the concrete floor, breaking the vitreous china inside them. Merle runs to the electrical switch on the wall and shuts down the line. We spend twenty minutes clearing the line jam before Merle can switch the line back on.

At lunchtime I'm glad to see Lily waiting for me at the toilet tester. I greet her heartily.

"Hi," she says. Her voice sounds somewhat subdued.

As we walk to the breakroom, I ask, "Where were you this morning?"

"I was talking to Jessie."

"Where've you been the last three days? I've missed you. Were you sick?"

"No. I took some personal days."

She seems reticent about telling me why, so I drop the subject.

At lunch I tell her about the line jam. She barely says a word.

"Lily, you're awfully quiet today."

"I am?"

Peering into her eyes, I notice that she looks sad. "Is something wrong?"

Suddenly, tears well up in her eyes, and she nods her head.

"What's wrong?"

She sets her peanut butter and jelly sandwich down on the table. "My ex died," she answers almost inaudibly. A fat tear rolls down her cheek.

"What?" I ask incredulously.

"Donny died Saturday," she says louder. Her lower lip starts to quiver. "Poor Donny..." she groans, and the tears gush down her face.

"Jesus..."

She sniffles. Then whispers, "He killed himself..."

I'm horrified...

She sniffles again.

"Oh, God, Lily. That's...that's terrible. I'm...I'm sorry," I stammer lamely. I don't know what to say or do to console her...

Since she's sitting with her back toward the other people in the breakroom, nobody else notices. Composing herself, she wipes her nose and dries her red eyes with her napkin; then crumples up the napkin into a ball and tosses it in the trash barrel at the end of the table. Staring into space disconsolately, she says, "It's been a real nightmare, Leo…"

"I can imagine." I put down my sandwich.

"First Gladys told me he accidentally shot himself in a hunting accident. Then—"

"Gladys?"

"His mama. She called me late Sunday night. Woke me up. Told me she had bad news. Donny was dead. The safety on his gun was broke, and it accidentally went off when he was climbing down the ladder at his tree stand. I was so shocked…I could barely understand a word she said…I…I just couldn't believe it. I never dreamed he'd get killed in a hunting accident. He knew how to handle guns from being in the army.

"I worried all night about how I was gonna tell my kids. I didn't know if I had the strength. But I had to tell them. He's their dad. And I wanted them to hear it from their mama. I told them first thing in the morning. It was awful…" she trails off in utter dismay.

In a low voice, I ask, "Did you tell them he killed himself?"

She whispers, "No. I told them he accidentally shot himself when he was hunting. I didn't know he killed himself when I told them…"

I nod like I understand why she told them that. "I…I can't imagine telling them."

Wringing her hands, she tells me, "It was the hardest thing I ever done. Sarah took it really hard. She cried all morning. But I think she's gonna be okay. I think she cried it all out. Rachel, she's so young she don't really understand what happened. And she was just a baby when I left him, so she don't remember him. It's Sean I worry about. He didn't show any emotion. He just went outside and rode his dirt bike."

God…those poor kids…

"I didn't find out the truth till his sister, Angie, called last night. She told me the police in Texas said he shot himself. They found him sitting on the ground, leaning against the tree with his shotgun in his lap. They could tell he shot himself by the way he stuck the gun in his mouth and used a stick to push the trigger."

God, he blew his brains out. I visualize myself sticking a shotgun barrel in my mouth, pushing the trigger with a stick, the gun discharging, and my head exploding—I shudder.

"So...are you gonna tell them the truth?"

"I don't know what to do. They've had to deal with so much shit in their lives. His drinking. The divorce. And just when things was starting to get better, he has to go and do this to them. I'm so mad at him. How could he do this to them?"

Shaking my head, I answer, "I don't know...the mind is a labyrinth..."

She cries pitifully, "This'll fuck them up for life, Leo."

Between the divorce, Donny's alcoholism, and now his suicide, I figure it'll be a miracle if her kids turn out normal. But, trying to console her, I reply, "Not necessarily. Kids are pretty resilient."

"Damn you, Donny! You can't do nothing right. You can't even die right. You always do what you want and leave me to pick up the pieces," she says bitterly.

I'm struck by how angry she is with him.

"Leo, what do you think I should do? Tell them the truth? Or just let them think he died accidentally?"

Pondering her predicament out loud, I reply, "Should you be honest? Or spare them the pain? That's a tough question, Lily. I...I don't know..."

"I'm thinking maybe someday I'll tell them when they're old enough to understand. But not now. They're too young."

I nod in agreement. Then I just sigh...

"You better eat your lunch," she says.

While I eat my sandwich, I morbidly visualize Donny blowing his brains all over the tree trunk. Try as I may, I cannot block out the gory image.

"Boy, this summer's just flying by," she remarks.

"Yeah. It's almost the Fourth of July."

As we make small talk, the shock of his suicide slowly recedes.

Recalling the way she cried when she first told me, I suspect that she still has strong feelings for him.

While I pack after lunch, I contemplate why he killed himself. What the hell drove him to blow his brains out? What was he thinking and feeling the days, hours, and minutes before he pulled the trigger?

I recall how angry she was with him for doing this to their kids. Despite sounding harsh, I understand her anger. Knowledge of his suicide would undoubtedly scar them for life. It might be better if she never tells them the truth.

I stew over what I should do. I realize Lily is my friend. She's helping me get through this summer. Now I need to be her friend and help her get through this tragedy. At the same time, I don't want to get sucked into her tragic life. I need to try to be supportive, but I don't want her to think I'm the answer to her problems—her savior. This consternation reinforces my decision not to get involved with her emotionally because of her kids.

At afternoon break, I ask her, "So is there gonna be a funeral?"

"Yeah."

"Where?"

"Here in Mansfield. Sunday afternoon."

"Are you going?"

With a tormented look in her eyes, she disregards my question. "He...he tried to get back together with me."

"He did?"

"Yeah. He called me the night before he killed himself. Told me he still loved me and needed me and really missed the kids and wanted to come home. Said he'd quit drinking this time for good. He'd found Jesus and was going to AA meetings..."

"So what'd you say?"

"I told him no. It was over. Then he begged me to give him one last chance. He told me he couldn't live without me. I just kept telling him, 'No, Donny—I don't love you anymore.' He was crying. I...I hung up on him..."

She sighs deeply. "I never dreamed he'd kill himself. He always said that's a coward's way out. Now I feel guilty. I wish I hadn't hung up on him…"

"It's not your fault, Lily."

She holds her face in her hands in anguish.

"You didn't make him do it. It was his choice. An act of free will."

Lifting her face from her hands, she nods feebly…

She rubs her eyes and says wearily, "I don't wanna go to the funeral. His whole family will be there. I can't face them. They blame me for not standing by my man. After I left him, Gladys called me and reminded me of my wedding vow—till death do us part. Then she spent an hour telling me how she's stood by Harold through his drinking problem."

I figure Harold must be Donny's dad. I advise, "Don't go. You're divorced."

"I have to. Like Mama says, he was my husband and my kids' dad, even if he never paid no child support."

"Are you going alone?"

"No, I'm taking Sean and Sarah. Mama says it'll give them a chance to say goodbye to him, and they need to see him dead, so they know he ain't ever coming back. But I ain't taking Rachel. I think she's too young to go to a funeral. It'd probably freak her out."

While I personally believe the custom of viewing the decedent's embalmed body in an open casket at a funeral is an anachronism, I nod in sympathy.

Back at my press after break, I think about Donny telling Lily that he wanted to get back together and couldn't live without her. This answers the question why he killed himself. I mutter, "Damn, Donny—you really couldn't live without her." I can't imagine killing myself over a woman. As long as you're alive, there's always a chance of falling in love with another woman.

After work I walk Lily out to her car. Sitting in the driver's seat with the engine idling, she rolls down her window. "Leo, I'm taking tomorrow off. I just gotta somehow get through this."

"Hang in there, Lily. Take it one day at a time. Just get through the funeral."

She nods sorrowfully as she drives away.

As soon as I get home from work, I check the Obituaries. Immediately, I spot Donald Wyatt's obituary. There is a photograph of him in his army uniform. His obituary says he died in a hunting accident; he was a veteran who honorably served his country in the U.S. Army during the Vietnam War and was awarded a Purple Heart; he graduated from Mansfield Senior High School and was the captain and quarterback of the varsity football team; he loved rock and roll music and played lead guitar in The Mustangs rock band. It identifies his family members who have survived him, including Sean, Sarah, and Rachel; but it doesn't identify Lily.

At morning break on Monday, Lily is waiting for me at the toilet tester. Walking down the corridor, I ask, "So...how'd the funeral go?"

"Awful. I would've walked out if I hadn't had Sean and Sarah with me. The preacher didn't know shit about Donny. He didn't say one word about his life. That he had kids. Or that he fought for his country. All he did was read Scripture and talk about salvation and Donny's soul. He said he was a lost soul till he found Jesus. He got his house in order by accepting Jesus as his Savior in the nick of time. Now his soul is in Heaven with Jesus and God, and that everybody needs to get their house in order before it's too late. All he wanted was to save souls. Donny would've hated it."

"Did he say anything about how he died?"

"Huh-uh. Nobody said anything about it. Angie acted like she never called me."

In the breakroom, I sit across from her at our table with my soft drink. She's drinking her orange juice out of her thermos cup.

"So how'd your kids handle it?"

"Well, they didn't actually see him laid out dead in his casket cuz it was closed. But I think they know he's dead and gone forever."

Closed casket—that shotgun must've blown his head off.

"After the funeral, we went to the cemetery for the burial service. An honor guard fired rifles at his grave. Sean thought that was cool."

"Did his family give you a hard time?"

"No, not really. After we left the cemetery, we went to a gathering at their church. Gladys told me she wished she could see her grandkids more. I told her I'm afraid to bring them over to her house cuz of Harold's drinking problem. It ain't safe for them to be there. So we worked out an arrangement. I'm gonna bring them over when he's at work."

"That's good."

"Harold didn't speak to me. He looked like he'd been drinking."

She tells me the church ladies brought food. It was good, old-fashioned home-cooking. Her kids got to see their cousins on that side of the family.

I realize I need to ask her about her feelings, but I'm uneasy talking about emotions. Taking a deep breath, I ask, "So, uh…how're you coping?"

"Okay. I'm getting through it."

"How do you feel?"

She reflects momentarily. "Part of me feels sad. I once loved him. We had three kids together. I feel really bad for them cuz they've lost their dad.

"But part of me feels relieved. I've dreaded that phone call for years. I always feared he'd die from driving drunk. I think he had a death wish. He always said he should've died in Vietnam. Now I finally got it over with…"

Impassive, she adds, "The truth is he died in my heart a long time ago."

I nod like I understand.

Break time ends. She screws the lid and cup back on her thermos. "Life goes on," she says stoically.

While I'm packing, I think about her marriage to Donny. I realize she has ambivalent feelings toward him. She said she once loved him, but her emotionless words "he died in my heart a long time ago" echo in my mind.

I wonder why they got divorced. Obviously, he had a drinking problem. I read somewhere that most marriages break up over infidelity. I wonder if he cheated on her or she cheated on him.

At lunch my curiosity gets the better of me, and I ask, "So, uh…how long were you and Donny married?"

"Five years."

"So why'd you guys get divorced?"

"Why do you ask?"

"I just thought it might help for you to talk about him."

She looks at me uncertainly…

"Lily, you helped me make it through my first day here. You're helping me make it through the summer. You've been my friend. Now it's my turn to be your friend."

She's wavering…

Her hand is resting on the table.

Touch her.

I place my hand on hers.

She glances at it; then looks into my eyes and smiles…

"C'mon, Lily. Tell me the story of your marriage," I coax.

"It's a sad story. You sure you wanna hear it?"

"Yeah. The greatest love stories are tragedies. *Madame Bovary. Wuthering Heights. Anna Karenina. The Red and the Black.*"

"Never heard of them."

"Take my word for it. I minored in English in college. *Romeo and Juliet.* You've heard of it, haven't you?"

"I seen the movie." With a twinkle in her eye, she asks, "Like *Bonnie and Clyde*?"

I chuckle. "Yeah, like *Bonnie and Clyde.*"

"Okay…you asked for it."

Lifting my hand off hers, I resume eating my sandwich.

She stares with brooding eyes ahead, recollecting…

"I first met Donny in junior high. He and my brother, Luke, was best friends. He'd come over to our house to see him. I could tell he liked me—he'd tease me.

"He was a year ahead of me in school. We started dating in high school the summer before my junior year, his senior year. He was the star quarterback on the football team. I was a cheerleader. At pep rallies, he'd tell me he was gonna score a touchdown for me. I thought that was romantic—"

Suddenly, the image of a cinnamon-haired cheerleader leading cheers for Mansfield Senior High School at a basketball game against my alma mater, Malabar, flashes through my mind. "Wait a minute. I remember you. I saw you cheerleading at the Mansfield-Malabar basketball game. You were drop-dead gorgeous."

She smiles.

"I never saw you cheerleading again."

"That's cuz I had to quit. You know— cuz I got knocked up."

"Right…"

"Anyway, all the girls was chasing after him. I knew he wasn't that smart, but I fell in love with him cuz he was so nice. Everybody liked him. And he was so handsome. I thought he looked like Robert Redford."

I picture his photograph in the newspaper. "Damn—he does look like Robert Redford."

"And…well…." she pauses. Smiling in a naughty way, she says, "We started doing it. You know—screwing. Donny didn't like to use a rubber. He said it was like taking a shower with a raincoat on."

I laugh.

"And…I got pregnant. It was a big scandal. I was only sixteen. They pressured me to drop out of school when I started to show."

"Who?"

"The principal and some guidance counselor. They told me and Mama how kids can be cruel, and I'd be the laughingstock of the school. So I dropped out…

"I stayed home and watched my belly grow bigger and bigger. We sort of had to get married. I didn't wanna give up the baby for adoption. I was afraid I'd always wonder what happened to it. I told Donny he didn't hafta marry me—I didn't wanna trap him. I'd raise our kid by myself. Mama said she'd help me. I was young and naïve. But he said he truly loved me and wanted to marry me and raise our kid together. We thought love would conquer all. So we got married. Everything happened so fast. We had a shotgun wedding the weekend after he graduated. Sean was born two weeks later…

"Then one day he and Luke got drunk and joined the Army.

They wanted to fight for their country like their dads. I got pregnant with Sarah before he went to Vietnam. I had her while he was there.

"He and Luke was in the infantry. They called themselves brothers in arms and swore they'd come home together."

She takes a deep breath. "Luke got killed…"

Aghast, I ask, "Your brother got killed in Vietnam?"

"Their platoon went out on patrol, and he stepped on a landmine. Donny was walking in front of him. Somehow he missed it. He got shrapnel in his back and legs. They both won Purple Hearts. He threw his away. Mama has Luke's."

"They were war heroes."

"This…this is kind of weird…" she hesitates to tell me.

"What?"

"Do you believe in ghosts?"

"Not really. Why?"

"I…I felt Luke's presence at the funeral yesterday. You know— like…like he was there watching…"

"Huh…"

"Anyway…the war changed Donny. It…it really messed him up. When he came home, he was a lost soul. He felt so guilty. He thought he should've been the one that stepped on the landmine. That's when he really started drinking. He'd drink to blot out the guilt and sorrow…"

Yeah, my dad really started drinking after the war.

"From then on, our marriage went downhill. After Vietnam he got stationed at Fort Hood, Texas. I moved there with Sean and Sarah. I shouldn't've got pregnant again. Rachel was an accident.

"When Donny got discharged, he went to work at the post office in Dallas. They hired him cuz he was a vet. He got fired there cuz he backed his mail truck over a little, old lady walking down the sidewalk. He was drunk. After that he never could hold a regular job. He always got fired for drinking on the job.

"Then he took up the guitar and joined a rock band called The Mustangs. He practiced till his fingers bled and got really good. He played lead guitar. I swear they played every dive bar in Texas. He'd stay up all night drinking and carousing. I remember one night this groupie had him autograph her tit. Some groupie was always following him back to his motel room to try to have sex with him. The funny thing is I don't think he ever cheated on me with other women. Just the bottle…"

"Huh."

"Finally, they kicked him out of the band cuz he was always drunk. I tried to tell him he had a drinking problem. He needed to go to the VA hospital and get help. But he wouldn't listen. He didn't think he had a problem. He thought he could quit whenever he wanted. But he couldn't."

Yeah, that's what my old man says—he can quit whenever he wants to. But he can't.

"Things really turned to shit after that. We was broke. He had to hock his electric guitar. That about killed him. After that he was just a drunk. He loved the bottle more than he loved me. When we was first married, he loved to screw me. But after he got hooked on booze, he'd rather get drunk than screw me. He'd drink gin all night. I'd find him passed out on the living room floor in the morning with an empty bottle next to him. I couldn't lift him. The kids would find him lying there. I'd tell them he was just sleeping, but they knew something was wrong.

"I remember one morning I found him lying on his side, cradling his bottle in his arms. I tried to take it from him. He woke up, and we started fighting over it. Somehow I got it away from him. I was gonna pour it down the drain."

I remember pouring Dad's bottle of booze on the ground while mowing the yard.

"He begged me, 'Please, Lily, gimme back my bottle.'

"I told him, 'You love your precious bottle more than you love me.'

"Then I heard Sean crying. He was standing in his bedroom doorway watching us the whole time. It broke my heart, Leo."

It's still so painful to her that she has to close her eyes and pause…

"Right then I knew I should leave him, but I tried to save him. I thought I owed him that.

"After that fight, he quit drinking at home and started drinking at bars. He got a DWI. Lost his license. Then he got a second DWI when his license was suspended. He did thirty days in jail. I visited him there. I could see his face through a dirty glass window. I had to talk to him through these little holes in the door. It was awful."

I think about my dad's DWI a few years ago. He and my mom think that they hid it from us kids. But Jack found out about it and told me, and I told Olivia. Dad's lawyer, Tom Moore, who's supposed to be the best criminal defense lawyer in town, got it reduced to Reckless Operation. Dad had to go to driving school but not to jail.

"After Donny got out of jail, I got a job working at a bar. We lived in this apartment that was a dump. I couldn't make enough money to pay the rent. We was getting evicted. All I had was like thirty bucks to feed the kids. He'd steal my money out of my purse to buy booze, so I hid it in a shoe. He was supposed to watch the kids while I went to work. Instead, he found my money and left Sarah and Rachel with the babysitter next door."

She pauses. I can tell by the expression on her face something bad happened.

I just look into her eyes sympathetically.

"He drove Sean to the football field to play catch. Afterward, he stopped at a bar on the way home and got drunk. Then drove his truck into a tree. The cops found him passed out behind the wheel. Sean was in the front seat crying with blood running down his face. He hit his mouth on the dash—it knocked out his two front teeth. Luckily, they was just baby teeth."

I see this intensely painful realization in her eyes. With raw anguish in her voice, she says, "He could've killed him, Leo. He could've killed my little boy…"

I feel her intense pain…

Holding her forehead in her hand, she stares despondently at the table and mutters to herself, "I was a bad mother. I let him down. I let my little boy down…"

"No, you didn't."

Racked with guilt, she says, "Yes, I did. I'm his mama. I'm

supposed to protect him."

"It wasn't your fault. You were at work. It was Donny's fault. He's supposed to protect him too."

The expression on her face is that of a cornered animal. "I was torn. I was afraid something bad was gonna happen sooner or later. But...but I didn't wanna break up my family. I had to choose between him and my kids."

I know the feeling when you have to choose between loved ones.

"You were caught between a rock and a hard place," I commiserate.

With a crazed look in her eyes, she replies, "I was caught in a living hell. All I can say is, Thank God he didn't kill him..."

Believe me, I know the feeling.

She solemnly says, "I chose my kids. And that's when I stopped loving him..."

She starts peeling her banana.

"So what'd they do to him?"

"They threw his sorry ass back in jail. After what happened to Sean, I knew I had to leave him. God gave me another chance to save my kids, and I took it. The night before the landlord was gonna evict us, we moved in with my friend, Tina. Which turned out to be a disaster. One night she got drunk and told me she was a dyke and loved me. I had to tell her I wasn't a dyke. I just liked her as a friend. It broke her heart. After that I couldn't stay there.

"So I called Mama. She told me to load the kids in the car and come straight home. Dad wired me two hundred dollars. I drove all day and all night. The kids slept in the car. My Camaro just barely made it. The engine had an oil leak. I didn't have enough money to fix it. I had to put two quarts of oil in it every time I got gas..."

She drops her banana peel in the trash. Looking at me steely-eyed, she says, "And then I got my shit together. I made up my mind to divorce him. Dad hated to see me do it. He really liked him cuz they was both vets. He and Donny and my brothers loved to go deer hunting together. But he told me I had to do it—for my own good and the kids. He told me Donny was an alcoholic and would pull us all down in the gutter.

"So I filed for divorce in Ohio, and the judge gave me custody of my kids. First, we lived with my folks at the farmhouse. Then Mama gave us a trailer to live in. She owns the trailer park where I live. She saved us. My mama is my rock. I don't know what I'd do without her.

"That's the story of my marriage…"

I'm at a loss for words…

"We didn't live happily ever after."

Packing on autopilot after lunch, I ponder the story of her marriage. It is truly heartbreaking. Obviously, it was Donny's alcoholism that destroyed it. I keep picturing the crazed look in her eyes when she told me that she was caught in a living hell and thanked God he didn't kill Sean. I can relate to her pain and sorrow. We share the pain and sorrow of having loved ones with drinking problems. Since she confided in me about Donny, I'm tempted to confide in her about my dad. But I don't feel comfortable telling her—we're not close enough yet.

I can relate to her dilemma of having to choose between Donny and her kids. Sometimes I feel like I have to choose between my dad and mom. I love my dad and feel like I need to support him, but I love my mom and sometimes feel like she needs to divorce him for her own wellbeing.

Lily's tragic life—teenage pregnancy, shotgun marriage, Donny's alcoholism, their divorce, his suicide—makes me realize just how easy my life has been. The only adversities I've faced are my dad's drinking problem, my breakup with Beth, and worrying about getting drafted to fight in the Vietnam war. It makes me feel like she's an adult, and I'm still a kid.

I'm free with a bright future ahead of me; she's trapped in her tragic past.

At afternoon break, Lily says, "Leo, thanks for listening to me. It made me feel better. You're the first person I've ever told about me and Donny. I feel like I can talk to you. You know—tell you the truth."

I just smile at her…

She just smiles back at me…

CHAPTER SIX

Beth and I are screwing passionately in my psychedelic room in Granville. I feel my climax approaching—

I wake up.

Longing for her, I stare into the darkness…

Downhearted, I admonish my subconscious, "You hafta stop dreaming about her, or you're never gonna get over her."

"There's only one way to get over her—find Lara," Liam Incognito replies.

"I hope I find her at law school," I reply.

∞◊∞◊∞◊∞◊∞◊∞

"Hot damn, Lily. Salami with mustard. Mom packed my favorite sandwich."

"Your mama still packs your lunch?"

"Yeah. It gives her existential meaning," I joke.

Rolling her eyes, she replies, "Even Sean can pack his own lunch."

While I heat my sandwich in the microwave, I wonder if Lily is seeing anyone privately. She never talks about dating.

"So…tell me about your love life, Lily."

"What love life? I ain't got no love life."

"I can't believe you don't have a boyfriend."

She scoffs, "You gotta be kidding. I got three kids. The only guys interested in me are losers. Or have a screw loose."

"C'mon, a pretty woman like you has to have a boyfriend."

"I was seeing an older man. A cop. But I ended it."

"Why?"

"He's a cheater."

"A cheater?"

"He likes to screw around. He's a good-looking guy and really funny. Women love a good-looking, funny guy in a uniform, and he can't tell them no. He's been married twice.

"And he drinks too much. I ain't making the same mistake again. Like my mama says, 'Fool me once, shame on you. Fool me twice, shame on me.' "

"Your mama's right."

"He asked me to marry him. I told him no. I ain't that desperate for a man."

I nod like I believe her.

"I know what I'm looking for. I just can't find him," she tells me.

"What are you looking for?"

"Just a decent guy. Somebody that's going somewhere in life. And likes to have fun but ain't no alcoholic. And…sexy," Grinning coyly, she says, "Somebody like you."

I'm thrilled that she thinks I'm sexy. I take a bite of my sandwich, trying not to chew with my mouth open.

"So what about you? You got a girlfriend?"

"No."

"I don't believe it. A good-looking, college guy like you must have girls beating down your door."

"I wish."

"You really don't have a girlfriend?"

"Nope." I don't want her to think I'm a homo, so I tell her, "There was a girl at Denison—Beth Brooks. I dated her all through college, but we broke up when we graduated."

"So why'd you break up?"

I don't know how to explain it without telling her about

Incognito's Folly and my secret romantic dream of finding Lara, which I doubt she'd understand. Trying to evade, I tell her, "It's a long story."

Glancing at the clock on the wall, she replies, "We got time."

"I don't really like to talk about it. It resurrects sad feelings."

"I told you about me and Donny."

"That's fair. Okay...maybe it'll be therapeutic for me to talk about it."

I picture Beth the first time I saw her...

"I saw Beth on my first day of college. She was in my Biology 101 class. I noticed she was really pretty. She has doe eyes and long, lustrous, chocolate brown hair. And she looked smart.

"Then I saw her a few days later at the university pool swimming lengths in the lane next to me. She looked really hot in her Speedo swimsuit. I struck up a conversation about how fast she swam butterfly. It turned out we'd both been on swim team in high school and were trying to stay in shape. So we started working out together.

"Then we became lab partners in Biology. There's nothing more romantic than dissecting an earthworm together," I joke.

She laughs.

"We both majored in Biology. I was pre-med. I thought I wanted to be a doctor. She minored in Education so she could teach high school Biology. We started studying together at the library. After we'd finish studying, I'd walk her back to her dorm late at night.

"Then one night we stopped by the sundial in front of Swasey Chapel. I remember it was fall and the leaves were swirling all around us in the moonlight—it was bewitching. I kissed her and, just like that, it turned romantic."

Lily's intrigued.

"After that we saw each other exclusively. We ate together. Studied together. Worked out together. Did everything together."

Don't tell her that we smoked pot together.

"We took Astronomy together the second semester of our freshman year. One night—I remember it was spring and real balmy out—we were up in the observatory looking at the rings of

Saturn through the telescope. They were magical. And I told her I loved her. And she told me she loved me.

"Over the summer, I went to her house in Cleveland and met her mom and dad. They live in a stone mansion in Shaker Heights. Her dad's a doctor. He really liked me because I was pre-med. Then she came to my house and met my mom and dad, who really liked her. They thought she was very smart and had common sense, and they hoped we'd get married someday."

Don't tell her that you lost your virginity to her that summer.

"In my sophomore and junior years, I took all the pre-med courses. Human Anatomy and Physiology, Molecular Biology, Inorganic and Organic Chemistry with their four hour labs. They're some of the hardest courses in college.

"My grades and MCAT score were high enough to get into med school. All I had to do was apply.

"In our senior year, we started talking about getting married someday. I was just talking abstractly—someday in the distant future. She was talking concretely. She had everything planned out. She wanted to get married after graduation. Have a big summer wedding. Then I'd go to med school. She told me she'd support me by teaching while I was in school. And then, after I became a doctor, I'd join her dad's practice, and she'd quit teaching, have three kids, and stay home and raise them. And, when her dad retired, I'd take over his practice. We'd live happily ever after in a ritzy house in Shaker Heights."

I feel this dull heartache…

I can't believe it. A year later it still hurts…

She's looking at me with a puzzled expression on her face. "So what went wrong?"

"Me. I changed. I started having serious doubts about whether I really wanted to be a doctor. Her dad's an ear, nose, and throat specialist. I started questioning whether I wanted to spend my life examining people's ears and noses and throats. I thought I'd get bored looking up their orifices."

"I don't get bored sticking my arm up horses' orifices."

"That's why you should be a vet."

She doesn't reply.

"Anyhow, I kept procrastinating on applying to med school. She kept asking me, 'When are you gonna apply?' I kept telling her, 'Don't worry. I got things under control.' And then one day it was too late—I missed the deadline. When she found out, she asked me—'Why?' I told her, 'I'm not sure I really wanna be a doctor.' That's when she started having doubts about us.

"Then things really started to fall apart. She was waiting on me to propose and give her an engagement ring. But I just couldn't commit. Finally, she got tired of my stalling. She told me she wanted an engagement ring by graduation. If I wasn't ready to marry her after four years, maybe it was time for her to move on."

With a smirk on her face, Lily remarks, "She told you to shit or get off the pot, huh?"

I nod, wincing.

"I remember we broke up on the weekend we graduated. It ruined graduation for both of us. She was moving her stuff out of my apartment, loading it in her car to take home, and I was helping her. I told her I'd call her later about getting together. She asked me if I was ever gonna marry her and go to med school. I told her, 'I don't know.' Then she told me, 'You're lost. I don't wanna be with you until you find yourself and are ready to commit. Don't call me until then.' "

Mesmerized, Lily asks, "So what'd you do?"

"I never called her. We haven't spoken to each other since then," I say sadly.

"You didn't try to work it out?"

"No. I didn't think it was possible."

"Why?"

Tell her why. She confided in you.

Setting my sandwich down on my paper plate, I look into her eyes intently. "Truthfully, I started to rethink my life after I saw the movie *Dr. Zhivago* over Christmas break in my junior year. It was so compelling I saw it three times. It's an epic romance set in Russia during the Bolshevik revolution. Dr. Zhivago is both a doctor and a poet. He falls in love with this beautiful, passionate woman named

Lara. There's a scene in the movie where they run away to Varykino to escape the civil war. Varykino is an enchanting country house with onion domes covered with snow. There he's inspired by her to write the Lara love poems, and she loves him because of what he creates for her. I don't know why, but this idea of a man being inspired by a woman to create things and her loving him because of it...just...just really stirred me emotionally. To me, this personifies romantic love.

"After I saw it, I took a creative writing course and wrote a short story. At the end of the semester, the class voted it their favorite story. Then I took an art class and drew illustrations for the story. My art teacher, Mrs. Zimmerman, really liked them. She told me I had more natural art talent than any student she'd ever had and tried to persuade me to become an artist.

"That's when I realized I didn't want to be a doctor. What I really wanted to do was write stories and draw pictures for Beth, and for her to love me because of what I created for her.

"But whenever I tried to tell her about my short story, she always fell asleep or at least yawned—she had no interest in it. And then when I showed her my illustrations and told her that Mrs. Zimmerman said I should be an artist, she thought that was a bad idea.

"I lived off campus in an old house in Granville. I loved to walk around town late at night and look at the quaint, old homes in the moonlight. It was so quiet and peaceful you could hear a train or a dog barking on the other side of town. One night I remember hearing a kid in bed ask his mom for a drink of water through his open window. I'd fantasize about living in this one really pretty Gothic Revival house. It's the last house on a dead end street and is perched high atop a bluff overlooking the town. I imagined writing stories and drawing pictures for Beth there.

"So one night I took her there and told her it was my dream to live here someday and write novels and draw pictures for her. She asked me how we would live. I told her I could get a job at the grocery store, and she could teach. I can still picture the look on her face when I told her that—she looked at me like I was crazy.

"That's when I realized she was in love with me because she mistakenly thought I wanted the life of a doctor. She didn't love the real me. So that's why I broke up with her."

"So you think it was her fault you broke up?"

"Not really. If it's anyone's fault, it's mine. My first three years of college I thought I wanted to be a doctor. That's the guy she fell in love with. But, in fairness to me, I didn't mislead her intentionally. I was only seventeen when I decided to go pre-med. Biology is primarily memorization. I have a photographic memory, so it comes easy to me. That's why I majored in it when I started college. I didn't really know myself and didn't discover my dream until my senior year.

"She has a right to her dream. But so do I. I had to be true to myself. To quote Shakespeare, 'To thine own self be true.'

"Honestly, I don't think it was anyone's fault. We just had incompatible dreams. If we'd gotten married, one of us would've had to give up his or her dream. Either I'd be unhappy being a doctor, or she'd be unhappy being married to a struggling writer. I knew it'd be best for us to go our separate ways after graduation before we got married and had kids. I didn't wanna end up divorced with our kids growing up in a broken home."

"Didn't you miss her?"

"I missed her a lot. Still do. I dreamed about her last night. But I learned a valuable lesson."

"What?"

"Don't fall in love with the wrong woman. It hurts too much when you break up. I learned my lesson the hard way."

"It sounds like that movie means a lot to you."

"I was so captivated by it I took Russian as my foreign language requirement at Denison."

"I'd like to see it."

"The truth is I'm looking for Lara—figuratively speaking. She's the imaginary woman who inspires me to create things and loves me because of what I create. That's my secret romantic dream. You're the first person I've ever told this to."

"I am?"

"I feel like I can confide in you. To understand me, you have to understand the power of the dream. It's so powerful it drove me to change what I wanted to be and to break up with Beth. It drives me to find Lara."

"You think it's written in the stars you'll find her?"

"Not really. I don't believe in fate. To quote Shakespeare again, 'It's not in the stars to hold our destiny but in ourselves.' "

"I believe it's written in the stars I'll find the love of my life someday."

"In our own ways, I guess we're both hopeless romantics," I say in jest.

She doesn't laugh. "So what'd you do after you broke up?"

"I tried to make it as an artist by taking a job as a pastelist at Cedar Point."

"What's a pastelist?"

"I drew people's portraits with pastels."

"I seen them artists on the midway."

"That was me. I had a great time. Lived the life of a bohemian. I resided in a dorm with all these college kids that Cedar Point hired for the summer to be ride attendants and work the concession stands. On our days off, we'd go to the park and ride the rollercoasters. Or go to the beach. We threw some hellacious beach parties."

"You make much money?"

"Nope. I found out the hard way I couldn't make a living as an artist. I draw too slowly because I draw too many details. And I draw women realistically. Some women wouldn't want to pay if you didn't make them look beautiful. I wouldn't make them pay if they didn't like their portrait.

"Now, the guy I worked with—Johnathan was his name—could actually make a living doing it. He could draw fast. He really cranked them out—I mean mass production. And he could make unattractive woman look attractive. They liked their portraits. He always told me to draw portraits for a living you gotta be able 'to make a silk purse out of a sow's ear.' "

She laughs.

"He confided that he was a homo and tried to talk me into moving to Key West with him. He draws portraits there over the winter. I had to tell him I like women. Actually, he was a really nice guy. He used to steer customers my way to help me make it."

"How long did you work there?"

"Till the park closed in the fall. Then I moved back home. I worked at the Y—at the front desk and as a lifeguard—while I expanded my short story into a novel."

"You wrote a novel?"

"Yeah."

"Are you gonna publish it?"

"I sent it to a literary agent in New York City. She liked the story but told me I needed to significantly change it to make it marketable."

"So did you change it?"

"No."

"Why not?"

"I gave up and applied to law school."

"Leo, I don't get it. If you wanna be a writer and an artist so bad, why are you going to law school?"

I sigh. "I tried and failed."

"You didn't try hard enough."

"I haven't figured out a way to make a living doing it. And I'm sick and tired of living at home—sponging off my dad. He says law school will make me a better writer because it teaches you to write succinctly. And he convinced me I don't wanna be a starving artist. He's implied there's a job waiting for me in his law firm if I become a lawyer. So I took the LSAT just for the hell of it and got a high enough score to get into Toledo State Law School."

"So is there any chance you'll get back together with Beth? You know—when she finds out you're going to law school?"

"Nope. She found what she was looking for. She married her high school boyfriend who's gonna be a doctor. They'll live happily ever after in Shaker Heights."

Back at my workstation, I reflect on confiding in Lily about my love affair with Beth and my secret dream of finding Lara and my novel. Much to my surprise, I feel comfortable divulging my innermost feelings and secret dreams to a woman who's so different from me.

I'm also struck by how enthralled she was with my love story, which I don't understand. I don't think mine is half as compelling as hers.

At lunch the next day, Lily asks, "Leo, would you draw my portrait?"

"Sure."

"How much does it cost?"

"At Cedar Point I charged twenty-five dollars for black and white and forty dollars for color."

"I'd like black and white."

"I'll need a photograph of you. If you want it to look like you, I need you to sit for me or I have to work from a photograph. It's a fallacy that artists can draw portraits from memory. Even though I'm an Eidetiker, I can only—"

"A what?"

"An Eidetiker. It's someone who has an eidetic memory. It's like a photographic memory." Pointing at my temple, I explain, "I can take a mental photograph of you. But I can only retain the photographic image in my memory for a few minutes. Then it starts to fade. This enables me to draw portraits using either a live model or a photograph. A photo will be more convenient than sitting for me. Pick out a favorite one that features your face."

She nods. "So tell me about your novel."

"It's sort of a science fiction story. The main character, Craig Hardesty, is thirteen years old. He makes friends with a really weird kid at school named Carl Mueller, who all the other kids ostracize because he looks deformed—they think he has major birth defects. It turns out Carl is really an alien from outer space, whose parents are alien scientists stationed on Earth to do field studies of Earthlings in their natural habitat. Their scientific mission is to only observe them, not to help them. Carl's dad has an anti-gravity machine, which looks like a motorized tandem bicycle. His dad and mom use it to float around town at night and peep into people's bedroom windows to study the mating habits of Homo sapiens. After Craig befriends Carl, they use it to float around town at night on a series of misadventures."

"I think Sean would like that. What's it called?"

"Incognito's Folly."

"How'd you come up with that?"

"Craig has an alias—Liam Incognito."

"Why does he have an alias? Is he a secret agent?"

"No. He tells the story in first person. It's like he has two voices living in his mind: Craig Hardesty's voice, which tells people what he wants them to hear after his brain edits it; and Liam Incognito's voice, which says what he's really thinking without any editing. Liam is the true him."

"So why Incognito?"

"Because Liam Incognito is traveling in disguise in Craig Hardesty's body."

"So why Incognito's Folly?"

"You hafta read the book to find out."

"So when can I read it?"

"You wanna read it?"

"Yeah. Just cuz I'm a high school dropout don't mean I don't know how to read."

I grin. Even though I've been saving my novel to give to Lara if I ever find her, I'm curious to hear what Lily thinks of it, so I decide to let her read it. "I'll bring it to work tomorrow."

"You promise?"

"Promise."

The next day I take *Incognito's Folly* back to Lily's workstation. "Lily, I want you to know you're the first person I've let read my novel."

She makes a face like she feels honored. Opening the accordion folder, she looks at the manuscript. "Wow, it's long."

"Two hundred and four type-written pages."

"I can't imagine writing something that long. You're the first author I've ever met."

"Whatever you do, don't lose it. That's the only copy I have. It would break my heart if you lost it."

"I'll guard it with my life."

She gives me a photograph of her from the shoulders up wearing a cowboy hat. "I like this picture. Karen took it after we went riding."

Scrutinizing it, I reply, "I like the expression on your face…"

CHAPTER SEVEN

When I walk out of the plant at quitting time on Friday, July 2, I feel good. Today I packed over six hundred toilets and earned the additional piece rate for the first time. I don't mind working at Boals-Corrigan anymore. I'm in the best shape of my life and am used to the heat and physical labor. There's not one ounce of fat on me—just hard, lean muscle. Since the Fourth of July is on Sunday, I get Monday off as a paid holiday.

Conversing with Lily on the way to our cars, I ask, "So you got any plans for the Fourth?"

"I'm going to my mama's. She has a family shindig every year. What about you?"

"My family's having a cookout too. Well, have fun. See ya Tuesday."

"You too. See ya."

I wonder what a family shindig in Little Kentucky is like—compared to a cookout in Woodland...

On Monday night, I'm not depressed about having to go to work tomorrow like I usually am on the last night of the weekend because I'm looking forward to seeing Lily.

I'm disappointed when she's not on break Tuesday morning; but I'm glad to see her waiting for me at the toilet tester at lunchtime. She tells me she had a doctor's appointment this morning.

During lunch, I ask her, "So how was your mom's shindig?"

"Fun. Me and Karen went horseback riding. We raced Derek back to the barn. He was on his motorcycle."

"Who's Derek?"

"Karen's boyfriend. He's a pipefitter in Johnson City, Tennessee. She's living with him. Mama says they're living in sin. You know— cuz they ain't married. They came home for the holiday."

"So who won?"

"We did."

"Horses are faster than a motorcycle?"

"He had to drive around logs on the ground. We jumped over them," she explains with a smirk. "My brother, Tommy, fixed barbecued chicken in his smoker. It was so good."

"I love barbecued chicken."

"You should come sometime. You'd like Tommy. He's a good guy."

"Is he single?"

"Married."

"Maybe I will," I reply, even though I doubt I'll ever do it. Curious about her family, I ask, "So how many brothers and sisters do you have?"

"I got five sisters and two brothers. Karen and Grace and Nancy came. They live here in town. And my other brother, Ray, came."

"Is he married?

"Divorced. He brought his new skank. He's a fool when it comes to women. He's always falling in love with some skank."

I find it amusing that she calls his girlfriend a skank. She tells me this story about how his last skank tried to throw lye on him and his new skank when she caught them in bed together.

Wincing, I reply, "Hell hath no fury like a skank scorned."

She laughs. "So how was your cookout?"

"It was fun. My sister and I shot off fireworks."

"What's her name?"

"Olivia."

"Olivia—that's a pretty name."

"Yeah. My mom named her after the heroine in *Twelfth Night.*"

LILY

"Twelfth Night?"

"It's a play by Shakespeare."

"My mama named me Lily after her favorite flower—the daylily."

"I like Lily. It's really feminine. I was named Leo after my Dad's younger brother, who was killed in the Korean War. So what's your middle name?"

She answers what I think is Leigh.

I spell, "L-e-i-g-h?"

"No, L-e-e," she spells.

"Lily Lee. I like the way it flows," I tell her, smiling.

"So what's your middle name?"

"Julien. Spelled with an *e* instead of an *a*. My mom chose the French spelling instead of the English spelling because she thought it was more romantic."

"Leo Julien Locke. It sounds like a lawyer. So you got any other brothers or sisters?"

"Yeah. An older brother—Jack. He's married to Lynn. They just had a baby—Josh. They had to eat and run. He just graduated from law school and has to study for the bar exam."

"Holy cow, it sounds like everybody in your family is a lawyer."

"Yeah. I guess it's in our genes."

"He must be smart too."

"Yeah. But he gave my parents some gray hairs. The first time he went to college he flunked out."

"Why'd he flunk out?"

"He partied too much. I guess he wasn't ready for college and had to sow some wild oats first. After he flunked out, he joined a rock band called The Sleepers as their lead singer. Not only does he have a good voice, he's a real ham. They hauled their instruments and amps around in a used hearse and practiced down in our basement. I'd sit on the steps and listen to them play for hours. They actually cut a demo record called 'Time Will Tell,' which was played on the radio in Cleveland, but it didn't chart.

"Once he realized the band wasn't gonna make it big, he married Lynn, who was his high school sweetheart. She straightened him out. He went back to college at Ohio State and graduated summa cum laude."

She looks as though she doesn't know what that means.

"It's Latin. It means 'with highest honor,' Then Jack decided he wanted to be a lawyer like my dad, so he went to law school."

"What's Lynn do?"

"She's a grade school teacher."

"She went to college too?"

"Yeah."

"So what's Olivia do?"

"She's going to college at Ohio State."

"Dang! Everybody in your family went to college. Nobody in my family went."

"Everyone except my mom. She was a gifted piano player. She actually got accepted at the Juilliard School of Music in New York City, which is one of the most prestigious music schools in the world. But she never went because she fell in love with my dad and ran off to marry him."

"Really?"

"Yeah. It was during World War Two. My dad had just completed his flight training to become a naval aviator—he'd just got his wings. My mom took a train all by herself from Mansfield to Pensacola, Florida, to see him before he went off to fight. He proposed to her the minute she stepped off the train, and the base chaplain married them an hour later. She told me they acted impetuously because they didn't know if he'd survive the war. They spent their honeymoon riding on a train across the country to Santa Barbara, California, where he was stationed before he shipped out to the Pacific. She said they spent the whole trip in their sleeping berth—screwing. That's where Jack was conceived."

Looking at me with wonder in her eyes, she replies, "I think I'd like your mama."

"You two have something in common," I observe.

"What?"

"Instead of going to school, you both had babies."

LILY

∞◊∞◊∞◊∞◊∞◊∞

As I'm heading out the door to go to Jack's place on Friday night, Dad stops me, looking very upset. He informs me that Olivia has been arrested by the police and is being held in the booking area at the Richland County Sheriff's Department. He needs me to drive him there to bail her out. Even though he's trying not to slur his words, I can tell he has been drinking. He must afraid he'll get a DWI if he drives. I ask him why they are holding her, but he doesn't know.

I chauffeur him to the Richland County Jail in his pearl white Cadillac Eldorado convertible. It's so hot out that I turn on the air-conditioning. When I try to turn on the radio, he turns it off testily. He instructs me to park on the street adjacent to the jail entrance and wait for him in the car. Before going inside, he pops a breath lozenge in his mouth.

I wait an hour, listening to the radio. Finally, Dad and Olivia exit the building. Fuming, he climbs into the front passenger seat and lights a cigarette. She climbs into the back seat and slinks down into the shadows.

"So what happened?" I ask them.

"Your sister got arrested trying to smuggle contraband to an inmate in the jail."

"Really?"

"She climbed up on a ledge on the outside of the building and tried to pass it through a window."

I wonder if it was drugs. "What kind of contraband?"

"It was just brownies," Olivia answers.

"Brownies?" I ask.

Before she can reply, Dad says, "Don't you ever pull a stunt like that again. You hear me?"

"I won't," she says meekly, looking out her window.

"You need to have your head examined—pulling a harebrained stunt like that. You could've fallen—"

"I didn't," she interjects.

He angrily warns her, "You heard Sheriff Miller. Next time he'll throw the book at you. And I'm telling you right now—I won't bail you out again. I'll let you sit in jail and learn your lesson the hard way. You're just damn lucky he's a fellow ex-Marine. That's the only reason he let you off with just a warning."

I hear her sigh…

"And why the hell are you smuggling contraband to a drug dealer in jail?" he asks.

"Dad, he's not a drug dealer."

"Sheriff Miller said he pled guilty to drug trafficking."

"He says he's innocent."

"That's what they all say," Dad scoffs.

"He's an old friend of mine. When I heard he was in jail, I felt sorry for him. The jail has visiting hours on Friday night, so I visited him last Friday and—"

"You visited him last Friday? How many times have you visited him?" It's like he's cross-examining her.

"Just twice. Last Friday he told me he loves brownies. So me and Janie baked some for him and tried to give them to him during visiting hours tonight, but the guards wouldn't let us."

I figure she means Janie Strickland, who's her college roommate.

"So Janie was with you?" Dad asks.

"Yeah."

"Why didn't the police arrest her?"

"She took off in her car when the cops arrested me. She drove me there."

"So how do you know this loser?"

"I went to high school with him."

"So there's nothing going on between the two of you?"

"No."

"No hanky-panky?"

"No. I told you—we're just friends."

"There'd better not be."

"What's his name, Olivia?" I ask.

"Joel Crawford," she answers.

"I don't know him."

"He's not a bad guy. He's—"

Dad cuts her off by saying, "Listen to me, young lady. This guy's a criminal. He's a born loser. You stay away from him."

"No, he's not, Dad. He's—"

"He's a convicted drug dealer. I will not allow my daughter to associate with a convicted drug dealer. Do not visit him at the jail again. Do not talk to him on the telephone. Do not write him. You're not to have any contact whatsoever with him. If you do, I'll find out. Sheriff Miller will tell me. You understand me?"

She doesn't respond.

"Olivia, I'm serious. I will not allow this loser to ruin your life. If you try to see him, I'll cut off your money so fast it'll make your head swim. I'm not wasting my money on your college education if you're just gonna throw away your life on some loser. You hear me?"

Grudgingly, she answers, "Yeah…I hear you."

In the rear view mirror, I see her glaring at him.

We ride in silence. I think about the lecture my old man would give me if I was going out with Lily. Since he grew up on the wrong side of the tracks, he wouldn't hold that against her. But, because she's poor and uneducated, he'd suspect she's a gold digger looking for someone to support her and her kids. He'd never approve of a divorced high school dropout with three kids. He'd say the relationship is destined to fail.

Lily, this is why I couldn't go out with you.

By the time we pull into our driveway, it's going on midnight. When we go inside, Mom is waiting for us in the kitchen with a distressed look on her face. Cornering my sister, she says, "Olivia, you and I need to have a talk."

"Please, Mom, not right now. I'm really tired and have a splitting headache."

"Then first thing in the morning."

Olivia goes straight to her bedroom. Dad goes straight to the bar and fixes himself a stiff one; then he and Mom go back to their bedroom. I fetch a bag of potato chips out of the pantry; then knock on Olivia's door.

"Who is it?"

"Me."

"Come in."

I enter her room. She's reclining on her bed with the light on, listening to James Taylor's *Sweet Baby James* album. Her eyes are red from crying.

I sit down at the foot of the bed. Munching on the chips, I offer her some.

"No thanks. I'm not hungry."

"So…you actually tried to smuggle brownies into the jail?"

Smiling ruefully, she nods.

"How?"

"Joel's housed in the trustee range since he's not a violent offender. It has glass windows with bars. The jail doesn't have air-conditioning. Since it's so hot out, the guards had opened them. I sneaked up the fire escape. From there I climbed onto a ledge that runs underneath the windows. It was so narrow I had to hug the wall and inch my way sideways to the closest window."

"That takes balls," I comment.

"The brownies were in a paper bag. I figured I'd toss it to him through the window, which was right above my head, but I couldn't see inside. So I started calling his name, and a guard inside heard me. That's how they caught me. They drew their guns and ordered me to come down."

"Jesus Christ, Olivia. You're lucky you didn't get shot."

"I'm lucky I didn't fall. It was high up. Then they arrested me. They suspected I was trying to smuggle a gun or drugs to him."

Shaking my head incredulously, I tell her, "You're crazy. So what happened to the brownies?"

"The cops confiscated them."

"I hope they don't have marijuana in them."

"I'm not that dumb."

"So who is this guy really?"

"He's just a friend of mine. He was in my music class at Malabar. He's a nice guy. I really like him."

"So he's not really a drug dealer?"

"No. He's a musician. He plays the guitar professionally. It's a bum rap. He was playing a gig at a bar, and an undercover narc tricked him into selling him a joint for a dollar. That's the only time he ever sold drugs to anybody. They charged him with drug trafficking, and he pled guilty. For one lousy joint, the judge threw the book at him—sentenced him to one year in the county jail. It's not fair."

"You're right. That's shitty."

"Leo, he shouldn't be in jail. He's not a criminal."

"It doesn't sound like it. So how long has he served?"

"Just two months. He's a model prisoner."

"I think he can get time off his sentence for good behavior."

"I hope so. I wanna help him. But I don't know how," she frets.

"You better not. You heard what Dad said. No more climbing on ledges at the county jail. I don't feel like visiting my kid sister in jail," I rib her.

Grinning, she replies, "You can smuggle brownies into me."

∞◊∞◊∞◊∞◊∞◊∞

At lunch on Monday, I tell Lily about Olivia's escapade on the weekend. She thinks it's funny. "I think I'd like your sister."

"Why?"

"She's daring."

"You two are kindred spirits—both fearless."

I imagine taking Lily home to meet my family. I'm sure Olivia and Jack would like her, and even my parents would like her—until they found out she's a divorced high school dropout with three kids.

While Lily and I are eating lunch the next day, a silver-haired, distinguished–looking man in a tan suit enters the breakroom. I recognize him—he's Mr. Verekee. This is the first time I've seen him come in here. He buys a frozen sandwich out of a vending machine and puts it in the microwave. While it's heating, he spots me and comes over to our table.

"Hi, Leo."

"Hi, Mr. Verekee."

"I just had a hankering for a cheeseburger today. So…how do you like working here?"

Grinning, I answer, "I don't—it's hot and boring. But I like having money for law school."

"This is the reason why you go to law school. So you don't have to work in a factory, doing a menial job."

"That's what my dad tells me all the time."

"How's he doing?"

"Fine."

"Your pop's quite a guy. Marine Corp Fighter Pilot. Ace. Won the Distinguished Flying Cross."

I nod.

"I flew a B-29 Superfortress Bomber. He and I like to swap stories about how we single-handedly won the war."

I laugh. "He has some great war stories." Everyone in the room is noticing that the President of Boals-Corrigan is talking to me.

Mr. Verekee glances at the microwave. "And I found out he also fought in the Korean War."

"Yeah. He had to learn how to fly a jet."

"He told me he got recalled to active duty after he started practicing law and had a wife and son. I figure he probably could've got out of it on a hardship case, but he didn't," he says with admiration.

"He once told me he believed it was his duty. Dad loves his country."

"They don't make them like your pop anymore. He's a true patriot."

"He is."

"You tell him I said hi."

"I will."

Smiling at Lily, he says, "Hi, Lily."

"Hi, Mr. Verekee."

"I have some good news for you. Hank Peters just approved your bid on the job in the warehouse."

"Really?"

"Forklift operator, right?"

"Right."

"Yeah. He just signed off on it. He told me Jessie Thompson specifically requested you to fill the position."

"Great. Thank you. I really want that job."

"You earned it."

Turning to me, he asks, "Can you believe we actually have a young lady this beautiful working here?" His eyes are undressing her.

"No. I still think she's a mirage."

He laughs. His cheeseburger is ready. "Good luck at law school, Leo."

"Thanks, Mr. Verekee."

He fetches his cheeseburger out of the microwave and leaves.

Lily is thrilled. "Leo, I got the job. I'm gonna be driving a forklift. It's skilled labor. Two dollars more an hour. Thank you, Jessie, for coming through for me. I love you!"

"Congratulations, Lily. I'm happy for you." It's weird. I feel slightly jealous of Jessie. It vexes me that she feels gratitude to him for helping her and especially that she said "I love you!"—even though I don't think she meant it literally.

I'm suspicious of Jessie's motives. I wonder why he specifically requested her to work for him. Is he trying to get in her pants? But then I remind myself I don't care if he's trying to get in her pants because I'm not interested in her romantically.

"So how do you know Verekee?" she asks.

"My dad's his lawyer. I met him on a case involving Boals-Corrigan. He came to our house one night. My dad told me about it after he left. He figures I need to learn about real cases since I'm going to law school. I'm not supposed to talk about it because it's confidential—attorney-client privilege…"

She's intrigued now, and I'm itching to tell her about it. I figure I can trust her, so I say, "I'll tell you about it if you promise not to tell anyone."

"I promise."

"Mr. Verekee hired him to defend Boals-Corrigan during the strike last fall after it turned violent. He had hired scabs to cross the picket line. The strikers had retaliated by torching a scab's car—which is arson. He needed a lawyer who's not intimidated by violence, so he hired my dad. My dad got a T.R.O. against the union."

"A T-R-O?"

"A Temporary Restraining Order. It's a court order restraining the union from doing illegal acts."

"So…it was your dad who sued me."

"Technically, he sued the union," I point out.

"I'm in the union. I went on strike and manned the picket line. He sued me," she insists.

"Okay, you're right. So…I'm curious. Who torched the car?"

"I don't know."

"It was probably Bill Barnes. Or Herb."

"I wouldn't rat on them if I knew. I ain't no snitch."

Awkward silence…

"My dad was just doing his job. He was trying to prevent violence. Stop people from getting hurt."

"He was trying to break us. All we wanted was a small raise and better health insurance. We was just peacefully picketing."

"Peacefully picketing? My dad got anonymous phones calls in the middle of the night threatening to burn down our house."

"Was he scared?"

"No—he's fearless. His comment was 'They ain't shooting bullets at me.' He just left the phone off the hook and went back to sleep."

"I think I'd like your dad."

"I think he'd like you too because he admires courage. He always quotes Winston Churchill: 'Courage is the first of human qualities because it is the quality that guarantees the others.' "

But I doubt he'd like me getting involved with you romantically.

"So…did you get your raise and better health insurance?" I ask.

"Most of it."

"All's well that ends well."

"So was your dad really a war hero?"

"As a matter of fact, he was. He flew a F4U Corsair off the

Bennington Aircraft Carrier and was an ace—he shot down seven enemy aircraft. He won the Distinguished Flying Cross for shooting down two Zeroes in a dogfight over Tokyo Bay."

"Wow!"

"He flew into aerial combat wearing my mom's yellow silk pajamas around his neck and Jack's blue booties on his helmet. He'd never seen Jack. My mom had him in Santa Barbara while he was on the aircraft carrier. That's a true story. I read it in a newspaper clipping in the Chicago Tribune."

"That's so romantic…"

"He was lucky to have survived the war. He actually got shot down over the Sea of Japan and had to land his plane in the water. He radioed his coordinates to his wingman right before he ditched and floated around the ocean in a rubber raft until a rescue ship found him at dusk. If the sun had gone down and he'd drifted all night, they probably would never have found him. And Leo Locke would never have been born.

"Dad once showed me a picture of him and four other fighter pilots in his squadron standing in front of a Corsair in their flying suits. He told me only he and Stoney made it home. The other three guys were killed in action—he said 'they crashed and burned.' Then he told me, 'I should've died when I was twenty years old. That's why I live every day like it's a gift.' "

"He sounds like Luke."

"My dad's a real character. They broke the mold after they made him. So…what about your dad? You said he's a vet. Which war did he fight in? World War Two or the Korean War?"

"World War Two. He fought the Germans. He took part in D-Day."

"He stormed the beach?"

"Uh-huh."

"Damn…I'd like to hear about that."

"He…he don't like to talk about the war…so, uh…Verekee and your dad are friends, huh?"

"Yeah…" I notice that she changed the subject. I wonder why.

"Must be nice."

"It is. That's how I got hired here—friends in high places. He seems like a decent guy. He drives a black Corvette. He actually let me take it for a spin."

Smirking, she replies, "He's a dirty old man. He tried to get me to go on vacation with him to the Bahamas."

"Are you shitting me? How?"

"One day last winter Mr. Castor stopped by at my workbench and told me Mr. Verekee wanted to see me in his office in the annex. The whole way there I'm wondering, 'Why does he wanna see me?' I mean he's the President of Boals-Corrigan. I just make ballcocks. I thought I'd done something wrong and was scared shitless they was gonna fire me.

"But it turned out he just wanted to lay me. He beat around the bush for a while. Asked me about my job. If I was happy working here. And if there was anything he could do for me. He even cracked a dirty joke about ballcocks. He told me he just wanted to make sure all the men was treating me right—since I was the first woman they ever hired to work in the shop. I told him they was treating me okay—even though practically every guy here was trying to lay me.

"Then he shut his door and pulled a bottle of Crown Royal out of his desk and offered me a drink. That surprised me cuz they can fire you if they catch you drinking on the job. I told him I better not since it's against company rules. He told me that's the best thing about being the president—he can break the company rules. So I had a drink with him—it ain't every day I get offered Crown Royal.

"Then he showed me a travel brochure about some fancy resort at Paradise Island and asked me if I wanted to go on vacation with him. He said he'd pay my way. We could gamble and go scuba diving.

"But all he really wanted was some pussy. The whole time he's trying to talk me into going with him I'm looking at this picture of his wife and kids on the table behind him…"

"So what'd you say to him?"

"I told him, 'No thanks. I don't think your wife there would appreciate it.' Then I thanked him for the drink and left." With a disdainful look on her face, she adds, "He thought I was just some dumb hillbilly girl who'd screw him for a free vacation in the Bahamas."

"Damn...so the President of Boals-Corrigan is a dirty old man..."

She nods.

"He's old enough to be your dad."

She nods again.

"My respect for him just went down. I don't like infidelity. I believe in true love," I say.

"You do?"

"Yeah. That's just the way I was brought up. My dad has his character flaws, but I think he's always been faithful to my mom."

"So has my dad."

"So has Verekee ever said anything to you about it?"

"No. He acts like it never happened."

"Jesus Christ, Lily—everybody in this damn factory from the president down to the janitor is trying to go to bed with you."

"Everybody except you. That's what I like about you. You're the only guy here not trying to get in my panties."

I just laugh.

With a coquettish expression on her face, she asks, "Why don't you take me scuba diving in the Bahamas?"

She's flirting with me again.

"I will—as soon as I get rich. So who else has hit on you?"

"Herb. He actually groped my tit once. I whacked him on the hand with a ballcock so hard he had to have four stiches. He ain't gonna try that again. Now all he tries to do is get me to pose nude for him. He tells me he'll send the pictures to *Playboy*, and I'll get picked Playmate of the Year and win lots of money and a sports car."

Chuckling, I reply, "He's right."

She bemoans, "I swear I can't even look at a guy around here without him trying to lay me. I...I just attract men—cuz...cuz of my body. I can't help it. Mama says it's both a blessing and a curse. Some guy's always asking me to go out for a drink. All they want is a one-night stand. Nobody wants a relationship cuz of my kids.

Except Beanie."

"Beanie?"

"Yeah. Poor Beanie…he thought he was in love with me. It was so sad. He bought me a diamond ring and proposed to me in sign language right at this table. I had to tell him no—I didn't love him. I just liked him as a friend." Then she makes an exasperated face and says, "In sign language."

I laugh.

"It wasn't funny, Leo. I didn't know the sign for 'friend.' So I had to write it on a napkin. He was crushed. He's so sweet. I felt awful."

"What about Jessie?"

"No. He's happily married with two kids. He's like a big brother to me."

I'm glad to hear that.

CHAPTER EIGHT

At lunch on Friday, I ask Lily, "So what are you doing this weekend?"

"Tomorrow I'm going to Lake Erie."

"Where?"

"Gem Beach."

"Gem Beach…I love Gem Beach. My parents used to take me there when I was a kid."

"You wanna come? I'm taking my kids fishing. We love fried perch."

My heart wants to see how much it's changed since I was a kid. But my brain is telling me do not get involved with her kids. Fortunately, I've already made plans for Saturday. "I'd like to, Lilly, but I can't. I told Reese I'd go with him to the GMAC Championship."

"What's that?"

I explain GMAC stands for Greater Mansfield Aquatic Conference, which is a summer youth swim conference that eight local swim teams participate in. Reese and I used to swim for Stonehaven Country Club. "We're gonna watch his kid sister swim."

On Saturday, the tuition bill for law school comes in the mail. Tuition plus activity fees and fees for a parking sticker total over six hundred dollars. The letter also contains information about on-campus dormitory housing and cafeteria meal plans. Since Reese and I plan on renting an apartment off-campus, I toss it in the waste basket. To save money I'm tempted to take my chances and not buy the student health insurance, but Dad makes me buy it. The letter makes me feel anxiety—I realize law school is looming on the not-too-distant horizon.

∞◊∞◊∞◊∞◊∞◊∞

"Tell me about your fishing trip," I say.

"There ain't nothing to tell."

"Did you catch any fish?"

"Nope. They wasn't biting. Want a celery stick with peanut butter? I got too many."

"Yeah, thanks." It's weird—it's as if she doesn't want to talk about it.

"So did you watch the Olympics last night? You see Nadia Comaneci score a ten?" she asks.

"I did."

"Wasn't she amazing?"

"She was."

"It was crazy the way they couldn't show her score."

"The announcer said the scoreboard couldn't display it because the manufacturer thought it was impossible to score a perfect ten. They thought wrong."

"I love to watch the gymnastics. I was on the tumbling team in grade school. And I love the equestrian. You know—cuz of the horses."

"I love to watch the swimming—because I was a swimmer. Mark Spitz is my favorite athlete. It'll be a long time, if ever, before somebody breaks his record of winning seven gold medals at one Olympics."

"I seen the picture of him in his sexy swim suit with all them gold medals around his neck." She fans her face like he makes her hot and bothered.

Grinning, I reply, "That picture of him in his Speedo changed everything for swimmers. It turned us into sex symbols."

"So how was the swim meet?"

"It was fun. Reese's sister got first place in the Girls Fifteen through Seventeen Backstroke. She set a new GMAC record."

"Wow! She must be fast."

"Yeah. It's in the genes. Reese holds all of the boys' GMAC records in backstroke. He placed second at the high school state championship and went to college on a swimming scholarship."

"So you was a swimmer, huh?"

"Yeah. I was on swim team in high school and college. I swam breaststroke." Just saying the word breaststroke makes me imagine stroking Lily's beautiful breasts.

If you knew what I was thinking right now…

"Was you a star?"

"I was a star in high school. In college I was just average. The competition was a lot stiffer."

"Did you like it?"

"I liked the camaraderie. That's how Reese and I became good friends. We both swam on the medley relay. He swam the backstroke leg. I swam the breaststroke leg.

"But I hated practice. Swimming is just a battle with pain—how much you can endure. And there's no glory in swimming. It's not a big spectator sport. They don't have cheerleaders at swim meets. It's not like football where the gorgeous cheerleader falls in love with the star quarterback," I razz her.

Friday rolls around. "You doing anything tonight?" Lily asks.

"I'm planning on going to my brother's house."

"You wanna go with me to the drive-in?"

It occurs to me that she and I could have sex in the back seat at the drive-in. "What're you going to see?"

"*Jaws.* I promised Sean I'd take him to see it for his birthday."

Not with Sean in the car. "I've already seen it."

"I hear it's really scary."

"The opening scene is terrifying. The rest is pretty far-fetched."

Back at my press, I think about her invitation to go to the drive-in with her and Sean. This is the second time she has asked me to do something with him. I get the distinct feeling that she wants me to meet Sean and start doing things with him like play catch in the back yard. I suspect that she may be looking for a surrogate father to him. Just the thought of being a surrogate father to her kids makes me anxious.

In general, I like kids. I'd probably have fun playing games with hers and would become attached to them over time, so I don't want to go down that road.

∞◇∞◇∞◇∞◇∞

"So did you see *Jaws?*" I ask.

"Yeah. It scared the shit out of me. I'm having nightmares about getting attacked by a Great White shark."

"Lily, the odds of getting attacked by a shark is less than getting struck by lightning."

"I don't care. I ain't ever going swimming in the ocean."

"So what's your favorite movie?" I ask.

"I don't know…*Night of the Living Dead.* I seen it at the drive-in, and it really scared me. I love scary movies. What's yours? Besides *Dr. Zhivago.*"

"From an artistic standpoint, I think the greatest movie is *Citizen Kane.*"

"I ain't seen it."

"I love *The Graduate.*"

"I seen it. It's funny."

"It is. I like the music by Simon and Garfunkel. 'The Sound of Silence' is one of my favorite songs. What do you think of Mrs. Robinson?"

"She looks sexy. But she's really just a high-class skank."

Chuckling, I reply, "True. My all-time favorite movie is *Casablanca.* Humphrey Bogart is my favorite actor. Have you seen it?"

"Huh-uh."

I can't believe it—I thought everyone has seen *Casablanca*. I tell her my other favorite movies: *The Endless Summer, The Godfather, 2001: A Space Odyssey, Easy Rider, Butch Cassidy and the Sundance Kid,* and *Dr. Strangelove.* The only ones she has seen are *Butch Cassidy and the Sundance Kid,* which she thought was funny, and *Easy Rider,* which bummed her out. Then I try to tell her about the great Swedish film director, Ingmar Bergman, and his art film, *Persona,* but she's never heard of him. I figure when it comes to movies, we don't have much in common.

She explains, "I don't go to the movies. Not with kids. I can't afford it. I only go to the Springmill Drive-in. You know—cuz it's cheap. I pop my own popcorn. And take pillows and blankets so the kids can sleep in the car."

"That sounds like fun."

"I like *The Sound of Music.* Cuz of the kids singing."

"You like rock?"

"I love rock."

"What's your favorite record album?"

"I don't buy albums. They're too expensive. I listen to the radio. It's free."

"So who's your favorite band?"

"When I was a girl, I liked The Beach Boys. Now my favorite is James Taylor. I love 'Fire and Rain.' Who's yours?"

"The Beatles. They just have so many great albums. Who else do you like?"

"Ummm…Credence Clearwater. And Lynyrd Skynyrd. Ray turned me on to them."

"I like them. They're my favorite American bands. Along with the Allman Brothers Band and the Eagles."

"I like the Eagles. I like 'Desperado.' "

"Yeah. That's a good song. I like the British bands too. You know—like the Rolling Stones. And the Who. And Led Zeppelin. So what's your favorite song?"

"Ummm…'Joy to the World.' My kids love it cuz it's about a

bullfrog." She looks up from her peanut butter and jelly sandwich, smiling.

"I saw Three Dog Night in concert in Columbus. They played it for their final encore."

"Right now my favorite is 'Crazy On You.' I love Heart. That song turns me on."

"It turns me on too," I reply, grinning.

"So what's yours?"

"Right now my favorite album is *Bustin' Out* by Pure Prairie League. I like Craig Fuller's songwriting."

"What's your favorite song?"

I think about it for a moment. "If I had to pick my all-time favorite, I'd pick 'Baba O'Riley' by the Who. I love that song."

She gives me a quizzical look.

I hum the power chords and sing the chorus.

"Oh—'Teenage Wasteland.' I like that song."

"The power chords send a chill right down my spine. I saw them play it at the Richfield Coliseum last December. Pete Townshend was amazing."

"Who's he?"

"He's their lead guitarist. He's a maniac on stage. He windmills his arm when he plays the chords," I tell her, demonstrating. "And Keith Moon is said to be the fastest drummer in the world. And their bass player, John Entwistle, is said to be the greatest bass guitarist. I think they're the best live band in the world. They were really loud. I swear my ears are still ringing, and my viscera are still vibrating.

"'All Along the Watchtower' by Jimi Hendrix is my second favorite. I think he and Eric Clapton and Jimmy Page are the greatest electric guitarists.

"So what's your favorite love song?" I ask.

"'Summer Rain' by Johnny Rivers. It always gets me right here," she says, touching her heart. "I like country music. I'm a country girl at heart."

"I like country music. I love Emmylou Harris."

"So what's your favorite love song?" she asks.

"Uhhh…that's a tough one. I have a lot of favorites. My favorite happy love songs are Jackie Wilson's 'Higher and Higher' and the Beatles' 'Got To Get You Into My Life.' They make my heart soar. 'In My Life' by the Beatles and 'Brown Eyed Girl' by Van Morrison make me feel nostalgic."

"Yeah. I like that song. It reminds me of making out with Donny behind the stadium."

I smile. "The best songs take you to a time and place. My favorite sad love songs are 'Yesterday' and 'For No One' by the Beatles."

"'Crying'—that's the saddest song for me. I remember my dad playing that record a thousand times when I was a girl."

"I like Roy Orbison. I love 'Pretty Woman. So, uh…your dad likes Roy Orbison?"

"Uh-huh," she mumbles.

I can tell by the look on her face that she regrets having mentioned her dad. She quickly asks, "So what do you think is the saddest love song?"

I wonder why she doesn't want to talk about him. "For me, the saddest love song is 'Heart Like A Wheel.' "

"I ain't ever heard of it."

"It's by Kate and Anna McGarrigle. They're obscure Canadian folk singers who are sisters. I found their album in the dollar bin at the Magnolia Thunderpussy Record Store. Isn't that a great name?"

Grinning, she replies, "Sounds dirty."

"It's on High Street in Columbus across from the university. It's my favorite record store because it has esoteric records. You wanna listen to it?"

"Sure."

"You got a record player? I'll loan you the album."

"Huh-uh. I got a cassette player."

"I'll make you a cassette tape."

That night I record the album for her. When I give the cassette to her at work the next day, I tell her to also check out "Talk To Me Of Mendocino"—that it's exquisitely beautiful.

She thanks me.

I guess we do have something in common—we both love rock

and roll.

∞◊∞◊∞◊∞◊∞◊∞

"I listened to 'Heart Like a Wheel' last night. You're right, Leo. It's really sad."

"It's so sad it almost makes me wanna die," I reply facetiously.

"And the other song about Mendocino is really beautiful. It makes me wanna go there."

"It makes me wanna live."

∞◊∞◊∞◊∞◊∞◊∞

Lily shows me a book she's reading on astrology. "This book says you can use the position of celestial objects to divine what's gonna happen in your life."

"Right," I reply sarcastically.

"You don't believe it?"

"Nope. It's pseudoscience."

"I believe it, Leo. My horoscope is the only thing I read in the paper. You're Scorpio. I think you got a lot of Scorpio male traits."

"Such as?"

"You're intense. Passionate."

I reply grudgingly, "I hafta admit—that's true. So what else?"

"They got magnetic sex appeal."

"That's me," I joke.

"Your element is water."

"What's that mean?"

"You go as deep as you can sexually cuz you're ruled by testosterone."

Laughing, I scoff, "No, I'm not. I'm ruled by my brain. Rationality."

She just looks at me skeptically.

"So what's your sign?" I ask.

"Aries. The Ram."

"What are Aries female traits?"

"They're fearless. Independent. Fiery."

"That's you."

She smiles smugly.

"So what about your sexuality?" I ask.

She quotes from her book: "The sign of Aries is governed by fire. Like other fire signs, an Aries woman is passionate. She is often the seducer in the game of love."

"Interesting…"

"Has a woman ever seduced you?"

"Only in my wildest dreams. It doesn't happen in real life. It only happens in the movies. You know—like *The Graduate.*"

"Would you like to be seduced by Mrs. Robinson?"

"I hafta admit I fantasized about being seduced by her. She looks incredibly sexy for her age. But the reality is she's neurotic and an alcoholic, and she's old enough to be my mom. I'd rather be seduced by a woman my age."

She just smiles.

"Boy, oh, boy, it's really hot out," Lily remarks.

"We're having a heat wave."

"It's so hot I couldn't sleep last night."

Fortunately, our house has central air-conditioning, so it's not a problem for me. "You don't have air-conditioning?"

She looks at me like that's a dumb question. "I live in a trailer, Leo."

"I thought you might have a window air-conditioner."

"No. All I have is a fan, and it don't work for shit. I sleep naked. It just blows hot air across my body."

Envisioning that titillates me…

"Leo, I finished reading your book last night."

"So…what do you think?"

"I think it's really funny. You know—the trouble Craig and Carl get into on their flying machine. And I love the old wino that pulls the wagon around town collecting aluminum cans to sell to the junk yard."

"Dewey."

"Yeah, Dewey. He's so sad. He's broken-hearted, huh?"

"He is. The death of his wife of forty years drove him crazy."

"Love can do that."

We talk about my book all through break and lunch. I really enjoy talking with her about it because she listens intently as I expound. After work she returns it to me. She had it locked safely in her car.

∞◊∞◊∞◊∞◊∞◊∞

Lily drops by my press a few minutes before morning break. Holding a plump, fuzzy, golden-rose peach in front of my mouth, she says, "Have a bite."

I bite into it. The sweetest, juiciest nectar gushes out and runs down my chin.

"Oh man, Lily, that's luscious. Where'd you get it?"

"My mama's orchard." She takes a bite out of it; then holds it in front of my mouth again.

I take another bite. "Mmm…I think that's the best peach I've ever eaten."

Lily beams. "We just picked them last night."

I notice her eyeing the pornographic picture on my packing press.

"You like dirty pictures?" she asks.

"Yeah…I like erotic pictures," I admit.

With a daring smile on her face, she says, "I wouldn't mind doing that."

My heart skips a beat. While we take turns eating bites of her peach, I visualize her posing like that. I get a hard-on…

She tosses the peach pit into the trash barrel.

"Two points!" I exclaim.

Chatting amiably with her at our table during break time, I can't get rid of my hard-on. Fortunately, the tabletop hides it.

Back at my packing press, I keep seeing her daring smile and hearing her say "I wouldn't mind doing that" in her sensual country twang and picturing her posing like that for me.

Man, oh man—I'd love to see that. It would be so exciting.

I can't believe she told me that—how bold she is. She's intimating that she wants to have sex with me.

I imagine that...

Oh, God—I'd love to have sex with her.

I realize she's not just flirting with me anymore. She's trying to seduce me. Why? Is she just wild and likes to have sex? Or is she interested in me romantically? Or is she interested in me because she's poor and needs someone to support her and her kids and thinks I'm going to be a rich lawyer someday? Or is it all these things?

When I go to bed at night, the image of Lily posing like the woman in the photograph on my packing press reappears in my mind. Aroused, I toss and turn. I can't erase it from my mind's eye...

I possess one dirty magazine—the February, 1973 issue of *Penthouse*—which I've hidden underneath my mattress because my parents disapprove of pornography, fearful that it'll corrupt Olivia. "Our house, our rules," they say. I take out the magazine and turn to the photo spread of the Pet of the Month—Karen Sather, "Soothsayer." She's a gorgeous redhead with milky white skin. For some inexplicable reason, deep inside the core of my being I desire her. She's the only fantasy lover I have; I stay true to her. I'm a monogamous masturbator. I fantasize she's Lara. I pretend the room in which she's posing is located in the Gothic Revival house in Granville, and I'm writing *Incognito's Folly* for her. She falls in love with me because of it. The photograph that excites me to the brink of orgasm is of her standing in a white turtleneck sweater nude from the waist down—the bushy red mound between her legs looks so erotic.

At the moment of my climax, my subconscious desire manifests itself and I visualize Lily posing for me like the woman on my press—this causes me to have a stupendous orgasm.

Damn you, Lily—you're engrained in my libido now.

∞()∞()∞()∞()∞()∞

"So…do you really like the picture of that woman on your press?" Lily asks.

"Yeah. I like beaver shots."

Giggling, she replies, "Beaver? That's a silly thing to call it."

"You're right. It doesn't do it justice. So what do you call it?"

"Pussy."

"That's dirtier. So what about vulva? Or female genitalia? Those are the correct anatomical terms."

"No. Anatomical terms turn me off. I only use them at Dr. Hall's office. I like dirty words. I love to say them. It turns me on."

I theorize, "That's because it's taboo for women to say dirty words, and it's exciting to break taboos."

"You analyze too much. Who cares why? All that matters is it does."

I realize she's flirting with me again. I can't resist flirting back—it's too much fun. "So what do you think is the dirtiest word?"

"Cunt," she answers without a moment's hesitation.

Nodding my head, I reply, "I agree. Of all the dirty words in the English language, it's my favorite. I love that word."

"Why's that?"

"I love how it sounds. It sounds like what it means."

She says it out loud to herself. Grinning, she replies, "You're right, Leo."

"I think it's the most erotic word. It really turns me on. So what do you call a man's penis?"

"His cock."

"You don't call it a dick? Or a peter?"

"No. Those are men's names."

"What about pecker?"

"Nope. That sounds like a bird. I like cock cuz it looks cocky when it's hard."

"Right…okay, from now on, we'll call yours a pussy and mine a cock."

She nods.

My cock is purring. "So what do you call an erection?"

"A boner."

I laugh.

"What's so funny?"

"That's what me and my friends called it in junior high."

"That's what us hillbillies call it."

"It's a good word. It's another word that sounds like what it means."

"Yeah. It does. So what do you call it?"

"A hard-on. Well…I'm glad we've established the nomenclature for our sex organs. It's been weighing heavily on my mind. Now I can sleep at night."

She laughs.

Man, oh man—just talking with her about our sex organs has given me a boner. I love that she loves to say dirty words. It means she has a dirty mind like me. I tease her, "You have a dirty mind."

She nods. "So do you like me to talk dirty?"

"Yeah…I…I have to admit—it turns me on."

"What turns you on most in the world?"

"A woman coming…"

She smiles at me provocatively…

I have to stop flirting with her. I'm leading her on.

"Jack's taking the Ohio Bar Exam this week. It's the big test you gotta pass to become an attorney."

"I thought you just had to go to law school."

"No. If you graduate from law school, you earn the Juris Doctor degree—J.D. You still hafta pass the bar exam to be admitted to practice law in Ohio. I'm a little nervous for him."

"You think he'll pass?"

"Yeah. He has my dad's genes."

∞◊∞◊∞◊∞◊∞◊∞

On the Friday night after the bar exam, I go to Jack and Lynn's duplex in Woodland. We smoke a joint and watch Ingmar Bergman's *Wild Strawberries*. He doesn't even mention the bar exam. After the movie ends, my curiosity gets the best of me, and I ask, "So…how'd the bar exam go?"

"Okay. I lived to tell about it."

"Was it hard?"

"It wasn't hard answering the questions. I felt like I was prepared since I took the bar prep course. The worst thing was the pressure. You've got a thousand nervous people packed like sardines in one room knowing three years of law school go down the drain if they fail this test. It felt like you could cut the tension with a knife. I saw a guy crack under the pressure. The proctors handed out the first two essay questions. He took one look, then stood up and walked out. And he didn't come back."

"Damn…"

"It's grueling. It's three days long. The first day is a full day of essay questions. The second day is a half day of multi-state multiple choice. The third day is another full day of essay questions. You gotta grind it out. Pace yourself. Take it one day at a time. Don't get too high or too low."

"So when do you find out the results?"

"End of October."

"You think you passed?"

"I hope so. I don't wanna hafta take it again."

"So if you fail, they let you take it again?"

"Yeah. They give you three tries to pass. If you fail three times, you can't be a lawyer. You gotta be a claims adjuster for an insurance company or work in a trust department at a bank. Just imagine if you failed twice…the pressure on your last try…"

I get pins and needles in my stomach just thinking about it.

"Guess what," Lily says with a sly smile on her face.

"What?"

"Dakota and Appaloosa did it yesterday."

I know what she means, but I play dumb and ask, "Did what?"

"Mated. I could tell Dakota was in heat. I saw the signs. When Appaloosa went past her stall, she backed up against the door and raised her tail and opened and closed the lips of her vulva."

"Really?"

"Yeah. It's called clitoral winking."

"Clitoral winking—that's an interesting biological term. I wish some woman would wink her clitoris at me," I joke.

"Maybe if you'd hit on a woman, she would."

I realize I'm flirting with her again. I can't help it. I love flirting with her—it's stimulating.

"Then I let them out in the pasture, and Appaloosa got laid. He reared up and mounted her from behind. He's a real stud," she says proudly.

"I'm happy for him. He lost his virginity."

Awestruck, she exclaims, "Leo, you should've seen his boner. I bet it was two feet long."

"I'm envious."

She laughs. "They did it multiple times. Now I just hope she gets pregnant," she says, crossing her fingers for good luck.

"When will you know?"

"I should have a pretty good idea in two to three weeks. That's when I'll look for signs she's in heat again. Which means she ain't pregnant."

"What signs?"

"Like if she's carrying her tail up or opening and closing her vulva or squirting urine when Appaloosa's around her."

"So if she's pregnant, when will she show?"

"Not for a long time and some mares never show. In sixteen to eighteen days, I'll perform a transrectal palpation on her."

"Rectal—that sounds like it involves the anus."

"It does. I'll insert my hand up her rectum and check the size and shape of her uterus and any swellings of her ovaries for indications of pregnancy," she explains matter-of-factly.

"That's what I like about you, Lily. You've got the balls to stick your arm up a horse's anus. You're not afraid to get your hands dirty."

"I wear a sterile glove. I don't wanna cause an infection."

"I don't know anyone who could do that. Most people would think it's gross."

"I don't. I love what I do, being a vet assistant. I love animals."

"Don't get me wrong. I'm not knocking it. On the contrary, it makes you interesting as a person. You know what you are?"

"What?"

"You're a horse gynecologist. That's what you are."

She smiles. "I guess so. I never thought of it that way."

"As a matter of fact, I think you're really intelligent. You should go back to school. Get your diploma."

"That's easier said than done. It's hard to go to school when you got two jobs."

"You could go to night school."

"That ain't easy when you're raising three kids."

"Where there's a will, there's a way."

"Now you sound like my mama."

"You could do it. Anyone who can perform a transrectal palpation and artificial insemination is smart enough to do it. Night school is your ticket out of here."

I can tell she's thinking about it. I sing to her the chorus to "We Gotta Get Outta of this Place" by the Animals.

She laughs.

Back at my workstation, I marvel that she has the nerve to perform transrectal palpations. I truly admire her for her love of animals and because she has found a way to do what she loves and get paid for it. That's what I want in life. I meant what I said when I told her she should go back to school and get her diploma. There's no doubt in my mind that she's smart enough. Hell, I'm starting to think she's smart enough to go to college.

It sounds like it's her kids that are stopping her. Between raising them and working two jobs to support them, it's too difficult.

LILY

I sigh.

Her kids. They're always the obstacle. They're the reason she can't go back to school and I can't fall in love with her.

I sigh again.

If only she'd never met Donny…

Lily is absent, so I sit with Percy and Mel at lunch. Mel went to the county fair last night. He animatedly tells us about watching two motorcycle stunt riders ride in circles at the same time inside the "Globe of Death Steel Ball" with a "hot babe" in a star-spangled, sexy outfit standing in the center of the ball; centrifugal force kept the motorcycles pinned in midair against the side of the sphere without colliding into the woman. He was impressed by how dangerous it was; he got dizzy just watching them.

"Hey, hippie, where's Lily?" Percy asks.

"I don't know. She's not here today."

"So what's going on between you and her? I see you eating lunch with her every day," he razzes me.

"Nothing. I just like eating lunch with her."

"Man, that woman's some fine pussy," he remarks.

"Damn fine pussy," Mel echoes.

Eyeing me slyly, Percy asks, "You fucking that pussy?"

"Nah…we're…we're just friends."

He looks at me incredulously. "Man, what the fuck is wrong with you? I see the way she looks at you."

"She has three kids."

"Shiiit…and this man went to college?" He's looking at Mel like I'm an idiot. "Mel, did I say he should marry her?"

"No, Percy."

"A man has to be a fool not to fuck that pussy if he has the chance. Right, Mel?"

"Right, Percy."

Looking me straight in the eye, Percy says, "Let me give you some advice, Leo. Pussy like that only comes along once in a lifetime. Fuck her while you have the chance."

"Just don't knock her up," Mel chimes in.

"I'll think about it. You guys know anything about her dad? She seems reluctant to talk about him."

"That's cuz he's in a coma," Percy answers.

"A coma?"

"Yeah, man. He's brain dead. That's what Merle told me."

"Jesus…how did that happen?"

He shrugs.

That must be why she doesn't talk about him. But she told me about Donny. So why doesn't she tell me about her dad?

At lunch the next day, I ask Lily, "So where were you yesterday?"

"Rachel was sick. I had to stay home since Mama couldn't watch her. So did you miss me?"

"I hafta admit I did. The day seemed twice as long without you here to talk to."

"Who'd you sit with at lunch?"

"Percy and Mel. We had an enlightening conversation. They gave me advice about women and love."

Rolling her eyes, she scoffs, "That's the blind leading the blind."

I summon up my courage and say, "And, uh…I heard something really terrible about your dad…"

Looking at me apprehensively, she asks, "What?"

"Mel said that…that he's in a coma."

She turns her face away from me and stares blindly into space…

"So it's true?" I ask.

When she looks back at me and nods, there are tears in her eyes.

"So…how'd it happen?"

"I don't wanna talk about it." She looks away again.

"Why not?"

"I can't."

"Why not?"

"It…it's too painful."

"You told me about Donny, and it made you feel better."

"This…this is different. I just can't."

"Why?"

"I have my reasons."

More than her words, I can see she's adamant. I drop it. I figure she must be so devastated that she can't talk about it. If my dad was in a coma, it would be a living nightmare.

On Friday, I pack bidets. They require special cardboard boxes that Merle brings me. Before I pack them, he tests each one at a special water faucet on the line to make sure they spray properly. He discovers that three of them are defective, so he scraps them. He makes me haul them out to the scrap pile of discarded vitreous china behind the parking lot. I don't mind—it gives me a chance to go outside in the sunshine and fresh air.

At lunch I say to Lily, "Guess what I packed today."

"What?"

Snickering, I tell her, "Bidets."

Snickering back, she tells me, "That ain't what us hillbillies call them."

"What do you hillbillies call them?"

"Pussy-washers."

I laugh. "Merle said they're shipping them to France. Apparently, French women like them."

She sings:

"There's a place in France where the women wear no pants.

There's a hole in the wall where the men can see it all."

Laughing, I ask, "So have you ever used one?"

"Nope. I ain't ever been to France."

"They were a pretty Aqua color. I think I want one."

"What for? You ain't got no pussy."

"I just think it'd be cool to have an aqua bidet. You know—as a novelty. I collect novelties."

She makes a face like I'm weird. "Hey, you wanna go to the fair tonight?"

Caught off-guard, I hem and haw while I think of an excuse to get out of going without hurting her feelings. "I can't. I told Reese I'd go to the Ski Lodge with him. They've got a live band playing there. So you're going to the fair?"

"Uh-huh. I'm taking Sean to see the Demolition Derby. He loves to watch the cars crash into each other. And we'll look at the animal exhibits. Sarah loves to see the horses and the rabbits."

I can tell by the look on her face that she knows I lied.

At lunch on Monday, Lily eyes me curiously as she munches on a carrot. "Leo, you ain't queer, are you?"

"Me? Queer? No." I realize she must think I'm queer because I haven't put the moves on her.

"So you like sex with women?"

"Yeah. Sure. I love sex with women. The truth is I'm a sybarite at heart."

"A what?"

"Sybarite," I enunciate. "A person who likes sensuous things. I like sex, food, music, and color in that order."

"So...did you and Beth do it?"

Just for amusement I play dumb. "Do what?"

"You know—screw."

I casually take a sip of my drink. "Yeah. We lived together our junior and senior years."

"Was she good?"

"Good?"

"You know what I mean—good in bed. Did she like to screw?"

In my mind, I hear Beth moaning with pleasure when I screwed her. I feel this pang in my chest and realize I still miss her. "Yeah. She liked sex. I was lucky. She was on the pill, so I didn't have to worry about getting her pregnant."

"Did she like to do dirty things?"

I recall how I could usually get her to do my sexual fantasies—especially if she smoked pot first. "Yeah. She liked to experiment sexually. Being a biologist, she was fascinated with the anatomy and physiology of sex. The bedroom was her laboratory. This reminds me of a funny story."

I tell her about a dirty trick Beth and I played on her roommate,

Ava, in Anatomy and Physiology class. Ava had confided in Beth that she was having sexual intercourse regularly with her boyfriend. She told Beth that they were using condoms for birth control. Beth had responded that she should get on the pill like her; that condoms aren't as reliable as the pill because they can come off or tear. So one day in lab class each student was required to bring a urine sample to look at under the microscope. I'd read somewhere that all male urine has dead sperm floating around in it. So I secretly poured some of my urine into Ava's urine sample. Poor Ava turned white as a ghost when she saw dead sperm on her slide under the microscope. When Beth told her the truth, she wanted to strangle me.

Lily thinks it's funny.

Then I tell her about Beth giving me a blow job late one night when we were alone in the lab at the Biology Department. After I came, she spit a drop of my semen on a slide, and we looked at living sperm under the microscope. Lily listens fascinated.

"You know how many sperm are in one drop of semen?" I ask.

"I don't know. Hundreds?" she guesses.

"Thousands. It's incredible how many sperm are swimming around in one drop of semen."

"I'd like to see that. So...did she come easy?"

"Yeah—if I rubbed her...in the right spot."

"So you know about a woman's clit?"

"Yeah. I took Anatomy and Physiology. It's your pleasure spot." She nods.

"It's like the gas pedal on a car. It revs a woman's motor. And takes her to her destination," I cleverly analogize.

Chuckling, she replies, "You have a way with words, Leo."

"In my humble experience, just screwing won't make a woman come. You gotta stimulate her clitoris."

"Uh-huh...so was she a quiet comer?"

Her question makes me laugh. I recall Beth's cries of pleasure when she came. Thinking of the volume dial on my stereo, I answer, "I'd say medium volume. So what about you? Are you a quiet comer?"

"Nope. I'm loud. I love to go wild. What about you?"

"I guess I'm pretty high volume."

"That's good."

"Why's that?"

"Cuz, in my humble experience, men that are quiet comers ain't no fun in bed."

I just laugh again.

CHAPTER NINE

The "Marines' Hymn" blaring over the intercom speaker in my bedroom jars me out of peaceful slumber early Saturday morning. Having smoked pot and stayed up late watching Ingmar Bergman's disturbing movie *The Virgin Spring* at Jack's place last night, I groggily carry on a conversation over the intercom with my old man. He invites me to go flying with Mr. Verekee and him in Mr. Verekee's airplane today. He twists my arm by saying it's like playing golf with the boss—it will insure that I'll be offered a job at Boals-Corrigan next summer. He also says he'll buy me breakfast. Even though I don't want to return there next summer, I realize he's right, so I drag my ass out of bed and tag along.

We meet Mr. Verekee at the restaurant at the airport. Dad is wearing a baseball cap with his Wolfpack Fighter Squadron insignia on it; Mr. Verekee is wearing one with the Shield of the Eighth Air Force on it—they are "brothers in arms." I eat a large breakfast of pancakes with bacon and eggs and listen while they nostalgically talk about the war and flying in combat. For sheer adrenaline, they say flying as a civilian pilot doesn't hold a candle to flying as a bomber pilot in a bombing raid over Berlin or as a fighter pilot in a dogfight over Tokyo Bay.

With Dad as his copilot and me sitting in the back seat, Mr. Verekee taxis his Cessna Skyhawk out of the hanger, and we take off down the runway. Gaining altitude, I look out my window at the miniature toy city below. We fly southwest over lush cornfields and green forests toward Clearfork Lake. On the way, Mr. Verekee magically pulls out a flask, which he and Dad pass back and forth. Dad offers me nips. Wanting to be one of the guys, I join in and drink slugs of liquor.

Arriving at Clearfork, Mr. Verekee turns over the airplane controls to Dad. While circling the lake, my old man performs power-on stalls by climbing rapidly and steeply. The airplane almost grinds to a halt at the peak of its ascent; then shudders and plummets in a nosedive straight downward toward earth. I feel my stomach in my mouth. When the airplane picks up enough speed, it levels out and I see the horizon again. Dad insists it's a safe aerial maneuver as long as you have enough altitude. When I was a kid, I begged him to do it—I loved the way it tickled my stomach. Today, it makes me woozy.

On the way home, my old man repeatedly buzzes our house trying to needle my mom. He flies extremely low over Mr. Bletz's house, who is our next door neighbor. We appear to just miss hitting the TV antenna on his roof. Then I spot Mr. Bletz standing in his front yard—angrily shaking his fist at us. Intoxicated, my old man and Mr. Verekee think it's funny.

After we land safely, a wave of nausea hits me. While exiting the hangar, I blow lunch in the bushes. This is the first time that I've ever experienced air sickness. I don't know if it was caused by my large breakfast or my old man's aerial stunts—I suspect it was probably the liquor. After I finish puking, I spit the string of vomit dangling from my mouth, wipe off my lips, and curse my old man to myself, "Goddamn, son of a bitch…I swear this is the last time I go flying with you." Snickering, he razzes me for not being able to hold my liquor.

Before we go home, they stop at the airport bar and order a few more rounds of drinks. Still feeling nauseous, I order a ginger ale to settle my stomach. Mr. Verekee tells me Mrs. Peters will be bringing her daughter's Girl Scout troop to Boals-Corrigan to tour the factory next week. Mrs. Peters is the wife of Hank Peters, who is the plant manager. Blaming the women's liberation movement, Mr. Verekee complains to my old man that women want to get out of their kitchens and inside his factory where they don't belong. Dad asks Mr. Verekee how his son is doing as a lawyer. He answers that he's getting rich working for a high-powered law firm in Columbus doing estate work.

In his cups, Mr. Verekee says, "John, your son did a helluva job this summer. Bob Castor said he's a hard worker. Quite frankly, I was surprised he stuck it out. Like I told you, most college kids couldn't cut the mustard. Your son did."

Smiling proudly, Dad slurs, "I told ya he could cut the mustard. I didn't raise my son to be a quitter. He's a man."

"Leo, if you want a job next summer, stop in and see me."

Reminding myself that I'd get to see Lily every day, I reply, "Thank you, sir. I may take you up on it."

By the time we leave, Dad is so inebriated that I have to drive us home. On the way, I tell him that Mr. Verekee is a dirty old man. He discredits Lily's story by saying, "Floyd Verekee fought for his country. He's true blue and a yard wide. If I had a dollar for every disparaging story told about him by some disgruntled worker after the strike, I'd be rich enough to retire."

"I believe her. She tells the truth," I retort.

As we open our lunch sacks, Lily asks me what I did on the weekend. I tell her I went for an airplane ride with my old man in Mr. Verekee's airplane. She's interested in hearing all about it. I recount the whole story except about getting air sickness—that's embarrassing.

"I'd love to fly. I ain't ever flown in an airplane."

"You haven't? Not even on a commercial airliner?"

She shakes her head. "It's on my list of things to do someday."

"So what else is on your list?"

"Go to the ocean."

"You've never been to the ocean?"

"Nope. I dream about it."

I can't believe she's never flown in an airplane or been to the ocean. "What else?"

"Go on a date with you." She winks.

"Lily, I ain't going on a date with you."

"Why not?"

"You'd steal my heart," I kid her and change the subject.

Lily proudly announces, "Leo, I'm pretty sure Dakota's pregnant. Appaloosa's gonna be a sire."

"Really?"

"Yeah. I done a transrectal palpation last night and it felt like she's pregnant. And she's moody. She ain't receptive to Appaloosa at all. She ain't showing her rear or raising her tail. The average gestation period for a horse is 320 to 362 days. If I'm right, she should foal right around the Fourth of July next year. And I'll get my stud fee. I'll be rich."

"Congratulations."

The Girl Scout troop tours the plant on Friday morning. Mr. Peters is their tour guide. He leads the Girl Scouts to my packing press, where he herds them into the space between my press and Mr. Machine's press. Standing with his back toward the side of my press, he explains the packing department to them. I show off by packing as fast as I can. Several girls start to snicker.

Oh, shit—I realize they're snickering at the photograph of the woman shooting the beaver taped to the side of my press.

Mrs. Peters spots the picture. Outraged, she whisks the girls away.

When Mr. Peters realizes what happened, he angrily asks me, "Who put that filthy picture up there?"

I don't rat on Herb. "I don't know. It was here when I got here.

I'm just summer help."

He storms off.

Shortly, Merle appears at my press and grumbles, "Mr. Peters was furious. I warned them not to let women in the plant. But, hey, they wouldn't listen to me."

I sing Bob Dylan's "The Times They Are A-Changin'."

He takes down the picture, tears it up, and throws the pieces in the waste basket.

I look at the blank spot on my packing press and sigh.

At lunch I tell Lily how the Girl Scout troop saw the pornographic photograph on my press.

Snickering, she remarks, "I bet the Girl Scouts don't got a merit badge for that."

I laugh. Acting heartbroken, I pine, "Merle tore it up. I'm gonna miss her, Lily. I've grown quite fond of her."

"That's cuz you're one of us now. You're a blue-collar worker. You like blue-collar porn."

I chuckle. "What's white-collar porn?"

"*Playboy.* Hey, I know where there's more porn. C'mon, I'll show you."

Exiting the breakroom, she leads me past her workstation to the warehouse.

I'm hesitant to enter Jessie's domain. "Lily, I don't know about this. Jessie doesn't like me. Remember when I forgot to glue the bottom of the box?"

"That was all show. He was just trying to scare you so you wouldn't do it again. I told him you're a nice guy. He likes you now."

"Where are you taking me?"

"You'll see."

The cavernous warehouse is comprised of long aisles and storage bays. In the storage bays, skids of boxed and unboxed ware are stacked to the ceiling. She leads me through the maze of lanes to a secluded storage room. On a skid, boxes of ware are stacked like stairs. We climb up them to the height of the roof of the storage room; then leap over the chasm onto the roof. In a cubbyhole in the wall back in the corner are mattresses.

Grinning, she says, "We call it the Hole-in-the-Wall Hideout. You know—like Butch Cassidy and Sundance Kid's hideout. Guys on the night shift sleep here."

"It's a good hideout."

"See—there's more porn."

We check out the centerfolds that wallpaper the wall.

"Wow, Leo. This woman's got big tits. You like big tits?"

"Personally, I prefer women with smaller breasts. I think they tend to have the sexiest asses and legs. I'm more turned on by a shapely butt and legs than big breasts."

"I thought all men love big tits."

"I'm not your typical male. You know what I find most erotic about her?"

"What?"

"Her cat-eye glasses."

She snickers.

"They really turn me on," I say only half-joking.

"You are weird. But that's what I like about you."

"Really?"

"Really. It turns me on."

That makes me feel like I'm glowing.

She looks into my eyes temptingly…

I look downward at her plump, rose-colored lips. My lips are drawn irresistibly toward them—

Suddenly, we hear a forklift approaching and duck out of sight.

Jessie goes whirring by on his electric forklift with a skid of ware.

Glancing at my watch, I exclaim, "Shit, it's ten after."

We rush back to our workstations.

Packing feverishly, I think about almost kissing her. If Jessie hadn't come along, I would have. I couldn't stop.

I picture the tempting look in her eyes…her enticing lips…

Arguing with myself, I say, "Man, oh, man—I wanna kiss her. I am so physically attracted to her.

"Do not kiss her. Do not turn the relationship romantic."

As I apply glue to the bottom flaps of a box, I sing "Temptation

Eyes" by the Grass Roots and analyze for the umpteenth time whether she could be Lara. When it gets right down to it, I couldn't care less that she lives in a trailer. That's better than living in my parents' basement.

And I don't care that she's a high school dropout. She's smart. She could always go back to school and get her diploma.

The only real obstacle to her being Lara is her three children. Not only do I not have the time and money to help her raise them, I fear they'll have behavioral problems as a result of the divorce and their dad's alcoholism and suicide. I imagine that Sean gets arrested for drunk driving, and I have to bail him out of jail and go with him to juvenile court—like father, like son. Then I imagine that Sarah or Rachel gets pregnant in high school, and Lily has to help raise the child—like mother, like daughter.

I have to stop leading her on. I tell myself no more sneaking back to the hideout with her. I'm afraid I won't be able to resist her next time.

∞◊∞◊∞◊∞◊∞

September arrives in no time. Law school starts in less than three weeks. As I drop my tuition check in the mailbox on the way to work, I ruefully think I could do something a hell of a lot more fun with the money—like buy a Triumph Bonneville motorcycle.

At lunch Lily asks me, "So when's your last day, Leo?"

"September tenth. I only have seven workdays left since we're off next Monday."

"When do you start law school?"

"September twentieth. I plan on taking a week's vacation."

"What are you gonna do?"

"Take it easy."

"So where's my portrait?"

I've procrastinated drawing it all summer. "I plan on drawing it over the three-day weekend and giving it to you on my last day."

"I'll believe it when I see it. So what'd you do this weekend?"

"Nothing."

"C'mon, you must've done something."

"Nope. My life is boring."

"Don't you ever wanna do something wild?"

Yep. I'd love to go wild.

"Nope. I'm Mr. Rational. I always do what's reasonable and sensible. That's why I'm going to law school."

"That ain't no fun."

"You're right. I live like a monk."

"You know what you need?"

"What?"

"A good lay," she jokes.

I laugh. "True."

Turning coy, she asks, "So…do you think I'm sexy?"

She's flirting with me again, and I can't resist flirting back.

"No, Lily. I think you're erotic."

"If only I could get you in the right place at the right time…" she sighs.

"What would you do?"

"Why don't you ask me out and find out?"

"Cuz I'd fall madly in love with you, and then you'd break my heart," I reply in jest.

She doesn't think I'm funny. "Why don't you ask me out, Leo?"

"Because now's not the time for me to become involved with someone romantically. I wanna be free when I go to law school. No emotional entanglements. It's nothing personal."

"You liar. You'd never ask me out. I ain't good enough for you."

"That's not true. You're my best friend here."

"You think I'm a dumb hillbilly. Trailer trash."

"No, I don't. I don't think you're dumb. I think you're just uneducated. You're certainly smart enough to go back to school. As a matter of fact, I think you're smart enough to go to college. And I don't give a damn that you live in a trailer. At least you have your own place. That's better than me living in my parents' basement."

"So why won't you ask me out?"

I don't want to hurt her feelings by telling her the truth—it's because she's not Lara. "Let's talk about something else."

"Tell me," she persists.

"Because I'm not the right guy for you, Lily."

"Why?"

"Because I'm going to law school."

"So?"

"So I'm gonna be moving to Toledo. You live in Mansfield. How would we see each other?"

"It ain't that far away. We could see each other."

"Lily, I have just enough money to pay for my first year of law school. I wouldn't be able to take you out to eat or to a movie. All my time will be spent studying law, so I wouldn't be able to pay attention to you. The law is a jealous mistress. I hafta put my nose to the grindstone. You need someone with similar circumstances. Someone who lives here in town. Someone who has a job and can pay his own way. Someone who can woo you."

"Woo me?"

"You know—someone who has the time and money to win your heart. I'm the wrong guy for you, Lily. If we start seeing each other, you'll wanna do something together, and I'll have my nose stuck in a law book. It's just a matter of time before you'll become unhappy with me. Then the right guy will come along and steal you away. I'll end up with a broken heart…"

She looks like she doesn't believe me.

"Believe me, if I was looking for a girl now, you'd be the first one I'd ask out."

"I ain't buying this," she scoffs. "It's my kids, ain't it? They always scare away the good ones."

I hesitate to answer her.

She puts down her apple and looks into my eyes. "It's okay, Leo. You can be honest."

I let out a long sigh. "Don't get me wrong, Lily. I want kids someday. I'm just not yet ready for a family. Hell, I can barely support myself. I couldn't support your kids even if I wanted to. And you sure as hell don't need another mouth to feed.

"You need someone who can be a stepdad. You know—go to Sean's Little League games. And read bed-time stories to them. And go to PTA. I wouldn't be able to do that."

"Leo, I ain't looking for a husband. I don't think that far ahead."

I look at her skeptically.

"I already had one, and it didn't turn out so great."

"That's because you had a bad one. An alcoholic. You need to find a good one. You know—someone like Jessie."

"He's already taken. If they ain't scared away, they're already taken or going to law school."

"There's someone out there who's right for you. Sooner or later, you'll find him. He'll give you what you need…"

"Leo, you don't know what I need."

"What do you need?"

Grinning, she answers, "I just need to have some fun. And get laid. I ain't had a man in a long time."

Her answer makes me chuckle, but I don't believe her. "Having fun and getting laid leads to emotional feelings. When I have sex with a woman, I fall in love with her."

"Really?" She is genuinely surprised.

"That's my experience."

"You're the first guy I ever heard say that."

"I told you—I'm not a typical male. I'm not like James Bond. I can't love 'em and leave 'em. Could you?"

"Leo, I'm going nowhere in life. I don't care about tomorrow. I live for today."

"That's not true, Lily. You're going somewhere—you're raising your kids."

"I ain't talking about their lives. I'm talking about my life."

"You could go somewhere in life—if you'd just go back to school and get your diploma."

"I don't wanna talk about school."

I sigh. "So what are you doing on Labor Day?"

"We're having a cookout at my mama's. Tommy's fixing barbecued ribs. They're lip-smackin' good."

"Mmm. I love lip-smackin' barbecued ribs."

"You wanna come?"

I'm afraid meeting her family could send the message that I'm interested in her romantically. "I'd like to come, but I promised Olivia I'd help her pick out a stereo system on Labor Day."

Disappointed, she drops it.

Back at my press, I realize she just implied that she wants me to lay her. I imagine taking her to a motel and having sex with her. I'm so turned on by the fantasy that I'm tempted to do it…

So what is stopping me? What am I afraid of?

Essentially, I'm afraid she's looking for a husband and a stepfather for her children. Maybe she's not consciously looking for a mate, but I suspect she's subconsciously looking. She needs a partner, and her kids need a father figure.

What is she looking for—sexual pleasure or love? She said that she just wants to have fun and get laid. While I admire her audacity, I doubt she could have sex just for pleasure; sooner or later, she'd want sex for love. She's deluding herself if she thinks she could have sex without paying some emotional price.

When I asked her if she could have sex without love, she answered she's going nowhere in life; she lives for today. This makes me feel depressed. Here is this ravishing, smart, unique woman who feels hopeless about her future because of her past. As her friend, I want to help her. All I can do is encourage her to go back to school, but she doesn't want to talk about that.

Then again, maybe she truly isn't looking for love. Maybe all she really wants is to get laid. When I told her that having sex with a woman causes me to fall in love with her, she was genuinely surprised. Maybe she could have sex with a guy without falling in love with him. I recall Reese advising me to get with the times—it's the '70s, the sexual revolution, women's liberation, free love. I'm missing out on it.

I say to myself, "Maybe I should take her to a motel and have a one-night stand. If I'm gonna to do it, I need to do it soon. I'm leaving for law school shortly…"

∞()∞()∞()∞()∞()∞

"Leo, I thought about what you said yesterday. I know the real reason you won't ask me out. It's cuz I ain't Lara."

Not this again. I sigh…

"Leo, we tell each other the truth. Don't we?"

"Yeah."

"So tell me the truth."

I feel cornered. "Okay, Lily. That's the real reason. You aren't Lara. But not because you're not good enough for me. Because of our circumstances."

"You're right, Leo. I'm Lily…I'm just a wild hillbilly girl…"

At this moment, I perceive a subtle light in her eyes revealing a hidden inner wildness. Her words—accentuated by this wild glint—send a shiver down my spine…

"Leo, let's have an affair."

"What?"

Looking at me ingenuously, she says, "Let's have a love affair. I'm dying of boredom. I need some spice in my life. I read in *Cosmo* an affair can be good for your mental health."

"I don't think that's a good idea, Lily."

"Why?"

"Because one of us will end up with a broken heart."

"You worry too much about the future."

"True."

"Do something fun in your life."

"Like what?"

"Let's go to the drive-in tomorrow night. Just me and you," she says suggestively.

This arouses me…

"C'mon, Leo, take me to the drive-in…we can get naked in the back seat…"

She's daring me.

I imagine getting naked and screwing in the luxurious burgundy leather back seat of Dad's Cadillac. Just the thought of it gives me a hard-on…

Despite being sorely tempted, I know it would be a mistake.

I exhale deeply. "Lily, as much as I'd love to take you to the drive-in and get naked in the back seat, I don't wanna ruin our friendship by having an affair."

"I don't understand. Why would it ruin our friendship?"

"Like I told you, I'm going away in two weeks. I don't wanna lead you on. It's not fair to you."

"You ain't leading me on. I'm leading you on."

I smile…

"Leo, you're going away forever. It's now or never…"

"I don't wanna hurt you, Lily."

"Ain't you ever heard the saying, 'Better to have loved and lost than never to have loved at all?' "

Grinning, I reply, "Yeah. It's a famous quote from the poet Alfred Lord Tennyson. I'm just not sure it's true. Actually, I think 'Tis better to have loved and won than never to have loved at all.' "

Undeterred, she gazes intently into my eyes and says in her sensual voice, "Leo, I want you…"

My heart throbs…

Placing her hand on mine, she says, "I know you want me. You wanted to kiss me in the hideout…"

I do want you. Oh, God, do I want you…

Suddenly, I become aware that we're the only people in here and look at the clock. "Shit, Lily, we're late."

We run back to our workstations.

Packing with a bulge in my pants, I picture that wild glint in her eyes—it sends a shiver down my spine again.

I marvel at the way she ingenuously proposed having an affair; then brazenly said we could get naked in the back seat of the car at the drive-in.

Again and again, I feel her hand on mine and hear her sensual voice saying "I want you…"

She wants me. This wild hillbilly girl wants me.

Man, oh, man…she stirs my blood…

I want her. I want this wild hillbilly girl so badly…

But then I recall her saying the word "love." I realize she's not talking about a one-night stand. She's looking for love.

Not me. Not with her. I know what would happen if we had an affair—I'd fall madly in love with her. Then I'd want to be her knight in shining armor and rescue her and her kids. But the prospect of taking on another man's three kids is too daunting. I might be willing to take on one but not three.

I toy with the idea of having a torrid affair and then dumping her when I go off to law school. But I couldn't use her just for my sexual gratification. I like her way too much to do that.

So…that settles it once and for all. I'm not going to have an affair with her and become lovers. I'm going to remain friends. Having made up my mind, I no longer feel torn. In fact, my hard-on is gone, and I feel surprisingly at peace with myself.

After clocking out at the end of the day, she and I walk to our cars together. Neither of us mentions our earlier conversation. At my parking spot, she looks at me expectantly. I suspect she's hoping that I'll ask her to go to the drive-in, but I act like it never happened. I plan on telling her goodbye on my last day of work and never seeing her again.

∞◊∞◊∞◊∞◊∞◊∞

On Saturday morning, I get out my twelve-piece Monarch Graphite Drawing Kit and sharpen my drawing pencils. Then I select the 17 inch by 14 inch smooth surface Strathmore Artist 500 Series drawing tablet; I prefer smooth paper for female complexions. To avoid my parents' nosy questions about Lily, I work at the game table in my guest suite. Propping her photograph against a picture frame, I select the 4H drawing pencil and begin drawing Lily's portrait. As usual, I start with her eyes, trying to capture the way they sparkle when she smiles; but I have to scrap my first try—they look dull, lifeless. Flipping the page of my drawing tablet, I start over. By painstakingly erasing specks of dark graphite in her irises and pupils with my sharpened eraser, I'm able to create tiny flecks of light. I draw her blue eye slightly lighter than her green eye. Wholly absorbed, I'm oblivious to time. At midnight, I finally finish her eyes and appraise them…

I tingle with excitement. They look alive—like they're sparkling from within.

Obsessed with the drawing, I work all day Sunday. I shade her pretty nose and high cheekbones. Then move on to her sensual lips, trying to portray her daring smile. I carefully draw each of her teeth and breathe a sigh of relief when I finish without screwing them up. After I finish sketching the outline of her face, I call it a day.

Eyeing my handiwork before I go to bed, I tell myself, "She's coming to life…"

On Labor Day, my parents have a cookout. Jack and Lynn come with Josh. After supper Mom, Olivia, and Lynn play with Josh in a rubber swimming pool in the back yard. Dad, Jack, and I sit at the picnic table on the screen porch talking law. Jack is working at Dad's law firm while he waits on his bar exam results. I listen as they talk about their cases.

"So, Leo, are you ready for law school?" Jack asks.

Shrugging, I answer, "I guess I'm as ready as I'll ever be. Got any advice?"

He takes a drag on his cigarette. Exhaling contemplatively, he advises, "The worse thing about law school is it attracts a lot of competitive jerks all fighting to get high grades so they can get hired at the most prestigious law firms. It can get pretty cutthroat."

"I'm not very competitive," I acknowledge.

"You'll do fine. You have Dad's genes."

"Sometimes I think I have more of Mom's genes."

Inebriated, Dad slurs, "Aaah, don't sweat it, Leo. It ain't war. They ain't shooting bullets at ya. Just put your nose to the grindstone."

As Mom would say, Dad is "on his muscle" tonight. I notice that he's definitely becoming more antagonistic when he drinks. "Dad, you're starting to sound like a broken record."

Smiling cynically, Jack says, "Leo, you don't hafta worry about grades and class rank. Dad will hire you no matter what. Right, Dad?"

"As long as he doesn't blow it," Dad answers.

Dad leaves the porch. Jack and I look at each other like we know where he's going—for a nip.

"So tell me, Jack…what made you decide to be a lawyer?"

"One day I just woke up with a burning desire deep down to be a lawyer. Don't you have that?"

"Not really. Sometimes I think I chose it just because it's the easiest path in life. You know—since Dad will hire me," I confide. I don't confide that I only have one burning desire—to write and draw for Lara. I doubt he would understand.

CHAPTER TEN

When I go to work on Tuesday morning, I feel great. All I have to do is make it four more days at Boals-Corrigan, and I'm free. As I pack, I sing "Take It Easy" by the Eagles.

Still, I feel a little melancholy, realizing that this is my last week to see Lily. I know I'm going to miss her.

At a quarter after seven, Merle shows up at my press with my replacement whose name is Kenny Turner. I quit packing and shake his hand. Merle tells me to train him. With his rosy cheeks and practically no beard, he looks like a kid. He's only eighteen and so scrawny I doubt he'll make it.

I figure my last week will be easy now that I have someone to split the work with. Taking him under my wing, I advise him to drink plenty of water, take salt tablets, and wear a cold sponge headband. Then I show him how to stamp the boxes and pack, and we take turns packing. He packs ten; I pack thirty. He's out of shape. By morning break time, he's exhausted.

He accompanies me to the breakroom. I don't see Lily, so I sit with Percy and Mel and introduce Kenny to them. When I tell them it's my last week, they're happy for me.

At lunchtime Kenny has to go to the bathroom, so I head to the breakroom without him. Lily is waiting for me at the toilet tester.

"It's your last week," she observes.

"Yep. Come Friday I can kiss this place goodbye."

She tries to look happy for me. "So…are you coming back next summer?"

"I hope not. Actually, I'm hoping my dad hires me as an intern at his law firm."

I see the disappointment in her eyes.

At lunch I ask her what she did over Labor Day weekend. It's like pulling teeth to get her to answer me.

"Are you mad at me?" I ask, smiling unsurely.

"No."

"You're awfully quiet."

"I…I just feel down."

"Why? What's wrong?"

"My life."

"What do you mean?"

"I don't have any fun anymore. All I do is go to work and assemble ballcocks. Then go home and fix supper. Do the dishes. Do laundry. Clean the trailer. And go to bed. Then get up and do it all over again."

"What…what are you talking about? You do lots of fun things."

"Like what?"

"You go fishing. Horseback riding. You're always doing something with your kids. You have way more fun than I do."

"That's…that's easy for you to say. You're getting out of here."

I can't help it you're trapped here, and I'm escaping…

I don't want to argue with her—I don't want to spoil our friendship before leaving for law school, so I just sigh…

"I'm sorry, Leo. I'm glad you're getting out of here. I really am." Sighing deeply herself, she tells me, "I just feel sad cuz…cuz you're leaving…and I'm stuck here alone…I won't have anybody to talk to at lunch…"

I can't think of anything truthful to say that will make her feel better, so I just look at her sympathetically—

She blurts, "I hate this place. I gotta get out of here, Leo."

Her words—spoken with sheer desperation in her eyes and voice—distress me.

Oh, Lily, I wish I could save you. But I can't. I'm not your knight in shining armor.

"I feel like I'm trapped here," she says bitterly.

Even though I fear she's trapped by her circumstances and doubt she'll ever go back to school, I tell her, "Listen to me, Lily. There's only one way to escape this place. Go back to school. Get your diploma."

She looks at me blankly.

Trying to encourage her, I say, "It's a free country. You could be whatever you wanna be. You're intelligent enough to get your high school diploma. You could even go to college. You don't hafta be that smart to go to college."

She gives me a dirty look for implying she's not that smart.

"Sorry. That didn't come out right. Believe me, you're smart enough. You're smarter than most people I knew in college."

Staring hopelessly at her peanut butter and jelly sandwich, she says, "I just feel like my life is over…"

God…she's only twenty-five years old and she feels like her life is over. I feel so sorry for her.

Suddenly, a light bulb goes on in my head. "Hey, you know what you need?"

"What?"

"A vacation. That'll cheer you up. You got any vacation time?"

"Yeah…I got two weeks. I haven't taken a vacation since I started here. I always work over my vacation—so I get paid double-time."

"You know what they say—'All work and no play makes Jack a dull boy.'"

She thinks about what I said for a moment. Then I see a faint glimmer in her eye. "Maybe you're right."

"I know I'm right. Take your kids up to the lake. Go to Cedar Point. Go to the beach. Go fishing."

The glimmer becomes a gleam. "You're right, Leo. I need to go somewhere. Do something fun."

"Have an adventure," I urge her.

Kenny enters the breakroom with his lunch pail, looking lost. I wave at him to come join us. He plops down beside me wearily. I introduce him to Lily. He's tongue-tied and keeps staring at her—he's probably intimidated by her beauty. She's lukewarm toward him. I can tell she's not happy that I invited him to sit with us—I suspect that she feels like he's intruding on our privacy.

Back at our workstation, Kenny exclaims, "Gosh, that girl's the prettiest girl I've ever seen. Is she married?"

"No. She's a widow." I inform him of her circumstances.

"Is she your girlfriend?"

"No. We're just friends."

"Does she have a boyfriend?"

"Nope." Obviously, he's developing a crush on her.

After work I drop Red off at Lester's Auto Shop for an overhaul. Lester says it'll take two days; she'll be ready after work on Thursday. Mom has to come pick me up.

After supper I start work on Lily's hair. Using the softer graphite pencils, I draw broad strokes in the direction her hair is flowing and shade the cinnamon-red tones in gradients. Using the eraser to streak the graphite and the drawing stub to blend it, I create highlights. Her hair is so long it runs off the bottom of the page.

On Wednesday, Kenny is so sore and stiff from packing yesterday that he can hardly move. So I pack for him. Using him as my helper, I try to pack a thousand toilets today—I want to earn a big payday. All morning he stamps the cardboard boxes, feeds them to me, and refills my glue bucket. I stand in front of my press and pack as fast as I can. I need to pack approximately two toilets per minute. By lunchtime I've packed 550 and am on track to make it.

During lunch Lily asks, "Hey, Leo—have you ever been to the ocean?"

"Yeah. I've been to the Atlantic Ocean lots of times."

"Where?"

"Saint Simon's Island, Bar Harbor, Maine, Cape Cod, Cape Hatteras, Hilton Head—"

"You've been to Cape Hatteras?"

"Yeah. I've been there twice. Beth and I went there over spring break of our junior year, and my folks took me there when I was in junior high. My dad wanted to see Kitty Hawk where the Wright Brothers flew the first powered airplane—the Wright Flyer. They flew it there because of the wind and the sand dunes."

"What's it like?"

"It's named the Outer Banks because it juts way out in the ocean. It's really just a sand bar that runs a couple hundred miles along the coast of North Carolina. It gets big waves, so you can bodysurf there."

She replies dreamily, "I wanna go to Cape Hatteras to see the wild horses of Currituck…"

"The wild horses of Currituck?"

"Yeah. Dr. Hall told me they're these wild horses that roam the sand dunes—free. They've lived on the Currituck Banks for four hundred years. You know how they got there?"

"Huh-uh."

"They swam ashore from Spanish shipwrecks in hurricanes."

"Interesting." I realize I need to cut lunchtime short if I want to reach my goal. "Lily, I gotta go. With Kenny's help, I'm trying to pack a thousand toilets today. Come on, Kenny."

"I really wanna see them, Leo."

"Go see them. Cape Hatteras is not that far away. You can get there in a day," I call over my shoulder.

Packing straight through afternoon break, by the end of the day, I pack 1,001 toilets. That's my personal record.

"Kenny, I'm a lean, mean, packing machine," I brag.

He looks at me in awe.

When I get home from work, there's a thick envelope addressed to me from the law school. In my bedroom, I sit down at my desk and open it. The administration sent my schedule. My first year courses are all mandatory: Civil Procedure 1, Contracts 1, Torts 1, and Criminal Law. I notice that orientation for first-year law students is scheduled for next Friday and Saturday with social events, including a faculty-student softball game and a cocktail party, on Sunday. The materials read: "Orientation is optional; however, attendance is strongly recommended." I figure I'd better attend. Enclosed is a thick stack of cases that I'm supposed to brief for orientation. Shit—I have homework to do before I even start law school, which will impinge on my vacation. Procrastinating, I shove everything back in the envelope. I don't even want to think about law school until next week.

After supper Reese calls me. "So are you ready to start law school?" he asks.

"Ready as I'll ever be."

"We'll make it together."

"It'll be just like old times—me and you swimming the medley relay. We'll finish the race together."

Reese and I arrange to attend orientation together. Our tentative plan is to drive to Toledo on Thursday and find a cheap motel to stay at until we can find an apartment. I tell him I'll call him to work out our final plans next Wednesday night.

After I hang up, I breathe a sigh of relief. Going through this law school ordeal with a friend calms my nerves.

On Thursday, Merle scolds me for not making Kenny pack yesterday. I explain that he's out of shape. Merle replies that he won't get in shape if I don't make him pack. I definitely won't miss mean Merle.

At morning break, I say, "Hey, Lily. Could you give me a ride to pick up my car after work?"

"Is it broke?"

"No. I'm having her overhauled before I go to law school since I'll be driving back and forth between Mansfield and Toledo for three years."

"Yeah. Sure."

"Thanks."

"I wanna ask you something too," she says mysteriously.

"What?"

"I'll wait till lunch when we have more time."

While Kenny goes to the pop machine, she says, "Leo, I wanna eat lunch with just you today. Okay?"

Intrigued, I answer, "Yeah. Sure. I'll tell Kenny. It sounds mysterious."

She smiles coyly.

At lunchtime I tell Kenny that Lily wants to ask me something in private and suggest that he sit with Percy and Mel today. Not following my suggestion, he sits at a table by himself.

Sitting at our private table back in the corner, I take a bite of my chipped ham sandwich. "So...what do you wanna ask me?"

Looking at me eagerly, she says, "Leo, I wanna go to Cape Hatteras and find the wild horses of Currituck. You wanna go with me?"

With my mouth full, I ask, "You...you want me to go with you to Cape Hatteras to find these wild horses?"

Her face turns animated. "Yeah. Me and you—let's go find them."

I swallow. "Uhhh...I don't know, Lily. When?"

"Tomorrow. We could leave right after work."

I'm taken aback...

"Please, Leo. Take me to the ocean. My life's passing me by. I'm twenty-five years old, and I've never seen the ocean. I wanna see it."

Hope is burning in her eyes. Knowing how much she loves horses, I want to help her find these wild ones. And I feel sad that she's never seen the ocean, never experienced its wonder. I'd like to show it to her.

But I leave for law school next Thursday and have to get ready. I have cases to brief for orientation.

While I hate to let her down, I need to tell her no without hurting her feelings.

"Lily, I...I can't afford it. I need all my money to pay for law school."

"I have the money. I saved it. I'll pay for everything."

"I don't wanna owe you."

"You won't owe me. I don't care about the money. I just wanna go to the ocean and find them horses..."

"Cape Hatteras—that's the coast of North Carolina. That's a long ways away."

"You said it ain't that far."

"It's a twelve hour drive. How would we get there?"

"Your car. It'd be really cool to ride there with the top down."

"I don't know, Lily. I don't think Red could make it that far. She'd probably break down somewhere on the Pennsylvania Turnpike in the mountains in the middle of the night. We'd be stranded. She's not too reliable."

"But you're getting her overhauled."

"You…you don't understand. These British sports cars are temperamental—they love to break down. It's their favorite pastime."

"Like my mama says, 'sometimes you just gotta take a little risk in this world. No risk, no reward.' "

"Even if Red could make it, I still can't go. I hafta go to law school."

"What day do you leave?"

"Thursday. I'm going to orientation with Reese. And we gotta find a place to live temporarily. And look for an apartment."

"That's a whole week away. We got time."

"They sent me a big packet of cases I'm supposed to brief for orientation."

"You know what they say—'All work and no play makes Jack a dull boy,' " she throws back at me.

"Lily, I'd love to help you find those horses, but I can't. I'm sorry…"

She looks crushed.

I stare at my sandwich unhappily…

"It's okay, Leo. I understand…"

The light in her eyes is gone. Trying to make her feel better, I say, "It's just bad timing for me. You know—starting law school next week. Maybe some other time. Maybe next summer…"

She looks at me like she doesn't believe me.

I change the subject by asking, "So…are your kids ready to go back to school?"

For the remainder of lunch, we make small talk about Sean's playing flag football and Sarah's joining the tumbling team.

After lunch Kenny and I take turns packing. He slowly packs twenty; I quickly pack twenty. On his turn, I sit on the glue drum, thinking about going to Cape Hatteras with Lily. I picture myself sprinting down the beach and diving into the surf, bodysurfing in the waves, floating in my army raft in the sea, and climbing Jockey's Ridge. I realize I'd much rather go to the ocean with her than stay home and get ready for law school.

It occurs to me that we'd stay at a motel, which means we'd probably sleep together, which means we'd probably have sex. Fantasizing about having sex with her, I become aroused—

"Oh my God!" Kenny exclaims. Gaping in revulsion, he's pointing at the closest toilet on the line.

I stand up and look—a huge turd is floating in a pool of piss.

"Who did it?" he asks.

I look up the line. Herb is grinning at us. "Herb. He plays that prank on all the new guys."

Kenny is bewildered. "What…what do I do?"

"I'll tell you what you don't do. You don't tell Merle."

"Why not?"

"He'll make you clean it out."

In dismay, he asks, "So what should I do?"

I check to make sure Kenny already applied glue to the bottom flaps of the box. Then I carefully lift up the toilet, so the turd and piss don't spill out, and gently lower it into the box. Then I grab his glue brush, apply glue to the top flaps of the box, and carefully shove it into the press.

Grinning sardonically, I tell him, "That's what. Some innocent victim remodeling his bathroom is gonna be in for a big surprise when he opens that box. Unless you feel like cleaning it out."

He shakes his head emphatically.

"You're a fast learner, Kenny. You just might make it as a toilet packer."

Glaring at Herb, I mutter, "I'd like to get even with that son of a bitch before I go…"

At afternoon break I say, "Hey, Herb. Thanks for the farewell present."

He plays dumb.

"Ya know, Herb, someday your little prank is gonna backfire on you."

"I don't know what the hell you're talking about, hippie."

After work Lily gives me a lift to Lester's in her old, beat-up Oldsmobile Cutlass. I hop in the front bucket seat. Feeling something under my butt, I pull out a nude Barbie Doll.

"Just throw her in the back seat," she says with a grin.

Holding her up on display, I ask, "You know what Barbie's measurements would be if she was a real woman?"

"What?"

"She'd have a thirty-nine inch bust. An eighteen inch waist. And thirty-three inch hips."

"How do you know that?"

"I read it in a magazine. The article said she's the reason little girls grow up to hate their bodies. Because they don't look like Barbie. That's why they get breast implants."

"I don't believe it. I had a Barbie when I was a little girl, and I didn't grow up to hate my body. I love my body."

"You're the first female I've ever heard say that."

"I ain't your typical female," she says with a grin.

"Mattel should've used you as her prototype. What are your measurements—if you don't mind my asking?"

"I don't mind. 34B-24-35."

"Damn, I don't believe it. That was my locker combination in twelfth grade. Those numbers."

"Really?"

"Really."

"I knew it…"

"Knew what?"

"Nothing." She smiles like she knows something I don't know.

At Lester's she waits while I see if my car is ready. Inside his shop, I ring the bell on the counter. Lester comes out of the back in his greasy overalls and slowly adds up my bill. I'm dreading it. I just about have a heart attack when I see it's five hundred dollars. Initially, he defends his bill by saying it's a foreign sports car; parts are expensive. Then he explains that he had to replace the head gasket, install a new brake line and new brake pads, turn the rotors, put four new tires on the car, and completely tune up the engine. I protest, but there's nothing I can do about it—he won't let me have my car keys until I pay him. I have to write a check—it takes a big chunk out of my savings.

In the parking lot, I tell Lily, "It's ready. You can leave. Thanks for the ride."

"What's the matter? You look sick."

"The bill."

"How much did he charge you?"

"Five hundred dollars."

"Five hundred dollars?" She has me show her the bill. "That's highway robbery. You should've taken it to Tommy. He would've done it for a lot less."

"Your brother's a mechanic?"

"Yeah. He's got his own auto repair shop. He can fix anything. And when he fixes something, it stays fixed. And he don't fix something that ain't broken. Some shops pad the bill."

"I'll remember that next time."

After supper I put the finishing highlights in Lily's hair and draw her felt cowgirl hat. Appraising the drawing, I'm quite pleased with how it turned out—she looks ravishing. I name her portrait *Lily after Riding Appaloosa* on the back, sign and date it on the front, roll it up, and put it inside a cardboard tube for safekeeping. Rather than take it into the plant where it could get smudged, I plan on leaving it in my car and giving it to her after work tomorrow.

On my last day, I loaf. I prep Kenny's boxes for him and spell him when he needs a breather. When I pour his glue for him, an idea comes to me. Grinning deviously, I say, "Hey, Kenny. You wanna get even with Herb?"

Grinning back at me, he nods eagerly.

I tell him my plan. At break time every Friday morning, the inspectors check out Herb's literature at his workstation. I figure right before break time, when he goes to the cooling area to fetch a cartload of toilets, we'll go pour glue on his chair.

About fifteen minutes before break time, Herb goes to the

cooling area. I grab the glue bucket, and Kenny and I sneak up to his workstation, where I pour a big puddle of clear glue on the seat of his plastic chair. We run back to our packing press.

At break time Kenny wants to stick around and watch what happens, but I tell him that'll incriminate us. He tags along with Lily and me to the breakroom and sits beside me, mooning over her. She barely notices him. I tell her about the prank that Kenny and I pulled on Herb. "This I gotta see," she says. We go back early to my press to observe what happens. Herb and his buddies are sitting in their chairs, perusing the literature. Break time ends. When Herb stands up, his chair sticks to his ass. It's hilarious watching him trying to remove it. Everyone laughs their butts off at him. After he finally succeeds in detaching it, he gives Kenny and me the finger.

"He got a dose of his own medicine," Lily laughs.

Smirking, I reply, "Revenge is a dish best served cold."

I ask Percy to sing a request since it's my last day—"When a Man Loves a Women" by Percy Sledge. He sings it soulfully—it sounds great.

A few minutes before lunchtime, Percy yells to me, "Hey, hippie, you wanna go to Burger Chef with me and Mel? We'll treat you since it's your last day. It's our going-away present to you."

That sounds a hell of a lot better than a baloney sandwich. "Can Lily come?" I ask.

"You gotta hurry. We ain't got much time."

I run back to Lily's workbench and invite her to go with us. She says she has to pee first. I tell her she doesn't have time. She grabs her lunch pail and runs after me.

Mel drives. Lily and I sit in the back seat. On the way, Percy produces a joint out of thin air. Firing it up, he takes a hit. "Hey, hippie, want a hit?"

"Sure."

He passes the joint to me over the back of his seat. Lily looks surprised when I take a toke. I offer her a hit, but she declines.

At Burger Chef, Percy and Mel practically trip over each other to hold the door open for Lily. Percy holds it gallantly and says, "After you, darlin'."

LILY

She makes a bee line to the women's restroom. While we order, Percy asks me, "So did you fuck her?"

"No. Like I told you, we're just friends."

Shaking his head in disbelief, he says, "You're a fool, man."

Mel nods his head in agreement.

Stoned, I order two Big Shefs, fries, and a large beverage, which they generously pay for. Lily joins us with her lunch pail at our table by a window. Since it's Friday, she pours herself a Bloody Mary from her thermos.

While we wolf down our lunches, we talk about my going to law school. Percy says if he ever gets busted, he'll hire me. Lily just listens.

"I'm gonna miss you guys," I tell them.

They scoff.

"You know who I'm gonna miss the most?"

Percy and Mel look at me like I'm going to say Lily.

"Mr. Machine."

They laugh.

"I love the sounds he makes while he packs. He sounds like a racecar. Before I go, I have one question. Has anyone ever heard him say a word? I haven't heard him utter one word all summer."

They all shake their heads.

Percy says, "That fucker's nuts." Then he tells a crazy story about him. One day Mr. Machine got a burr up his ass—nobody knows why because he never says a word—and failed to catch a long line of toilets that Herb pushed down his roller conveyor. When the speeding toilets hit the bumper, they fell like dominos, breaking over thirty toilets. Shards of vitreous china were scattered all over the floor along the line. Management was furious with him; but, because he's such a fast packer, they didn't fire him—they didn't even deduct the cost from his pay. All they did was make him clean up the mess.

After we finish eating, we race back to the plant. On the way, Lily says, "Hey, Leo…"

"What?"

Shaking her head like she changed her mind, she says, "Never mind."

We clock in at twelve noon on the dot.

After lunch I sit on the glue drum and existentially observe the operation of the factory. I start thinking Boals-Corrigan is a microcosmic universe. I'm stoned out of my mind…

When Percy shouts "Break time" I tell Kenny, "Only ninety more minutes and this sweatshop is history."

He looks envious.

In the breakroom, I shake hands and say goodbye to everybody. They all wish me good luck at law school and give me shit about someday becoming a shyster and an ambulance chaser. Flashing me the peace sign, Percy says, "Peace, brother." Lily just sits at our table, watching me from a distance. I smile at her. She smiles back faintly.

When I come to Herb, he says, "You fucker, you ruined my pants." Then he stands up and shows me the dried glue on the seat of his pants.

"I don't know what the hell you're talking about, Herb."

At two fourteen, I walk back to my press for the last time feeling philosophical. Each day felt like an eternity; but the summer went by in the blink of any eye.

At quitting time, while I'm helping Kenny tally his toilet count on his time sheet, Mr. Castor and Merle stop by to say goodbye. It's payday. They give me my paycheck; then shake my hand and wish me good luck at law school. Pointing at my packing press, Mr. Castor says, "Son, there's the reason why you go to law school. So you don't have to pack toilets the rest of your life."

"Yes, sir. That's what my dad says."

"If you need a job next summer, come see me. You're a good worker."

Not wanting to burn any bridges behind me, I smile. "Thank you, sir. I'll keep that in mind."

Not if I can help it.

Lily stops by my press on her way out. Just in case I want to get in touch with her someday, I say, "Hey, Lily, let me have your address. So I can write you."

She scribbles down her telephone number and address on a piece of paper, and I stick it in my wallet. "You'll have to write me. Keep me apprised of things here."

I stroll to the exit with Lily. I'm sky-high. Everybody is lined up in front of the time clock. I get in line behind her. The time clock hits three thirty. As I shuffle toward it, I count down the last ten seconds out loud while I'm waiting on her to clock out—then punch out at three thirty-one.

I made it.

I proved to everyone I could cut the mustard.

I'm free...

Walking out the door with Lily, I start singing "Free Bird" by Lynyrd Skynyrd.

"I love that song," she says.

"Hey, I got a surprise for you."

"What?"

"It wouldn't be a surprise if I told you. It's in my car."

We walk to my car, where I get her portrait, remove it from the tube, and unroll it on the hood.

Gazing at it in wonder, she murmurs, "Oh, Leo..."

"I named it *Lily after Riding Appaloosa.* You like it?"

"I do..."

"I think I captured your sparkling eyes and daring smile, if I say so myself."

Her finger to her lips, she examines her portrait. "How'd you make them sparkle?"

"A magician never reveals his secrets."

"Let me pay you."

"Nope. It's my farewell present to you for helping me make it through this summer. I couldn't have done it without you."

"This is the nicest present anybody has ever given me. Thank you so much. I'll think of you when I look at it..."

I smile. Then I roll up her portrait, put it back in the tube, and hand it to her.

We both realize it's time to say goodbye. We stare at each other glumly...

Looking at me poignantly, she says, "I really like you, Leo."

"I really like you too, Lily."

"I really like talking to you."

"I really like talking to you too."

"I'm really gonna miss you."

"I'm really gonna miss you too."

"No, you won't."

"Yes, I will. I was just kidding about Mr. Machine at lunch. You're the one who I'm gonna miss the most."

"You're just saying that."

I feel a bitter-sweet pang in my chest. "No, I'm not. You're my best friend."

"I ain't ever gonna see you again."

Even though she's probably right, I assure her, "You'll see me again. When you're least expecting, I'll drop in here and say hi to you."

"You liar."

Her eyes are so sad I have to look away...

My eyes drift to the scrap pile of discarded vitreous china behind the parking lot where I spot the aqua bidets. "Hey, I almost forgot. I'll be right back."

"Where you going?"

"I'm gonna get me one of those pussy-washers."

"What for?"

"For my apartment. I want a souvenir of this place. I'm gonna use it as a pot for my jade plant."

"You're weird."

"No, I'm not. I just have a warped sense of humor. You want one?"

"No thanks."

I deadpan, "All the trailers featured in *Better Homes and Gardens* have a pussy-washer. It's vogue."

She just laughs.

I lug an aqua bidet to my car and set it on the passenger seat; then walk around to the driver's door. I hate drawn-out goodbyes. Forcing a smile, I say, "See ya, Lily."

"Bye."

I reach for the handle on my car door.

"Leo, wait."

"What?"

"Umm…are you free tonight?"

"Yeah. Why?"

"It's not a date. I…I just wanna take you out to eat at the Cameo. I wanna treat you. It'll be my goodbye present to you."

"The tavern on Springmill Street?"

"Yeah. Have you eaten there?"

"No. I've seen it on my way to the country club."

"I used to work there. They have the best cheeseburger and fries in town."

Since I'm high, that sounds really good. "Okay."

She looks like she can't believe it.

"Want me to come pick you up?" I ask.

"I'd love it. I'm dying to ride in your sports car with the top down."

"What time?"

"How about five thirty?"

"I'll be there."

She gives me directions to her trailer park; tells me she lives in the trailer with the white picket fence and pink awnings at the end of Rose Lane. "I hope you don't get lost. I live in the boonies. You probably won't be able to find it."

"I'll find it."

"You ain't gonna stand me up, are you?"

"Nope. I'll see ya later."

"See ya."

As I barrel out of the place, I lay on the horn.

After cashing my paycheck at the bank, I have enough money to pay for a motel room and food until Reese and I can find an apartment.

At home I store my aqua bidet in the garage and get ready to go out with Lily. I shower, shave, and put on my favorite Raccoon Creek Swim Team T-shirt, cutoff jeans, and tennis shoes; then roll a joint in case I feel like getting stoned. What the hell—she knows I smoke pot now. With my headphones on, I recline on the sofa, listening to music, until it's time to go.

CHAPTER ELEVEN

Heading out the door, I remember that Lily is dying to ride in my car with the top down, so I put it down and remove the side windows.

Driving through Roseland on Trimble Road, I see Stonehaven sitting high atop Country Club Hill to the east. I smell a faint, acrid odor—beyond the country club, yellowish-gray smoke is billowing out of the smokestacks at the steel mill. The tow truck in front of me turns into Smoyer's junkyard.

Looks like Lily lives near a junkyard.

Woodland is zoned residential, which keeps out factories and junkyards. I figure this area is either zoned industrial or has no zoning at all. I recall reading an article in the newspaper that said Roseland didn't have sanitary sewers until a few years ago. County officials constructed them after the Health Department reported several cases of cholera caused by raw sewage leaking from outhouses into a nearby creek.

As I drive further north, I begin to see some ramshackle houses on lots cluttered with rubbish; several have junk cars without wheels parked on cinder blocks in either the driveway or front yard. A few houses are falling down and appear to be abandoned—their windows are boarded shut, their paint is peeling, and their grass has not been mowed. I start humming "Dueling Banjos" from the movie *Deliverance.*

On the outskirts of town, I cross another railroad track and drive past modest homes that appear to be well-maintained.

Emerging into the countryside, I come to a T-intersection. Turning onto Wolf Road, I see a sign up ahead that says "Roseland Trailer Park." Turning onto Rose Lane, I weave my way up a tar and chip road through the park. All of the side lanes are named after flowers. Several trailers display deer statuary—bucks, does, and fawns—in their front yards. At the intersection of Daisy Lane, two young boys riding a minibike run the stop sign—I have to slam on the brakes. They think it's funny. Continuing slowly on Rose Lane, I go by a trailer with a pair of pink flamingo statues in the front yard.

Damn, I wish I had them to go with my aqua pussy-washer— that would be so eclectic.

I go past a trailer where skinny kids are swimming in an above-ground swimming pool in the front yard. They stop playing and gape at me as I drive by in Red. I flash them the peace sign. At another trailer, a burly guy with a butch haircut is mowing his front yard on a riding mower, while simultaneously smoking a cigarette and drinking a can of beer. He's wearing clodhoppers and bib-overalls without a T-shirt. His hairy beer belly is hanging grossly out of the sides of the bib. His yard is the size of a postage stamp— he barely has enough room to turn around. I chuckle—Americana.

I stay on Rose Lane all the way to the back of the park where the road dead ends. Up ahead I see a white trailer with pink awnings and a white picket fence enclosing the front yard. Lily is waving at me. Wearing her cowgirl hat, she's sitting on her front stoop. Flower beds are on each side of the stoop, and pretty flower boxes are underneath the front windows. Her place looks charming from the outside.

Her Olds Cutlass is parked in the carport. I pull in the driveway and park behind it. Hopping out of my car, I announce, "Here I am. I made it."

She stands up and walks down her front walk toward me.

Holy shit…

She's wearing a red bikini halter underneath a tight, blue and white checkered tie-front top. Her top buttons are unbuttoned far enough to show off the cleavage between her creamy-white breasts, and her shirttails are tied in a knot so you can see her cute belly-button. She's wearing tight blue jeans cut off right below her crotch that show off her butt and legs. She has on red, open-toed high heels; her toenails are prettily painted with red polish. Her long, cinnamon hair flows in curls down over her shoulders almost to her breasts. I've never seen her in anything but work clothes. She looks so incredibly sexy that I get a lump in my throat.

"How do I look?" she asks.

Gulping, I answer, "Irresistible."

"I hope so."

She's carrying her purse in her hand and has a leather saddle bag slung over her shoulder. "Can I put my bag in your trunk?"

"You mean the boot," I kid her.

"The boot?"

"Yeah. That's what the limeys call the trunk."

She doesn't get my sense of humor.

"It's a British sports car," I explain. Grabbing the car keys, I open the boot for her. "So what's in it?"

"I ain't...I'm not telling. It's a surprise."

"Now you got me curious."

"I'll tell you when the time is right."

Playing along with her, I reply, "You're gonna keep me in suspense, huh?"

Smiling, she nods and makes me lock the boot.

"How about showing me your trailer?" I suggest.

"You really wanna see it?"

"Yeah. A woman's trailer is her castle," I quip.

She smiles.

She gives me a grand tour, explaining that her dad and brothers are welders and custom-made the trailer for her by connecting two Fleetwood trailers side by side lengthwise. The front trailer is comprised of a utility room, kitchen, dining room, kids' bathroom, and Sean's bedroom; the back trailer is comprised of Lily's bedroom and bathroom, living room, and the girls' bedroom. Lily's bedroom and bath are on the opposite end of the trailer from the kids' bedrooms and bath.

"So it is a doublewide mobile home," I point out.

"It ain't...isn't a doublewide mobile home. It's two trailers that was joined together by cutting out and welding walls with an oxyacetylene torch."

"Same difference. I like it. The floor plan is very functional. You have your own private bedroom and bath. And I like the wood beams on the ceiling and the built-in hutch in the dining room. Those are nice aesthetic touches."

"The Fleetwood Festival's top of the line."

She has decorated the place with houseplants—it smells like a greenhouse—and has photos of her family, pets, and horses on display. "And I like the way you've decorated it. It feels homey."

"Thanks."

Opening a sliding glass door in the living room, she takes me outside on the cement patio where I survey her fenced back yard. Near the patio is a birdfeeder. A swing set and sandbox are in the lawn. On the back of the lot are several tall maple and oak trees. Beyond the fence is a dense pine forest, which I presume is her mom's farm.

"Wow. This is huge," I remark.

"It's almost two acres. The kids and dog have room to play."

"I could live happily ever after here…"

She smiles.

I want to meet her kids and dog. "So where are they?"

"They ain't—aren't here. They're at my mama's house."

We go back inside.

"So…are you hungry?" she asks.

"I'm starving."

"Let's go."

On our way out, she locks the front door behind her. I walk her to the car. Trying to be a gentleman, I open the door on the passenger side for her. As she climbs in, I can't resist admiring her shapely legs.

Sitting in the passenger seat, she reaches outside the car and touches her hand on the pavement. "This car sits really low to the ground."

"It does."

"I love sports cars. Can I drive it?"

"Can you drive stick?"

She looks at me like that's a dumb question.

I open the door for her, and she climbs out, and I get in the passenger side. She strolls around the car and hops over the door into the driver's seat. Reaching down, she takes off her high heels. "I can't drive in these," she says, dropping them in my lap.

"Can you drive barefoot?"

She looks at me like that's another dumb question.

She starts the engine, puts the car in reverse, and backs out of her driveway into the street. Shifting deftly into first gear, she revs the engine—then pops the clutch and lays rubber up the street.

I guess so.

"Your trailer park is nice," I comment.

"That's cuz my mama has rules. You gotta mow your yard. And she don't allow no trash or junk cars."

"I like that the streets are named after flowers."

"She loves flowers."

Exiting the trailer park, we come to the railroad tracks again. Far away a train is slowly approaching the crossing. Disregarding the warning lights, she steers around the lowered gate and crosses the tracks.

"Hey…that's dangerous."

"It ain't dangerous when the train is far away and coming slow. I done it lots of times."

"That's a bad habit."

"These tracks are busy. I can't wait on every train. I've learned how to do it so it ain't risky. I only do it when the trains are far away and coming slow and the kids ain't in the car."

"Famous last words."

"You don't live near railroad tracks."

"You must not have seen the same driver's ed movie I saw."

"I missed driver's ed cuz I dropped out."

As we approach the Cameo on Springmill, I point out the country club up on the hill. "Hey, how about treating me to a gourmet dinner at the country club?"

"I can't afford it."

"I'm just kidding. They wouldn't let me in. They got a dress code for men—sport coat and tie."

The parking lot at the Cameo appears to be full, which I figure is a good sign. Circling behind the building, she finds a tight parking place next to the dumpster and zips into it. Turning off the engine, she hands me the car keys; then takes her high heels from my lap and straps them back on.

I follow her into the bar. Watching her butt swivel in front of me, I feel my pulse quicken. Inside, the place is packed to the gills with factory workers. All the booths are taken, so we sit at the bar until one opens up.

"So…you used to work here, huh?" I ask.

"Yeah. I started out as a waitress. Then worked as a bartender. I know the owner—Pete Watkins. He's a friend of mine."

The bartender spots Lily and comes over to us. Bleary-eyed, he says to her, "Hi, Beautiful."

"Hi, Pete," she replies, flashing him a big smile. "Pete, this is my friend, Leo."

"Nice to meet you, Leo," Pete says, extending his hand. In his other hand is a cigarette. Physically, he's a big guy. He looks like the owner, bartender, and bouncer rolled into one.

I shake hands and say hi.

Pete asks, "So what can I get ya?"

"I'll have a Bloody Mary," Lily answers.

I decline a drink. Pete leaves to fix Lily her drink.

"You sure? I'm treating," she reminds me.

"No thanks. I don't like to drink."

"I don't get you."

"What do you mean?"

"You don't drink, but you smoke pot. That don't make sense to me."

"The truth is I prefer marijuana over alcohol."

"Why?"

"Well, first of all, marijuana is not addictive. Alcohol is highly addictive, which I don't hafta tell you. Second of all, I'd rather get high than drunk. Alcohol dulls my brain and senses, and I don't like feeling hungover the next day. Marijuana stimulates my brain and senses without feeling hungover the next day."

"I can't believe somebody going to law school smokes pot."

"Why not?"

"It's illegal. Ain't you supposed to respect the law?"

"I don't respect the law when it comes to marijuana. It's unjust. Pot needs to be decriminalized. It's not as dangerous as alcohol, which is legal."

"So...you got any other vices I don't know about?" she teases.

"Yeah."

"What?"

A painting of a voluptuous woman with long curls of golden hair, lying nude in bed, is on the wall behind the bar. "Her."

"You like her?"

"Yeah. She looks dreamy."

"She used to work here. Pete has a friend that's an artist. He painted her."

I don't tell her that I drew Beth lying nude in bed.

"Pete tried to talk me into posing nude for his friend. He told me I got a better body than her."

I eye the painting; then eye her body. I deadpan, "I can't tell with your clothes on. Why don't you take them off?"

"Ha, ha. Very funny." She slugs me in the arm playfully. "He said he'd hang my painting over the bar in place of hers, but I didn't do it. I was afraid it'd make the customers try to pick me up when I was tending bar."

"That was probably wise."

Pete brings Lily her Bloody Mary and tells her that Gloria is getting the booth in the back ready for us. She thanks him. Then he puts his hand on my shoulder and says, "Leo, my friend, if I ever hear of you mistreating her, I'll kick your ass."

Okay…

"You won't," I assure him.

"See ya, Beautiful," he says to Lily, and he goes back to bartending.

Cocking my head at her, I ask, "So tell me something. Why do all your friends threaten to kick my ass?"

"Don't mind him. He's just being protective like a father."

A sultry waitress with coal-black eyes and jet black hair ambles up to us. She looks Italian. She says to Lily, "Hey, kiddo."

Lily introduces me to Gloria. "I work with him at Boals-Corrigan. I guess I should say I used to work with him. Today was his last day cuz he's going to law school."

"Really?" she asks like she's impressed.

"I'm gonna be an ambulance chaser," I joke.

She doesn't laugh. "You know any good divorce lawyers?"

"Ben O'Brien's supposed to be the best divorce lawyer in town. But he's high-priced."

"I don't care how much he costs. I just want somebody who'll fight for me. Me and my husband are battling over custody of my little girl. I don't want that asshole to get her."

"O'Brien has the reputation of being a fighter."

"Thanks." She winks at me.

She leads us to a black leather booth in the back corner by the kitchen door, and we slide into it across from each other. Lily explains that Pete reserves this booth for his friends, so they don't have to wait long for a table. The table is already set with two paper napkins and silverware. Lily takes off her hat and sets it beside her on the seat. Then she orders another Bloody Mary with her dinner. I order ice water.

I scan the menu—it looks like standard bar food. "So what did you say I should order?"

"The Italian Stallion. It's the best cheeseburger in town. Frieda puts a thick slice of grilled salami on it. And get the fries. They have the best fries too."

Following her recommendation, I order the Italian Stallion and fries. Lily orders a Cobb salad.

"So why didn't you order the Italian Stallion?"

"I'm watching my figure."

"What for? You got a great figure."

"And I wanna keep it that way."

I smile.

Sipping on her Bloody Mary, she remarks, "I love your car, Leo. What is it?"

"It's a '57 Triumph TR3A."

"Where'd you get it?"

"At an antique car auction at Hale Farm outside of Akron."

"It's an antique?"

"No. To be considered an antique car, it has to be over fifty years old. But it is almost a classic. To be considered a classic, it only has to be twenty-five years old."

I tell her the story about how I got in a bidding war with some guy, but I won. I ended up paying three thousand dollars for it— over half of my life's savings.

"It's a blast to drive," she says.

"I affectionately nicknamed her Red. I have a love-hate relationship with her."

"I love red. It's my favorite color."

"I think she's sexy. But, like most sexy women, she's high maintenance," I kid.

"I'm sexy."

"You are."

"I ain't—I'm not high maintenance. I'm a cheap date."

"True. You're the exception to the general rule."

"I'm like my Cutlass. Low maintenance."

"You're a Cutlass with a body like my Dad's Jaguar XKE, which I think is the sexiest car in the world."

She smiles.

Gloria brings us our dinners. The Italian Stallion is so big I can hardly fit it in my mouth. In addition to the huge cheeseburger and grilled salami, slices of tomato and onion and dill pickles are on it. It's drenched in Italian dressing and held together by a steak knife stuck through the bun. I take a bite. "Mmm—you're right. This is delicious."

She smiles.

I devour my Italian Stallion. Juice is running down my chin and fingers—I have to wipe my face and hands with a napkin. Talking with my mouth full, I ask, "So when do you start your new job in the warehouse?"

"Let's not talk about work."

"Okay. What do you wanna talk about?"

"Guess what I did."

"What?"

Smiling proudly, she says, "I passed the GED test."

I swallow my bite and open my mouth. "You got your diploma?"

"Yeah. It's a Certificate of High School Equivalency. I've been going to night school at Mansfield Adult Education for a year."

"Wow. Why didn't you tell me?"

"I kept it a secret. Only Mama knew cuz she watched the kids for me when I went to class. I didn't wanna tell anybody till I passed my last tests. I just found out yesterday I passed."

This surprises me. Clearly, I underestimated her. Extending my hand across the table, I say, "Congratulations. I knew you could do it."

Shaking my hand, she replies, "I still can't believe it. I'm no longer a high school dropout. I'm a high school graduate."

"This is exciting news. It could be your ticket out of Boals-Corrigan. I'm really happy for you."

Beaming, she says, "I was dying to tell you."

"Next you'll be going to college."

She laughs.

"What's so funny about that?" I ask.

"I couldn't go to college."

"Why not?"

"I ain't—I'm not smart enough."

"Lily, I don't care if you say ain't."

Flustered, she replies, "I'm trying not to say it. I know it's bad English, but I just can't help it. Everybody I know says it."

"Just be yourself. I like you as you are."

She smiles.

"I don't give a rat's ass if you don't use proper English," I say.

"I ain't proper."

"That's what I like about you. Just because you say ain't don't mean you ain't smart enough to go to college. The truth is I think you're really smart. I've seen it time and time again. I saw it that day you stood up to Merle. You knew the law and articulated it quite clearly. You read veterinary books and know how to breed horses and do artificial insemination. I bet there ain't no English teachers who know how to do that."

"I'm interested in animals and learning how to do things like that."

"That's what I mean. You have useful knowledge. Don't sell yourself short."

"But I ain't smart like you."

I scoff. "I ain't that smart. All I have is book knowledge, and I can bullshit."

"You can go far on that."

I laugh. "You know what I think?"

"What?"

"The only reason I went to college and you didn't is socialization. My parents indoctrinated me to believe that I'd go to college when I grew up. If you'd been indoctrinated like me, you probably would've gone to college.

"Believe me—you could do it. I think you could go to vet school and become a vet if you set your mind to it."

She looks doubtful.

"You just lack confidence when it comes to formal education."

"So…tell me about law school," she replies, changing the subject.

Shaking my head, I reply, "I don't even wanna think about it. I'm on vacation now."

"So am I."

"You are?"

"Yeah. Mr. Castor let me take it on short notice. He likes me."

"What are you gonna do?"

"I'm going to Cape Hatteras to find the wild horses of Currituck."

"Really?"

"Really."

"Did you find someone to go with you?"

"Huh-uh."

"You're going all by yourself?"

"Uh-huh."

I realize she must really want to see them if she's willing to go there all by herself. "Seeing those horses must really mean a lot to you, huh?"

"I dream about them, Leo. See them galloping wild and free down the beach."

Imagining it, I reply, "That would be really cool."

"I gotta go find them. You sure you don't wanna come with me?"

I admire her grit to go by herself all the way to Cape Hatteras in search of them. The thought of her searching for them alone makes me feel sad and somewhat guilty. I'd like to help her find them. "Lily, I'd love to go with you on a quest for the wild horses of Currituck…"

Excited now, she exclaims, "We could go sightseeing, Leo. I went to the Triple A and got all these travel brochures. After we see the horses, we can go see a shipwreck and the lighthouses. And I wanna see the National Seashore. Have you seen it?"

"Yeah. Beth and I explored it."

"What's it like?"

"It's wilderness. The Atlantic Ocean and endless, desolate beach are on the east side of the cape. The sound and miles and miles of marsh are on the west side. The only signs of civilization are the highway and the telephone poles running down it. There are no hotels and restaurants. No billboards. No tourist traps. Just pure, unadulterated nature. In some places, the cape is so narrow that during storms the breakers actually wash over the highway to the sound. They hafta close the road."

She listens in wonder…

"Just thinking about it stirs my soul…" I trail off.

"Come with me, Leo," she coaxes.

Longing for some adventure in my life, I'm tempted to blow off studying for orientation and go with her; but I know that would be irresponsible. I sigh deeply. "It's tempting, Lily. It really is. I wish I could go with you, but I can't. I hafta get ready for law school. Study for orientation…"

She nods glumly. "I'll think of you when I'm exploring."

I eat my last French fry. "I'll think of you when I'm studying. Believe me, I'd much rather go to the ocean than brief cases."

She slugs down the rest of her Bloody Mary.

"Send me a postcard if you find those wild horses. Better yet, send me a photograph—"

"You guys want any dessert?" Gloria asks.

"They make a great homemade lemon meringue pie here," Lily tells me.

"Let's split a piece," I suggest.

She shakes her head.

"C'mon."

"Nope."

"Man, you've got will power—I'll say that."

I order a piece and take a bite. Smiling, I say, "That's sublime."

I put a bite on my fork and dangle it right in front of Lily's mouth. She can't resist. She licks her lips and rolls her eyes in pleasure. We end up splitting it.

Gloria brings me the check.

Snatching it out of my hand, Lily says, "I told you—I'm treating."

"Then let me cover the tip."

"Leave her a big one. She's my friend."

"Thanks for treating me. That really was the best cheeseburger I've ever had."

Pleased, she says, "You're welcome. Mama says, 'The way to a man's heart is through his stomach.' What do you think?"

"I think there's some truth to that saying."

"You know what I think?"

"What?"

Grinning provocatively, she says, "I think the way to a man's heart is through his cock. And the way to a man's cock is through his stomach."

I consider what she said. "Right…that's probably truer."

I leave a five dollar tip. "Is that enough?"

"That's too much. She'll think you're hitting on her."

Putting back on her cowgirl hat, Lily waves goodbye to Gloria. Outside, looking at the lavender sky, she says, "Boy, is it nice out. Let's go for a ride out in the country."

This sounds like a good idea to me. "Okay."

"Can I drive again?"

"Yeah. Sure." I toss her the car keys.

In the car she takes off her cowgirl hat and high heels and drops them behind her seat. I turn on the radio—she cranks up the volume.

As we drive past the Windsor estate on the outskirts of town, we gaze at the beautiful horses grazing in the pasture.

"Dr. Hall said them are prize-winning Tennessee Walkers. The Windsors breed them. I'm gonna inseminate one of their broodmares," Lily tells me.

"I'd be interested in hearing about that."

We cruise up and down the rolling hills and wind our way through the valleys. Smiling with pleasure, she says, "Mmm, I love to feel the wind blowing through my hair."

I admire her long tresses streaming in the wind behind her.

"I'm thinking about coloring my hair blonde. They say blondes have more fun. You think I should?"

"Nope."

"Why not?"

"I like your hair just the way it is. It's fiery—like you."

Rolling her eyes, she says, "You're full of shit."

"No. I really like it, Lily. But I'm partial to women with red hair. My first crush was a redhead."

"Who was she?"

"I don't know. Just some girl I saw when I was a kid. So where are you taking me?"

"To Sunset Point."

I feel like getting high. I light the joint and take a hit.

Glancing at me, she asks, "Is that what I think it is?"

"What do you think it is?"

"Pot."

"You guessed it. So you wanna get high?" I ask and offer her a hit.

"No thanks. I don't do drugs. They lead to heroin."

"Lily, I've been smoking pot on and off since my senior year in high school, and I've never tried heroin, and I never will. I know lots of people who smoke it, and none of them do heroin."

"Maybe. But that smoke can't be good for your lungs."

"I can't argue with that. But at least I don't smoke cigarettes."

"I don't wanna get busted for drugs. I'm a mama. I don't want Children Services saying I'm an unfit mother and trying to take my kids away from me."

Nodding like I understand, this sounds to me like another reason why I shouldn't get involved with her kids.

By the time we reach Clearfork Lake, I'm as high as a kite. Gazing at the passing scenic lakeshore, I feel so mellow…

At Sunset Point, Lily drives up the gravel lane toward the secluded lookout. I toss the roach—the last thing I need before I go to law school is to get busted. The lane dead-ends atop a ridge affording a scenic view of the lake. She parks the car at the guardrail, leaving the radio on. Her left hand is on the steering wheel, her right hand on the gearshift.

"Amie" by Pure Prairie League is playing.

"I love this song. Their harmonies," I say.

"Me too."

We sing along.

We are the only people here. The situation feels intimate…

Gazing serenely across the lake, she says, "I love to come here and watch the sun go down…"

Sunlight is shimmering on the water. Mesmerized, I say, "It looks like the water is on fire…"

"Leo…"

I turn toward her.

She looks deeply into my eyes. Her blue and green eyes are ablaze. They bewitch me…

She places her hand on my hand. Her touch turns my body on…

She looks downward at my lips, drawing my lips toward hers. We kiss. Her lips feel exquisitely soft. The sensation is thrilling…

With a dreamy expression on her face, she says, "Leo, we can get a motel room at Cape Hatteras. I'll take off my clothes. Show you my body…"

Oh, man…

I look at her cleavage exposed by her low cut bikini halter. The sun is shining on her partially bare breasts—they're a beautiful rose-ivory color.

I wonder what her nipples look like.

I imagine slipping off her halter…kissing her breasts…sucking her nipples…

My eyes are drawn downward past her belly button to the tantalizing V-shaped mound hidden inside her tight, cutoff blue jeans.

I wonder what her pussy looks like…

I imagine pulling down her jeans and panties…seeing it…feeling it…

Aware of my tremendous hard-on, I pry my eyes off her and look out the windshield at a pontoon boat that is cruising across the lake toward the dam…

We need to go our separate ways right now once and for all, or one of us will end up with a broken heart.

Tell her no.

Facing her, I avert my eyes from her body, but they cannot resist…

Oh, God—I want to see and feel her naked body so badly.

I can't say no.

"Don't you wanna see my body?" she teases.

"I'd love to see your body," I answer breathlessly. "But…but I have orientation on Friday," I stammer feebly.

"If we leave right now and drive all night, we'll have Saturday, Sunday, Monday, and Tuesday at the ocean. We'll drive home Wednesday in time for orientation…"

Just the thought of staying four nights with her in a motel room makes my heart race. My resolve is crumbling…

Moving her hand off my hand, Lily slides it downward onto my inner thigh—so that her fingertips are resting on the fringe of my cutoffs almost touching my hard-on. In her country twang, she says, "Leo, if you take me, I'm yours…"

Man, oh, man—she'll fuck me.

I visualize her lying nude on the bed, gazing at me with desire. Pure lust is surging through my body…

Out of the blue, Percy's advice pops into my mind: "A man has to be a fool not to fuck her if he has the chance. Pussy like her only comes along once in a lifetime."

Percy's right. Lily is once in a lifetime. I'd be a fool not to fuck her.

Gently holding my cheek in the palm of her hand, she turns my face toward her. Looking intently into my eyes, she exhorts, "C'mon, Leo! Take me!"

I feel intoxicated. Images of her nude body and fucking her and bodysurfing in the waves and searching for the wild horses are whirling through my mind…

"Let me be your wild hillbilly girl…"

At this moment, I see it again—the same wild glint in her eyes that she had when she told me—"I'm Lily. I'm just a wild hillbilly girl."

I want her. I want this wild hillbilly girl more than anything in the world.

All at once I feel this dam break inside me, and I go wild. Slapping my hand on the dash, I exclaim, "Okay, Lily! I'll take you!"

She is so excited—her eyes are sparkling brightly. "You will?"

I feel exhilaration. "Let's go find the wild horses of Currituck!"

She lowers her hand from my face onto my arm. "Right now?"

I nod my head eagerly.

In the blink of an eye, she reverts to innocent Lily. Slipping her other hand off my thigh, she says, "Oh thank you, Leo. Thank you so much for making my dream come true."

I'm grinning from ear to ear…

Wrapping her arms around my neck, she kisses me passionately.

My head is spinning. I feel so…so alive…

"Oh, Leo, I'm so excited. I can't wait to get there. Let's get out of here." She starts the engine.

Patting Red on the dash, I whoop, "Hot damn, Red! We're going on a road trip to Cape Hatteras. I'm counting on you. Don't let me down."

As we drive back down the lane, I ask, "So…uh…what do you need to do to get ready?"

"Nothing."

"What…what about your kids?"

"That's all taken care of. They're staying with my mama."

"Well, uh…don't you need to pack?"

"No. I got my bag in the boot. I got money. I'm ready to go."

Wait a minute…

I recall her saying "It's a surprise" about her bag. I stare at her with my mouth open…

"What?" she asks.

"You must've been pretty sure you could talk me into it."

Smirking slightly, she replies, "I figured my body would do the trick."

I just shake my head in disbelief.

"So what do you need to do to get ready?" she asks.

"I need to pack, get my money, and tell my parents where I'm going."

Lily pulls out onto the highway, the tires throwing gravel behind us, and speeds silently toward town.

Still dizzy, I replay in my mind the scene at Sunset Point. I visualize her bewitching eyes; her hand touching mine; then her boldly initiating our first kiss. Closing my eyes, I feel the thrilling sensation of her soft lips and hear her tell me she'll take her clothes off and show me her body; then feel her hand resting on my inner thigh, her fingertips a fraction of an inch from my hard-on, and hear her sensual voice say "Leo, if you take me, I'm yours…"

You ignited a lust that drove me to the verge of taking you.

I distinctly envision the wild glint in her eyes when she held my cheek in her hand and said "Let me be your wild hillbilly girl."

But it was that wild glint in your eyes that pushed me over the brink. It was the catalyst that made me take you on this madcap adventure of finding the wild horses.

You are wild, Lily. You make me wild.

What did you tell me at the Cameo?

"The way to a man's heart is through his cock. And the way to a man's cock is through his stomach."

That's exactly what you did.

I smile wryly.

You seduced me, Lily. You were so confident you could seduce Mr. Rational that you had your bag packed and were ready to go.

I marvel at her audacity and supreme confidence in her sexuality.

Feeling like I'm coming over the top of the first hill of a rollercoaster, I take a deep breath…

There's no turning back now. I guess I'll just have to love her and leave her. I start singing "Carolina in My Mind" by James Taylor.

Grinning at me mockingly, she remarks, "Looks like you ain't Mr. Rational after all."

I smile and reply, "You took the words right out of my mouth."

We arrive at our house at dusk and pull into the semi-circular driveway. Gaping in awe at the house, she says, "Wow…your house is really cool. I knew you was rich but…" she trails off.

The garage door is up. Dad's car isn't here; Mom's car is. I figure either he's not home from work yet, or he came home and took her out to eat. Just in case she's home, I decide not to take Lily inside. There's no way my parents would approve of my taking her to Cape Hatteras, so I tell her, "I'd give you a quick tour, but we'd better get going."

I direct her to stop at the front door. While she waits in the car, I run into the house and bound down the steps to my bedroom. As fast as I can, I pack my Hang Loose pro surfer swim trunks, a few T-shirts, a pair of jeans, some white socks and underwear, and my leather sandals in my bullhide duffel bag; then run into the bathroom, gather up my toiletries, and cram them in my bullhide travel kit. Scrounging all my cash, I have almost five hundred dollars. I fetch my pot out of my secret hiding place and stash it in my duffle bag; then grab my aviator sunglasses off my dresser and stick them in the pocket of my T-shirt. I'm ready to roll.

With my duffle bag slung over my shoulder, I run back upstairs into the den and scan the bookshelves until I find the road atlas.

To avoid an argument, I figure I'll just leave a note on Mom's kitchen desk that says I'm going to the ocean and will be back in time for orientation. As I scribble the note, Mom startles me by coming up behind me and saying, "Hi, Leo."

"Oh, hi, Mom. I didn't realize you were here. I was just writing you a note telling you I'm going to the ocean."

"What?"

"I'm going to the ocean."

"Where?"

"Cape Hatteras."

"Cape Hatteras? What…what about law school? Don't you have orientation next week?"

"Yeah. But it's not till next Friday. I'll be back in plenty of time."

"I…I thought you were planning on going with Reese to Toledo to look for an apartment."

"I am. On Thursday. If he calls, tell him I'll be back in town Wednesday night. I'll call him as soon as I get home."

With a worried expression on her face, she replies, "I don't like this, Leo. I don't understand why you suddenly hafta go to the ocean."

"Mom, I just wanna go to the ocean before I start law school. Have some fun before I put my nose to the grindstone."

"Cape Hatteras—that's a long ways away. How are you getting there?"

"Red."

Shaking her head, she says, "I don't like it. I don't trust your car."

"I just had it overhauled."

"What if it breaks down again?"

"Mom, sometimes you just gotta take a little risk in this world. No risk, no reward."

"Why don't you just go to Lake Erie? It's only an hour away."

"Mom, Lake Erie's not the ocean. I wanna go where there are big waves. I wanna bodysurf."

"Are you going alone?"

"No. I'm going with a friend. We're splitting the costs."

"Who?"

"Just someone at work."

"What's he do?"

"Assembles ballcocks."

"Ballcocks?"

"They go inside toilet tanks. It's the valve that turns the water on and off after you flush. Mom, I gotta go. We're gonna drive all night."

"Leo, I don't think this is a good idea. I think you should talk to your father about it."

No way. He'll say no.

"Where is he?" I ask.

"He's at the office working late tonight. He had to meet with Dr. Blair who got sued today. There's a big article about it on the front page of the paper."

I want to get the hell out of here before he gets home. "I can't wait. I wanna hit the road right now. So I can get back in time for law school."

"He should be home any minute."

"Mom, I'm twenty-two years old. I'm a college graduate. I don't need to get my dad's permission anymore to do something. Hell, at my age he was married and had a kid and was getting shot down."

She looks at me fretfully.

"Don't worry, Mom. Everything will be fine. Nobody's shooting bullets at me."

"You tell your friend no drinking and driving."

"I will."

"I mean it, Leo—no drinking and driving."

"Right. See ya Wednesday." I kiss her cheek quickly.

I beat it out of the house. Lily climbs out of the car barefoot and pops the boot for me, and I load my duffle bag in it.

"Who's driving?" she asks.

Knowing it would be safer for Lily to drive until the pot wears off, I answer, "I'm still high. You drive the first leg. I'll navigate."

She hops in the driver's seat. I hop in the passenger seat and smile broadly at her. "Let's hit the road."

As she steers around the driveway, I remember something. "Hold on. Wait a second. I almost forgot something. Pull over by the garage."

I jump out of the car and run into the garage, where I dig my army raft and wood paddle out of a storage cabinet and haul them out in the driveway.

"What's that?" she asks.

"My army raft. Could you open the boot again for me?"

She climbs back out of the car and unlocks the boot. While I cram my army raft and paddle in it, she observes, "It sure takes up a lot of room."

"We can ride the waves in it."

"Not me. I ain't getting attacked by a shark."

"No shark is gonna attack you."

We hop back in the car. She hooks her purse around the gearshift and pulls out of the driveway. Revving the engine, she peels out— the tires squeal.

Before we get on the interstate, we stop at a gas station. While the attendant fills the tank, I warn Lily that the needle on the gas gauge drops quickly after it goes below a quarter of a tank, so we need to exit the highway and get gas before the needle gets that low.

Using the road atlas, we take interstate freeways south-east across Ohio and a sliver of West Virginia into Pennsylvania. The car sits so close to the pavement and has such a lousy suspension that I feel the bump of every expansion crack in the concrete freeway.

LILY

Between the roar of the engine, the noise of the tires, the wind streaming through the car, and the radio blaring, we have to shout just to hear each other. She has a lead foot and passes semi after semi. I look up at the silhouettes of the truck drivers in the cabs as we go by. They look like they're about three stories above me. Then I watch the long trailers go by. The bottom edge of the trailer between the front and back wheels is level with my neck. If we get in a wreck, I fear I'll be decapitated.

I shout, "I JUST HOPE I DON'T END UP LIKE JAYNE MANSFIELD."

"WHO'S THAT?" she shouts back.

"AN ACTRESS WHO GOT DECAPITATED IN A CAR ACCIDENT WITH A SEMI."

"I LOVE PASSING SEMIS. BLOW THEM TRUCKERS OFF THE ROAD," she shouts.

God, what the hell did I get myself into?

She's passing another one. We're flying along about seventy miles per hour right next to it.

She reaches over and feels my chest. With a lascivious grin on her face, she says something I can't hear—the tires on the truck are roaring right in my ear.

Holding my ear, I shout, "WHAT? I CAN'T HEAR YOU."

"YOU'RE HARD AS A ROCK," she shouts louder.

"THAT'S FROM PACKING A THOUSAND TOILETS A DAY," I shout back.

The car is vibrating and shimmying all over the place. She has one hand on the steering wheel and her other hand on my chest. I see her ogling me in the glow of the dashboard.

She shouts, "I BET YOU COULD FUCK ME ALL NIGHT."

Man alive! She's a nymphomaniac.

We're so close to the truck I feel like I could reach out and touch it.

I shout back, "NOT IF WE END UP IN BODY BAGS! PLEASE, LILY—JUST KEEP BOTH HANDS ON THE STEERING WHEEL AND YOUR EYES ON THE ROAD."

She laughs. "LEO, THAT'S WHAT I LIKE ABOUT YOU.

YOU'RE FUNNY."

She steps on the gas and we fly past the semi.

CHAPTER TWELVE

We drive through the night. When we get on the Pennsylvania Turnpike, the rhythm of the road makes me drowsy…

A hard bump jolts me. I realize I dozed off.

Lily is barreling down the turnpike.

I check the gas gauge—the needle is way below the quarter mark. I shout over the road noise, "WHY DIDN'T YOU STOP AND GET GAS?"

"I DON'T STOP TILL I'M ON EMPTY. I HATE TO STOP AND GET GAS. IT SLOWS ME DOWN. I JUST WANNA GET THERE," she yells back.

"WE'RE NOT GONNA GET THERE IF WE RUN OUT OF GAS."

"DON'T WORRY. WE'LL MAKE IT."

I look out the window—see the massive black shadows of the mountains silhouetted against the dark night sky. This is the last place I want to run out of gas in the middle of the night—we'd have to walk for miles. I check the road atlas—the next exit is Breezewood.

God, I hope we make it.

I yell, "WHY ARE YOU FLOORING IT?"

"I'M TRYING TO GET TO THE GAS STATION FASTER," she yells back.

"NO, DON'T. YOU NEED TO SLOW DOWN. DRIVE SLOW.

CONSERVE GAS."

She slows down for a few miles but then speeds up again. I have to keep telling her to slow down. I sit on pins and needles, expecting the engine to sputter and die and the car to coast to a halt. Finally, we exit the turnpike at Breezewood and coast on fumes into an open gas station. I let out a huge sigh of relief.

"See—I told you we'd make it," she says.

"That was too close for comfort."

"You worry too much."

Realizing that she's right, I drop it.

After filling up and going to the restroom, we argue over paying for the gas. "I'm a man. I'm supposed to pay for everything."

"That's old-fashioned. I'm a working woman. You don't need to pay for me."

"I tell you what. Let's take turns buying gas. Fair enough?"

"Fair enough."

I drive the next leg of the trip. Lily goes to sleep. It's smooth sailing from here. There is hardly any traffic driving around Washington, D.C., in the middle of the night.

In the faint predawn light, we arrive at Point Harbor, North Carolina. I smell the heady aroma of salt water; then see a black expanse of water to the east.

"Lily, wake up. We're almost there."

Sitting upright and craning her neck to see, she asks excitedly, "Is that the ocean?"

"No. I think it's the Albemarle Sound—the body of water between the mainland and Cape Hatteras."

We come to a bridge. "This is the bridge to the cape."

"Oh, Leo…I can't wait to get there…"

As we cross it, we strain our eyes to see the sound, but it's too dark. All we can see is moonlight reflecting off the water.

On the other side of the bridge, I announce, "We're here. This is Cape Hatteras."

"Yay!"

We roll into Kitty Hawk predawn. Needing gas, we pull into a gas station and wait for it to open. Lily curls up in the passenger seat and goes back to sleep. I try to sleep but can't get comfortable sitting behind the steering wheel. By the time it opens at seven, the sun is up.

Traveling south down Highway 12 into Kill Devil Hills, I notice that the Outer Banks is more commercially developed since the last time I was here—in fact, it's starting to look downright tacky in places. We stop at a diner and order bacon and eggs for breakfast. While we eat, we check out the motels in her Triple-A book. Immediately, we get into another argument. I want to stay at the Ocean Ranch Motel in Kill Devil Hills, which is where I stayed when I came here with Beth and when I came with my family. "Look, Lily, it's oceanfront. I wanna be right on the beach with a view of the sea. And it has a heated pool, a restaurant, and a high rating."

She wants to stay at The Beachcomber, which is located on the west side of the beach highway with beach access. "Leo, it's got a heated pool too. And look—it's a lot cheaper."

"That's because it's not oceanfront. You gotta cross the highway to get to the beach."

"I don't mind crossing the highway if I can save money."

"You might get run over."

"I'll take my chances."

"Lily, it took you twenty-five years to make it to the ocean. Who knows when you'll make it back? So live it up."

She gives in.

The waitress brings us our check. Before she can hand it to me, Lily takes it from her and says, "I got this."

I sigh. "Lily, we need to talk about money. Get this settled once and for all."

"There ain't nothing to talk about, I told you I'd pay for everything."

"I wanna pay my own way."

"Why? I thought you needed all your money for law school."

"I'm not a freeloader. It's a matter of self-respect," I answer. But this is only partially the reason. The primary reason is I want to be free to kiss and say goodbye without feeling beholden to her.

"This is my vacation. I talked you into coming here, so I'll pay for it. I've saved the money."

"This is my vacation too. I'm gonna bodysurf and ride my army raft."

She doesn't reply.

"I got an idea. Let's each pay our own way and split the motel bill equally," I propose.

"It's a deal."

We shake hands on it.

She needs to buy some things for the beach. We find a store at a strip mall called Cheap Beach Stuff, where she buys a tube of expensive sunscreen, explaining that she has fair skin and doesn't want to get sunburned. I've never heard of sunscreen. I've only heard of suntan lotion, which I don't need since I went to the pool all summer and have a good tan. She buys a pair of red flip-flops. I buy a pair of blue ones.

As we drive to the Ocean Ranch Motel on the beach highway, Lily keeps trying to see the ocean in between the oceanfront motels but only catches glimpses of water. In the parking lot of the motel, we can hear the waves crashing on the beach. She tells me she'll wait in the car while I inquire as to the availability of a room. She is dying to see the ocean. I make her promise to wait for me—I want to see the look on her face when she sees the ocean for the first time.

Inside the lobby I tell the motel manager I just got married—my wife and I eloped and are on our honeymoon. I figure this will explain why I don't have a wedding ring. He grins like he knows what we'll be doing the whole time we're here. I ask him for a room overlooking the ocean. He doesn't have any vacant oceanfront rooms, but he has an oceanfront efficiency on the second floor of the new addition—"the honeymoon suite." It has an extra-large bedroom with a king-size bed, a sofa bed, and a color TV, a deluxe bathroom, and kitchenette. He says it's their most expensive accommodation, but he'll only charge us half-price since it's off-season now—forty-nine bucks a night, not including tax. I rent it for four nights. He tells me we can't get in the room until three o'clock, but I can check in now. I fill out the registration form—"Mr. and

Mrs. Leo Locke." He gives me two room keys, and says we can use the motel beach until our room is ready.

I tell Lily I rented the honeymoon suite. She's amused that I told the motel manager we eloped. She says, "Lily Locke...I like it."

When I tell her that we got the room at half-price, she's pleased but still thinks it's too expensive. She's delighted to hear we're allowed to use the beach until our room is ready.

I park as close as I can to our room. Kissing the steering wheel, I say, "Thank you, Red. You didn't let me down."

Lily puts on her cowgirl hat and grabs her purse. "Last one there's a rotten egg!"

We jump out of the car and race around the side of the building to the beach. I let her beat me. Standing side by side in the sand, we gaze at the Atlantic Ocean in all its splendor. Waves are curling and crashing on the shore thunderously. Sea gulls are flying in circles above the white caps.

I look at her—her eyes are sparkling with joy. She closes them, takes a deep breath, and says, "Umm, I love that smell."

I take off my shoes and socks and walk into the shallow surf. Foam swirls around my ankles. Barefoot, she follows me into the water.

I'm exhilarated. Impetuously, I take her in my arms and kiss her.

Surprised, she asks, "What was that for?"

"For talking me into coming here."

She just grins.

I return to the car to put on my swimsuit. Burning the soles of my feet as I hotfoot it across the asphalt, I fish my trunks out of the boot; then furtively change into it in the passenger seat of the car.

In my new flip-flops, I dash back to the beach.

Lily is watching a sandpiper peck at the wet sand.

I toss her the car keys. Stepping out of my flip-flops, I sprint into the surf and dive into a breaking wave.

She watches me bodysurf from the shore. Aiming her camera at me, she shouts, "Hey, Leo. Smile."

I smile and wave.

Pointing at her wrist, she shouts, "Your watch."

"It's waterproof. It's a skin diving watch," I holler and wave for her to come in.

She just stands there.

Wading into shore, I reach for her hand. "Come on in."

She shakes her head.

"What's the matter? Don't you know how to swim?"

"I know how to swim. I just don't wanna swim in the ocean."

"Why not?"

"Sharks."

"You gotta be kidding."

Raising her chin, she replies, "Nope. I ain't ending up like that girl in *Jaws*."

"Lily, the odds of getting attacked by a shark are infinitesimal. You had a greater risk of dying in a car accident driving here."

"You ain't afraid of sharks?"

"Actually, I'm more afraid of rip currents. A lot more people drown in rip currents here than get attacked by sharks."

"All I know is I ain't gonna end up shark shit."

Shaking my head in disbelief, I mutter, "I can't believe you came all the way to the ocean and you're not gonna swim in it—all because of *Jaws*."

I bodysurf by myself. After a while I get tired and rejoin Lily, who's sitting on the beach near my flip-flops. I sit down beside her, letting the sun and wind dry me off. Recalling that I've been awake for thirty hours, I curl up on my side in the soft, warm sand, close my eyes, and doze off…

"Hey, Leo."

I open my eyes.

"Would you put sunscreen on my back?" Lily asks. She has taken off her blue and white checkered top and her cutoffs and is sitting in the sand in her red bikini.

I gaze in awe at her body. In spite of having had three kids, her belly is as flat as a pancake. The curves of her hips, thighs and calves are so pleasing to the eye. "I'd be glad to."

She hands me her tube of sunscreen.

"Man, Lily, you could be in the *Sports Illustrated Swimsuit* issue."

"You think so?"

"I know so."

Smiling, she unties the strings on the top of her bikini that go around her neck, so I can apply sunscreen to her shoulders and the back of her neck. Her firm breasts hold up her top. The titillating sight gives me a hard-on.

"That's remarkable," I observe.

"What?"

"Your breasts defy gravity."

"That's even after breast-feeding three babies."

She swivels sideways so her back is facing me. Sitting up, I squirt some cream in the palm of my hand; then rub it all over her shoulders and down her back. Even the curve of her back is sexy.

"My mama had nine kids and still has a good figure. She says the good Lord made McFarlane women to make babies."

"Obviously, you inherited her genes."

I slather more and more cream on her body. I could do this all day…

"Okay, I think that's enough—you're gonna use it all up. Thanks," she says.

"My pleasure."

She swivels around and faces me. "Now you put it on."

"I don't need suntan lotion."

"Yes, you do. And it ain't suntan lotion. It's sunscreen. It protects you from the sun's ultraviolet rays. They're really bad here at the ocean."

"But I won't burn. I already got a tan."

"You wanna get skin cancer?

"No."

"Don't argue with me."

"Okay, okay." I figure it's not worth getting into an argument.

"Jeez, you're as bad as Sean."

She makes me apply it to my arms, chest, and legs.

"Let me have it."

I hand her the tube.

"Turn around," she orders.

I turn around.

She applies it to my back and shoulders. "My God, you're lean, Leo. You don't have an ounce of fat on your body. I bet you're a real stud," she teases.

"Me and Appaloosa."

"Now let me do your face."

I swivel around and face her.

She gently rubs the cream on my face—first my cheeks, forehead, and chin; then my nose and lips. Her fingertips feel wonderful. A bead of sweat runs tantalizingly down her cleavage. My hard-on gets harder.

"Close your eyes." She delicately applies cream around my eyes.

"You college kids don't know nothing. Dr. Hall told me sunscreen prevents skin cancer. He says it needs to have a sun protection factor of at least twenty. And he knows cuz his wife died of melanoma caused by sun poisoning when she was young. There. Now you ain't gonna get skin cancer."

"Huh. Learn something new every day."

"Oh, look." She's pointing at a large boat going by far out in the ocean. Grabbing her camera, she stands up and takes a picture. Then she swings the camera around and snaps a picture of our oceanfront motel; then snaps a picture of me, reclining on the beach. I try to hide my hard-on.

Handing me her camera, she says, "Take a picture of me." She poses by the water's edge with the waves crashing on the shore behind her.

I snap the shot with one hand, while I nonchalantly hide my hard-on with the other.

"Did you bring a camera?" she asks.

"Nope."

"Why not?"

Pointing at my temple, I answer, "I don't need one. I take pictures in my mind."

She looks at me skeptically. We plop back down on the beach. While she happily sunbathes, I sit here acutely aware of my hard-on, counting down the minutes until we can get into our room—

now all I want to do is screw her. I avoid looking at her body, but my hard-on won't go away because I can't stop picturing it in my mind.

At five till three, I stand up, brush the sand off, and step into my flip-flops. "Hey, Lily—it's almost three. Let's go check out our room."

"I know what's on your mind. It shows," she replies, pointing at the bulge in my swimsuit with a smirk on her face.

Grinning sheepishly, I explain, "It's an involuntary response stimulated by the sight of your sexy body."

"Save it for later."

She stands up and brushes the sand off her butt—it ripples sublimely under the pressure of her hand. I can't wait to see it bare. She puts her top, cut-offs, and flip-flops back on; then gathers up her things and heads toward the motel. Enthralled by the sight of her butt cheeks peeking out of the bottom of her cutoff jeans, I'm dying to feel them.

We walk back to the car, get our bags out of the boot, and carry them inside the motel to room 216 on the second floor. I unlock the door and open it for her. She starts to step inside—

"Halt!" I order.

She looks at me perplexed.

"Mrs. Locke, allow me to carry you over the threshold."

Sweeping her in my arms, I carry her into the honeymoon suite and toss her onto the bed.

She squeals with delight.

Anticipating sex, I dash back out in the hall and grab my duffle bag; but, by the time I come back inside the room and lock the door behind me, she has climbed off the bed and is checking out the appliances in the kitchenette.

"Look, Leo—a dishwasher."

In the broom closet, she finds an electric skillet and a radio. She hugs me. "I love it, Leo. We can save money cooking in, instead of going out to eat."

In the bedroom, I set my duffle bag on top of the dresser. Opening the drapes, I discover sliding glass and screen doors that exit onto a balcony overlooking the ocean. Sliding them open, I step out on the balcony where I discover two chaise lounges, a small dining table with two chairs, and a grill.

"Hey, Lily, come look at this."

She comes out on the balcony and gazes at the majestic ocean. "Oh, Leo, I love this view."

"Aren't you glad I talked you into oceanfront?"

Nodding, she replies, "I wanna get a picture of this."

She gets her camera and snaps a few pictures of the ocean from our balcony; then sets it down on the table and joins me at the railing.

Driven by lust, I take her in my arms and kiss her. I press my bare chest against her breasts and my hard-on against her mound—

All at once she pulls away from me. "I ain't in the mood for sex right now."

I look helplessly at the bulge in my swimsuit.

With mock pity, she says, "Oh, you poor boy."

"I'm gonna get blue balls."

"You'll live."

"You said 'I'm yours' if I took you to the ocean."

Looking at me sympathetically, she says, "I am. But not right now."

"You said you'd take off your clothes and show me your body. I'm dying to see it."

"I will. Tonight. But we got things we gotta do first."

"Like what? We're on vacation," I argue.

"I wanna unpack."

She goes back inside. I give up on getting laid and follow her. She unpacks by dumping the contents of her leather saddle bag on the bed. I see a pink polka dot bikini, some lingerie, and a smaller bag. "Is that all you brought?"

"I travel light. I got everything I need right here."

"Where are your clothes?"

"I don't need clothes. I'm gonna live in my bikini."

"Sounds good to me."

She puts her stuff in the top drawer of the dresser. Since we're only going to be here for a few days, I don't bother to unpack—I'll live out of my duffle bag. She takes her smaller bag into the bathroom. I follow with my travel kit. Much to our delight, we discover his-and-her sinks.

"Now I need to call home," she tells me.

"What for?"

"I need to tell my mama where she can reach me. You know—in case of an emergency."

No, I don't know.

"Right," I reply.

She sits down on the bed beside the nightstand, picks up the telephone, and makes a long-distance, collect phone call, while I sit down on the sofa and wait for her. Acting like I'm watching the ocean, I eavesdrop.

"Hi, Mama. I arrived safe and sound. I'm staying at a motel in Kill Devil Hills."

I wonder if her mom knows that she came here with me. She gives her mom the information on how to reach her. Next, she wants to talk to her kids, but it sounds like Sean is outside playing football and Rachel is taking a nap.

I hear her say, "Hi, Pony Girl."

I figure she must be talking to Sarah.

"Yeah. I seen it. It's wonderful."

She must be talking about the ocean.

"No. I ain't seen them. I just got here. If I find them, I'll take a picture of them for you."

She must be talking about the wild horses.

She listens to Sarah…

"He's just a friend from work. His name is Leo. Like your lion. He's helping me find them. Honey, I gotta go. I love you. Tell Sean and Rachel I love them."

After she says goodbye and hangs up, she comes over and sits down on the couch beside me. Smiling, she says, "I'm glad I got that taken care of. Now I can forget about being a mama and just be free."

By this time, my hard-on has wilted. Her telephone call had the same effect on my libido as taking a cold shower.

"So, uh…does your mom know you came here with me?"

"Yeah. I told her the truth."

"What does she think?"

"She told me to go. That I needed a vacation to get away from work and being a mama."

"How does she feel about you and me sleeping together?"

"I don't know. We didn't talk about it."

"Who's Pony Girl?"

"That's my pet name for Sarah. She loves horses too."

"I overheard her asking about me."

"She's curious about you. I told her I was coming here with you. C'mon, let's go to the store. We need groceries. We hafta eat."

She puts on her checkered top and cutoffs over her bikini. I put my shirt on and switch out of my flip-flops into my leather sandals. Since my swimsuit is almost dry, I don't bother to change back into my cutoffs. On our way out the door, I grab my wallet.

Driving around the beach town looking for a supermarket, I can't stop thinking about her telephone conversation with her mom and Pony Girl. I'm struck by how deeply they love each other—I could almost feel their love being transmitted back and forth over the telephone line. I'm especially affected by Pony Girl asking about me. Her telephone call has made me realize that her mom and kids are not abstractions; they are real people who know Lily is here with me. As such, I don't want them to think I'm a bad guy and to dislike me. Consequently, I don't want to do anything that would hurt either Lily or them—

"Leo, stop!"

I spot the red light and slam on the brakes. We skid to a stop in the middle of the intersection…

Fortunately, no one was coming. Shifting into reverse, I back up. I was so absorbed in my thoughts that I almost ran a red light. "Sorry. I didn't see the light."

We find a supermarket. Rather than paying separately for groceries, we agree to split the entire cost.

"So what do you wanna fix for dinner?" she asks.

"I don't know. I don't know how to cook. Truth is I've never had to learn."

"Your mama always cooked for you, huh?"

"Yeah."

"What'd you do in college?"

"I had a meal ticket at a dining hall."

"You rich, college kids don't know jack shit," she mocks.

"What can I say? Girls took Home Ec in high school. Guys took Shop. I do know how to grill. My dad taught me."

"Well, you're lucky. I like to cook."

"Great."

"But I don't feel like cooking tonight. Let's go out to eat somewhere cheap. Tomorrow I wanna find a seafood store and fix a homemade seafood dinner."

"Sounds good to me."

While I push the cart up and down the aisles, she selects the basic staples for breakfast, lunch and dinner for a few days and the ingredients for her Bloody Marys. I get a bag of charcoal and charcoal lighter. She acquiesces to me getting a dozen glazed donuts for breakfast and crème sandwich cookies for a treat, even though she says she won't eat any because they are too fattening.

Back at the motel, we put away the groceries. Then we find a nearby pizza place. We try a pizza with clams on it—it's delicious. She informs me that she loves pizza; it's the only food she can't resist and one of her two vices. I ask what her other vice is, and she replies that it's vodka—that pizza and vodka are both loaded with calories.

"So what about sex?" I ask.

"Sex ain't a vice. It burns calories."

I laugh.

While we eat, we make plans for tomorrow. She hopes it doesn't rain because she wants to get up early and go in search of the wild horses. Pulling a tourist map of Cape Hatteras out of her purse, she spreads it out on our table. It shows where all the lighthouses and shipwrecks are. Pointing at the wilderness area north of Duck, she informs me, "That's where the wild horses live."

After dinner we go back to the motel. Determined to get her money's worth out of staying here, Lily wants to go for a dip in the pool. The pool is deserted, probably because the kids are all back in school. The lights in the pool make the water luminous, which looks inviting. At the shallow end, she descends the steps into the water, swims a few strokes of freestyle, then rolls over and floats on her back.

Showing off, I do a racing dive into the shallow end, swim a length of freestyle, do a flip turn, and swim a length of butterfly. Taking a deep breath, I push off the wall and swim two lengths underwater.

She mounts the diving board. Hanging onto the buoy rope in the middle of the pool, I watch her curiously. She does a perfect jackknife, ripping into the water. Then she does a front flip, an inward dive, and a back flip. Each time she has to rearrange her bikini halter before she climbs out of the pool.

I'll be damned—she knows how to dive.

Joining her at the diving board, I ask, "So where'd you learn to dive?"

"Emerald Lake."

"I didn't know you knew how to dive."

"Leo, there's a lot you don't know about me."

Trying to one-up her, I mount the diving board and attempt to perform a forward one and a half somersault; but this diving board doesn't have as much spring as the one at the country club. I under-rotate and smack my belly, floating on the surface in pain…

Bouncing on the end of the board, she laughs and razzes me, "That was a beautiful belly-smacker."

Treading water in front of the board, I grin like I'm not fazed. I swim over to the ladder and climb out. My chest, stomach, and the front of my thighs are pink.

She performs a perfect forward one and a half somersault.

I shake my head in admiration.

At ten o'clock, management turns off the pool lights, signaling that the pool is closed.

We go for a walk down the beach. The sky is overcast, so we

can't see the moon or stars. As we meander past a row of illuminated oceanfront motels, Lily tells me how much she loved seeing the ocean for the first time today. The sea breeze and crashing waves stimulate my senses. Feeling horny, I eagerly anticipate having sex with her tonight.

Back in our room, she goes into the bathroom; then I hear the shower running.

To create a romantic atmosphere, I open the drapes and the slider door to the balcony—so we can lie in bed and watch the ocean, listen to the rhythmic waves, feel the breeze, and smell the salt water. I turn on the nightstand light—I want to see her nude body. I hang the Do Not Disturb sign on the door, lock the door, and fasten the chain.

I strip. I pull back the covers, prop the pillows against the headboard, and climb into bed. Reclining against the headboard, I pull the sheet up to my waist. Then I wait expectantly for her to come to me. Picturing her in her bikini on the beach, I get a hard-on again—

Suddenly, I'm startled by the ringing of the telephone on the nightstand. Wondering who's calling at this hour, I answer the phone. The hotel desk clerk informs me of a long distance call and connects me to the caller. It's Mrs. McFarlane, who asks to speak to Lily.

Fearing an emergency, I tell her, "Ma'am, she's in the shower right now. You want me to get her?"

"It ain't an emergency. I just need to speak to my daughter."

"Sure. I'll get her."

I slip into my swim trunks, run to the bathroom, stick my head in the door and say, "Lily, your mom's on the phone. It's not an emergency. But she needs to talk to you."

Sticking her head outside the shower curtain, she says, "Tell her just a minute."

I return to the phone and tell Mrs. McFarlane she's coming. We chat pleasantly about the weather here and in Mansfield.

Lily comes to the phone with a towel wrapped around her, and I hand her the phone. Sitting on the side of the bed, she converses with her mom. From their conversation, I gather that Sarah had a nightmare and couldn't be consoled.

Mrs. McFarlane puts Sarah on the phone, and Lily listens to her nightmare.

"Honey, I'm fine. It was just a bad dream. We're gonna go look for the wild horses tomorrow. I'll be home in a few days and tell you all about it. Now go back to bed."

She listens to Sarah.

"I miss you too, Pony Girl. Good night. Sleep tight. Don't let the bed bugs bite."

She hangs up and exhales deeply. "She just had a bad dream. She thought I was killed in a car accident and wouldn't go back to sleep. I ain't ever been gone over night before. Everything's okay now. She just needed to hear my voice. Know that I'm still alive and kicking."

I nod like I understand. I figure her daughter's nightmare was probably triggered by Donny's suicide—the trauma has made her insecure.

"Don't go away. I'll be right back. I just gotta dry my hair," she says, disappearing to the bathroom.

Sitting on the end of the bed, I ponder her phone calls with her family. I realize the calls are "Coming Attractions" for us if I become involved with her romantically. Already I feel like I'm being pulled into her home life against my will, which is exactly what I was afraid would happen if I came here with her.

I have second thoughts about having sex with her. If I start having sex with her, sooner or later she'll want to be my exclusive girlfriend. Then she'll want me to get emotionally involved with her kids because they are a family. Listening to her on the phone with Sarah has made that abundantly clear to me. But I definitely do not want to be dealing with countless child problems like Sarah's nightmare when I'm starting law school.

If we have sex and fall in love, Lily will want me to be true to her. But I want to be free to find Lara at law school. I won't call her and see her again. I'll hurt her. She'll think I just used her for sex and will be upset with me. I'll ruin our wonderful friendship.

My conscience is telling me I should not have sex with her unless

I'm willing to be true to her and become involved emotionally with her kids. I'm ashamed of myself for planning on loving and leaving her and feel guilty about using her for my sexual gratification.

My hard-on is long gone. The last thing I feel like doing is having sex with her. I turn on the TV, sit down on the sofa, and watch the local news. The weatherman is giving the forecast for tomorrow—it's going to be sunny and in the 70s. This should please Lily.

She comes out of the bathroom singing "Crazy on You" and enters the bedroom with a bath towel wrapped around her. The end of the towel is tucked in above her breasts. As she walks past the TV, she turns it off.

Standing right in front of me, she smiles seductively and unfastens the towel and lets it fall. Her eyes gleaming, she says, "I told you I'd show you my body…"

It takes my breath away…

Gazing amorously into my eyes, she tells me, "I'm yours."

Strangely, I find her fabulous body only aesthetically pleasing—it doesn't make me get a hard-on. I don't think I could get it up even if I wanted to.

Sighing deeply, I say, "Lily, let's just be friends."

"What?"

"Let's not be lovers."

"Leo, I didn't come here just to be friends. I told you I'm yours if you took me to find the wild horses. You took me, so I'm yours."

Looking at her skeptically, I reply, "You may feel that way now, but you'll feel different if we have sex. Sooner or later, you'll regret it."

"No, I won't. I'll cherish it."

"Yes, you will. Sex has consequences. It causes love. That's why they call it making love. If we make love, we'll fall in love, and you'll want me to love you. It's like that song "Will You Love Me Tomorrow." The guy and girl make love. Then the girl asks the guy will you love me tomorrow? If we make love, you'll want me to love you tomorrow. But I won't love you tomorrow. I'm going away. I wanna be free."

"You don't hafta love me tomorrow. Just love me tonight," she replies with a mischievous smile. She takes my hand and tries to lead me toward the bed.

Embarrassed, I tell her, "Lily, I…I can't do this."

She sits down beside me on the sofa. Now distressed, she asks, "What's wrong?"

"Me. I'm wrong for you. I can't have sex with you."

"You don't want me?"

"Believe me—I want you."

"You don't like my body?"

"I think you have the sexiest body I've ever seen."

She looks at me like she's confused. "I don't understand you. This afternoon you wanted me. I seen your boner. Now you don't want me…"

"That was because I was blinded by lust. That was before I heard you talk to your daughter on the phone. That changed me."

"Changed you?"

"You know how we tell each other the truth?"

"Uh-huh."

"The truth is when I came here I wanted to have sex with you. I sexually desired you more than any woman in this world. I was planning on loving and leaving you. Because I…I'm not willing to take on your kids."

"I don't care, Leo."

"Lily, listen to me. After listening to you talk to Sarah on the phone today, your kids finally became real to me. I can't pretend they don't exist. They come with you. You're a family. For me to have sex with you, I have to be willing to take on your kids. It's only right. You're like a package deal. But I'm not willing to do it. I wanna be free when I go to law school. So it would be wrong for me to have sex with you. A decent guy would not take advantage of you. Only a cad would do that…"

Frustrated, she replies, "Now I wish I hadn't stopped you earlier. Why do you hafta make everything so damn complicated?"

"I'm just trying to do what's right. I don't wanna have a guilty conscience."

"To me it's simple. If you really like somebody and wanna have sex with them, just do it. Then see what happens."

That's probably how you got knocked up.

"I can predict what'll happen. I'll hurt you. I can't do that to you. You're my dearest friend, Lily."

"I am?"

"It's true. If I love you and leave you, it'll ruin our friendship. So I don't wanna become lovers. I just wanna stay friends. You understand?"

She looks at me with sad eyes. "I…I guess so," she mumbles. Then she sighs and says, "I knew it was too good to be true. So does this mean you wanna go home?"

"No. Like I said, I'm your friend. I wanna help you find these wild horses. Make your dream come true. That's what we came here for. We'll go look for them tomorrow. Okay?"

Her shoulders slumping, she nods half-heartedly.

"You'll be glad to hear the weather forecast for tomorrow is sunny and warm. We're gonna have perfect weather to look for them."

"That's good."

"So…are we still friends?"

"Yeah."

"Good."

"Well, if we ain't gonna do it, I guess I'll just go to bed."

She stands up and walks over to the bed. I suggest that she take the side of the bed next to the phone in case she gets any more calls from home. She pulls back the covers, climbs in, and pulls them back up over her nude body. Smiling coyly, she tells me, "I told you—I sleep naked."

"That's fine with me. I think I'll take a shower now."

In the shower, I keep picturing her nude body. Her body truly is aesthetically perfect. As an artist, I'd love to draw her nude. Despite my noble intentions, the image of it gives me a hard-on again. I have to turn the water colder and colder to make it go away. I picture her sad eyes when she realized we weren't going to have sex. While I regret having hurt her feelings, I believe it was the right thing to do in the long run.

Brushing my teeth, I look in the mirror and tell myself, "Well, Leo, looks like you ain't a stud like Appaloosa after all." My eyes look sad. I'm definitely disappointed. I tell myself we can still have fun. We'll go search for the wild horses tomorrow; go sight-seeing on Monday; go to the beach on Tuesday, our last day; and go home on Wednesday.

I didn't bring anything to sleep in, so I wear my surfer trunks to bed. Lily has gone to sleep without turning off the light on the nightstand. Before I turn it off, I look at her face lying on her pillow. Initially, I think she looks angelic; then I think she looks devilish. It's strange—actually, she looks both.

I leave the drapes and sliding glass door open; then turn off the light and climb in bed. A mercury light that illuminates the boardwalk to the beach is shining into the room—it creates a soft nightlight to find the bathroom in the middle of the night. Even though I'm dead-tired, I have trouble falling asleep. I'm conscious of Lily's nude body only inches away from me. In my mind, I hear Percy call me a fool.

All night I keep waking up with a hard-on.

CHAPTER THIRTEEN

I'm awakened by the sun shining in my eyes through the sliding door. Lily is lying on her side with her head propped on her elbow, studying me...

"Morning, Lily."

"Morning, Leo."

"So...what're you looking at?"

"You. You're really good-looking."

"I am?"

"Yeah. I really like your face." Peering into my eyes, she says, "You got beautiful brown eyes. They got little specks of gold in them. And I like your wavy hair."

This makes me feel good. Except for my mom—who is biased—she's the only female who has ever told me this. Admiring her eyes, I reply, "I really like your eyes, too. They're psychedelic."

"Psychedelic?"

"The colors sparkle when you smile. And I like your face. It's ravishing. And I like your ivory skin. And cinnamon hair. It looks like a horse's mane."

She smiles.

I recall not having sex with her last night and am glad that she doesn't appear to harbor any resentment. "What time is it?"

"Seven forty. Time to find the wild horses."

Since we're going to get all hot and sweaty hiking through the wilderness, we don't bother to get cleaned up. I put on my swim trunks, a T-shirt, and tennis shoes and wear my aviator sunglasses, so I look cool. Lily wears her pink polka dot bikini and flip-flops.

For breakfast I eat a half a dozen glazed donuts, dunking them in my coffee.

Lily eats a bowl of oatmeal with a sliced banana on top. Watching me critically, she comments, "Them donuts ain't very nutritious."

"Yes, they are. The dextrose produced by the metabolism of the carbohydrates in these donuts will give me energy."

She rolls her eyes.

After breakfast, we set off in search of the wild horses of Currituck. She's the pilot; I'm the navigator. Using the road atlas, I direct her north on Highway 12 toward Duck.

"So how do we get there?" she asks.

"It's easy. Just drive till we come to the end of the road."

At nine thirty we arrive at Duck, which is a quaint coastal village. North of Duck the paved highway turns into a gravel road, which ultimately ends at a barricade. A sandy lane provides motor vehicles access to the shore. A road sign warns motorists against beach driving unless their vehicle has four-wheel drive. Disregarding the road sign, Lily barrels straight toward the sandy lane.

"Stop!" I yell.

She ignores me and drives off the gravel—plows right into the sand.

My Triumph slowly sinks to a standstill in the soft sand...

Putting the car in reverse, she tries to back up...

Spinning, we go nowhere.

"Whoops..."

"God damn it, Lily. Why didn't you stop?"

"I thought we could cover more ground in the car than on foot."

"My Triumph can't drive in sand. It's got rear-wheel drive, and the chassis sits too low to the ground."

She grins sheepishly. "Sorry..."

I let out a long sigh. "I'm gonna hafta get out and push."

I climb out and survey the situation. The car is stuck in the sand half way up the spoke wheels. Crouching against the front bumper, I try to push the car back onto the asphalt while she hits the gas in reverse. My feet can't get any traction in the loose sand. Rocking the car back and forth between forward and reverse gears, the rear wheels spin impotently, and the car sinks deeper and deeper until it's resting on the chassis. I fall to my knees...

"Fuck!" I gesture for her to shut off the engine. Standing up, I brush off the sand; then wipe the sweat off my brow. With a stoic expression on my face, I go inform Lily, "We're stuck."

"What do we do?"

"We're gonna hafta walk back to Duck and find someone to tow it." I exhale deeply. "Ya know, Lily, if you don't mind my saying so, sometimes you're too impetuous. Next time when I say stop, stop."

"Next time I'll be driving a jeep."

Even though I doubt anyone could steal my immobile car, I grab the keys. She grabs her purse. We start walking back to Duck.

"Well, we're off to an auspicious start," I banter.

"Auspicious?"

"Never mind. I was just trying to be humorous."

"I don't get it."

"It doesn't matter. Forget it."

After trekking a mile or so down the road in the hot sun, we see a car approaching. Lily flags it down. A local fisherman in a jeep pulls over and asks if we need help. I explain what happened. He informs us we have to have four-wheel drive to drive on the beach—like the sign says—and thinks it's funny that we tried to drive a sports car in the sand. I can tell he views us as typical dumb tourists.

I offer to pay him if he gives us a lift to Duck. Then Lily shows him the bloody blisters on her feet from walking in her sandy flip-flops. Feeling sorry for her, he tells us, "Hop in. I'll give you a lift for free."

On the way to Duck, he asks us why we tried to drive on the beach—if we were going fishing. When we tell him we're looking for the wild horses, he says, "Good luck. They're really hard to find. They roam the banks all the way to Corolla."

"How far is that?" I ask.

"Fifteen miles."

In Duck he drops us off at a gas station-convenience store. The attendant kindly lets us use his phone. We try calling tow companies in Kill Devil Hills and Nags Head, but none of them are open since it's Sunday morning. Finally, the attendant informs us that Outer Banks Towing in Kill Devil Hills opens at one o'clock on Sundays.

To kill time, we explore the village. There are some tackle shops and an art gallery, which are closed, so we window shop. Smiling wryly, I point out to Lily a bumper sticker that adorns a parked car—it reads "Stuck in Duck."

Returning to the convenience store, we eat steamed hot dogs for lunch. Then we try calling Outer Banks Towing again. It rings and rings. Finally, the proprietor answers the phone. Since it's Sunday, he charges emergency rates—one hundred dollars. I accept and arrange for him to pick us up here.

After I hang up, Lily complains, "He gouged you."

"He had us over a barrel. What did you want me to do?"

"Negotiate. You're gonna be a lawyer."

"Next time I'll let you handle it."

We wait and wait for the tow truck. Finally, around two o'clock it arrives. The driver is a fat, bald-headed guy in greasy overalls. I don't even have to give him directions to my car. Smirking, he remarks he makes a decent living off tourists who regularly drive their cars into the sand—although he's never actually seen anyone attempt it in a British sports car.

He hitches a chain to my car and tows it out of the sand. Huddling, Lily and I discuss how to pay him. She says she'll pay for it since it was her fault, but I insist on paying half—I tell her we're in this together. While she gets money out of her purse, I notice that he's looking down her bikini halter at her cleavage—he's practically drooling on her. After he drives away, I comment on it contemptuously. She says she doesn't pay any attention—she's used to it.

It's past two thirty. "Now what?" I ask.

With her jaw set, she answers, "I ain't giving up. Let's go on foot."

We park on the gravel by the road barricade. Heading north, Lily leads the way across the grassy sand dunes. She has trouble walking because of her blisters. Entering an area of shrub thickets, the breeze dies.

All at once we are attacked by a swarm of huge, blood-sucking mosquitos. They land all over our bodies—I spot several on her back. We swat at them frantically. I'm cursing. She's shrieking.

"Let's get out of here," I exclaim.

We run all the way back to the car and jump in. They chase after us as we drive away. I drive back to Duck and pull into the gas station. Scratching my mosquito bites, I tell her, "Damn, Lily, those are the biggest mosquitos I've ever seen."

"I seen bigger ones in Canada."

"They were eating us alive. That does it. I'm not going back there."

Even though she hates to give up, she doesn't argue with me. Crestfallen, she replies, "I come here to find the wild horses and get laid, and I ain't gonna do neither. All the way here for nothing…"

I don't know what to say. I've totally let her down.

"What time is it?" she asks.

"It's almost three."

"We wasted the whole day."

"Not necessarily. We still have a few hours of sunlight left. Let's go to the beach," I venture to say.

"Okay. I need a drink."

On the way back to the motel, she tells me to keep an eye open for a liquor store. She wants to fix herself a Bloody Mary at dinnertime.

We stop at the beach store and buy more beach apparel. She buys a beach blanket, two beach towels, a beach bag, a small cooler, and a new magazine called *People*. I check out the boogie boards, which are short, light surfboards ridden in a prone position. I want to buy a fiberglass one called Hard Slick, but it's too expensive. The towing bill took a big chunk of my cash. I look at a cheap plastic one. She remarks that it looks flimsy. After I tell her it's all I can afford, she buys Hard Slick for me, saying it's her way of thanking me for her portrait. I thank her. She asks the cashier for directions to a liquor store.

On the way out of the store, Lily spots a pair of red, heart-shaped sunglasses. She tries them on and asks me, "How do I look?"

"Like a red candy apple."

Since she generously bought me Hard Slick, I buy them for her.

We both walk happily out of the store.

At the liquor store, she selects a cheap bottle of vodka off the bottom shelf.

"That stuff is rot gut. Go for top shelf. My old man says it's smoother and doesn't give you a hangover," I recommend.

"Your old man's rich and can afford it. It's too expensive for me."

"Splurge. You're on vacation."

"Why do you care? You ain't gonna drink it."

"True."

I see the gears turning in her head. "Leo, I tell you what. I'll indulge and buy top shelf if you indulge and have a drink with me."

I figure one drink won't hurt me. I counteroffer, "I'll have a drink with you if you smoke a joint with me."

"Okay. Deal."

"We may salvage this day after all."

She pays for the vodka since she'll drink most of it. The sales clerk makes her show him her driver's license. When she tells him she's the mother of three kids, he doesn't believe her.

On the way to the car, I spot a sign that says Fresh Seafood Market in the same shopping plaza. We go in the store and browse the merchandise. I ask the proprietor what he recommends. He gives us his recipe for Maryland Blue Crab Cakes with Hollandaise sauce and hush puppies. Then he shows us the fresh Maryland Blue Crab in his display case.

Lily checks the price and says, "It's too expensive."

He explains that it's expensive because little, old German ladies have to painstakingly extract by hand the delicate crab meat from the blue crab shells—it's very labor intensive.

This induces her to buy it.

I buy a half pound of unshelled, uncooked shrimp and the ingredients to fix shrimp cocktails for appetizers. Before we go, the proprietor talks me into buying a yellowfin tuna steak, which is also pricey. He tells me it tastes just like filet mignon if you grill it properly. He instructs me to brush melted butter on each side of the fish steak; then sear each side for thirty seconds, stressing it should be almost raw inside. Lily whispers in my ear, "You got expensive tastes."

Back at the motel, I race to the beach and try out Hard Slick. Propping my chest upright on my elbows on the boogie board, I catch several big waves for long, speedy rides. The board is very buoyant and durable, and the velvety surface is comfortable to lie on—definitely worth the money.

I spot Lily standing in the backwash, snapping pictures of me. Waving to her, I holler, "Come on in. Try it. It's a blast."

Acting like she didn't hear me, she returns to her new beach blanket and reads her magazine.

At dinnertime we go back to our room. Having salvaged some of the day, we're both in a good mood again. Before we start dinner, she calls home. Reclining on the bed, she talks to her mom and kids one by one, while I sit on the sofa and watch TV. I can't help overhearing her conversation. Having decided not to take advantage of her sexually, I don't feel guilty when she talks to them now. This reassures me that I made the right decision to just be friends. Without going into the details of today's debacle, she tells Sarah that we didn't find the wild horses; then they talk about Mrs. McFarlane taking her to Sunday school today. Speaking to Sean, she tells him about my body surfing and boogie boarding and promises to take him to the ocean someday. I realize just how much this trip to Cape Hatteras means to her, and my heart swells.

After she hangs up, she fixes Bloody Marys for both of us. I turn on the radio and find a local rock station. Standing at the kitchen counter, she stirs her drink with a carrot stick; then sips it. "Mmm, I gotta admit, Leo, this vodka is smooth."

I sit down on a barstool across the counter from her and have a sip of mine. "Tasty," I remark.

"I make a mean Bloody Mary. The secret is the right mixture of Tabasco, Worcestershire sauce, and horseradish."

"I remember the last time I drank these was the first time I ate lunch with you at Boals-Corrigan. I got tipsy and dropped a toilet. Remember?"

Smiling nostalgically, she replies, "I remember."

"So are you gonna get stoned with me?"

"Yeah."

I fetch my pot and roll a joint. Spotting my derringer-lighter, Lily asks, "Is that a real gun?"

"No, it's a lighter."

"Where'd you get that?"

"A novelty shop in New Orleans."

"New Orleans…I'd like to go there."

"The French Quarter has a lot of character."

"It sounds like you been everywhere."

"My parents have taken me to a lot of places on vacation."

"Let me see it."

I hand her the lighter.

Aiming it at me, she says, "Stick 'em up."

I raise my hands.

She pulls the trigger, and the gun barrel emits a flame.

I light the joint and take a toke; then offer her a hit.

She takes the joint and examines it curiously. Mockingly, she asks, "Is this gonna turn me into a wild woman?"

Chuckling, I answer, "No. You're already a wild woman. The effect is subtle. Most people don't get high the first time they try it."

"So what does it do to you?"

"Personally, I think it enhances your senses. When you're stoned, food tastes more delicious. Music sounds more beautiful." I don't tell her I think sex feels more pleasurable; it's best to let sleeping dogs lie.

She takes a small puff and coughs.

"You gotta hold the hit." I take a hit—show her how to hold it.

She takes another hit and doesn't cough. "I think I got the hang of it."

After we finish the joint, we start fixing dinner. While she makes the crab cakes and hush puppies, I peel and devein the shrimp. When I tell her I'm fixing shrimp cocktails as an appetizer, she tells me she once had a shrimp cocktail when Donny took her out to eat on her birthday. She says she loved it. I can't believe she's only had a shrimp cocktail once in her life. She acknowledges that she hasn't gone out to eat at fancy restaurants very often. I boil the shrimp; then put them on ice in the refrigerator to chill.

Next I fix the cocktail sauce, mixing in several teaspoons of horseradish.

"That's a lot of horseradish," she observes.

"I like it hot."

"You sure it ain't gonna be too hot?"

"It could never be too hot for me. I love spicy food."

Skeptical, she mixes some extra tablespoons of ketchup in her sauce.

I light the grill. While she fries the Maryland Blue Crab Cakes and hush puppies in an electric skillet, I set the kitchen table. At the last minute, I grill the yellowfin tuna. Lily wrinkles her nose at the thought of eating raw fish, so I grill each side for a minute. Flipping the tuna steak, I notice how nice it is outside this evening. It's dusk. There is a pleasant ocean breeze, and the waves are breaking on the beach harmoniously. There are no bugs or humidity. Suddenly, I have an idea. Sticking my head inside, I holler, "Hey, Lily. Let's eat on the balcony. It's really nice out here."

"That's a good idea," she yells back.

We carry everything out on the balcony and sit down at the table. The food looks and smells so delectable. "Are you high?" I ask.

Smiling blithely into space, she answers, "I think so."

We feast, starting with the appetizers. I dip a shrimp in my cocktail sauce—so that it's liberally coated—and pop it whole into my mouth. My sinuses burn so badly it makes my eyes water.

Smirking, she asks, "What's the matter? Too hot?"

I just grin and bear it.

She loves her shrimp cocktail. Dipping the shrimp in her cocktail sauce, she savors each bite.

Next, I eat a bite of yellowfin tuna. "Mmm—this is really good. The guy at the store was right—it tastes just like filet mignon. Except I think I overcooked it—it's too well-done. I should've listened to him. He said to sear it only thirty seconds."

Lily tries a bite. Looking unsure about it, she comments, "It's a little too rare for me."

Then we eat the main course—the crab cakes.

She squeezes lemon on them; then takes a bite. "Mmm. You like them?"

I try a bite. "I don't like them. I love them. You're a good cook."

"Thanks. I like to cook if I can try new recipes. But my kids hate it when I try new things, so I get discouraged and give up."

After supper she fixes Bloody Marys for both of us again. While we load the dishwasher and clean up the kitchen, she swills hers. I think she's a little tipsy because she starts acting racy. She keeps brushing her body against me in her bikini.

During twilight, we stand at the railing on the balcony, our shoulders touching, silently watching the waves break on the shore. The sky is an intense indigo color, and the air is balmy...

At dark, I say, "Hey, let's go swimming,"

I teach her how to do a can-opener off the diving board. She keeps trying to make a big splash, but her cute butt just isn't big enough. When she hits the water, it forces her bikini bottom to go up her butt crack—exposing her cheeks. She has to keep extracting it—it's comical.

We horse around in the shallow end. She rides piggyback on me. I feel her soft breasts pressing against my back and her muscular thighs locked onto my waist. Diving underwater, I swim like a submarine with her on my back. Next, I dive underwater behind her and surface between her legs with her sitting on my shoulders; then carry her around the pool. Eventually, I grab hold of her heels and dump her backwards into the water—she squeals with delight.

After the pool closes, we go for a walk on the beach. While we smoke a joint, we talk about whether we'd rather live at the ocean or in the mountains. Lily tells me, "I'd live in the foothills of the mountains in eastern Kentucky. When we lived there, my dad took me horseback riding. We rode all day up and down the hills and through the hollers. Summertime we galloped across the meadows through the wildflowers. They was such pretty colors. In the fall, when the leaves was changing, we rode miles through the forest. I seen deer and eagles and black bears. Once I even seen a bobcat…"

"Wow…"

"You can go places on a horse you can't go in a car. You can ride across a creek. And through a ravine with sandstone cliffs. And you can ride a lot farther than you can walk."

I envision myself riding a horse through the woods—it stirs my imagination. "I'd like to do that."

"Sometime I'll take you horseback riding at Mama's farm."

"It'd make me feel like I'm a frontiersman."

"So what about you? Where would you live?"

"I'd live at the ocean because of the waves. I love waves. I find them hypnotic—the way they dynamically curl and then violently crash on the shore. If I lived at the ocean, I'd learn how to surf. I've always dreamed of being a surfer."

"Really?"

"Yeah. When I was in high school, Reese and I saw this movie, *The Endless Summer*. It's about two surfers who go on a surfing adventure, traveling to beaches all around the world in search of the perfect wave. They surf incredible waves in Africa, Australia, California and Hawaii. Man, I'd love to go on an adventure like that."

"You should do it."

I sigh. "But, instead, I'm going to law school. It seems like I always postpone my dreams for my career."

We stop walking and talking and just gaze at the moon and the stars. A pleasant breeze is blowing from the ocean. Facing it, she feels it blow through her hair…

"Boy, oh, boy, Leo—that breeze feels nice."

"Uh-huh."

Back in our room, she goes into the bathroom to take a shower. I strip down to my swimsuit, turn on the TV, and wait for my turn. Reclining on the bed, I watch the end of the news and the weather forecast. We get lucky again—it's going to be sunny and warm tomorrow.

While I'm watching Johnny Carson, she enters the bedroom nude again.

I try not to look at her but can't resist—her naked body is an eye magnet.

"It's all yours," she tells me.

While I take a shower, the image of her nude body keeps reappearing in my mind, and I get a hard-on. Tonight it won't go away. The marijuana has made me horny, and I have trouble controlling my thoughts.

I think about how much fun we had horsing around in the pool. Even though our search for the wild horses was a total fiasco, I had fun doing it with her. Truth is we have fun together.

I remember her talking about going horseback riding with her dad and realize that she opened up to me about him. Perhaps she'll tell me what happened to him now.

I recall her inviting me to go horseback riding at her mom's farm. If I wasn't going to law school, I truly would like to do that.

My hard-on is gone. I put on my swimsuit and return to the bedroom. I'm surprised to find her lying in bed under the covers wide awake. She has turned off the TV but left the nightstand light on.

"You're still awake."

"I ain't sleepy."

I climb into my side of the bed and pull up the covers.

We lie on our sides with our heads on our pillows, facing one another.

"Last night I had a dream about you," she says coyly.

"What'd you dream?"

Smiling in a devilish way, she says, "I shouldn't tell you. It was really dirty."

I'm curious. "Tell me. I love erotic dreams."

"I dreamed me and you was screwing and it felt so good…when I woke up, I was so turned on I was wet down there."

Man, oh, man…

Imagining this, I get a hard-on again.

"It's hot in here," she says.

"Want me to open the sliding door?" I ask.

"Yeah."

I hop out of bed and open the drapes and the sliding glass door. As I turn around and face her, she kicks off her covers exposing her nude body.

The ocean breeze gently rustles the drapes. Lying on her back, she spreads her legs. Closing her eyes, she sensually feels the breeze blow across her body. "Oooh, that feels good…"

Standing at the foot of the bed, I am enamored with her. Her breasts are perfectly shaped and a beautiful ivory-seashell color where her bikini has covered them. But it's her nipples that are especially erotic. They look like pink wild strawberries budding from large, rose-colored areolae.

My eyes are drawn downward to her cinnamon mound…

She opens her eyes and gazes at me alluringly. "You like my body?"

"Yes…"

"You like to look at my pussy?"

"I do. It's so…womanly."

"I love showing it to you…"

Spotting the bulge in my swimsuit, she grins. "I see your boner."

"I can't help it. It has a mind of its own."

Chuckling, she says, "I wanna see it. Show it to me…"

That wild glint is in her eyes again—it drives me wild.

My fingers fumble excitedly with the drawstring on my swimsuit—it ends up in a knot. Frustrated, I yank my swimsuit down and kick it off.

Beaming, I show it to her…

She eyes it lustfully. "It's so manly…I wanna touch it…"

Heart racing, I crawl onto the bed between her legs and kneel facing her.

She feels it. "It's hard. But soft…you wanna feel mine?"

I reach down and feel her…

"What's it feel like?"

"Like…like…" I struggle to find the right words. "It's indescribably wonderful. They're made for each other."

Her fingers caress the pleasure spot on my boner…

"Oh, God, Lily…that feels so good…"

In her sensual twang, she says breathlessly, "Oh, Leo…I'm on fire…stick it in me…"

Desire overpowers us. Together we stick it in her. Gazing ardently into each other's eyes, we utter long, deep moans of pleasure.

"Ohhh, Leo, fuck me…"

I thrust in and out slowly. Her heels high in the air, she thrusts her hips up and down in unison with me…

Clawing her fingernails into my backside, she exhorts, "Harder."

Panting, I thrust as hard as I can…

Her face twisted, her teeth bared, she's panting and grunting and groaning like a wild animal. Her heels are digging so hard into my back it hurts.

My brain disintegrates and I thrust wildly.

With each thrust, she cries, "Oh!"

Her cries of pleasure spur me to come. The indescribably pleasurable sensation in my cock intensifies into an uncontrollable urge to explode, and I thrust as deep as I can inside her. Grimacing, I groan loudly, "Oh, Lily, I'm coming…"

My cock ejaculates in the most exquisite sensation of pleasure I've ever felt.

Pleasure radiates throughout every nerve in my body. Breathing heavily, I lie on her in a state of bliss…

As she fondles the back of my neck, I smile at her with my eyes.…

She looks at me expectantly.

I realize she didn't come. "Make yourself comfortable, Lily," I say with a wink.

Her eyes gleaming in anticipation, she reclines against the pillows.

I rub her hard nipples gently…

Closing her eyes, she savors the pleasure she's feeling. Soon, she begins to breathe heavily and sigh…

She opens her legs, inviting my fingers to caress her. Her hips thrust up, down, up, down…

I rub her clitoris in a circular motion matching the rhythm of her hips…

"Oh, Leo—that feels so good…"

Her eyes roll back into her head and her irises disappear in pleasure—which excites me immensely.

"Harder…" she groans.

As I rub harder, her eyes and mouth open wide in ecstasy, and she starts thrusting vigorously against my hand. Panting and moaning, her eyes lock onto mine…

All at once her eyes clamp shut, her face grimaces fiercely, and she starts panting maniacally through clenched teeth. Lifting her head off the pillow and arching her hips off the bed, her whole body goes rigid, her thighs lock together around my hand, and she groans huskily, "Ohhh, Leo, I'm coming…"

With each pulse, she groans loudly and contorts her body convulsively, while her fingers claw the mattress and her feet jerk spasmodically…

Gradually, her groaning and panting subside and her body goes limp on the bed…

God Almighty!

Opening her eyes, she gazes at me with an expression of blissful wonder and murmurs, "Wow…"

In the afterglow of sex, I hold her in my arms and kiss her shoulder lightly.

She turns off the light on the nightstand, pulls up the covers, and says, "'Night, Leo."

"'Night, Lily."

I close my eyes and fall into a deep, contented sleep.

CHAPTER FOURTEEN

I wake up early in the morning with a piss hard-on. Standing at the toilet, I cannot piss because I'm still turned on by the memory of having sex with Lily last night. Only by concentrating on the seashell pattern on the wallpaper am I able to lose my erection and pee.

In my mind I feel her fingernails clawing my backside while we screwed. Examining my backside in the mirror above the sink, I discover claw marks on my butt.

God, she's a wild woman.

I love it.

I return to the bedroom. Without waking her up, I slip on my swimsuit and go outside on the balcony. The sun has risen and is shining brightly on the ocean. Standing at the railing watching the waves break on the shore, I recall it all started when she told me her dirty dream. Then I opened the sliding glass door for her, and she kicked the sheet off her body to feel the sea breeze. I vividly picture her lying nude on the bed with her legs spread, gazing at me alluringly.

"Damn, Lily—you seduced me again."

I picture the wild glint in her eyes when she told me that she loved showing her pussy to me and asked me to show her my boner. "That's when I threw caution to the wind."

LILY

I recall how indescribably wonderful her pussy felt. And when she caressed the pleasure spot on my boner, it felt so good I couldn't stop. "How did she know where to touch me so I couldn't stop?"

Closing my eyes, I replay us having sex—the entire scene is recorded indelibly like a sound film in my eidetic memory. I hear her tell me that she's on fire and to stick my cock in her and marvel at us sticking it in her together...

I feel the ineffable pleasure of being inside her, and I relive us fucking like wild animals, culminating in my having the most powerful orgasm of my life...

Last, I visualize her stupendous orgasm...

I utter, "Man alive, Lily..."

Smiling drolly, I tell myself, "So much for just being friends. She and I are lovers now."

Oh, Lily, you are sexual heroin. I want another fix of you more than anything in this world.

Reliving sex with her has given me a hard-on. I want to go back to bed and do it again.

Out of the blue, I recall Mel saying, "Just don't knock her up." I figure the odds are small that she'll get pregnant from having sex one time. Still, I realize I'm playing Russian roulette. Heeding his advice, I decide to hold off on having any more sex with her until I buy some condoms—

I hear the sliding screen door open behind me. Turning around, I see her stepping out on the balcony in her red bikini.

She smiles warmly. "Morning, Leo."

I smile back. "Morning, Lily."

Standing side by side at the railing, we watch the waves. I wait for her to say something about our sex last night, but she doesn't mention it. Neither do I. I don't feel like having a heavy talk about it right now. I just want to have fun with her today. I figure we can talk about it later.

"It looks like it's gonna be a nice day today. What do you wanna do?" I ask.

"Go sight-seeing."

"What do you wanna see?"

"The Laura Barnes shipwreck. The Bodie Island lighthouse. The Hatteras lighthouse. I wanna climb to the top of it. It's the tallest brick lighthouse in the United States."

"Cool."

"So what do you wanna do?" she asks.

"I wanna climb Jockey's Ridge. It's the tallest sand dune on the east coast."

"Cool."

"Sounds like we have an itinerary."

"Let's get going."

"Make up for lost time."

For breakfast I eat the other half dozen glazed donuts. She fixes herself a shrimp cocktail from the leftover shrimp. Before she can criticize me for having donuts for breakfast again, I ask, "You're eating a shrimp cocktail for breakfast?"

"Uh-huh. I love shrimp cocktail. And shrimp don't have that many calories."

I say facetiously, "Lily, you're gonna get gout eating so much shrimp. The uric acid in shellfish gets deposited in your joints. The joints in your feet and toes are gonna swell. It'll be so painful you won't be able to walk."

She gives me a dirty look and pops a whole shrimp in her mouth.

To go sightseeing, she puts on her checkered top and cutoffs over her bikini and wears her cowgirl hat and sunglasses. I change into my cutoffs and put on a clean T-shirt and sunglasses.

Before we go, she fixes tuna salad sandwiches out of the leftover tuna and packs them, carrot and celery sticks, and apple juice in the cooler.

She wants to drive, so I navigate. Looking at her map of Cape Hatteras, I direct her to take the bypass around Kill Devil Hills to avoid all of the stoplights on the beach highway. We cruise with the top down at a leisurely speed so we can hear each other talk.

At Nags Head I spot a mountainous sand dune off in the distance to the west. People are climbing up it—they look like ants. Pointing at it, I say, "Hey, Lily, there it is. Jockey's Ridge. Stop!"

She drives right past it.

"You went right past it," I complain.

"Ooops. I accidentally missed it. Sorry," she says with mock sorrow.

"Accidentally on purpose."

Grinning, she says, "That's why I like to drive. I have control of the steering wheel."

"I'll remember that."

I've already climbed Jockey's Ridge twice—once with my family and a second time with Beth. Since she's never been here before, I'll do whatever she wants to do.

We drive south on Highway 12. Lily lets out a whoop when she sees a sign on Bodie Island that says Cape Hatteras National Seashore.

The road is hedged by grassy sand dunes to the east and wooded forest to the west, so we can't see either the ocean or the sound. Eventually, we come to signs that say Coquina Beach and Site of the Laura A. Barnes Shipwreck. Lily starts fretting over how much they're going to charge us to see the shipwreck.

"I think it's free, Lily."

"Leo, there ain't nothing free in these tourist traps."

There are only three other cars in the parking lot. She looks around for a ticket booth but doesn't see one. "I guess you're right," she concedes.

"See—I occasionally know a useful tidbit of information."

She picks up her camera. We follow a winding path over and through the dunes. Tiny, invisible bugs keep biting our ankles. Finally, we reach the shipwreck. All we see are a few rotten wooden beams and boards almost buried in the sand with a plaque commemorating the shipwreck. Several tourists are taking snapshots of it.

Lily whispers to me, "I see why they don't charge. There ain't nothing here to see. C'mon, let's go."

"Aren't you gonna take a picture?"

"Heck, no. I could take a picture of this any day at the junkyard down the street from my trailer park."

"What were you expecting? Skeletons?"

She looks at me like very funny. "I was expecting a little more wreckage."

"So what's next on the agenda?"

"The Bodie Lighthouse."

She drives to the lighthouse, which is located in the marshes on Bodie Island near the sound. She loves the black and white horizontal striped lighthouse and takes several pictures of it.

"You just like it because it's a phallic symbol," I kid her.

"What's that?"

"Something that resembles a penis."

Eyeing the 156 foot tall lighthouse, she replies mockingly, "You wish."

We go inside and climb the narrow, spiral stairs to the top. She counts all two hundred and one steps. She reads about the high-powered light and takes its picture. Outside on the metal catwalk that circles the pinnacle we have a bird's eye view of the Atlantic Ocean, the Bonner Bridge, the surrounding marshes, and Pamlico Sound. While I walk around the catwalk with one hand on the railing, she runs around it, snapping panoramic pictures in every direction. She has no fear of heights.

Back on the ground, she asks an elderly man to take our picture in front of the lighthouse. At first she won't let me put my arm around her but finally relents because she doesn't want to keep the nice man waiting.

Driving south down Highway 12, we come to the Herbert C. Bonner Bridge, which spans Oregon Inlet. As we cross the long, high bridge, we look at the boats passing to and fro between the ocean and the sound. At the apex of the bridge, she gapes at the water far below. "I love going over high bridges. It tickles my stomach. Don't you?"

"I'd like it more if you kept your eyes on the road."

She laughs.

We cruise down the national seashore, admiring the pristine nature. Sand dunes with sea oat tassels swaying in the breeze are on the east side of the road. Emerald and beige waves of marsh grass and the Pamlico Sound are on the west side. I point out how it's not spoiled by human development and advertising. We go through the picturesque fishing villages of Rodanthe, Salvo, and Avon.

We travel to the Hatteras lighthouse at Buxton. Lily wants to climb to the lantern room. She's disappointed when she learns that it's closed to the public due to structural cracks in its foundation—we drove all the way down here for nothing.

At a picnic table in the shade, we eat our lunch. I tell her the fresh tuna salad sandwiches taste delicious. Propping her sunglasses on her head, she paraphrases her brochure on the Hatteras lighthouse: just offshore Cape Hatteras is Diamond Shoals, where the warm Gulf Stream collides with the cold Labrador Current, creating ideal conditions for powerful ocean storms and sea swells; over six hundred ships have run aground on the shifting sandbars, causing Cape Hatteras to be nicknamed the Graveyard of the Atlantic; to prevent shipwrecks, the lighthouse was constructed using over a million bricks. She finds all this really fascinating.

After we finish eating, we stroll down the beach, sandals in hand.

"Hey, Leo."

"What?"

"I just wanna thank you for taking me here. I'm having a really good time now."

"Yeah. Me too, Lily."

"I'm happy I got to see the ocean. I seen everything I wanted to see. Except the wild horses."

"At least we tried."

With a mischievous twinkle in her eye, she says, "And I got laid."

I laugh. "You seduced me. I couldn't resist your charms."

She smiles. "So…did you like screwing me last night?"

"Yes. You're a wild woman," I tease her.

"You love it."

"I do. You made me go wild." I picture her eyes rolling back into her head when I masturbated her. "You're really sensual."

Snickering, she replies, "That was a really powerful orgasm I had."

Visualizing it, I remark, "Damn, Lily—it was the most erotic thing I've ever seen."

She looks at me curiously. "Why do you say that?"

"I love the way your body contorted and you cried out my name and told me you're coming. It's forever filmed in my eidetic memory."

That puzzles her.

"I may have a civilized veneer, but I'm a caveman at heart. I think a lot of women are afraid to express their orgasm. Beth thought she didn't look pretty when she came. You know—she thought it wasn't feminine. Nothing excites me more than making you come like that. It was phenomenal."

"You brought out the animal in me. Bitches and mares don't care what they look like when they do it. Neither do I. Like Dr. Hall says—we're all animals. I ain't ashamed of it. I love it."

"I love you being an animal."

"It must look like I'm in pain when I come. But I ain't."

I'm curious if her orgasm feels like mine. "So…what does it feel like?"

"Pure pleasure." Snickering, she says, "I'm getting wet just thinking about it."

Immediately, I get a hard-on.

"You wanna fuck me again tonight?" she asks.

"Yes. Now that we've let the genie out of the bottle, I want to experience more of its magical powers."

"I understand why you don't wanna get involved with my kids. I really do. They're a big responsibility. I know you're going away to law school. It's okay. I don't care if you love me and leave me. I just want you to love me here at the ocean…"

Figuring it's a fait accompli, I nod.

"Let's just have a wild fling. Then kiss and say goodbye," she says.

"Okay."

We smile at each other like we've come to an understanding. She stops and picks up a shell. After examining it, she places it back in the sand.

"So, uh…let me ask you something, Lily."

"What?"

"Out of all the eligible bachelors in the world, what made you ask me to take you on this trip?"

Musing, she tells me, "I don't know…when Jessie told me they was hiring a college guy, I was curious about you. I didn't know any college guys, so I wanted to see if you was different…

"And my horoscope said I was gonna meet someone…someone tall, dark, and handsome. You're tall, dark, and handsome…

"I remember I first saw you at lunch. You looked so…so lost. You couldn't even work the microwave."

Grinning, I reply, "That's because I was lusting for your body."

That makes her smile. "And then at afternoon break I heard Barnes talking shit about you, calling you a pussy, and saying you was gonna quit. So I went to check on you. You looked like you had heat exhaustion."

"You revived me."

"And then you smiled and thanked me. You got a really nice smile, Leo."

"Thanks."

"Everybody said you wouldn't make it a week. You know—they called you a hippie college kid. Your dad's a rich lawyer. I gotta admit—I thought you'd quit. But you didn't."

"Thanks to you."

"I started sitting with you at lunch every day. I really liked eating lunch with you…just talking to you. You're funny. You made me laugh."

"I think I have a good sense of humor."

"And you actually listened to me."

"That's because I liked listening to you. You're interesting."

"I liked listening to you, too. Then I realized you…you are different…"

No woman has ever told me this before—it makes me feel special.

"All morning I'd just watch the clock—counting down the minutes till I could eat lunch with you," she reveals.

"I looked forward to eating lunch with you too."

"And then one day I realized…" she stops. With a big grin, she declares, "Leo, you got a sexy body."

"You really think I have a sexy body?"

"Uh-huh."

This is music to my ears. "I've always wanted to be sexy. You know—like Steve McQueen."

"You look like…like a thoroughbred racehorse. You got fine bones. A broad chest. Long legs. Lean haunches."

"Lean haunches?"

"You know—a sexy butt."

I laugh. "You're the first woman who's ever told me that."

"Your body turns me on."

I love hearing her say that my body turns her on.

"I shouldn't be telling you this. I'll give you a big head."

"You're giving me a big boner," I wisecrack.

She laughs. "And you got beautiful hands."

Looking at them curiously, I reply, "I've never thought of my hands as beautiful."

"They are. I imagined them feeling my body one night…" She stops talking in the middle of her sentence.

I'm listening intently now. "What?"

"I shouldn't tell you this."

"Why not?"

"Cuz it's something good girls don't do."

"Tell me."

She hesitates…

"C'mon. Don't leave me hanging. I wanna know you intimately. Hear your innermost secrets."

"Okay, you asked for it."

She stops walking and faces me. Looking guilelessly into my eyes, she tells me, "One night—I remember it was the Fourth of July. Mama took the kids to see the fireworks at Emerald Lake. I stayed home alone and went to bed early but couldn't fall asleep. I was really horny…and I pictured you kissing me…and feeling me up…and then I…I fingered myself while I fantasized you was screwing me…and I had a super powerful orgasm…"

Snickering, she says, "I had my own fireworks. And then the rest of the summer, whenever I fingered myself, I just fantasized about me and you having sex…"

My heart is fluttering…

"And then I started dreaming about going to the ocean with you…and I realized you was gonna go away and I'd never see you again…and I wanted to screw you so bad for real—not fantasy."

I feel this pang in my heart and look out at the ocean…

"That's why I picked you. What…what's the matter?"

I'm taken aback by her honesty. "Nothing."

"Did I say something wrong?"

"No." I turn and quickly smile at her.

"Yes, I did. I shouldn't've told you I like to finger myself. You think I'm bad, don't you?"

"No, absolutely not."

"Yes, you do."

Clutching my heart, I say, "You…you pierced my heart, Lily. You know—like the song 'Cupid' by Sam Cooke. You just shot an arrow straight into my heart." I sing the first verse of the song to her.

She laughs, relieved.

"I love the thought of you masturbating to me. It makes me feel so…so incredibly sexy." Her honesty makes me feel like I can be honest with her, and I confide, "Lily, the truth is I, uh…I fantasized about screwing you…

"And I beat off to you. After you told me you wouldn't mind posing like that woman on my press, I beat off to the image of you doing it…"

She smiles. She likes it.

I smile back because she likes it.

"So you don't think it's a sin? Our preacher says it's a sin. Cuz the Bible says it's fornication," she says.

"No. I mean I did when I first started doing it. But not anymore. I figure God couldn't care less if we pleasure ourselves."

"Me too. I figure if it feels good and I ain't hurting anybody, do it. So…how often do you do it?"

"I beat off when I don't have a girlfriend and get horny. Usually to a nude centerfold."

"Which one? *Playboy*?"

"Yeah. I've beaten off to *Playboy*. But, actually, I prefer *Penthouse*. It's more explicit. It shows pubic hair. I really like this one *Penthouse* Pet. Karen Sather. She has red pubic hair like you."

"My brother, Ray, calls them skin magazines. He likes *Hustler*."

Laughing derogatorily, I reply, "*Hustler*—it's really explicit. I think the women look hard. I think the *Penthouse* Pets are the most erotic."

"How so?"

"Because they look real to me. You know—like the girl next door."

She scoffs, "Real? Them *Penthouse* Pets ain't real. They ain't the girl next door posing naked for you. They're models doing it for the money."

"I know. But I fantasize that they're doing it for me."

"You wanna know what's real?"

"What?"

"Me—I'm real. I ain't the girl next door. I'm the girl from the poor side of town taking my clothes off for you for free."

"You are."

"You know why?"

"Why?"

"Cuz I love getting naked for you. I love to show you my body. You should be beating off to me."

"I should."

"I'm as sexy as them *Penthouse* Pets."

"Sexier. But I don't have any nude pictures of you."

"Want me to pose naked for you?"

"I'd love it if you posed nude for me."

"You got a Polaroid camera?"

"Huh-uh."

"You don't wanna use an Instamatic."

"Why not?"

"I used to be a cutter at Quick-Prints where they process film. I cut prints. It's amazing how many people take dirty pictures and send in the film to have prints made. They take dirty pictures of everything—and I mean everything. Management confiscates them. They have thousands of dirty pictures in trash containers. They look at them at office parties."

"That's not right."

"That's why you need a Polaroid. If you get a Polaroid, I'll pose naked for you."

I wonder how I can get my hands on a Polaroid camera. Then I remember that I'd love to draw her nude. "You know what I'd really love to do?"

"What?"

"Draw you nude. Your body is aesthetically perfect. I'm inspired by it. I wanna immortalize you for posterity."

Smiling provocatively, she replies, "I'd like that. I told you I can be dirty. I mean really dirty. I love to be dirty. It turns me on. You think of dirty things for me to do, and I'll do them for you…"

Dirty sexual fantasies pop into my brain. Snickering, I tell her, "I hafta warn you. I have a really dirty mind. I'm erotically creative."

Her eyes brighten in anticipation. "Good. I'll go crazy on you."

"Like the song?"

"Like the song."

She puts her sunglasses back on. "C'mon, let's go home."

On the way back to the car, I marvel that she just touched my heart like no other woman has. I imagine taking nude pictures of her, and drawing her nude, and her doing my sexual fantasies and going crazy on me. But how could we do this if we kiss and say goodbye?

As we pull out of the parking lot, she asks, "So…what about you? What made you take me here?"

Smiling fondly, I answer, "From the moment I first laid eyes on you, I've believed you're the sexist woman I've ever met. It's not just the way you look. It's the way you are. You…you personify sexy.

"But it's more than that. Ultimately, you have this wild spirit. I see it in your eyes. It drives me wild, and I can't resist you."

Glancing at me through her red, heart-shaped sunglasses, she flashes me her sexy smile. Then she steps on the gas and zooms north up the highway. Taking off her cowgirl hat, she lets the wind blow through her hair.

I gaze at her in wonder with her long, red hair streaming behind her—and I feel so happy…

In Kill Devil Hills, we stop at the Fresh Seafood store, and I buy another yellowfin tuna steak. She buys more shrimp. The proprietor tells us about a great carryout seafood diner around the corner.

At the bakery next door, Lily buys a loaf of garlic bread. I buy a banana cream pie that was just baked today. Lily says she won't eat any of it because it's too fattening.

On the way back to the motel, I remember that I need to buy some condoms.

"Hey, Lily. I need to stop at a drugstore."

"What for?"

"I need to buy some condoms."

"Don't worry about it. I had my tubes tied after Rachel."

The thought occurs to me that she could be lying, but then I realize that she has always told me the truth, so I believe her.

At the motel we change into our bathing suits. Lily makes cocktails, which we take to the beach. Sitting in the sand at the water's edge, we sip our drinks and talk as the waves wash over our legs. Between the sun and the surf and the ocean breeze and the alcohol, I feel a happy buzz.

"Ya know, Lily, life doesn't get any better than this."

She smiles, nodding.

At dinnertime we go back to our room and turn on the radio in the kitchen. She fixes fried shrimp, home fries, and fried green tomatoes. I grill my yellowfin tuna.

After smoking half a joint to whet our appetites, we eat on the balcony. Her fried shrimp is delicious. I think my tuna steak is cooked perfectly; she thinks it's too rare inside.

Basking in the setting sun, we have another round of cocktails, which causes me to let down my guard. Feeling like I can confide my fears to her, I ask, "Wanna know why I don't ordinarily drink?"

"Yeah. Why?"

"Cuz I'm afraid my old man has a drinking problem."

"Oh..." she says taken aback. "You sure?"

"Yeah. He can't control his drinking any more. He's bombed pretty much all weekend now, and I found a half-empty bottle of vodka stashed in a tree in our back yard that he nips on when he grills."

Wincing, she replies, "Donny used to hide them from me in his toolbox."

"So...that's why I don't drink. I'm afraid alcoholism is in my genes, and I'll become an alcoholic. I don't wanna hafta go to AA meetings for the rest of my life. That'd be a real drag."

She nods with a wry smile.

"So...uh...now that I've told you about my dad, why don't you tell me about your dad?"

"Tell you what?"

"Like what happened?"

"I—I don't wanna talk about it."

"Why not?"

She turns her head away. "I just don't want to."

"I confided in you about my dad. I don't understand why you won't confide in me about your dad."

"All I can say is I really love him. He was a wonderful dad. And now he's in a coma at a nursing home. He's a vegetable..."

I see and hear the intense pain in her eyes and voice. "So how did it happen?" I ask quietly.

"I can't talk about it, Leo."

"Why not?"

"I just can't."

She's adamant, so I back off. I figure it's not worth getting in an argument and spoiling our romantic night. Since this is the second time she has refused to talk about her dad, I decide that I won't ask her about him again.

Trying to placate me, she says, "We're on vacation. Let's not talk about sad things here. Let's just talk about happy things."

"That's fine with me."

We smoke the other half of the joint.

"Speaking of happy things, I just remembered the banana cream pie. You sure you don't want a piece?" I ask.

"I'm sure."

I go inside to the kitchenette, cut myself a huge piece of pie, and take it outside on the balcony. While I savor each bite of the smooth, creamy banana-flavored pie, I notice that Lily can't take her eyes off it—she's practically drooling.

"Oh my God, Leo—that looks so good."

"It is. It's really fresh. You got the munchies. Have a bite." I extend to her a bite on my fork.

She can't resist.

After feeding her several bites, I notice some meringue on her mouth. Setting my fork down, I wipe it off her lips with my index finger; then hold my finger in front of her lips.

She licks the meringue off my finger, which makes me tingle all over.

Some meringue remains on her lips. "I missed some."

Leaning toward me, she puckers her lips. "Lick it off…"

Leaning toward her, I stick my tongue out and lick the meringue off her lips. Her lips feel so soft and plump. She sticks her tongue out and plays with my tongue. It sends a thrill through my body—straight to my cock.

The next thing I know, we're standing on the balcony—French kissing. Our tongues entwine…

Aroused, we go inside where we can get naked. She unfastens the clasp on her bikini halter and unties the ties around her neck; then lets her halter fall to the floor.

Stepping back, I admire her breasts…

Her eyes gleaming, she asks, "You like my tits?"

"Yeah. I love to just look at them. I'm very visual. Aesthetically speaking, they're shaped perfectly. And I love their beautiful ivory color. And I really love your large, prominent nipples. And their lovely rose color."

Looking at her breasts lovingly, she replies, "I think they're sexy."

"They're more than sexy. They're erotic. Smile—I wanna take a picture of you in my eidetic memory."

She gives me her daring smile.

Concentrating momentarily, I take a picture of her in my mind.

"Got it."

"Fooled Around and Fell in Love" by Elvin Bishop is playing on the radio. She starts dancing to the beat of the music.

I watch her, entranced...

She dances into my arms, I whip off my shirt, and we embrace. Thrusting her breasts into me, she rubs them back and forth against my chest.

I cup her breasts in my hands. "I love how they feel soft and light yet firm and heavy. It's a paradox."

I fondle her breasts, kissing them gently. "Hey, I just thought of something dirty to do."

Taking her by the hand, I lead her into the kitchenette. The banana cream pie is on the kitchen counter. Scooping fingers full of filling, I say, "Let's eat each other for dessert."

"That sounds like fun."

I spread filling on her nipples.

She dances around the kitchenette like a stripper wearing pasties.

"Come here. I wanna lick it off."

She shimmies up to me.

I lick the banana cream off her nipples...

"Mmm..." she moans. "Suck my nipples, Leo..."

When she is very aroused, she pulls down her bikini bottom. Thrusting her hips forward, she asks mockingly, "You like my pussy? Aesthetically speaking?"

"I do. It's striking in an exotic way. Smile..."

She smiles salaciously...

I take another picture of her in my mind.

Sticking my finger in the pie filling, I dab it on her clitoris—then lick it off. "Oh, man, Lily—you taste delicious..."

She yanks down my cutoff shorts and underpants and smears banana cream pie on my hard-on and licks it off...

Moving into the bedroom, we turn on the nightstand light so we can see each other's bodies. Lily climbs onto the bed on her hands and knees, presenting her shapely, ivory rump. Looking over shoulder at me, she says, "Let's screw like Dakota and Appaloosa."

While we do it "horsey-style," my hand is free to stimulate her clitoris, which makes her climax quickly, which makes me come.

Lying in each other's arms afterwards, I remark, "Lily, you come easily."

"I'm lucky. I read in *Cosmo* it's hard for some women to have an orgasm. Not me. Stimulate my clit and I come. I'm still horny, Leo. I think it's that pot."

"Some people say it's an aphrodisiac."

"Let's do it again…"

We screw again with her on top facing me. While we do it, she strokes herself to a climax. Watching her make herself come is so exciting it makes me come. Afterward, she rests her head on my chest. I venture to say, "Lily, I like the way you touched your clitoris. I find that extremely erotic."

"I figure God wouldn't've made it feel so good if he didn't want me to touch it."

Feeling sticky from the banana cream pie on our bodies, we decide to shower together.

"Hey, Leo, I got an idea. Let's take a bubble bath."

"You brought bubble bath?"

"Yep."

"Good idea." I mimic Do Ho singing "Tiny Bubbles."

While I fill the bathtub, she pours bubble bath under the spout. Bubbles foam. We sit down in the bathtub facing each other with her in the front of the tub and me in the back. We play with the bubbles—blow them in each other's faces.

After a while, she becomes uncomfortable sitting in the tub facing me—she can't lean backwards because of the spout. Turning around with her back toward me, she leans back in my lap with her head on my chest. Reclining against the back of the tub, I wrap my arms around her with my hands in her lap. She lets the tub fill almost to the top; then turns the faucet off with her foot. We just soak. I luxuriate in the feel of her soft skin against mine and the scent of her hair.

Massaging shampoo deeply into her scalp, I wash her hair. My fingers are entwined in her long red stresses, dripping with lather. Her eyes closed, she sighs with pleasure. Trading places, she washes my hair. Her long fingernails feel wonderful.

Lathering soap on our washcloths, we wash each other. She giggles and squirms when I wash her toes, saying it tickles.

After rinsing in the shower, we climb out of the tub and dry each other. She wraps her damp hair in a towel. The hot bath and shower have made me sleepy. Yawning, I ask, "You ready to go to sleep?"

"Huh-uh. I'll sleep when I go home. Let's do it again."

She tells me she's going to give me a full-body massage. Grabbing her bottle of skin lotion, she leads me into the bedroom and has me lie down on my stomach on the bed. Straddling me on her knees, she squirts lotion in the palms of her hands and proceeds to rub and knead the muscles on my backside from my neck to my feet. "So how does that feel?"

"Mmm...soothing."

She has me roll over onto my back. Starting at my shoulders, she works her way downward over my chest and stomach. Squirting lotion on my limp penis, she artfully strokes it until I'm fully erect again. As the exquisitely pleasurable sensations intensify toward climax, I moan in ecstasy...

"Don't stop, Lily...please don't stop..."

I have a tremendous orgasm...

"Man alive, Lily...you know exactly where my pleasure spot is."

Smiling, she brags, "I got magic fingers."

I remind her that one good deed deserves another and make her lie down on her stomach. Kneeling on the bed straddling the back of her thighs, I slather lotion on her body and massage it into her ivory skin. Starting at her neck and shoulders, I work my way down her back, over her buttocks, and down her legs to her ankles. Then she rolls over on her back, and I do her front side, paying special attention to her breasts. Slathering lotion between her legs, my magic fingers bring her to a climax again, and she loudly cries out my name and announces that she's coming.

Afterward, we lie awake, talking. "Leo, that's what I like about you. You know where my clit is. Poor Donny—he couldn't find it with a flashing neon sign. When he was drunk, I swear he was dumber than…than Peanut." She laughs, remembering.

"Who's Peanut?"

"A toy poodle we had. That dog was so dumb it fell asleep in the road and got run over by a garbage truck. Can you believe that? I mean how dumb can you get?"

"That's pretty dumb."

Staring absentmindedly, she says. "Boy, oh, boy…I'm kind of rambling…I…I think I'm really high…"

"No shit."

"You…you're really smart even though you don't know jack shit about anything useful."

"I know how to make you come—that's useful."

Grinning, she says, "That's what I mean—you're witty."

Sexually satiated, we start to drift off to sleep.

Before I go to sleep, I get up to take a leak. On my way back to bed, I hang the Do Not Disturb sign on the door and lock up. I want to sleep in tomorrow.

When I return to the bed, she turns off the light on the nightstand and pulls the covers up over us. I hold her in my arms, and she lays her head on my chest, sighing with contentment.

We kiss.

"'Night, Leo."

"'Night, Lily," I whisper in her ear and close my eyes—

Suddenly, the telephone rings and startles the hell out of me. At this time of the night, I figure it must be Lily's mom calling again. I hope it's not an emergency. Maybe Sarah had another nightmare.

Lily answers it. Handing me the phone, she says, "It's for you."

"For me?"

"Yeah. He asked for Mr. Locke."

"Hello?" I ask apprehensively.

"Hello, Mr. Locke. This is the night manager. Sorry to disturb you at this late hour, but we got a complaint from the man staying in the room next to you. He says your wife is, uh… too loud when you have sex. She keeps waking his wife up."

"Oh…sorry…we're on our honeymoon."

"I understand. But other people are trying to sleep."

"Okay."

I burst out laughing and hand the phone to her.

She hangs up. "What's so funny?"

"Uh…it was the night manager. He'd appreciate it if you'd come quieter."

"What?"

"The guy next door complained you're making too much noise. You're waking his wife up."

Embarrassed, she stammers, "I…I can't help it."

"It's okay. I told him we're on our honeymoon. That placated him."

Smiling sheepishly, she says, "I just go wild when I come."

"Trust me. It's not a problem. Go to sleep." I pat her on the butt.

"I can't."

"I wouldn't lose any sleep over it. She's probably just envious."

"Is something wrong with me? Am I oversexed?"

"There's nothing wrong with you. Believe me, you can't be oversexed."

"Leo, am I too loud when I come?"

"Nope. You can never be too loud when you come."

"You sure?"

"Yep. Women who are quiet comers ain't no fun in bed."

CHAPTER FIFTEEN

I hear an alarm buzzing.

For a moment I'm disoriented. Then I realize I'm lying in bed with Lily Wyatt in a motel room in Kill Devil Hills, North Carolina. It's almost surreal. The room is dark—except for the dim light emanating from the face of the clock radio, which continues to buzz obnoxiously.

Lily fumbles around with the clock radio until she succeeds in shutting off the alarm. I roll over and go back to sleep.

I feel her kissing my lips and hear her sensual voice whisper in my ear, "Leo…wake up…"

Without opening my eyes, I mutter, "Go back to sleep, Lily."

"Good morning, Leo. Time to get up," she says more insistently.

I open my eyes—see her face hovering over me. "What…what time is it?"

Not answering, she turns on the light on the nightstand.

Squinting, I check the time. "Lily, it's four thirty. It's not morning. It's the middle of the night."

"Get dressed." She's already in her bikini.

"What…what for?"

"I wanna go to the National Seashore."

"Right now?"

"Yeah."

"Are you kidding? That's a long ways away."

"That's why we gotta go right now. We gotta get there before dawn."

"Why?"

"I wanna watch the sun rise over the ocean. Then I wanna screw on the beach. It's my dream."

I point out to her, "I thought your dream was to find the wild horses."

"It is. This is my other dream."

"How many dreams do you got?"

"That's for me to know and you to find out. C'mon. Let's go."

"Lily, listen to me. I probably won't be able to get it up. My peter's petered out. It needs eight hours sleep to revive."

She goads me, "C'mon, Leo—I thought you was a stud. Like Appaloosa you said."

"I got an idea. Why don't we go back to sleep, then later open the curtains and do it right here in bed with a view of the ocean?"

"Cuz I wanna screw out in nature. You know—with the waves…and the seagulls…and the sun coming up. That really turns me on."

To appease her, I say, "That sounds cool. Let's do it at sunset."

"That ain't the same. The sun won't be rising over the ocean."

"Lily, I just wanna sleep in today." I pull the covers over my eyes to block out the light.

"Leo, quit wasting time." She rips the covers off the bed. "Get up!" she orders.

Lying uncovered and naked, I mutter, "Don't you ever sleep?"

"Every minute I sleep is a minute I ain't on vacation. Now get your ass out of bed. I'm a bitch in heat."

Suddenly, she grabs ahold of my cock and pulls me out of bed like a dog on a leash.

"Jesus Christ, Lily—you'll break it off!"

She releases me; then tosses my swim trunks to me. "I'll drive. You can sleep in the car. When I come back, you better be dressed and ready to go," she warns as she heads for the kitchenette.

I traipse into the bathroom and take a leak. I look in the mirror—

I look like hell. And I'm hungry…

"Hurry up," she hollers.

"I need to shower and shave and eat breakfast," I holler back.

"We ain't got time!"

I skip getting cleaned up and breakfast; put on my swim trunks, T-shirt, and flip-flops as fast as I can.

Holding her purse, camera, and beach blanket, she waits impatiently on me.

I grumble, "This…this is crazy…"

"C'mon, Leo. We ain't got all day."

"I'm on vacation. I just wanted to sleep in today," I complain.

"Don't be a spoilsport."

"Lily, I'm not a morning person. I'm more of a night owl."

"You'll be glad you went when we get there."

"Right," I say sardonically.

Lily speeds south down Highway 12 toward the National Seashore. There's hardly any traffic at this hour. Bleary-eyed, I try to sleep in the car, but it's too noisy and windy with the top down. We come to the sign on Bodie Island that says Cape Hatteras National Seashore. The dark sky is beginning to lighten in the east.

We reach the bridge at Oregon Inlet. As she flies across it toward Pea Island, I check the speedometer—she's doing almost eighty. I look over the railing—see dim boat lights flickering in the darkness far down below. I have this vision—a tire blowing, the car flipping over the guardrail, plunging into the black sea. Shuddering, I shout, "SLOW DOWN, LILY."

"I THINK WE'RE GONNA MAKE IT, LEO," she shouts back.

"NOT IF WE END UP IN DAVY JONES' LOCKER!"

As usual, she laughs.

Driving down the National Seashore, we don't see any cars—it's like we've entered an uninhabited world. Half way to Rodanthe we come to an isolated beachside rest area. She pulls in and parks in the empty lot. Grabbing her stuff, she jumps out of the car and heads for the beach with me following her. A few stars are still visible in the dim, pre-dawn light. Silently, we walk along a winding path through the beach grass across the sand dunes. The sound of waves crashing on the shore grows louder and louder. As we crest the last sand dune, silver breakers are tumbling on a desolate sand beach that stretches north and south as far as the eye can see. A gentle sea breeze blows through my hair. Screeching sea gulls are flying above the whitecaps and skipping along the shore. There is no sign of human life.

On the dry, soft sand near the water's edge, she spreads the blanket, and we sit down. Staring silently across the dark gray sea, I wait for the sun to rise…

The eastern sky becomes deep purple…then maroon…

Streaks of crimson light appear in the heavens…

Cirrus clouds brighten to a pastel pink…

On the horizon, a crescent-shaped sliver of red rises above the water. Soon, it becomes a fiery, blood-red ball; then orange; then yellow. A kaleidoscopic fan of orange and golden light shines across the sea, glittering on the water…

We gaze wonderstruck…

She whispers, "Ain't it beautiful?"

"It's truly magnificent," I whisper back.

As the sun rises higher and higher, the sky lightens to lavender blue.

"You know, Lily, cosmically speaking, this is how this beach has looked for thousands, maybe even millions of sunrises."

"And me and you are the only two people here on Earth to see it. Hey, I almost forgot—take my picture." Handing me her camera, she jumps up and runs down to the water's edge; then faces the camera and poses.

I stand up and frame the picture with the sun rising over the ocean behind her. "One…two…three…smile."

She smiles.

Click—I take the picture.

"Did you get the sun rising behind me?"

"Yeah. I don't know how it's gonna turn out with the sun behind you, but I got it."

Sitting back down on the blanket, I say, "I hafta admit, Lily, I'm glad you drug my ass out of bed. It was worth it."

She smiles smugly.

Smiling back, I ask, "So did I make your dream come true?"

She sits down close beside me; then takes her camera and puts it in her purse. Looking at me seductively, she replies, "Nope. We still got one more thing to do."

She looks around to make sure we're alone; then slips out of her bikini. As I peel off my shirt, she unties the drawstring on my swimsuit and tugs it off me.

I'm as limp as a wet noodle. Grinning sheepishly, I say, "You wore it out last night."

She looks at it like a doctor examining a patient's broken finger. "Don't worry. I can fix this in no time."

She curls up on her side in between my legs and lays her head on the inside of my thigh. Speaking to it like she's training a seal, she coaxes, "Up, up…"

Remarkably, it stands right up.

"Good boy," she praises it. "See—I fixed it. I got it up without even touching it," she brags.

"Damn…"

Fascinated, she studies it. "You know what it looks like? A German soldier standing at attention. Look—it has a German helmet. Achtung!"

It stands to attention.

She wriggles onto her back, and I straddle her waist on my knees. While she squeezes her breasts together with her hands, I slide my cock up and down the valley between them; then rub her nipples with it.

Reaching behind me, I rub her clitoris lightly.

With a fiendish snicker, she grips my cock in one hand and lightly flicks her tongue against the pleasure spot…

Oh my God—it feels so good…

Gazing into each other's eyes, we respond to each other exclusively by touch, trying to make the other climax first.

As I rub faster and harder, she flicks faster and harder…

She starts talking dirty to me, which immediately causes me to climax. I talk dirty back, which immediately causes her to climax.

We collapse into each other's arms, panting.

"Mmm...it tastes salty—like the ocean," she remarks, licking her lips.

"How would you know? You won't go in the water."

"I know. I've tasted it in my imagination."

Coming down from my sex high, my eyes refocus on the seashore, and I smell the briny air and feel the balmy breeze. Listening to the waves crashing rhythmically on the shore, I fall asleep...

Lily nudges me awake. Leaning over my face, she gives me a gentle kiss. "We better get dressed. I heard two cars go by."

"Now did I make your dream come true?"

"Uh-huh. Well, almost. We didn't actually screw."

"That's a technicality. We had sex on the National Seashore at sunrise."

"I guess I'll take a raincheck."

We get dressed and stroll back to the car. It's almost eight o'clock. The sun is fairly high up over the ocean, and it's starting to get hot.

"So now what do you wanna do?" I ask.

"Climb Jockey Ridge."

"Let's do it."

At Nag's Head we stop at a restaurant named Sea Shack and buy breakfast to go. We both get the Seafood Brunch Bake, which is made of croissants, shrimp, crab, eggs, bacon, and cheese, a side order of banana fritters to share, and lemonades. We savor them at a picnic table in Jockey's Ridge State Park. The ridge of sand dunes looks like a scene out of the movie, *Lawrence of Arabia*. There is no vegetation, just asymmetrical, wind-sculpted mountains of sand. I take a picture of Lily standing in front of them.

Climbing one step and sliding back a half a step, we scale the tallest sand dune. Our efforts are rewarded by spectacular views of both the ocean and the sound at the summit. She snaps several pictures.

On a smaller dune, a guy is giving a hang-gliding lesson.

"Leo, I wanna do that. I dream of flying."

We trek over there. The instructor is a young man named Zach. He has long hair and a beard and seems like a free spirit. He's instructing two teenage boys, who look like brothers; their lesson is ending. Zach has an assistant who photographed the boys' flights. The boys are buying the photographs.

We inquire about lessons. Zach tells us it costs a hundred dollars per person. We decide it's too expensive.

Eyeing Lily in her bikini, he offers, "I'll give you a free lesson if you model for me."

"Model?" she asks.

"My photographer will photograph you hang gliding. I'll use the photos in my advertising."

"What's a free lesson?"

"Three flights."

"Three flights for me and him," she counters, pointing at me.

"Lady, you got a deal."

She grins at me.

"Aren't you a wheeler-dealer? Thanks," I tell her.

The two boys stick around to watch.

Zach instructs us on how to steer, fly fast and slow, and fix our eyes on a target; then demonstrates techniques for launching, flying, and landing.

In her red, heart-shaped sunglasses and helmet, Lily poses clipped into the hang glider on top of the dune.

"She even looks sexy in a hang glider," I observe.

"Yeah, and sex sells," Zach replies.

He holds the hang glider steady and acts like he's instructing her while the photographer shoots pictures of them. Then she runs off the ridge into a flight. The photographer runs below shooting pictures of her flying. Since she's light, she glides about ten feet off the ground for a good distance and lands deftly on her feet.

It's my turn. Standing at the top of the dune strapped into the glider, I firmly grip the control bar below the sail. A strong wind is blowing from the sea. Sprinting barefoot down the steep face of the dune, the wind lifts my feet off the ground with my body suspended horizontally in the harness—I'm flying. It's quite exhilarating. Since I'm heavy, I fly only about five feet off the ground for a short distance; then land on my knees in the soft sand.

On her last flight, Lily hands her camera to me and asks me to photograph it. I take a picture of her posing in her launch position. Catching a big gust of wind, she launches and soars about fifteen feet high for a long distance. I run along snapping pictures of her. At the last second, she veers sideways and crash-lands in the sand. The crash forces her bikini halter to slip up around her neck— exposing her breasts. She fixes her halter as fast as she can.

Trying not to laugh, Zach tells her, "That's never happened before."

Grinning sheepishly, she replies, "You better warn women in your ad not to wear bikinis."

"A disclaimer," I joke.

Looking apprehensively at the photographer, Lily asks, "Did you take a picture of that?"

"No. Don't worry. I didn't take any pictures of you crashing," he assures her.

"I did. I captured it on film for posterity," I tease.

The two boys are snickering because they got an eyeful.

I do my last flight. Catching on, I fly pretty high and far and actually land on my feet. Lily takes pictures of me.

Afterwards, Zach takes Lily's name and address and tells her he'll send her prints of her pictures for free.

On the walk back to the car, she tells me, "Leo, I'm really glad you talked me into coming here. I got to hang glide. It was really fun."

"It was. That's what it feels like to fly. And you got your first professional modeling job."

"Yeah. It's like he paid me two hundred dollars."

"Ya know, you probably could be a professional model. You certainly got the looks. You should send your picture to a model agency. You could be the next Cheryl Tiegs."

"Who's she?"

"A supermodel. She made the cover of last year's *Sports Illustrated* Swimsuit Issue. I could be your agent. We'll get rich." I'm only half-kidding.

She laughs.

"That was hilarious when your top came off. Your bikini malfunctioned," I observe.

"They ain't designed for hang gliding. Did those boys see me?"

"I'm afraid so. They were snickering."

"Oh, dear."

"Don't worry. You made their day. I guarantee it."

We go back to the motel. After loading last night's dirty dishes in the dishwasher and cleaning up the banana cream pie on the kitchen floor, we decide to spend our last afternoon at the beach. We pack peanut butter and jelly sandwiches in the cooler and go sit on our beach blanket. While Lily happily reads her magazine, I eat my sandwich feeling contented.

A dad and mom spread out a blanket on the sand beside us with their little boy and girl. The dad plays with the little boy in the small waves close to shore. Holding him by his arms, he suspends him in the water. The little girl and her mom are playing with a bucket and shovel in the sand at the water's edge.

Watching them, Lily smiles and remarks, "I'd love to take my kids here someday…"

I imagine Lily making sandcastles with her girls on the beach; Sean and I body surfing and boogie boarding in the surf. We'd have a blast…

Don't even think of getting involved with her kids.

"You should. I remember my folks bringing me here when I was a kid. I loved it. I took Reese along and we body surfed all day. Hey, you wanna go for a walk down the beach?" I ask, changing the subject.

"Okay," she replies coolly. I sense she's disappointed because I didn't show any interest in bringing her kids here.

She grabs her camera, and we meander down the beach. She stops and examines all the dead animals on the shore that the tide has washed up—she's fascinated with them. She takes pictures of a horseshoe crab and a big sea turtle to show to Sarah. Spotting a dead shark, she runs over and takes its picture.

"See, Leo—I told you there're sharks here."

"That shark couldn't eat you, Lily. It's only two feet long."

"It could take a bite out of you."

A fisherman is casting his line into the surf.

"Catch anything?" Lily asks.

He proudly shows her a mackerel that he caught.

We continue strolling side by side down the shore. Feeling affectionate, I take hold of her hand.

She pulls it away. "Don't, Leo."

I look at her in a questioning manner.

"I don't wanna hold your hand."

"Why not?"

"I don't want your love. I came here just to have fun. All I want from you is sex. Pleasure. Orgasms."

"Sorry...I...I was just trying to be romantic. I thought women like romance."

She sees that she has hurt my feelings. With a sigh, she says, "Leo, I don't wanna fall in love with you. Tomorrow we're gonna kiss and say goodbye, remember?"

Nodding grudgingly, I sigh...

We turn around and walk back to our blanket in silence. She resumes reading her magazine. I sit down and ponder what she said.

Fun...pleasure...orgasms...

Okay. If that's the way you want it...

"C'mon, Hard Slick. Let's me and you go have some fun."

I have a blast boogie boarding by myself, but it would be even more fun doing it with Lily. Catching a good wave, I ride it all the way up the beach close to her.

"You're really missing out on some fun," I coax.

She doesn't look up from her magazine.

"You said you wanted to have fun," I remind her.

She's ignoring me.

"You can lead a horse to water, but you can't make it drink," I say to myself loud enough for her to hear.

"I heard that."

"Lily, come boogie board with me. This is your last chance. We're leaving tomorrow."

"If God wanted me to swim in the ocean, He would've made me a mermaid."

Picturing the red-headed sea creature, I reply, "That's a sight I'd love to see."

Suddenly, it occurs to me that I haven't taken my army raft in the ocean. I don't want to have brought it here for nothing, so I get it and the wood paddle out of the boot of the car. Kneeling in the sand beside our blanket, I blow up the raft. It takes twenty minutes to blow up by mouth. When I finish, I'm light-headed.

Eyeing my army raft curiously, Lily asks, "So where'd you get that?"

"At an army surplus store. You wanna float with me?"

"Nope."

"Lily, no shark's gonna get you in this raft."

"A Great White Shark got that kid on a raft in *Jaws*."

"That's just a movie. It's not real. It's fiction."

"It could happen."

"You could get struck by lightning but that doesn't stop you from going outside in a thunderstorm."

"Yes, it does. I go inside in a storm."

I can see there is no convincing her. Exasperated, I exhale noisily.

Holding a rope tied to a steel grommet on the front of the raft, I tow it out into the ocean, climb aboard, and paddle exuberantly around in the breakers. Eventually, I get bored floating by myself, so I paddle back to shore where Lily is sunbathing.

Trying to cajole her, I say, "I can't believe someone who's not afraid of horses is afraid of sharks."

"Horses don't eat you, Leo."

"Be rational, Lily. The chance of a shark attack is like one in a million. C'mon. Go for a ride with me. It's no fun riding by myself. Please…"

"I tell you what. I'll go for a ride with you in the pool. There ain't no chance of a shark attacking me in the pool."

I figure that's better than nothing. We move to the pool. Placing the raft in the water, I hold it against the gutter while she climbs aboard with her magazine and gets herself comfortably situated.

In a low voice, she says, "Leo, hand me my towel please. I don't like the way that guy's looking at me."

A middle-aged man reclining on a chaise lounge beside the pool is leering at Lily. He has a dark tan and is wearing a muscle T-shirt and a Speedo swimsuit.

I toss the beach towel to her, and she covers herself with it. I tell her, "I gotta go to the bathroom. Don't go anywhere. I'll be right back."

When I return, the man is gone. Lily is floating peacefully around the deep end, reading her magazine.

Sneaking onto the diving board, I shout "Bombs away!" and do a cannonball into the water right beside her.

She's drenched. Her sunglasses are dripping. She props them on top of her head. Glaring at me, she mutters, "You bastard. You got my magazine wet."

Grinning, I climb into the raft and recline beside her.

"You're like a big kid, Leo. I swear you're worse than Sean."

"Killjoy."

You want orgasms, Lily? I'll give you orgasms.

Slipping my hand under her towel, I slide it down inside the front of her bikini bottom. While we float innocuously around the pool, I rub her clitoris underneath her towel. Ladies are reading their books and magazines on chaise lounges. A pool maintenance guy is cleaning the pool filter.

Pretending like she's reading, she stares blankly at the page of her magazine, mouth half-open—trying to breathe quietly. Eyes half-closed, she reaches up and puts her sunglasses back on her face. Her hips are gyrating rhythmically underneath the towel—

All at once she lays her magazine in her lap. Quietly gasping, she clenches her teeth and locks her thighs together...

Her thighs relax and she sighs softly.

"Hey, lady, I checked under the hood. That's a well-lubricated machine you got there."

"Very funny."

"You said you wanted orgasms."

To cool off, I roll off the raft into the water and swim to the shallow end, where I stand in chest deep water. Lily climbs out of the raft and swims underwater to me. Surfacing, she wraps her arms around my neck and her legs around my waist. Her long, wavy red hair is slicked back behind her ears. She spits water in my face and grins at me with the devil in her eyes.

Man, is she sexy.

She fixes us Bloody Marys. Floating around the pool in my army raft, we sip our drinks and talk. I ask her what it was like growing up as a country girl on a horse farm in the foothills of the mountains in Kentucky. She tells me caring for horses was hard work. She and her brothers and sisters had to feed and water them twice a day three hundred and sixty-five days a year; they had to clean their stalls regularly. For a few years, her family had a riding stable, where she gave riding lessons and took people horseback riding on trails on their property. The horse farm was where she fell in love with horses.

She asks me what it was like growing up as a city boy. Nostalgically, I recount that I lived in a nice house on Mapledale Lane in Brinkerhoff throughout grade school. Brinkerhoff was the quintessential small-town neighborhood in the 1960s. There were lots of baby boomers my age to play with; we called ourselves the Mapledale Lane Gang. We hung out in our backyard in the summer and our finished basement in the winter. As young kids, we played games like hide-and-seek, spud, and kick-the-can. When we got older, we played kill-the-man-with-the-ball and capture the flag. Our neighbors tolerated kids traipsing through their backyards and hiding in their trees and window wells. I once hid my team's flag at the top of our next-door neighbor's TV antennae, and they didn't mind. In fifth grade, my friends and I got skateboards and skateboarded down Taylor Road, which was the steepest hill in Brinkerhoff.

Lily explains that she mostly played with her brothers and sisters because their neighbors' kids lived too far away. There was a pond on the farm, where they swam and fished in the summer and ice skated in the winter. Their main entertainment was breaking, training, and riding horses.

I point out that our bikes were our horses. We rode them to school, stores, parks, and the movie theater downtown. I could park my three-speed Schwinn Corvette without a lock in any of these places, and nobody would steal it. We knew roads based upon their hills, which were either hard to pump up or easy to coast down.

She tells me her folks sold the horse farm in Kentucky and bought their farm outside Mansfield when she started high school. From then on, they only had horses for recreational purposes.

I expound that as a result of my dad's successful law practice, we moved from Brinkerhoff to Woodland in the summer before I started junior high school. Unhappy about leaving my childhood friends, I protested vehemently, but it was to no avail. My dad informed me he was living his dream, and, as a kid, I was just along for the ride; when I grew up, I could live my own dream. That summer he joined the country club, and, from then on, I lived at the pool during the summers. At sixteen, I became a lifeguard and saved my money for a motorcycle—a Honda S90. The ninety cc engine freed me from pedaling. Simply rotate my right wrist on the throttle, and I had eight horsepower at my disposal. I drove my motorcycle everywhere—to work, school, Esposito's Pizza. On Saturday nights, I'd fill the gas tank and drive around town with Reese on the back—it got eighty miles to the gallon. We explored the old, gothic Ohio State Reformatory with its eerie stone towers and gables and the whorehouse on Main Street. Through the picture window, the prostitutes beckoned us to come inside, but we were too afraid. We traveled far out in the country to Mount Jeez and Pleasant Hill Lake and Mohican State Forest, where we rode the trails. I compare our cross-country motorcycle riding to her horseback riding. One Saturday we rode all the way to Gem Beach at Lake Erie, where we went swimming and played coin-operated games at the penny arcade.

Swim team at the country club was where I discovered girls. As soon as they saw my motorcycle, they'd beg me to take them for a ride. With their arms wrapped around my waist, they'd ride barefoot in their Speedo swimsuits. Reciprocating, they invited Reese and me to their dance parties, where I learned how to dance and make out.

Grinning, Lily says, except for a few crushes, she wasn't that interested in boys until she met Donny. He taught her how to kiss. She learned how to dance by watching the go-go dancers on *Upbeat* on TV and going to the Inferno dances at the Y.

We while away the afternoon happily reminiscing about our youth. Later, preparing to leave early in the morning, I deflate my army raft and load it in the boot of the car. I feel melancholy about leaving.

While Lily and I are getting cleaned up, we argue about dinner. Since it's our last night, I propose to take her out to eat at the Ocean Ranch Restaurant, so we can order seafood and not have any dishes to do on our last night. She reminds me she doesn't have a nice outfit to wear and doesn't want to spend the money going out to eat. Finally, we compromise by ordering carryout from the recommended seafood diner—the classic deep-fried seafood platter for two.

After smoking a joint, we sit on the balcony and stuff ourselves to the gills with deep-fried flounder, shrimp, bay scallops, and clam strips dipped in cocktail and tartar sauces; then watch the waves break on the beach…

"Leo, I have one more dream."

"What's that?"

With a wild gleam in her eye, she tells me, "I'll take my raincheck right now. I wanna watch the sun go down on the sound and do it in your car."

I chuckle.

"What's so funny?"

"Where do you get these ideas?"

"You gave me the idea this morning when you said let's do it at sunset. I have sexual fantasies too."

"I'd like to hear them. I'm curious about female sexuality."

"Not now. We ain't got time if we wanna get there before the sun goes down."

"Okay. I'm up for it. There's symmetry to it. We did it while the sun rose over the Atlantic Ocean this morning. We'll do it while the sun sets on Albemarle Sound."

We ride around the outskirts of Duck, searching for a secluded place to park with a view of the sound. Chancing upon a private lane, I spot a sign advertising the future site of a new condominium development. Turning onto the lane, we drive through a patch of uninhabited maritime forest into marshland. The road ends at an isolated cul-de-sac overlooking the sound. She parks the car at the water's edge. There is a gentle breeze, and the crickets are chirping melodiously.

We watch a golden ball of fire set on the distant mainland. The clouds are infinite shades of yellow, orange, red, turquois, blue and purple; the kaleidoscope of colors is blurrily reflected in the glassy water.

Lily's eyes are transfixed on the radiant vista.

"I'm not sure which is more beautiful—the sunrise or the sunset," I muse.

Smiling lasciviously, she wriggles out of the bottom of her bikini; I slip my swimsuit down around my ankles. Then she climbs over the gearshift and straddles me. She comes so loudly that she makes the nearby birds fly away.

Our lovemaking is interrupted by approaching headlights. While I scramble to pull my suit up, she climbs back into the driver's seat and casually drives away bottomless.

We drive around Duck, looking at the fabulous vacation homes and condos.

"Man, I'd like to stay here someday," I remark.

Gaping in awe at the homes, she declares, "This is where the rich people live."

When it gets too dark to continue exploring, we return to the motel. In the parking lot, she slips her bikini bottom back on. Still restless, we go for our last walk on the beach.

"Well, Lily, I'm sad our vacation is almost over."

"Just when we was starting to really have fun."

"Yeah. Did you get your money's worth?"

"Yeah, I guess so. I done everything I wanted to do except find the wild horses."

"Now you have a reason to come back."

"I wish we could stay longer. Try again."

"Yeah. Me too."

Before going to bed, we get ready to leave early tomorrow morning. We run the dishwasher, clean out the refrigerator, and take our showers tonight.

Lily needs a drink to forget about leaving tomorrow and fixes herself a Bloody Mary.

Instead of having a drink, I take the leftover banana cream pie out on the balcony and finish it off.

She joins me. "So what time do you wanna leave tomorrow?"

I want to get home by dark. I figure it'll take eleven to twelve hours to drive home. "Seven thirty."

"Leo, this is our last night together. Let's make it special."

Gazing at the shadowy whitecaps, I reply, "Hey, Lily, I got an idea. Let's sleep out here overlooking the ocean."

"Good idea." She polishes off her drink.

We lug the sleeper sofa out on the balcony and unfold the metal frame and thin mattress to make a bed. It's so warm all we need is a sheet for covers. Lying in bed with our arms wrapped around each other, we listen to the waves crashing on the shore and watch the moon rise over the sea—it's almost full. We kiss softly.

Lily drifts off to sleep.

I lie awake staring at the stars...

We're having so much fun I don't want to leave. It occurs to me that we could stay longer if I skipped orientation. I still have money left.

Orientation is not mandatory. It's optional.

But my old man will be unhappy if I skip it. And Reese is expecting me to go with him.

I don't care about them. All I care about is Lily. I just want to stay here with her.

I can't skip orientation. That would be getting off to a bad start. It would be foolish to skip it, and I don't want to be foolish. I have to go.

I sigh…

I never do what I want to do. I always do the sensible thing. This is the story of my life.

Resigning myself to leaving, I roll over and close my eyes…

Lily and I are wandering around an endless maze of sand dunes…

I see a herd of horses roaming across the swirling sand on the horizon.

It thrills me.

"Look, Lily! It's the wild horses. We found them."

Someone is shaking me. "Leo, wake up. It's raining."

Opening my eyes, I feel raindrops falling on my face.

Scrambling, Lily and I close the sleeper sofa and lug it back inside.

I remember I didn't put the top on my car. We throw on some clothes, dash outside, and put the top on.

Getting undressed again, we go back to bed. I don't tell Lily about my dream because I don't want to remind her that we failed to find the wild horses.

CHAPTER SIXTEEN

On Wednesday morning, I wake up at seven thirty. Lily is lying on her side facing me, sound asleep. I gaze fondly at her face…

Time to go.

I sigh. I feel so downhearted…

I don't want to leave you.

Softly stroking her tousled hair, I call her name louder and louder until she opens her eyes sleepily. "Time to get up."

We get up, go to the bathroom, and get dressed without saying a word. Before checking out, I step out on the balcony one last time. The sun is shining on the ocean. Fluffy, golden clouds are billowing across blue skies.

Lily joins me on the balcony.

"It looks like it's gonna be a beautiful day," I remark.

Glancing at the sky, she nods. Then she shows me the menu for the motel restaurant. "Look, Leo. They got toasted pecan rolls. I love toasted pecan rolls. Let's eat here before we go."

Just the thought of a toasted pecan roll makes my mouth water. "Sounds good to me."

We load our bags into the boot; then walk to the motel restaurant. Sitting at a table overlooking the beach, we order coffee and toasted pecan rolls.

Gazing wistfully at the surf, I tell her, "I don't wanna leave. It's a perfect day to go to the beach."

"So let's go to the beach," she proposes with a twinkle in her eye.

"It's tempting…"

"You said classes don't start till Monday."

"I have orientation on Friday."

"Do you hafta go?"

"No. The materials said it's not mandatory."

"Skip it," she dares me.

"But they said, 'Attendance is strongly recommended.' "

"Well, I strongly recommend you skip it. You don't need oriented. You need laid. That'll get you more ready for law school than orientation. It's hard to study when you're horny—I know."

Laughing, I shake my head and say, "You are a brazen hussy."

"Whatever that means—you love it."

"I do," I admit.

Our waitress brings us our toasted pecan rolls and coffee. Lily takes a bite of hers. "Mmm…there ain't nothing better than a toasted pecan roll."

I spread butter on the hot roll and watch it melt; then take a bite. It's delicious—so sweet and buttery and crunchy and sticky. Caramel and butter run down my chin. Wiping my mouth with my napkin, I quip, "I love sticky buns in the morning."

She laughs at my double entendre. Eyeing me, she sensually licks some caramel off her finger.

I can see her wheels turning…

"Ya know, Leo, if you skip it, we can stay till Sunday. Four more nights."

I ponder getting up early and driving back on Sunday. If we left at 6:00 a.m., I'd get home around suppertime and could drive to Toledo after supper; but then I realize I'd be letting Reese and my old man down, and I hate to disappoint them…

Smiling seductively, she says, "I bet you could think of more dirty things for me to do."

"I bet you're right. I'd like to go skinny-dipping with you in the sea."

"I ain't going skinny-dipping in the ocean. But I'd go in the pool tonight."

I imagine screwing in the pool tonight…

In her sensual twang, she says, "We'll just fuck and have fun for four more days."

I cannot resist you.

Sorry, Reese. Sorry, Dad. But, for once in my life, I'm going to do what I want to do. I'm going to skip orientation and stay here with my wild hillbilly girl.

"To hell with orientation." I get out my wallet and count my money. "I'm not sure I got enough money."

"I do. I'll cover you."

"If I run out, I'll pay you back."

"Don't worry about it."

I savor another bite of my toasted pecan roll.

Your sexuality always overpowers my rationality.

"Lily, I remember what you told me at the Cameo. 'The way to a man's heart is through his cock. And the way to a man's cock is through his stomach.' That's your modus operandi."

"My what?" she asks, her mouth full of gooey bun.

"That's your method. That's how you do it."

"Do what?" she asks ingenuously.

"Seduce me. You seduced me again. You are such a seductress."

Grinning playfully, she replies, "I couldn't seduce you if you didn't wanna be seduced. That's what *Cosmo* says."

"True."

I'm on cloud nine again.

After breakfast I enter the motel office and tell the manager we want to stay four more nights. He makes a wisecrack about charging me for two rooms since my wife drove out the couple next door; then says he's just kidding. He understands—we're honeymooners. Looking out the window at Lily, he observes, "She's a beautiful bride. You're a lucky man."

Having booked the honeymoon suite for four more nights, I walk out of the motel lobby singing "Wild Thing" by the Trogs. Lily knows I'm alluding to her and finds it amusing. We grab our bags out of the boot, go back to our room, and unpack. Then she calls her mom collect again. Eavesdropping, I hear her say we're staying longer. Her mom must not like it because I hear Lily respond that she hasn't taken a vacation in years and promise that she'll be home Sunday night. Then she asks how Sean and Sarah are doing at school.

After she hangs up, I ask, "Is everything okay?"

"Yeah. She was a little upset at first but got over it. She knows I ain't had a vacation in years."

Since my parents are expecting me to come home today for orientation, I need to call and let them know that I'm staying longer, so they don't report me missing to the police when I fail to show up. I want to talk to Mom, not Dad. Since it's way past eight o'clock, I figure my old man will have gone to work. I call home collect, and, just as I hoped, Mom answers the phone and accepts the call. I tell her I'm having so much fun I've decided to stay a few more days—like it's no big deal. Immediately, we get in an argument over my skipping orientation. I tell her that it's optional—the extra R and R will better prepare me for the grind of law school. She warns repeatedly, "Your father's not gonna like this." Finally, I remind her that I'm the one paying for law school, I'm an adult, it's my life, and I'll see them on Sunday. After a quick "Bye," I hang up on her. I'm glad I got that call out of the way.

Lily asks me if everything is okay. I tell her no—my dad won't be happy about my skipping orientation—but I figure he'll get over it once he realizes it's a fait accompli. She doesn't know what that means exactly but is glad we're staying longer.

I want to go to the beach now, but she says we have to go to the store first, so we go to the supermarket and buy enough groceries for another four days. Stopping in at the Fresh Seafood store, we buy another pound of fresh shrimp and a jar of cocktail sauce. The proprietor gives Lily a recipe for sautéed shrimp with garlic, stressing that one cannot use too much butter or garlic. Then we stop at a drugstore for more sunscreen and film.

Back at the motel, we change hurriedly into our swimsuits and dash to the beach. Today's waves are the biggest yet. Down the shore, I spot two guys who are surfing. I go watch them. After a while, they take a break and paddle into shore, where I strike up a conversation with them. Their names are Steve and Eric, and they are going to college at Duke University. Being from California, they love to surf. Noticing my interest, they ask me if I want to give it a try. I reply I'd love to. On the beach, Eric shows me where to place my front and back feet on the board; how to pop up by doing a pushup into a standing position with my knees bent; and how to catch an unbroken wave. Steve attaches the leash of his surfboard to my ankle. I am totally psyched to try this.

Paddling the surfboard in a prone position, I follow Eric to a spot several yards beyond where the waves are breaking and turn around so I'm facing the shore. Looking over my shoulder toward the horizon, I wait for the perfect wave. Soon I see a swell surging into an unbroken wave. As the wave propels me forward, I paddle…try to catch it before it breaks…but miss. I launched too early. I try again and again but keep missing, always too early.

Eric tells me I'm too far out.

So I paddle toward shore—closer to where the waves are breaking. This time the wave breaks onto my back, so I move a little farther out.

Wading out, Steve coaches me, "Lie in the center of the board. Wait for the moment you feel the wave pushing and lifting you up. Then paddle as hard as you can. You gotta paddle fast enough to match the speed of the wave."

After numerous attempts, I finally catch a wave. I stand up momentarily; then fall back into the water.

Steve points out that I was looking at my legs—I need to look straight ahead.

Eric instructs me, "Arch your back when you pop up. Don't lock your knees. Keep them bent."

"This is a lot harder than it looks," I admit.

They keep encouraging me.

I spot Lily on the shore taking pictures of me.

Determined to do it for her, I catch a wave, stand crouched with my weight on my back leg, and travel across the water—I'm surfing…

Waving at her, I holler "Hang ten!"—right before I plunge into the water.

When I surface, Steve and Eric whoop, "You did it. You surfed,"

"This is a blast," I yell.

"There's nothing like the feeling of dropping in on a wave for the first time," Steve yells back.

Each time I catch another wave I'm able to stand a little longer— I'm starting to get the hang of it. I'm having so much fun I keep telling myself, "One last wave."

Bobbing in the surf, I spot a huge wave coming. Paddling madly, I catch it and fly down the steep face of the foaming curl. The next thing I know I'm tumbling head over heels inside a waterfall. The wave crashes upon me in a thunderous explosion of whitewater and force. Driven downward, the back of my neck slams into the sand— I feel this electric shock sensation in my spine. The wave pins me underwater and drags me along the bottom until I run out of breath. The board wrenches my ankle. I pop up—gasping for air. Staggering to my feet, I recover the surfboard and stumble to shore.

Steve lopes up to me. "Wipe out! Are you okay?"

My nose burns from the saltwater that I took up it and my right shoulder stings. I gasp, "Man, that wave pinned me on the bottom. I almost ran out of air."

"You got worked," he chuckles. "You going back out?"

"No. I'm hogging your board."

I detach the leash from my ankle and return his surfboard; then thank them for the surfing lesson.

"We just might make a surfer out of you," Eric says, grinning broadly.

Walking up the beach with Lily, I ask, "Did you get a picture of my wipeout?"

"Yeah. I think so."

Rubbing the back of my burning neck, I exclaim, "Man, I did a somersault and hit my neck on the bottom." I show her the back of my shoulder.

"You scraped it. It's bleeding."

"It stings."

"That's the salt water. It should disinfect it."

"Man, you could break your neck surfing. I'm glad you're not rolling me home in a wheelchair."

"It's like horseback riding. You could break your neck falling off a horse. But it's worth the risk."

Back at our blanket, I relive surfing—feeling the exhilaration and freedom. Beaming proudly, I say, "I did it, Lily. I surfed."

"You did, Hard Slick."

Chuckling, I fantasize about using my summer earnings to become a surfer and travel around the world in search of the perfect wave—like the guys in the movie *Endless Summer*—instead of going to law school. "You wanna come with me? Be my surfer girl?" I ask only half-facetiously.

"I hate to burst your bubble, but I gotta work."

I just sigh.

At suppertime we go back to the motel and shower together. I make shrimp cocktails again. Lily sautés shrimp in almost two sticks of butter and several finely chopped garlic cloves; then pours it over toast. I think it tastes great, but she says shrimp cocktail is still her favorite.

We go for our evening swim in the pool.

After our late night walk on the beach, we sneak into the pool. They have turned off the pool lights, so it's dark. We take off our swimsuits and swim nude in the shimmering moonlight—it feels so free. Standing in the shallow end, I hold her—she's practically weightless. Facing me with her arms draped around my neck and her legs wrapped around my waist, we live my fantasy. After she comes, we beat it out of here—I'm afraid the hotel manager may have heard her.

Lying awake in bed, we talk about tomorrow.

"Let's go on a picnic at the National Seashore," she suggests.

"Okay. We'll have a campfire on the beach and a weenie roast."

CHAPTER SEVENTEEN

For our picnic at the National Seashore, Lily packs the cooler with cold shrimp and cocktail sauce, the ingredients for Bloody Marys, carrot and celery sticks, and a big jug of ice water. We borrow a pot, some silverware, and a flashlight from the kitchen. I take Hard Slick. The weather forecast is sunny with no chance of rain, so we put the top down.

On our way, we buy hotdogs, buns, baked beans, potato chips, marshmallows, half a watermelon, and roasting forks. When we go through the checkout line, Lily buys a National Enquirer.

Shaking my head incredulously, I needle her, "I can't believe you bought that. That's not journalism. That's sensationalism."

"It has an article I wanna read."

"What?"

"'Use Horoscope to Understand Your Child,' " she quotes from the cover.

I roll my eyes.

We stop at the beach store where she buys a beach chair without legs, and I buy a Frisbee and a kite.

Looking for a place where there are no other people, we drive far down the National Seashore. Halfway between Salvo and Avon, we park at a desolate public beach access. I blow up my army raft; then load all our stuff in it. Towing the raft by the rope, I haul our stuff over the ridge of sand dunes and far down the shore. We spread out our beach blanket in the virgin sand.

There is not a living soul as far as the eye can see. "Hey, Lily, I thought of something dirty to do."

"What?"

"Let's be nudists."

"Like Adam and Eve?"

"Yeah. No one will see us here."

We strip, exposing the untanned places on our bodies to the sun. She cautions me, "Be sure to put sunscreen on your wiener—you don't wanna burn it."

"I wouldn't wanna get melanoma there."

The sight of her standing on the beach with nothing on except her hat inspires me to sing "Cowgirl in the Sand" by Neil Young.

She does a cartwheel in the sand—her hat falls off.

"Nude gymnastics. That's erotic," I remark.

"I was the star tumbler on the tumbling team in grade school. Watch this…"

Extending her arms up in the air, she bends over and does a handstand—her legs are pointed gracefully straight upward to the tip of her toes. After a few seconds, she drops her feet back on the ground. Then she backs up several steps, takes a short run, and does a front handspring, landing on her feet.

I clap.

"Here's a back walk-over into a back handspring," she announces.

She does a backbend for several seconds. While arching her back, she kicks one leg up and over her head, with her other leg following, and lands so she's standing upright. Without stopping, she does a back handspring and lands upright on her feet—but she has so much momentum she has to hop backwards to keep from falling on her butt.

I whistle and cheer.

"One more. I did this trick when I was a cheerleader." She backs up; then dashes several steps forward, lunges, and performs a round off into a back handspring. But she has so much momentum that she over-rotates and lands on the back of her heels and falls backward onto her butt. Sitting in the sand, legs splayed, she laughs…

"Man alive, Lily, you never cease to amaze me." I pull her up and brush the sand off her backside.

"I'm a little rusty."

I bound into the waves. "Lily, this feels free. Come join me."

"A shark's gonna bite your wiener off."

I cringe at the thought. In a falsetto voice I reply, "I hope not."

I talk her into throwing the Frisbee with me in the shallow surf—the water is only up to her calves. Gradually, I arc the Frisbee farther and farther out into the ocean, forcing her to wade deeper into the water to catch it. Eventually, she catches on to what I'm doing and quits.

Standing in the shallow water, I gaze at her sitting nude in her new beach chair on the seashore, wearing her red, heart-shaped sunglasses and cowgirl hat, intently reading the tabloid for horoscopic advice on her kids. I'm struck by how winsome she is. Wanting to be near her, I go plop down on the blanket and air dry. Feeling the warm sun and cool breeze on my skin, I sing "By the Beautiful Sea:"

"By the sea, by the sea, by the beautiful sea

"You and I, you and I, oh how happy we'll be"

"Ya know, Lily, I like being a nudist—it feels natural to me. I think we should join a nudist colony," I kid.

"Donny once took me to a nudist camp."

Surprised, I sit up. "Really?"

"Yeah. We went with one of his army buddies and his wife as their guests in Texas."

"Tell me about it."

"It wasn't what I expected. I thought I'd see people having sex out in public, but that's against the rules."

"What'd you do?"

"We went skinny-dipping in the lake and played volleyball and shuffleboard with nothing on."

I picture myself playing shuffleboard in the nude. Finding the

WILD HORSES OF CURRITUCK

image comical, I chuckle to myself. "So what's it like playing shuffleboard naked?"

"Breezy."

"Were you self-conscious?"

"A little at first. But, after a while, I forgot I was naked. The worst thing was not having any pockets."

"Huh…that's what I like about you, Lily. You're practical."

"When we went back to our cabin, Donny's buddy and his wife wanted to swap, but Donny and me didn't want to. After that, we never saw them again. It ruined our friendship."

Her going to a nudist camp makes me realize that she's more unconventional than I thought; yet not so kinky as to participate in wife-swapping.

She goes back to reading her article.

So I fly my kite. In the steady wind blowing toward shore, it takes off, soaring and diving over the dunes.

Lily comes up beside me and watches.

"I'm getting into nude kite-flying. It's kind of kinky. You wanna try it?"

"No thanks." She heads down the beach.

"Where are you going?"

"I'm gonna look for shells."

Eventually, I get bored with the kite and tie the string to a large piece of driftwood, letting it fly itself.

Parking myself on the blanket, I read Lily's *National Enquirer*.

She walks far down the shore without any trepidation about running into a beachcomber while far away from her clothes. As she saunters back toward me, I'm struck by how she looks like a lone sea siren. She's carrying her hat full of seashells, which she dumps on the blanket for me to see. She found clam and conch shells and several broken sand dollars. Delighted, she tells me, "I'm gonna take them home for Sarah and Rachel."

Feeling hot and sweaty, I dive into the water and bodysurf. After cooling off, I float in my army raft. Wanting Lily's company, I paddle into shore and coax, "C'mon, Lily, go for a ride with me. When my dad got shot down, he floated around in the middle of the ocean for hours in a raft like this, and no sharks got him."

She's weakening.

"Please…" I beg.

"All right."

"Hot damn!"

Before she can change her mind, I drag my raft into the ocean where the water is up to my knees. "Hop in."

She climbs aboard apprehensively.

I tug the raft into the surf where the waves are breaking; then crawl in, facing her. Floating around in the whitecaps, she looks around continuously for a shark fin.

"Relax. You're safe with me," I assure her.

She leans back against the side of the raft with her legs dangling overboard in the water.

"Leo, this is fun. It's like riding the Tilt-A-Whirl."

"Just think what you've been missing."

We drift far down the beach…

All of a sudden, she sits bolt upright with a look of sheer terror on her face and shrieks, "Sharks!"

I look in the direction she's pointing and spot two fins in the water about thirty yards away—coming straight toward us…

Clutching onto me, she scrambles into the center of the raft.

I paddle toward shore frantically. Glancing back over my shoulder, I see the fins getting closer and closer until they're only a few yards away…

Then I notice that the fins are not staying level in the water—like shark fins. Instead, they're bobbing. "Wait a second. They got humps. Those aren't sharks. They're porpoises."

Astonished, she asks, "Porpoises?"

I nod, laughing.

Lily is thrilled. "Oh my God, Leo. I love porpoises."

Swimming around the raft in circles, they come so close to us we can hear their blowholes snort.

She leans over the side of the raft and tries to pet them, but they won't let her touch them. Eventually, they lose interest in us and swim away.

"Leo, I'm so glad I got to see them up close. They're my favorite animal after horses and dogs."

"They're one of my favorite animals too because they're one of the most intelligent mammals."

"*Flipper* was my favorite show when I was a girl."

"It's some consolation for not getting to see the wild horses."

"I just wish I'd got a picture of them to show Sarah and Rachel."

Walking in the backwash, we tow the raft back up the shore in front of our blanket; then drift down the shoreline again. We do this several times. Lily hopes the porpoises return, but they don't.

At suppertime I gather driftwood and built a campfire. I forgot to bring the charcoal lighter, so I use pages of her *National Enquirer* as kindling to start the fire.

"Don't burn my horoscope article, Leo."

Grinning sheepishly, I reply, "Whoops…too late."

"I wanted to take it home."

"Sorry."

Not convinced, she gives me a dirty look.

"You don't really believe in Astrology—do you?"

"Why shouldn't I? There ain't no harm in it."

"Because it's like believing a fortune teller."

"What's wrong with that? My sister reads tarot cards."

"Lily, no one can predict the future."

"Says who?"

"I say. Don't you see that astrologers and fortune tellers make vague untestable statements about you that could apply to almost anyone? Then you remember evidence selectively to reinforce your expectations."

Yawning, she retorts, "You sound like a lawyer."

I laugh. "Touche."

Before supper we smoke a joint and have the shrimp cocktails as appetizers. Then we roast hotdogs over the fire as our main course. While eating the baked beans, I describe the infamous scene in Mel Brook's western movie, *Blazing Saddles,* where the cowboys eat beans for supper; then sit around the campfire farting all night. "It's hilarious."

"Donny used to light his farts with a cigarette lighter. He thought that was funny."

"That's playing with fire."

"Why do men think farts are so funny, Leo?"

"Because men are inherently immature, and farts are intrinsically funny. Don't you think they're funny?"

"Sometimes. I remember one time Sean farted in church during the preacher's sermon. No matter how hard I tried I couldn't stop laughing. It was awful. I was so embarrassed."

I laugh. "That's because you're supposed to be reverent in church."

For dessert we eat the watermelon, which is sweet and juicy.

After supper I reel in my kite and stockpile driftwood for the campfire while there's still light.

Sipping our cocktails at dusk, we watch the stars come out. The mosquitos don't bother us because of the sea breeze.

When it gets dark, we roast marshmallows. Sitting stoned around the campfire, I pose hypothetical questions. "Who's the least sexually attractive man you know?"

"Bill Barnes."

"If you were stranded on a desert island, would you have sex with him?"

"Nope. I'd finger myself before I'd have sex with him."

I laugh. "Is there any man in the world you would have an affair with if you were happily married?"

"No. Why would I wanna cheat if I was happily married?"

"Not even with Robert Redford?"

"That would be tempting," she admits, smiling.

Furrowing her brow, she confides, "I was unhappily married and never cheated on Donny."

"You never were tempted?"

"I was once. When things got really bad between us, I was tempted to cheat on him with Eli Brown. But I didn't."

"Who's Eli Brown?"

"The drummer in Donny's band. Eli was really sexy. He told me he was madly in love with me. You know that song 'Midnight

Confessions?' "

"By *The Grass Roots?*"

"Uh-huh. They used to play it. He said he was like the guy in that song. When I'd hear it, I'd fantasize about having an affair with him."

"So what stopped you?"

She sighs. "I believed in being true to my husband."

"I admire that."

"I'm like my mama. She's been true to my dad through thick and thin. So what about you? If you find your dream girl, will you be true to her?"

"I believe so."

I feel like our conversation is getting a little too heavy. "Let me ask you a delicate question. Does penis size matter?"

She grins.

"Tell me the truth. Is bigger better?"

"There are other things that matter a lot more."

I scoff. "Women always say size doesn't matter. But I think that's bullshit. They don't wanna give men performance anxiety over penis size."

"So do you have performance anxiety over your penis size?"

"No. I know I'm longer than average. I measured it."

She thinks that's funny.

"I was a biologist. So...all things being equal, do you prefer a longer penis?"

"All things being equal?"

"If all the other characteristics about two guys are identical, would you prefer the guy with the longer penis?"

"Truthfully...yes. Cuz it penetrates deeper."

"I thought so. It's a matter of natural selection."

I get up and toss some more wood on the fire. "Let me ask you a metaphysical question. Which comes first—sex or love?"

"What do you mean?"

"You know—it's the proverbial question. Which came first—the chicken or the egg? Does sex cause love? Or does love cause sex?"

"Why are you asking me about love?"

"Because it's my favorite subject."

"I don't wanna talk about love."

"Not even theoretically?"

"Nope. I told you—I ain't falling in love with you."

"Okay..." Changing the subject, I ask, "What's your favorite sense?"

"Sense?"

"You know—sight, hearing, smell..."

"Touch."

"Touch?"

"Yeah. I love feeling...and being felt. I'm really physical. You know—hands on. It's how I talk to animals. Hands and words. Dogs can learn as many words as a two year old child. Horses can learn about ten words."

"That's fascinating..."

"So...what about you?"

"Definitely sight. My eyes love colors and shapes and lines—probably because of my eidetic memory."

She scoffs at my eidetic memory.

"The Good Lord gave you a sexy body. He gave me an eidetic memory."

"So why are you asking me all these questions?"

"It's enlightening. I like to get the female perspective on life."

"So let me ask you a question," she says.

"Shoot."

"Do you like me?"

"What do you mean—do I like you? Of course I like you. It goes without saying."

"What do you like about me?"

"I like your sparkling eyes. And your daring smile."

"Do you like me as a person?"

"Yes, I like you as a person. I like how you're fearless and wild."

"Is that all?"

"You're smart. And you're fun. And adventurous."

"What do you like most about me?"

I ponder her question. "Your zest for life. I should call you Miss

Zhivago."

"Miss Zhivago?"

"Yeah. Zhivago means life in Russian. So Dr. Zhivago means Dr. Life."

"Do you like me as much as a college girl?"

"Absolutely. I've never met a college girl as interesting as you."

"Really?"

"Really. I love talking to you, Lily. You think uniquely."

"What do you mean by that?"

"I mean you think in a way that belongs only to you."

This pleases her.

I stand up and walk toward the ocean.

"Hey, where you going?"

"I'm going skinny-dipping."

"You better not. You're gonna end up like that girl in *Jaws*. Night time's when it's most dangerous. That's when sharks feed."

"I'll take my chances."

I wade out chest deep in the surf; swim breaststroke for a while. The fathomless, black water is eerie.

Unable to resist, I fake like I'm being attacked by a Great White Shark. Thrashing around in the water, I let out a long, blood-curdling scream.

Silently, I sink into the swells so she can't see me…

"Leo, are you okay?" she cries out in the night. Frantically calling out my name, she shines the flashlight across the water, searching for me.

I hear terror in her voice and realize it's time to stop fooling. Wading into shore, I say, "God-damn, son of a bitch, Lily—you're not gonna believe what happened to me. A crab pinched my penis."

Shining the flashlight in my face, she replies furiously, "You liar."

"I ain't lying. It hurt."

"I don't believe you." She storms off.

I chase after her, trying to put my arms around her.

She angrily pushes me away. "That ain't funny, Leo. You scared the shit out of me. That's a dirty trick to play. You know I'm scared of sharks."

I can't help laughing. "C'mon, Lily, don't be mad. You gotta admit it was funny."

"No, it wasn't. Sometimes you are so juvenile."

"I can't help it. I'm just a kid at heart."

She won't speak to me.

"Okay, I'm sorry."

"You ever heard of The Boy That Cried Wolf? That'll be you. If a shark really attacks you, I ain't gonna help."

"I won't do it again. I promise."

"You better not. Not if you wanna get laid again."

Trying to make up with her, I coax, "C'mon, let's go for a nude walk on the beach."

She walks down the beach but won't speak to me.

She shines the flashlight ahead. Tiny protruding eyeballs are reflected in the light.

"What are those?" she asks curiously.

"Sand crabs."

As we approach them, they scurry sideways into the surf. She laughs. "They're really funny."

Strolling along, she talks to me again.

Suddenly, she stops. "Look, Leo, the wave is glowing."

The crest of the breaking wave is not white—it's glowing with a luminous blue-green light.

"It's magic," I say.

She gazes in wonder…

"Actually, it's bioluminescent plankton. They have biochemical enzymes that generate light."

"You really do know everything—don't you?"

"I took Marine Biology in college," I reply modestly.

By the time we return to the campfire, she's no longer mad at me. Sitting on our beach blanket, we enjoy the warm fire. The flames dance, and the coals pop and crackle. Sparks soar into the night.

Lying on our backs listening to the waves crashing rhythmically on the beach, we gaze at the stars. I remark, "Look how bright they are with no city lights to dim them. You can really see the constellations."

I show her the constellations I learned how to find in Astronomy class. The Big Dipper is low on the horizon in the northern sky. I explain it's not really a constellation. It's an asterism—a star pattern within the constellation Ursa Major. It leads me to the North Star. Using the North Star, I find the Little Dipper above the Big Dipper; it's also an asterism belonging to the constellation Ursa Minor.

I point out the Leo constellation, which I learned because it's my name and is the easiest constellation to find in the zodiac. I simply look for the large, orange star underneath it, which is actually Jupiter.

Continuing, I point to the Northern Cross within the Milky Way galaxy; the Orion constellation, which is very recognizable; and Scorpius, which I learned how to find because it's my astrological sign.

On the distant horizon, a sliver of orange emerges from the surface of the ocean.

"Look, Lily, the moon is rising over the sea."

A huge, orange ball rises—it looks like the sun. Slowly, it turns a creamy yellow.

"It looks like a full moon. You can see the dark craters on its surface," I observe.

Moonlight is shining across the silvery water from horizon to shore...

Lily leans against my shoulder.

"God's putting on a spectacular light show for us tonight," I remark.

"So you believe in God?"

"Yeah. I believe in a Creator who created the world and life. What about you?"

"Me too."

"Are you a Christian?" I ask.

"I'm a part-time Christian. I go to church on Christmas Eve and Easter."

"What church do you belong to?"

"The Mount Zion Baptist Church. What about you? Do you go to church?"

"No. My mom took me when I was a kid. But I stopped going in college."

"Why?"

"I became disillusioned with organized religion during the Viet Nam War. They were drafting guys to go to Nam, and I opposed the war. I wasn't against the guys who fought in it—you know like Donny and your brother. I respect them for fighting for their country—like I respect my dad and your dad for fighting for their country in World War Two. I just thought it was a civil war that we had no business getting involved in, and I didn't believe in the Domino Theory. I didn't know what I was gonna do if I got drafted. I basically had three bad choices—go to prison or go to Canada or go to Nam. So I asked our minister what was the morally right thing to do. His answer was 'Render unto Caesar the things that are Caesar's and unto God the things that are God's.' I was looking for answers, and the church didn't have any. After that I just quit going. Fortunately, I was able to avoid the draft with a high lottery number. Then Nixon ended the draft, and my moral dilemma was solved."

"I wish Donny and Luke had gone to Canada. Luke would still be alive. And Donny might not have become an alcoholic and killed himself."

I nod. I don't tell her that I fear they died for nothing.

There is a long silence...

"And I have theological doubts about Christianity. As an ex-biologist, I'm skeptical about the virgin birth of Jesus. You gotta have male chromosomes to make a male. And Jesus coming back from the dead is implausible. No one has ever come back from being medically dead."

"Ain't you scared of going to Hell?"

"A little. I wouldn't wanna be stuck in Hell for eternity with all the evil souls—that would be a drag. But I also wouldn't wanna be stuck in Heaven for eternity with all the righteous souls—that would get boring. Truth is I'd rather go to Purgatory—that's where God sends the sinners who were moderately bad but didn't really hurt anybody. They just liked to have fun and pleasure in life. Those are the souls I'd rather be with for eternity. They'd be more fun."

She laughs at that. "So you ain't a Christian?"

"Nope. I'm a Creatian."

"A Creatian?"

"I kind of invented my own religion. I think of God as the greatest artist of all because he created the universe. I call him the Cosmic Artist. He judges you on whether you create or destroy. You hafta create—not destroy—to get into Heaven. If there is a Heaven…"

She looks at me like I'm peculiar and comments, "You sure got some funny ideas. But that's what I like about you. I got some funny ideas too."

"Like what?"

"Like I kind of believe in reincarnation…"

"So what were you in your prior life?"

"A horse. A filly…and you're my stallion, Leo."

"That's cool. I always secretly wanted to be Tornado." I pronounce it in the Spanish way, Tor-NAH-do.

"Who's Tor-NAH-do?"

"Zorro's horse. *Zorro* was one of my favorite shows on TV when I was a little kid. Tor-NAH-do is how they pronounced it on TV. Did you watch it?" I ask.

"Yeah. He was a beautiful black horse."

"He was intelligent and swift as—"

At this moment, a meteor streaks downward in the sky.

"Oh, wow, Lily. Did you see that falling star?"

"Uh-huh. Make a wish and it'll come true."

"You know where that legend originated?"

"No, but I'm sure you do."

"I learned it in Astronomy class. The ancient Greek astronomer, Ptolemy, said occasionally the gods peer down on Earth from the heavens for their entertainment. Sometimes, while they're doing this, a star slips from the sky and becomes a falling star. Since the gods are watching at this moment, they may hear us and grant a wish."

"Makes sense to me."

"So did you make a wish?"

"Yeah."

"What did you wish for?"

"I ain't telling. If I tell, it won't come true."

"You're superstitious."

"It's getting late. What time is it?" she asks.

"Ten after eleven."

"Time to go home."

Being an ex-Boy Scout, I fill the water jug with sea water several times and thoroughly douse the campfire; then bury the ash in the sand. By the time we get dressed, find our way back to the car, and drive all the way back to the motel, it's past midnight. Drained, we fall into bed and go straight to sleep.

CHAPTER EIGHTEEN

"Lily, what's on today's itinerary?"

Eating peanut butter toast for breakfast, she looks longingly at the picture of the wild horses of Currituck on the cover of her brochure. "Find them."

Opening the brochure, she reads out loud: "'When the herd isn't roaming, the horses live near the marshes adjacent to the sound where there is marsh grass for grazing and pools of fresh water to drink.' " She shows me a photograph of the wild horses grazing in the marsh grass.

"Lily, the marsh is a breeding ground for mosquitos. I don't feel like getting malaria. Let's go to the Wright Brothers Memorial."

"I bet Hard Slick could find them."

I smile. "You have your heart set on seeing them, don't you?"

"It's my big dream in life, Leo."

"Let's do it then."

I love you!" She kisses me.

Sipping my coffee, I ask, "Have I ever told you I once was a Boy Scout?"

"No."

"I was. I didn't make it past Tenderfoot. Even though I liked scouting, I quit after one summer because I hated the saluting and standing at attention and marching. I only joined so I could go on my troop's expedition to Philmont Scout Ranch in New Mexico. We backpacked in the mountains and camped out with the rattlesnakes and scorpions. I had a riot. Anyhow, the Boy Scout motto is: 'Be prepared.' Let's go buy some bug spray, and get you some long pants and shoes."

"You think I need them?"

"Yeah. That marsh grass looks nasty. If we're gonna be hiking through it, we'll need long pants and shoes to protect our legs and feet."

I put my jeans on over my swim trunks and wear my tennis shoes. At the drugstore, we pick up insect repellant; then stop at a department store, where Lily buys a pair of tennis shoes, jeans and a T-shirt, which she puts on over her bikini. I look for a canteen but can't find one.

Now prepared, we return to the end of the road, avoiding where my car got stuck in the sand. As soon as we get out of the car, we spray the bug repellant all over our bodies, including our faces.

Coughing, I tell her, "Great. We'll probably get cancer from the DDT."

"Quit complaining."

"I'm not complaining. I'm joking. Humor is how I deal with adversity."

"Ha, ha. Let's go. Which way?"

"West. Toward the sound."

An impenetrable wall of shrub thickets and entangling vines bounds the marshes on the sound side of the cape, blocking us from going west. Grassy sand dunes interspersed with clumps of shrub thickets stretch endlessly to the north. "Let's head north across the dunes. See if there's a way to get to the sound," I suggest.

With camera in hand, Lily sets off across the dunes. As soon as we enter the shrub thickets, a massive cloud of mosquitos buzzes around my ears and flies into my face, but none actually land on my skin.

"Man, this bug spray really works. Hey, Lily, take a picture of them flying around but not landing on me."

"Nope."

"Why not?"

"That's a waste of film."

"No, it's not. I'll send it to the company, and they'll pay me big bucks for it. You know—like that bug spray commercial on TV of the guy who sticks his arm in the jar full of mosquitos and none of them light on him." I'm being facetious.

She ignores me, apparently not finding me amusing.

The heat is oppressive; in no time, I'm sweating like a pig.

Winding our way between the shrub thickets, we hike across sandy hills and ridges for over two hours. In some places the cape is so narrow we can hear the ocean to the east. Except for an occasional bird and the relentless mosquitos, we don't see a living creature.

Finally, the western terrain changes and openings appear in the wall of shrub thickets, which enables us to head northwest toward the sound. In this location marsh grass is growing in the depressions between the dunes. Up ahead are lush fields of marsh grass extending along the shore of the sound as far as the eye can see. Her hand shielding the sun from her eyes, Lily looks intently for the wild horses. Disappointed, she says, "I don't see them, Leo…"

"They must be roaming."

"Let's keep going."

The marsh grass is tall and dense. I'm apprehensive about entering it.

"I don't know, Lily…I don't like the looks of this. There could be snakes in there."

"I ain't scared of snakes. You don't bother them, they don't bother you."

"You ain't scared of venomous snakes?"

"There's poisonous snakes in there?"

"I don't know. There could be coral snakes. They're highly venomous. I know rattlesnakes live in the forests of western North Carolina. But I don't know if their habitat extends to the coastal areas."

"This is where the horses live. We gotta go in there if we wanna find them."

"It looks…inhospitable," I observe.

"You should feel right at home."

"Why's that?"

"Ain't you Tor-NAD-do?"

I can't help but chortle.

"Giddy up, Tor-NAH-do," she commands and slaps me on my butt.

Trying to stay on dry ground, I lead the way through the marshland. My feet continually get tangled in clumps of grass, tripping me. Sweat is dripping off my brow—

Suddenly, I stop. "Look, Lily. They've been here." I'm pointing at some old, dried piles of horse manure. "Looks like we're on the right track."

Examining it, she notes, "It ain't fresh. Here's their hoofprints. They went that way." She's pointing toward the sound.

We track their hoofprints and the trampled grass for a long distance to a large fresh water pool. They are nowhere in sight.

I let out a sigh. "They appear to have entered the water to drink."

I'm starting to get thirsty. The water in the pool looks tempting, but I know it's not safe to drink because of animal feces. I wish I had tracked down a canteen.

Circling the pool, we search for where they exited but can't find their tracks. As we approach the sound, the ground becomes soggy. Soon, our shoes are caked with mud—like walking with weights on our feet.

I stop. Wiping the sweat from my brow, I say, "We've lost their trail. You wanna keep going?"

"I'm gonna find them if it's the last thing I do," she declares with a look of determination.

We plod doggedly toward the sound without seeing any sign of them…

Coming to a halt, the infernal mosquitos hover like a black cloud over us. We're blocked from going forward or sideways by a swamp consisting of a vast carpet of marsh plants growing in brackish water. Beyond the swamp is the sound. The mainland is on the distant horizon.

"Phew!" She wrinkles her nose in disgust.

"Smells like sulfur."

Frustrated, she demands, "Where are they, Leo?"

"I don't know, Lily. All I know is they're not here."

"Shit…"

I spot a large, bluish-gray bird with a long neck and long legs wading in the water. Pointing, I remark, "Look, Lily—there's a cool bird."

"What is that? A stork?"

"Huh-uh—I don't think storks live in North America. I think it might be a heron."

"It's pretty." She takes its picture.

It flies away gracefully.

"Lily, I hate to say it, but I think we've reached the end of the line. The horses don't live in the swamp, and we can't go any farther because of the water. Let's turn around and backtrack."

Pointing northwest, she says, "Look, Leo. There's more marsh grass. If we could just get over there, we could keep going."

Another expanse of marsh grass is abutting the swamp off in the distance. "I see it. But to reach it we hafta cross this swamp."

"How deep do you think it is?"

"Not too deep. Wait a minute. Don't tell me you wanna keep going."

"Yeah. Why not?"

"You wanna wade in that water?"

"Yeah. I'll do it if you do."

"Lily, that's a bad idea."

"You say that about all my ideas. And then after you do it, you're glad you did."

"Not this time. This time it's really a bad idea."

"Why?"

"Because swamps are dangerous."

"What's the matter? You scared?"

Shaking my head incredulously, I say, "I don't get you. You're afraid to go in the ocean, but you're not afraid to go in a swamp. It makes no sense."

"Yes, it does. There ain't no sharks in there."

I scoff, "You're being totally irrational. Sharks aren't the only animals in water that attack you. I know for a fact that water moccasins inhabit the swamps of southeastern United States. This is a swamp in North Carolina."

Her eyes scan the lagoon for a water moccasin swimming across the water. "I don't see any."

"They're probably lurking in the reeds. Personally, I'm more afraid of water moccasins than sharks. You could walk right into a whole nest of them and sustain multiple bites. If that happened, the venom would kill you before I could rush you to a hospital and they could administer the antivenin. You'd be DOA—dead on arrival." I'm hoping this will dissuade her.

Peering uncertainly into the murky water, she replies, "I ain't ever heard of that. I've only heard of a duck hunter getting bit by one water moccasin. I don't think they nest together. I think you're making that up to scare me."

"No, I'm not. I read about a water-skier who was skiing near a swamp and fell into a submerged nest of water moccasins and got bit a hundred times and died." I don't tell her it was fiction; I have no idea if it's true.

"Where?"

"I don't remember. Some lake in the south."

She gazes at me tauntingly. "I dare you…"

You're challenging me to see if I have the balls to do it…

I'll show you I have the balls.

Feeling a surge of adrenalin, I reply cockily, "Okay, Lily. Follow me."

I wade into the water. My feet sink into muck over my ankles. Keeping an eye out for water moccasins, I lead the way through the tall reeds. As we ford the swamp, the brackish water gets deeper and deeper. Soon it's up to my knees; then my waist…

At this moment, it strikes me that I'm having a ball.

"Hey, Lily, believe it or not, I'm actually enjoying this. I feel like I'm Tim Kelly and you're Chick Chandler on *Soldier of Fortune* on

TV. It was my favorite show when I was a kid. They were always wading through a swamp."

"This ain't TV," she retorts.

As we get closer to the marsh grass, the muck on the bottom gets deeper and deeper. Our feet sink into it up to our calves; then our knees. Suddenly, I fear walking into quicksand and being sucked underwater.

The water becomes chest deep. Holding her camera above her head, Lily worries, "I hope I don't ruin my camera."

"Fuck the camera. I don't wanna sink over my head in quicksand..."

Aghast, she asks, "Is quicksand here?"

"I have no idea."

"I thought you knew everything."

"I know one thing."

"What?"

"We should've gone to the Wright Brothers' Memorial."

Now the water is up to her chin.

"Leo, you wanna turn back?"

I hear a trace of fear in her voice. I can see the marsh grass about a hundred yards away. Having come this far, I dread turning back.

"Nope."

The muck sucks off my shoe. "God damn it!"

"What's wrong?"

"The mud sucked my shoe off."

We stop. Ducking underwater, I grope around in the tangled reeds and algae and muck but can't find it. "Shit...it's lost."

After several more steps, the muck sucks off my other shoe. I don't even try to find it.

Lily loses both of her shoes too.

Gradually, the water and muck get shallower. Staggering out of the swamp, I slip-slide across a mudflat onto the soggy bank of marsh grass.

"We made it, Lily."

She's barefoot behind me. "See, Leo—I told you we could do it."

Soaked to the bone, we are coated with sulfurous-smelling,

brackish muck. My socks are coming off. When I pull them back up, I discover a leech on my ankle. "God damn, son of a bitch. There's a leech on me."

Lily looks at it, appalled.

Fortunately, it hasn't attached to my skin, and I'm able to peel it off. "You blood-sucking bastard," I snarl and fling it away. "Now I feel like Humphrey Bogart in the movie, *The African Queen*. Have you seen it?"

"Nope," she sighs.

"It's a classic starring Bogie and Katharine Hepburn. He plays Charlie, a gin-swilling riverboat captain, and she plays Rose, a prim Methodist missionary. It's set during World War I. They escape the Germans by shooting the rapids on the Ulanga River in Africa. Their boat gets stuck in a swamp like this one. He has to climb out and tow it. When he gets back in, he's covered with leeches. It freaks him out. She uses salt to detach them."

Shaking her head in disbelief, she says, "I can't believe you're talking about movies. Who cares about some dumb movie at a time like this?"

"I do. Don't you see—we're emulating Charlie and Rose?"

"I ain't emulating anybody. I'm just looking for the wild horses."

"I'm always trying to emulate the heroes in the movies. I feel like I'm an actor in the movie of my life."

Rolling her eyes, she retorts, "You and your damn movies. You ain't in no movie. You're in a for real swamp. Quit living in movieland."

I exhale deeply. You don't understand...

"So now what?" She's looking expectantly at me.

"How should I know? I live in movieland. I'm waiting for the director to yell 'Cut!' "

"You're the brains—when you ain't living in movieland. Think of something."

Pondering our predicament, I say, "Well...I figure we'd better head east through this marsh grass. That's the direction we came from."

Looking at the sun, I try to discern which direction is east. "It's gonna be tough-going—walking through that marsh grass without shoes."

"Lead the way, Tim," she mocks me.

I slog through the marsh grass in what I think is due east with Lily right behind me. She keeps stepping on my heels. Just as I thought, it's difficult without shoes. Without shoe treads, we can't get any traction in the slippery grass.

Because the water rinsed off the insect repellant, the incessant horde of mosquitos attacks us again. Fortunately, the insect repellant is in her pocket, and we spray ourselves again.

We continually get entangled in the marsh grass—it's maddening. My arms are scratched and bleeding. "Man, I wish I had a machete."

In the middle of the expanse of marsh grass, we stop and take a breather. Turning in a circle, Lily's eyes search in vain for the wild horses. In sheer desperation, she cries out, "Where are they?"

I shrug. "You heard that fisherman. He said they're really hard to find."

"I don't understand why they ain't here. The brochure says this is where they live. Cuz of the grass and fresh water."

"They must not have read the brochure," I wisecrack.

She smiles in spite of herself. "You are funny."

"Believe me—this safari is sorely trying my sense of humor."

"So where are we?"

"You're asking me?"

"Yeah. You're the navigator."

Exasperated, I answer, "How the hell should I know? You're the one leading this wild goose chase. Hell, we're probably in Virginia by now. Maybe even Maryland."

She gives me a dirty look.

I say testily, "I'll tell you where we are. We're in the goddamn middle of nowhere. That's where we are."

No reply.

"Face it, Lily—we're not gonna find them. Their habitat extends for fifteen miles. It's like looking for a needle in a haystack."

"I really wanna see them, Leo."

"I know you do. So do I. But the odds of our finding them are probably about one in a million. It'd take a miracle."

"I hate to give up."

"Look at the bright side—you got to see their manure," I joke.

She doesn't even crack a smile.

Trying to console her, I say, "At least we tried our best..."

Staring bleakly across the marsh grass, she lets out a long sigh.

I spot something crawling in her hair. "Hold still. You got something in your hair." While she stands still, I pick a bug off her scalp and examine it. "Damn, Lily—it looks like a tick. Luckily, I don't think it bit you. It's not engorged with blood." I crush it between my fingers and flick it away.

She shudders with disgust. Creeped out, she says, "That does it. I give up. I ain't getting Rocky Mountain Spotted Fever."

"Let's get out of here," I suggest.

"How do we get back?"

I consider our options...

"You think we should go back the same way we came?" she asks.

"Nope. I don't feel like wading across that swamp again."

"So what do we do? We can't stay here."

"If we keep going east, we should escape this marsh grass. Then we can turn south and go back toward where we entered the swamp. Hopefully, we can find our tracks in the sand and just follow them back to the car."

"Okay."

Silently, we soldier on...

Finally, the marsh grass thins and we break out into the grassy dunes. I lead us south. Wandering between the shrub thickets, I search for our tracks, but they are nowhere to be found...

I lose my bearings—the terrain all looks the same. Not wanting to wander aimlessly, I halt.

"Why are we stopping?"

"I'm lost..."

"Lost?"

"I don't know the way back to the car," I admit.

She sits down and rests...

I mutter to myself, "If I could just find a landmark..."

"You'll think of something."

"I got an idea. The Atlantic Ocean is east. If we head due east, sooner or later we hafta run into it. Then we can just walk south down the beach to the sand lane, which will take us back to our car."

"Sounds like a plan. So which way is the ocean?"

The sun is still so high in the sky that I'm not sure which direction is east. "Damn—I wish I had a compass."

Squinting at its position, I say, "Gauging by the sun, I'd say that way."

We head for the ocean. It's brutal. The blazing sun is beating down on us, and we keep stepping on sharp thistles. Cursing, we stop and remove them from the soles of our feet.

We trudge up and down countless sand dunes...

I'm very thirsty. "Lily, are you thirsty?"

"Yeah."

The thought of being lost in the wilderness without water is alarming. We risk dehydration. "I wish we'd brought water."

The farther we walk without reaching the ocean the more I fear that I'm leading us in the wrong direction...

What if we can't find it? I don't want to be lost on these dunes after nightfall.

I faintly hear waves. "Do you hear waves?"

"Yeah."

Relieved, I scurry toward the ocean with Lily right on my heels...

As I climb over the crest of the last sand dune, I stop dead in my tracks—

I don't believe it...

Lily walks right into the back of me—

"Oh my God, Lily...there they are...the wild horses of Currituck..." I whisper.

Her mouth open, she gazes at them in amazement...her psychedelic eyes are sparkling brilliantly...

I'm jubilant. "We found them!"

LILY

They are a beautiful sight to behold with their rough, shaggy coats glistening in the sunshine and long manes streaming in the wind. Lily counts fourteen horses—nine bays and four sorrels. She points out a chestnut foal near its mother. Quietly pulling out her camera, she photographs them. Three horses gallop through the shallow surf, splashing and snorting. Trying not to spook them, she slowly moves in closer and closer, snapping pictures, with me creeping behind her. They don't seem afraid of us. They seem almost docile. Lily cautions against getting too close because they are wild and we could get kicked.

Two horses are frolicking on the beach—one rears playfully.

She takes a picture of them.

The herd ambles north up the beach.

We follow…

"See that stallion out in front of the herd?" she points.

"Yeah."

"He's the leader. He's magnificent."

"He is."

She takes his picture. She keeps snapping pictures until she runs out of film.

The horses turn west and ramble over the sand dunes. We run after them but can't keep up. They vanish into the wilderness.

We return to the shore and strip down to our bathing suits. Sitting in the sand at the water's edge, we let the breaking waves wash over our legs. It cools us off and rinses the sweat and sulfurous-smelling, swamp muck off our bodies. The sharp-edged blades of marsh grass have cut our feet—especially Lily's since she was barefoot. We wash the cuts in the salt water—it stings, but we don't care. We're not even thirsty anymore. The wild horses are all we can talk about.

"Leo, they was so beautiful."

"Magical."

"I still can't believe it. I actually saw the wild horses of Currituck."

"We did it, Lily. We found them."

"Leo, you did it. You led us to them."

"It was luck."

"It was written in the stars."

"Whatever the reason, we were in the right place at the right time."

"Oh, Leo…you made my dream come true…"

Ecstatic, she kisses me.

My heart is soaring.

Lying entwined in the frothy backwash, we passionately kiss…

All at once a big wave crashing on the beach washes over us. Lily gets saltwater in her eyes and wipes them.

"Lily, this is really romantic. Now we're emulating Burt Lancaster and Deborah Kerr in *From Here to Eternity.*"

Again, she doesn't know what I'm talking about.

"It's a war movie about the Japanese sneak attack on Pearl Harbor."

"I ain't seen it."

"Burt Lancaster plays a soldier. Deborah Kerr plays an officer's wife. They commit adultery. They have a famous kiss scene on the beach, lying in the surf in their skimpy bathing suits. It was considered quite risqué for the times."

"Leo, that's another thing I like about you. You got a wild imagination…"

Later, as we walk down the beach back to the car, I recall Lily telling me it was written in the stars that we'd find the wild horses. The odds of finding them were very small, which makes me wonder if we are also destined to fall in love with each other…

A sign on the beach shows the location of the sand lane, so we have no problem finding the car. On the way back to the motel, we stop at an ice cream stand in Kill Devil Hills and buy root beer floats. While we quench our thirst, Lily continues to marvel at seeing the horses galloping in the ocean. Knowing how much she loves horses, I'm happy for her.

"I'd love to ride Appaloosa in the surf," she fantasizes.

"Aren't you afraid a shark would eat you?" I kid.

"We'd ride like the wind. They couldn't catch us."

Imagining it, I tell her, "That'd be a sight to see."

LILY

At the Fresh Seafood store, we buy ten pounds of long-neck clams, the store's breading mix, a jar of tartar sauce, and a special knife to shuck clams and oysters. For appetizers, she picks fresh shrimp for cocktails, and I pick fresh oysters for raw oysters on the half shell.

"You gonna try an oyster? I ask.

"Gross."

I make sure I save enough money to take her out to eat tomorrow night. Stopping at the bakery, we buy a loaf of French bread.

Back at the motel, Lily goes to our room. Meanwhile, I take a quick dip in the pool to rinse off the salt water. When I open the door to our room, I hear her singing in the shower. I hang my swimsuit outside on the balcony to dry and don't bother to get dressed.

Beginning dinner, I boil the clams in a big pot of water on the stove. As the shells open, I ladle them out into a pot of cold water. While I shuck them one by one, I reflect on what a good time I'm having and wish it would never end…

Lily comes out of the bathroom with just a towel wrapped around her and her hair pinned up on her head. She polishes off her Bloody Mary. "What'cha doing?"

"Shucking clams."

She looks impressed.

"See—I can do other useful things," I say.

"You forgot your clothes."

"No, I didn't. I feel like being a nudist tonight."

"Me too. I feel like getting wild tonight." She lets her towel drop.

Sitting at the kitchen table, I roll a joint while she fixes herself another Bloody Mary at the kitchen counter.

"Want one?" she asks.

"Please."

I light the joint and take a hit; then pass it to her. She hands me my drink. While I sip on mine, she slugs hers down.

I shuck an oyster and squirt some Tabasco Sauce on it—then slurp it down. "Mmm, I love raw oysters."

"I ain't ever had one."

"You wanna try one? They're indescribably delicious."

"What do they taste like?"

"They taste briny—like the ocean."

While I shuck another one, she watches curiously. I fold the glistening, fleshy raw oyster, so there is a deep crease in it; then show it to her. Grinning, I ask, "What's that look like?"

Grinning back, she answers, "You do have a dirty mind."

"I can't help it—visual similes and metaphors just pop into my head." Laughing coarsely, I remark, "Raw oysters are like eating pussy—they both look and taste so exotic. They're my two favorite things to eat. C'mon, try one."

"Okay. Just one."

I shuck an oyster for her and squirt a little Tabasco sauce on it.

She tries to bite it in half.

"Just eat it whole," I advise her.

She puts the whole oyster in her mouth and holds it there.

"Just chew it a little and swallow it."

"It's slimy," she mumbles.

"You like it?"

She nods her head and smiles. "Could I have another one?"

I shuck another one and show her the raw oyster lying in its natural juice in the half shell. "See this juice in the half shell? Chefs call that liquor. I like to slurp it down."

She slurps it down; then nods enthusiastically.

"That's how you eat a raw oyster," I pontificate. "Ya know, some people say they're an aphrodisiac."

"Gimme another one."

We devour the rest of the oysters. Then Lily fries the clams in a big cast iron skillet. Standing at the stove, I watch her cook in the buff. She wears an apron tied around her neck and waist, but her butt is still exposed. Occasionally, she opens the oven door to check on the French bread and bends over, which affords me a wonderful view of her ass. As soon as the clams are ready, she spoons them onto our plates. Then she takes off her apron, and we sit down at the table. We dip the fried clams in the Tartar sauce and munch on our French bread.

She has another Bloody Mary—she's tipsy now.

I turn on the radio and spin the dial until I find a rock and roll station that's playing golden oldies. While we are cleaning the kitchen, "Mony, Mony" by Tommy James and the Shondells begins to play.

"Oh, God, I love this song!" Flinging her dishrag into the sink, she cranks up the volume on the radio and dances wildly around the kitchen. Spinning around, she shakes her ass.

All too soon, "Mony, Mony" ends, and she stops dancing.

"Man, oh, man, Lily. You can really dance."

"Want me to dance for you?" she asks with that wild glint in her eyes.

"Do bears shit in the woods?"

"I need a stage."

We move into the bedroom, where she decides to use the dresser across from the foot of the bed as her stage. While I plug in the radio on the dresser, she draws the drapes on the sliding glass doors and turns on the lights. She puts on her sexy lingerie: a lacey, red bra, a red garter belt, red fish-net hose, and her red, open-toed high heels. To my delight, she does not put on panties.

"Lily, I love your garter belt. It's like…like a picture frame. It frames the work of art."

She snickers. Using a chair to climb on top of the dresser, her head almost touches the ceiling. Unpinning her hair, she shakes it so that it falls freely; then tousles it so that it looks a little wild. Hands on her hips, she waits patiently for a song with a slow beat.

Reclining on the bed, my heart is racing in anticipation…

"Me and Mrs. Jones" comes on. Lily's eyes begin to smolder. Swaying rhythmically, she gazes with heavy eyelids into my eyes and slowly runs her tongue across her upper lip.

"Puuussssy…puuusaaay…" she purrs.

Man alive…

She dances back and forth across the dresser sinuously.

Unfastening her bra, she lets it fall to the floor and runs her hands through her hair down her shoulders to her bare breasts. To the slow beat of the music, she caresses them; then slides her hands down her belly to her thighs, caressing them.

Spinning around backwards, Lily caresses her butt; then stands up straight and shimmies her body. Placing her hands against the wall, she spreads her legs, bends over, and slowly wiggles her butt; then smacks her butt cheeks with her hands, making them ripple.

Spinning around so that she's facing me again, she gyrates to the music. As she squats on the dresser, her butt knocks the seascape painting above the dresser off the wall, and it falls onto the dresser.

"Whoops!" She smiles sheepishly. Stooping, she picks up the painting, looks at the artist's signature, says "Sorry, Paul," and hangs it back on the wall.

"I ain't got enough room up here." She kicks off her high heels and springs like a cat off the dresser onto the bed. Standing on the mattress straddling my stomach, she slowly squats with her legs spread. Leaning backwards over my body with her elbows propped on the mattress, she undulates to the beat of the music with a sultry expression on her face.

I'm spellbound…

She stands back up and turns around backwards. Spreading her legs, she bends over and grabs hold of her ankles. She's looking at me upside down through her legs. Grinning wickedly, she says, "I'm an exhibitionist."

"No shit."

She stands and turns around so she's facing me again. "That's my dance, Leo," she says proudly and takes a bow.

I clap. "Bravo!"

She drops to her knees and onto my thighs, and we embrace with tremendous force…

After blistering sex, we lie in each other's arms panting contentedly…

"Lily, I love sex with you. You actually make me feel high. Metaphorically speaking, you are sexual heroin. If we keep doing it, I'm afraid I'm gonna become addicted to you."

Smiling like that's her secret stratagem, she replies, "It's okay Leo. I ain't like drugs or booze. I'm a healthy addiction."

CHAPTER NINETEEN

On Saturday, we sleep in. Trying to use up our bread, Lily fixes French toast. We eat brunch on the balcony and relive our adventure of finding the wild horses. I remark everything will be anticlimactic from here on. Having accomplished our mission, we decide to spend our last day just relaxing at the beach. Wearing her pink polka dot bikini, she sits in her beach chair reading a magazine about the Outer Banks that she found in our room. I sit beside her on the beach blanket, picturing her dancing for me last night.

"Hey, Lily…where'd you learn to dance like that?"

She acts like she didn't hear me.

I ask again louder.

"Leo, why don't you go ride Hard Slick?"

"I don't wanna ride Hard Slick. You've aroused my curiosity. How is it you dance like a pro?"

"I was afraid this would happen. I never should've done it. I get wild when I'm drunk."

"C'mon, Lily, tell me…"

"If I tell you, will you hold it against me?"

"No way."

"How do I know you ain't just saying that to get me to tell you?"

"Because I'm not like that."

"Most men would hold it against me if they knew what I done.

They'd think I'm a whore."

"I'm not most men. I'm not judgmental. Like Jesus said, 'Let he who is without sin cast the first stone.' "

Wavering, her eyes roam the ocean. "You promise you won't hold it against me?"

"Yes."

She lowers her magazine. "I was an exotic dancer."

"You mean a stripper?"

"Uh-huh."

"Where?"

"Dallas."

"I don't like Dallas. That's where Lee Harvey Oswald assassinated President Kennedy."

"It's the wild west. It's got a lot of strip clubs."

"Yeah. Jack Ruby owned one of them."

"It don't seem real now. It's like…like I was two people. During the day, I was a mama changing diapers. At night I was swinging around a pole."

"So…how did you become a stripper?"

"Why do you wanna know?"

"I've never met a real-life pole dancer, so I think it's really interesting. Tell me the whole story. I'm always looking for a heroine for my next novel. You know—a femme fatale."

She puts her magazine on the blanket and recollects for a moment. Sighing deeply, she begins, "You hafta understand I was broke after I left Donny. I was scared we was gonna starve. I had to buy food with food stamps. I needed a job bad. But I couldn't get a real job cuz I was a high school dropout.

"Then one day I seen a sign in the window at the Tequila a Go-Go saying they was hiring go-go dancers. I figured it was fate."

"Fate?"

"Yeah. I always knew I had a body. And I knew I could dance. At high school dances, kids would make a circle around me and watch me dance and applaud afterwards. It was my one talent. So I just walked in and told the manager I wanted to be a go-go dancer. He took one look at me and hired me on the spot. I didn't hafta audition like all the other girls.

"So I didn't start out as a stripper. I started as a go-go dancer. I wore a skimpy cowgirl outfit with sequins and danced in a cage hanging from the rafters. I liked dancing, but I didn't like the manager. He thought he was God's gift to women and was always hitting on me. I had to constantly fight him off.

"Then I met my friend, Tina. She was an exotic dancer at a strip club called Stilettos. She told me I could make a lot more money working there. It was owned by a guy named Bart Charles. She said the good thing about Bart was that he didn't hit on his girls cuz he was a queer.

"So I checked out Stilettos. It had a big stage with bright lights and a runway with a pole. I had to dance topless. I remember Bart's exact words—'Darlin', if you wanna work here, you gotta show them horny cowboys your pretty titties. That's what they pay to see.' I needed the money, so I went to work at his club. While the deejay played two or three songs, I'd strip to just a G-string. It turned out I was really good at pole dancing. I worked some of my tumbling tricks into my routines. I'd do the splits and back bends and swing upside down from the pole. Bart once told me I was the best dancer he'd ever seen, and he'd seen dozens come and go over the years. There's a high turnover rate for exotic dancers. He said I had the best body and the sexiest moves. And I had a sweet, innocent look. You know—I didn't look hard like a lot of his dancers."

"So did you like it?"

"What I liked was being my own boss. I only worked when I wanted to. On the nights I worked, Tina's sister babysat my kids. If she couldn't make it or one of them was sick, I just didn't go to work.

"So that's how I became an exotic dancer," she concludes with a shrug.

"Exotic dancer? Don't you mean erotic dancer?"

"Exotic dancers—that's what Bart always called us. He said that sounded classy. He gave us stage names cuz he said cowboys are sentimental fools—they love catchy stage names. Mine was

Cinnamon.

"Them cowboys loved Cinnamon. They'd come from miles around just to watch me dance. On Saturday nights, there was a line out the door. Bart had to turn people away. He called me a gold mine. I made damn good money—a lot more than assembling ballcocks. I remember on Super Bowl weekend I made one thousand three hundred dollars in one night."

"Wow…so what did it feel like being up there on the stage with all those men drooling over you?"

Staring into space dreamily, she answers, "I remember the first time I stripped it was such a rush. I mean pure adrenaline—like the most powerful drug was pumping through my veins. I had all them men eating out of the palm of my hand. I felt like…like a star. Oh, God, I loved it…

"Sometimes up on that stage I was so lost in my own fantasy world I forgot there was men out there…

"But then…after you do it night after night, the thrill begins to fade. It became like any other job. First, you get bored. Then it becomes a grind. Then you start hating it and just do it for the money.

"And it's risky. A crazy guy fell madly in love with me and started stalking me. Bart's bouncer had to scare him off.

"I had losers ask me to marry them. One fat, bald-headed guy always stuck these sweaty ten dollar bills under my G-string. He stopped tipping me after I turned him down.

"I had creeps offer me money to have sex with them. They thought I was a prostitute. Some girls turned tricks for extra money cuz they was hooked on drugs, but I never did that. I may have been a stripper, but I wasn't no whore. I couldn't perform sex for money. I knew that would spoil it—turn it into a job that I'd end up hating. Sex is something I always wanna do for pleasure.

"Everybody tried to use me. Guys tried to be my pimp. One guy from LA—he wore diamond rings on his fingers and gold chains around his neck—tried to get me to go to Hollywood. He said he'd make me a big porn star.

"The whole time I was living a lie. I didn't tell people I was a stripper. I told them I was a professional dancer working in the entertainment business. If you tell people a lie long enough, you start to believe it.

"I wanted to quit. The cops was always harassing Bart. I was afraid I was gonna get in trouble with the law. But I was making so much money, I couldn't.

"That's when my whole world came crashing down on me..."

"What happened?"

"The cops reported Sean getting hurt in Donny's car accident to Child Protective Services, and they investigated us for neglect. They found out he was in jail, and I was a stripper living with a dyke stripper. They threatened to take my kids away from me and put them in a foster home. I was scared shitless. I called Mama, and she told me to come home right this minute. As soon as I hung up, I grabbed the kids and ran. I left all that bad shit in my rear view mirror.

"That put an end to me being a stripper. I moved back to Ohio and started a new life for myself. I got me a regular job. I don't make near as much money, but I don't hafta worry about losing my kids. I found out the hard way there ain't nothing in this world worth losing your kids for."

"True..."

"So...are you happy now? Now that I told you the whole story?"

"Yeah. I feel like I know you better."

"You think I'm a whore?"

"No. I think you're a natural-born exhibitionist."

"I was really wild back then. I ain't that girl anymore. I ain't Cinnamon. I'm Lily."

But I love Cinnamon. I love your wild side...

"You really ain't gonna hold it against me?" she asks, searching my face with her eyes.

"No. The way I see it is you just did what you had to do to survive."

Shaking her head skeptically, she insists, "It's hard for me to believe that."

If I'm honest with myself, my feelings are ambivalent. Picturing her dancing almost nude on a stage arouses me sexually, but it also bothers me—I actually feel jealous of the men who were watching her. I remind myself that I don't care since we're going to kiss and say goodbye tomorrow. Still, it's disconcerting that I have possessive feelings for her that could make it hard for me to kiss and say goodbye.

"The funny thing is lots of men have seen me naked, but only three men have screwed me. Donny. That cop I told you about. And you. And that's the truth."

"Huh. That's… that's actually ironic."

"What's that mean?"

"That's when something appears to be a contradictory fact."

"You like your big words—don't you?"

"I do. I'm a sesquipedalianist," I say with a grin.

"A what?"

"A sesquipedalianist. That's someone who loves to use big words."

Returning my grin, she replies, "Well, I'd say it just goes to show 'You can't judge a book by its cover.' "

"Yeah, that too."

"I don't want anybody to find out I was a stripper."

"Were any pictures taken of you?"

"No. Bart wouldn't allow any cameras in the place."

"Then I wouldn't worry about it. If anyone ever says you did it, just deny it. It's your word against theirs."

"Leo, promise me you won't tell anybody. Nobody in Mansfield knows. Even Mama don't know. She thought Children Services was after me all because of Donny. I don't want my kids to ever find out."

"I won't."

"Say it."

"I promise, Lily—if you promise to be my private exotic dancer. You know—be Cinnamon for me."

Smiling, she replies, "I promise. So you must've liked my dance last night, huh?"

"I loved it."

"I loved dancing for you. I felt that rush again—only better. Cuz I was dancing for you."

I wonder how she's going to dance for me again if we go our separate ways.

Smiling ruefully, she says, "Leo, I have another confession to make."

"What?"

"I've smoked pot before. I used to smoke it with Donny in Texas. And I took acid."

I'm shocked. She's not as innocent as I thought. "You took LSD?"

"Uh-huh. It was far out. I saw Donny's cock turn into a snake. You ever take acid?"

"Yeah. Being biologists, Beth and I went on a 'field trip' and dropped tabs of Orange Sunshine LSD at Black Hand Gorge State Park. I had a psychedelic experience. For several hours, I forgot who and where I was and roamed the forest believing I was Hawkeye in *The Last of the Mohicans*."

"That don't surprise me."

"Fortunately, I remembered who and where I was when I looked at my driver's license. That was the one and only time I tripped on LSD. I figured my imagination is active enough without enhancing it with psychedelics."

She nods.

"So have you done any other drugs?"

"I done a little cocaine, but I quit when Donny started getting hooked on it. That was another reason why I left him. I quit all drugs when I came back to Ohio."

Suddenly, she grabs her groin and says, "I gotta pee. But I don't wanna walk all the way back to the room."

"Just go in the ocean. That's what I do."

She looks at the water like she's considering it.

"Just wade out up to your waist." I don't tell her that most shark attacks occur in waist-deep water.

She wades out waist-deep and pees.

I realize this is my chance to play with her in the waves, so I run into the ocean and grab her hand. Dragging her out into the surf, I cajole, "You can't go home without playing in the waves with me."

Holding hands, we play in the breakers. A huge wave curls and falls, crashing into her and knocking her down. Spluttering, she stumbles to her feet, wipes the water from her eyes, and realigns her bikini top. She loves it.

I show her how to bodysurf. Since she's light, she catches several waves and gets good rides. Swimming up to me, she wipes the salt water from her face. "Leo, this is really fun."

"Now you can tell your kids you went bodysurfing in the ocean and lived to tell about it."

Wrapping her arms around my neck and her legs around my waist, she kisses me.

"Hey, Lily, it's my dream to do it in the ocean."

She takes off her bikini bottom underwater, and I pull down my swimsuit. Bobbing face to face in the breakers, we fuck…

A man floats by on a rubber raft and gives a friendly wave.

We wave back, smiling.

Suddenly, with a distressed look on her face, she whispers in my ear, "Oh my God, Leo. I lost my bottom."

"You gotta be kidding."

"I ain't kidding."

I look around for it floating on the surface but don't see it.

"Jeez, Lily. You're always having a problem with your bikini."

"I can't help it. It must've slipped out of my hand."

"It's a damn good thing you're an exhibitionist."

"That ain't funny. Do something."

"I'll go back to the room and get your other bikini. Wait here."

"No, don't leave me."

"I know—I'll get your towel."

While she waits in waist deep water, I fetch her beach towel. Turning her back toward the shore, she wraps it around her waist; then wades into shore and walks back to the motel sopping wet.

Twenty minutes later, she returns in her red bikini, carrying two Bloody Marys. Floating happily in my army raft, we sip our drinks and talk about dinner. I want to take her out to eat since it's our last night. She tells me she doesn't have a nice outfit to wear. I insist on taking her out to eat tonight at the Ocean Ranch Restaurant whether she likes it or not. She says okay—but she'll have to buy an outfit. While she gathers up all our stuff and heads back to the motel, I deflate my army raft and load it in the trunk.

I shower and shave; then go sit on the balcony and wait for Lily. I hang our beach towels on the railing to dry. Finally, she comes outside and sits down with me. She is a rainbow of colors—blue mascara on her blue eye, green mascara on her green eye, rose blush, red lipstick, ruby ear rings, and her long, flowing cinnamon curls.

"So…how do I look?" she asks coyly.

"Dazzling."

"I gotta go buy a dress."

She drives to the strip mall where Cheap Beach Stuff is located. I tag along to keep her company. While she shops for a dress in a women's clothing store, I go into Cheap Beach Stuff. Browsing, I find a periwinkle blue T-shirt that says OBX in bold black letters. Since it's the end of the summer season, it's on sale for only four bucks. I figure it's a steal. Back in the car, I stick it in the glove compartment.

A few minutes later, Lily strolls out of the store wearing an amazing dress. It's tight, sleeveless, low-cut, and very short; but what makes it special is it's a kaleidoscope of bright colors and patterns. She's braless—her nipples embossed in the cotton fabric are visually tantalizing.

With a demure look on her face, she hops in the car and asks, "You like my new dress?"

"That's the coolest dress I've ever seen. It's psychedelic. It matches your eyes."

Snapping her fingers, she says, "Darn it, Leo, I forgot something."

"What?" I'm afraid she left her wallet in the store.

Looking at me ingenuously, she raises the hemline of her dress. "My panties."

"Wow…how does that feel?" I ask, wide-eyed.

"I love to feel a breeze down there."

I smile. "You really are a minx."

"What's that?"

"A girl who's sexually audacious."

"Audacious?"

"Bold."

"It makes me feel free."

"So what's in the bag?"

"I bought cute Cape Hatteras T-shirts for Sarah and Rachel."

When we get to the motel, I want to take a picture of Lily in her psychedelic dress. I park the car by the Ocean Ranch sign. It's dusk so there is still enough light outside to take her picture. Borrowing her camera, I make her pose standing in front of my Triumph with the motel sign in the picture frame—then count to three. She smiles in a winsome way. I snap the shot. "I want this picture for posterity."

Before we go to dinner, we sit out on the balcony, smoke a joint, watch the waves, and chat about frolicking in the ocean. Ravenous, we go to dinner.

Entering the restaurant, I tell the hostess that Lily and I eloped and ask for a table beside a window overlooking the ocean. Lily gets a kick out of my telling the hostess that we eloped. The hostess finds my story romantic and seats us at a table with a great view of the water; then lights the candle in the center of the table.

Lily orders a Bloody Mary; for variety, I order a martini. Perusing the menu, I pick the most expensive item—twin Maine lobster tails. She chooses deep-fried shrimp.

"You don't like lobster?" I ask.

"I ain't ever eaten it."

"You've never eaten lobster in your life?"

"No. What's it taste like?"

"Shrimp. Only richer."

"It's too expensive."

"Lily, you only live once. Try it."

She orders the twin lobsters tails. The chef butterflies them. Dipping the lobster meat into melted butter, it tastes sweet and succulent. As Lily eats hers, I watch curiously.

"You like it?"

Rolling her eyes in ecstasy, she declares, "This is the best thing I've ever eaten." Relishing each bite, it takes her forever to eat them.

For dessert, I talk her into splitting the house specialty—chocolate fudge cake, which is a brownie with vanilla ice cream, hot fudge, toasted pecans, whipped cream, and a Maraschino cherry. We devour it. We even share the cherry.

After dinner we reminisce about our vacation, laughing about her driving Red into the sand and losing her bikini top while hang-gliding and bikini bottom while fucking.

Smirking, she asks, "Ain't you glad I talked you into staying?"

"You mean seduced me into staying."

"We would never have seen the wild horses."

"True. So what was your favorite moment?"

"I liked hang gliding. And seeing the dolphins. But seeing the wild horses of Currituck was my dream come true. I'll remember it the rest of my life…"

"Believe it or not, Lily, I dreamed we found them."

"Really?"

"Yeah. The night it rained. Sometimes I think I'm clairvoyant."

"I told you it was written in the stars. So what was your favorite moment?"

"Seeing your erotic dance. That's truly a unique talent," I answer only half-kidding.

"Yeah…I bet'cha there ain't a lot of college girls that can do that," she wisecracks.

I laugh. "Seriously, I enjoyed the day we spent playing nudists on the National Seashore. I revel in being unconventional. And going surfing was a dream come true. But my favorite moment was seeing the wild horses galloping in the Atlantic Ocean. It was an extraordinary sight. One I'll never forget. I'm glad you talked me into trying again."

"I keep picturing them two horses playing on the beach. They're like me and you."

"They're a metaphor."

Holding up my glass, I propose a toast. She holds up her glass.

"To the 'Wild Horses of Currituck,' " I salute.

"To the 'Wild Horses of Currituck,' " she salutes in return.

We clink glasses and smile at each other, acknowledging that we'll share this wonderful memory for the rest of our lives.

Her smile broadens into a grin. "C'mon, Leo, let's go for a walk on the beach."

I pay for dinner; she covers the tip. On the way out of the restaurant, we both use the restroom. The sign on the door to the men's restroom says Mermen. Hanging on the door below the sign is a resin merman figurine. Afterwards, I wait for her in the fresh air on the front walk outside the restaurant.

Suddenly, she slinks out the front door. Hiding something in her hands, she makes a beeline for the car.

Curious, I follow.

"Open the boot," she orders.

"What've you got there?"

She surreptitiously shows me a resin mermaid figurine. The mermaid has long, red hair adorned with a circlet of pearls and a large emerald above her forehead. Her hair covers her bare breasts. From the waist down, she has a long turquoise tail with a teal tailfin.

Grinning, she confesses, "I stole it."

I glance around to make sure nobody's watching. "What for?"

"I want a souvenir of our trip."

"Why that?"

"I love it. When I was a little girl, I wanted to be a mermaid, and I think she looks like me." She hides it underneath my army raft.

"What are you—a kleptomaniac?"

"Just shut the trunk, Leo."

I close it. "Now I'm an accessory after the fact."

"We're Bonnie and Clyde."

"You're incorrigible."

On the boardwalk, it occurs to me that this is our last nightly walk down the beach. I quickly force the thought out of my mind—I don't want to think about tomorrow.

To my surprise, she takes my hand.

LILY

We stroll hand in hand down the shore…

"Lily, this is the best time I've ever had in my life."

"Me too, Leo."

We sit down in the soft, dry sand. I put my arm around her, and she lays her head on my shoulder. We watch the waning moon rise over the sea…

"I'm so happy," I declare with a sigh.

"Me too."

She lies back in the sand.

Gently holding her face in my hands, I gaze into her eyes and tell her, "I wish this would last forever."

She smiles and strokes my hair.

Closing my eyes, I kiss her passionately.

She kisses my eyes tenderly.

Lost in the moment, we kiss and caress amorously. Her soft lips, smooth skin, hot breath, and earthy scent stir pleasurable sensations throughout my entire body and feelings of love and affection. We meld together into one living being…

The wind begins to whistle; then thunder rumbles off in the distance. Pulling apart, we look up in the sky. Dark, ominous clouds are obscuring the moon and rolling over the sea toward us…

"Looks like a storm is coming. We better head back," I say.

Standing, we brush the sand off.

On the horizon, lightning flashes; then thunder claps.

"The top is down on your car," she reminds me.

"Shit!"

Scurrying back up the beach, big gusts of wind blow the sand against us—it stings like tiny needles. We run to the car, grab the top and side windows out of the boot, and quickly snap them back on as huge raindrops begin to fall.

We dash through the pouring rain to our room, where we open the sliding glass door to the balcony and swivel the sleeper sofa so that we're facing the water. Sitting in the dark with my arm around her shoulder and her hand on my thigh, we watch the storm rage over the ocean. Again and again, jagged bolts of lightning flash downward from the heavens to the surface of the sea. For a moment, the bolt lights up the entire seascape as bright as day—sheets of rain are pummeling the turbulent whitecaps. Then everything turns pitch-dark again, and a deafening crack of thunder shakes my insides. The pungent, metallic smell of ozone permeates the air.

After a while, the howling wind begins to whip the rain through the sliding screen door inside our room, forcing us to shut the sliding glass door.

In silence, we watch the storm until the lightning and thunder and wind and rain fade away to the west. I sigh. "Well…it looks like the show is over."

She replies by kissing me fiercely.

Pulling down the shoulder straps on her dress, I kiss her breasts and suck her nipples…

Cradling my head in her arms, she moans and groans…

I slide my hand up her supple, inner thigh and caress her soft, wet mound…

She whispers breathlessly in my ear, "Oh, Leo, fuck me…fuck me like there ain't no tomorrow."

She slithers out of her little psychedelic dress and moves onto the bed, waiting for me…

I strip as fast as I can and crawl onto the bed between her legs.

We make torrid love…

As our excitation builds to a crescendo, we lock eyes…

At the moment she climaxes, she moans, "Oh, Leo, I'm yours…"

I hear the emotion in her voice and see it in her eyes.

Climaxing, I reply, "Oh, Lily, I'm yours too…"

I truly mean it.

Still inside her, I caress her face, her eyes, her lips…

She gently runs her fingers through my hair…

She's mine and I'm hers.

I feel wonder…

Afterwards, I get a drink of water. When I return to the bed, she appears to be asleep.

Restless, I go outside on the balcony. Standing naked at the railing, I realize that something happened within my heart when I saw her climax and heard her tell me that she's mine.

Lily, I...I think I'm falling in love with you.

From nowhere, I think of Beth and me coming here on vacation. I don't feel any pain when I think of her, just a fond memory. I don't care about the past.

And I don't care about the future. I don't want to go to law school. I'm not interested in it.

All I care about is living in the present with Lily. I'm only interested in her. I want to learn everything there is to know about her.

Oh, Lily, I don't want to leave you. I love being with you. You are wild at heart. You make me wild at heart. I feel the most alive when I'm with you...

The sliding screen door opens, and she comes out on the balcony naked. Joining me at the railing, she asks, "What are you doing out here?"

"I can't sleep."

"Me neither."

All at once I take her in my arms and say, "Lily, I have to tell you something."

"What?"

Looking intensely into her eyes, I tell her, "I'm falling in love with you."

Impassioned, we kiss so hard it hurts my mouth—

Suddenly, she pulls away. "No, Leo! I ain't falling in love with you."

"Why not?"

"This is just a fling, remember? Tomorrow we kiss and say goodbye."

"Lily, I don't wanna kiss and say goodbye. Let's run away together," I say impetuously.

"Go where?"

"New Zealand."

"New Zealand?"

"I've seen pictures of it in National Geographic. It looks like it's the most beautiful country in the world. And they got great waves for surfing."

She chuckles.

"What's so funny about that?"

"Leo, you're crazier than I am."

"I'm a dreamer…"

"Sometimes I dream about running away with you and starting all over."

"Really?"

"Uh-huh…but then I realize it's just make-believe. We can't."

"Why not?"

"You know why. I have kids that I love more than anything in this world. I could never abandon them. And you gotta go to law school…"

She's right. She has to be a mother, and I have to be a law student. I can't back out of law school now. After backing out of med school, people will justifiably think I'm a quitter.

Her words bring me back down to earth. I must have told her "I'm yours" because I was in the throes of an orgasm when my brain was turned off. Now that my brain is turned back on, my reason tells me that I didn't truly mean it. It's time to kiss and say goodbye.

I sigh…

"C'mon, we got a long drive tomorrow," she says.

She leads me back to bed. She lies with her face on my shoulder and her arm draped across my chest and her leg draped over my leg.

I hold her in my arms like I never want to let go…

CHAPTER TWENTY

The next morning I wake up at ten after six. I let Lily sleep while I quietly get ready to go. I don't bother to shower or shave; just brush my teeth. After I get dressed, I wake her up, and she stumbles into the bathroom. I pack; then go in the kitchen and fix myself a piece of toast with peanut butter, leaving her the last piece of bread.

While eating my toast on the balcony, I notice the sky is overcast. I feel so melancholy…

To preserve my memories of our love affair, I stand at the railing and take a picture in my mind of the ocean; then turn around and take a picture of the balcony. Back inside, I take mental pictures of the bed, the living area, and the kitchenette.

I walk to the shore. Standing at the water's edge, I gaze at the waves crashing on the beach…the sea gulls circling overhead…

Lily joins me and slips her arm around my waist. I put my arm around her shoulders.

In my mind, I say, "So long."

Looking down the beach, I spot pink polka dots. Pointing at them, I say, "Hey, Lily, look."

We walk down there and find the bottom to her bikini tangled in the seaweed, washed ashore by the tide last night. She picks it up and shakes the sand out.

Hand in hand, we walk back to the room. I carry our bags out to the car and load them in the trunk, leaving the top and windows on. She gives me her half of the money to pay the hotel bill and check out.

She asks me to drive home because she doesn't want to drive away from here. It's not nearly as windy and noisy in the car with the top and windows on, so she's able to curl up in the passenger seat and sleep. As I cross over the bridge to the mainland, I feel my heart sinking.

I find myself continually glancing at her—she makes me feel happy inside. I reflect on what an extraordinary person she is. The more I get to know her the more I admire her qualities—her indomitable spirit of adventure, her curiosity and almost childlike wonder about nature, her passion for living creatures, and, most of all, her zest for life. I've always thought my dad and mom we're the most extraordinary people I've ever known, but I now realize Lily is the most extraordinary person I've ever met. Despite all of the hardship and tragedy in her life, she loves to live more than any person I've ever known.

I loved going with her on this adventure. I want to go with her on more adventures.

But I know we must kiss and say goodbye when we get home. She has to go back to work and raise her children. I have to go to law school and fulfill my life as a lawyer.

But I don't want to end my relationship with this extraordinary woman. I was afraid this would happen if we made love. I knew I'd fall in love with her.

I feel so torn...

At Richmond she wakes up and turns on the radio. We listen to the tunes silently.

Driving around Washington, D.C., an idea crystalizes in my mind. Given the right circumstances, perhaps there is a way she could be Lara. If she'd go to college, this could be a starting point for a future relationship.

On the Pennsylvania Turnpike, she says she's hungry so we stop for lunch at a truck stop. During our meal, I casually mention, "Lily, I got an idea. Why don't you quit Boals-Corrigan and go to college?"

"Leo, I told you—I ain't smart enough."

"Yes, you are. Hell, I'm starting to think you're smarter than I am. You have feminine wiles."

"Feminine wiles?"

"Yeah. You know how to get me to do whatever you want."

"That's just pussy power," she scoffs.

Laughing, I reply, "Whatever it is it works. You could move to Toledo and go to Toledo State. Now that you got your high school diploma you could go there. It's a commuter school."

"What's a commuter school?"

"Students live at home and have jobs and go to classes at night. You could get a job and go to night school. We could rent a house and live together."

"Leo, I can't. I gotta go to work tomorrow. I got three kids to support. I can't just yank them out of school and move all of us to Toledo with no job and no money. How would I support them and pay for college? I got a good job and a free trailer and free babysitting in Mansfield."

She's right. I'm dreaming. It always boils down to it's impossible because of her kids. Besides, I want my own kids someday. She can't have kids.

"I'm a mama, Leo. That's what women in my family do. We don't go to college. We make babies and raise them. Don't try to change me..."

What the hell am I thinking? I must be out of my mind to propose such an idea.

Resigned to the fact that we must kiss and say goodbye when we get home, I sigh deeply and reply, "Right...I guess it's a crazy idea."

Crossing the Ohio River at Wheeling, I see the Welcome to Ohio sign and realize our adventure is almost over, which bums me out.

I pull into her driveway after nightfall. Her trailer is dark inside—it looks like no one is here. I turn off the engine and say, "You're home."

She doesn't reply.

While opening the boot for her, I flash back to her putting her bag in it before she seduced me. Shaking my head incredulously, I say, "Lily, I still marvel you had your bag packed and were all ready to go."

"That's cuz I didn't want to give you the chance to change your mind."

I smile. "Don't forget your mermaid."

She fishes it out from under my army raft.

I spot Hard Slick and hand it to her. "Here, give this to Sean. He can boogie board when you take him to the ocean."

"I bought it for you."

"He'll get more use out of it. I don't think I'm gonna be going to the ocean anytime soon." I give her my kite to give to her kids.

She smiles and thanks me.

"Let me walk you to the door," I say.

Her front porch light is on. We stand dejectedly on her front stoop...

"Time to kiss and say goodbye," she breaks the silence.

"Right..."

She sets her stuff down beside her, and we embrace and kiss perfunctorily. I feel like I did when she wouldn't let me hold her hand on the beach.

Forcing a smile, I say, "Thanks. I had a great time."

"Yeah. Me too."

"Lily, I, uh...want you to know—it wasn't just the sex. It was more. I don't want you to think I was just using you for sex."

"I don't. I was using you for sex," she wisecracks.

I laugh.

Smiling, she says, "Leo, all I wanted was to get laid and find the wild horses. I got what I wanted. Thanks for making my dream come true."

"My pleasure."

At this moment, I flash back to when she asked me to go out to eat with her in the parking lot at Boals-Corrigan—it seems like eons ago. "I'm just glad you asked me to take you to the Cameo."

Nodding, she replies, "You drawing my portrait made me do it. I almost didn't. Every time I tried to ask you at work somebody was in the way. First Kenny. Then Percy and Mel. I almost gave up. It wasn't easy talking you into it…"

"It was the irresistible force paradox."

"The what?"

"What happens when the irresistible force meets the immovable object? You're the irresistible force, and I'm the immovable object. Now we know the answer. The irresistible force prevails."

"I ain't ever heard of that."

"Actually, now that I think about it, it was more like spontaneous combustion. You and I ignited in spontaneous combustion one night in a motel room at Cape Hatteras."

Rolling her eyes, she replies, "Whatever you say."

"You made me throw caution to the wind. Truth is, Lily, you make me go wild…"

"You love it."

"I do. I feel so alive with you…"

She smiles.

"And you said it wasn't a date," I remind her.

"I lied. I was afraid you wouldn't go if you thought it was a date."

"Man alive—that was some first date."

She chuckles.

I listen to the crickets chirping. "Man, it's nice out." I'm stalling…

"You better get going. Good luck at law school."

"Thanks. I'll need it."

"Bye."

"Bye," I say, lingering.

She picks up her bag and turns toward her trailer.

She's saying goodbye to me forever.

But I don't want to say goodbye forever.

"Lily, wait."

She turns around. "What?"

"Am I ever gonna see you again?"

"Leo, I gotta go." She turns to go again.

All at once I think of the photograph that I took of her leaning up against the hood of my Triumph in front of the Ocean Ranch sign. I imagine her delivering it to me at my new apartment—nude—and am instantly turned on again. Grabbing hold of her hand, I say, "Uh…I have this dream…"

"A dream?"

"Well, actually, it's, uh…more like an erotic fantasy."

"Something dirty you want me to do?"

"Yeah."

"What?"

"You know that picture of you I want?"

"Yeah."

I smile suggestively. "My fantasy is for you to personally deliver it to me—nude."

Then we're in each other's arms again kissing amorously—

Breaking away from me, she whispers breathlessly, "Stop, Leo…"

"Why?"

"Our vacation is over. I'm home. I gotta go pick up my kids. I promised my mama." She fishes her keys out of her bag and unlocks her front door.

"I dare you to deliver it to me naked," I taunt her, hoping that she won't be able to resist taking the dare.

Turning serious, she sighs, "No, Leo. I can't see you again…"

Her words make my heart sink. "You can't see me again?"

"Huh-uh."

"Why?"

"Cuz I'm falling in love with you, and I don't wanna fall in love with you."

"I don't understand. You were willing to take that risk and go to Cape Hatteras with me. Now you're no longer willing to take that risk?"

She collects her thoughts. Then she takes a deep breath and tells me, "Leo, we had a wonderful time at Cape Hatteras. But it was just a fling. It's over now. What you said about me and my kids is true. We come together. We're a package deal. And you ain't willing to get involved with them. So I don't wanna see you again. You loved me at Cape Hatteras. I got a happy memory. I'll cherish what we had forever. Now it's time for you to leave me. You're free. Go find your Lara. I ain't gonna let you break my heart…"

Moved by the poignancy of her words, I sigh deeply. In my heart, I know she's right. "I understand. You're right, Lily…"

She slings her bag over her shoulder, picks up her plastic mermaid, and says, "Bye, Leo."

Still, I'm so distressed by the thought of never seeing her again, I stammer, "Wait…wait a minute…"

"What?"

I realize I can't stall any longer. If I want to see her again, I must be willing to get involved with her kids. "All I know is I wanna see you again. What if I'm willing to get involved with your kids? Would you see me again?"

Staring at the mermaid, she considers it momentarily. "Yeah. But only if you really mean it."

My desire to see her again overwhelms my reluctance to get involved with her kids. Pressured to decide, I answer hesitantly, "I…I think so…"

"I don't wanna pressure you. Why don't you think it over?"

I realize she's right. This is a serious decision that I need to think over.

"If you don't really mean it, I don't wanna hear from you…"

I nod.

With a sly smile on her face, she says, "If you really mean it, send me your address."

"And you'll fulfill my fantasy?"

"Maybe. I'll hafta check my horoscope. See if it's written in the stars," she says teasingly.

"You don't hafta check it. I read my horoscope in your National Enquirer when you went for a walk down the beach."

"What did it say?"

"It said: A wild hillbilly girl will deliver a present to me nude."

She laughs. "I gotta go. Bye, Leo."

"See ya, Lily Lee."

She opens her front door, turns on a light, and disappears inside.

Cruising home, I think about her saying she's falling in love with me and doesn't want to see me again unless I'm willing to become involved with her kids. Damn—she wasn't kidding when she said all she wanted was to get laid and find the wild horses. I smile wryly, finding it ironic that all along I thought I would be the one who would end the relationship. In the end, I was the one who couldn't kiss and say goodbye—because I've fallen in love with her.

It's true, Lily. I fell in love with you at Cape Hatteras. When? Where? Was it the first time we had sex after you seduced me or the last time when we looked into each other's eyes and said "I'm yours" during our climaxes?

Maybe it happened at an earlier point in time...when we first kissed at Sunset Point...or the first time I saw that wild glint in your eyes when you said "I'm Lily. I'm just a wild hillbilly girl"...or when we shared your peach and you told me you wouldn't mind posing like the woman in the photograph on my packing press...or when we exchanged confidences at Boals-Corrigan...or maybe even the first time I saw you at the microwave...

Who knows? Trying to ascertain this is as impossible as trying to reach the end of the rainbow...

If I had to pick the exact time and place, I suspect I was inexorably falling in love with you while wading through the swamp at Cape Hatteras but for all intents and purposes fell in love with you the moment we found the Wild Horses of Currituck.

I visualize coming over the crest of the sand dune and seeing them on the beach. The mental images of them galloping in the surf and playing on the beach thrill me once again.

Now the question is do I want to fall out of love with you and search for Lara at law school. Strangely enough, by setting me free, you have become even more desirable. I love the way your mind and heart work.

I imagine her delivering her picture to me nude—it makes my heart beat faster...

Your kids might be fun to get to know.

I picture Lily in her psychedelic dress standing in front of Red by the Ocean Ranch Motel sign, smiling in her winsome way.

LILY

Humming "Falling In and Out of Love" by Pure Prairie League, I cruise home.

Wild Horses of Currituck

Wild Horses of Currituck
Book One in a four-book series

Lily
a novel by
Michael Justus Murray

Wild Horses of Currituck
Book Two in a four-book series

Caia
a novel by
Michael Justus Murray

Wild Horses of Currituck
Book Three in a four-book series

John
a novel by
Michael Justus Murray

Wild Horses of Currituck
Book Four in a four-book series

Leo
a novel by
Michael Justus Murray

.

ABOUT THE AUTHOR

Michael Justus Murray was a lawyer who metamorphosed into a writer.

Wild Horses of Currituck is his first series.
www.wildhorsesofcurrituck.com

He is also the author of a mystery novel, *Deuce Delaney*, which is available in e-book and paperback at Amazon.

Made in the USA
Middletown, DE
30 January 2022

60023237R00201